At the sound of broken glass and a scuffle on the platform outside their car, Sarah whispered, "Oh, I'm so scared. I think somebody's coming in here."

"Whatever happens, Sarah, stay hidden behind the seat." Anya tightened her hold on her gun and waited, while the door slowly opened, revealing the outline of a half-naked man.

He fired into the shadows, barely missing Anya, who immediately returned his fire. For a split second, he remained upright; then he slumped to the floor.

"I think I shot him," a surprised Anya said, not taking her eyes from the man's body. Cautiously, with the gun still in her hand, she left her place behind the Pullman seat and crept toward him to make certain he was dead.

"Sarah, you'll have to help me," she called. "We need to get him out of the car."

There was no response.

"Sarah?"

THE SILK TRAIN

Frances Patton Statham

FAWCETT GOLD MEDAL • NEW YORK

For Marie and Willa

A Fawcett Gold Medal Book
Published by Ballantine Books
Copyright © 1994 by Frances Patton Statham

All rights reserved under International and Pan-American Copyright Conventions. Published in the United States of America by Ballantine Books, a division of Random House, Inc., New York, and simultaneously in Canada by Random House of Canada Limited, Toronto.

Library of Congress Catalog Card Number: 94-94203

ISBN 0-449-14928-5

Manufactured in the United States of America

First Edition: September 1994

10   9   8   7   6   5   4   3   2

Acknowledgments

On a warm, Southern, April day, I departed from Atlanta, a city already heralding spring with its extravagant blossoms of dogwoods, tulips, and azaleas covering the landscape. My destination was North Dakota to research THE SILK TRAIN. I was a stranger, traveling out of season, when many of the places I needed to see were still closed. As I arrived at the airport in Bismarck, claimed my rental car, and began the sixty-mile trek west to Dickinson, the nearest town to Medora, it began to snow. I looked at my friend, Marie, whom I had persuaded to make the trip with me. Words were not necessary. We both realized that the trip was going to be more of an adventure than we had planned.

But despite the extremely cold weather and the snow, we found some wonderful people, whom I wish to thank for their warmth, friendliness, and hospitality.

Carol and Don Beckert, oil consultant from Dickinson, were most helpful in introducing us to those we needed to see and in arranging much of our itinerary. Don, acting as guide, first took us in his four-wheel drive through the wilderness areas of the Theodore Roosevelt National Park, with Carol keeping in touch by mobile phone. The previous week, an enthusiastic tourist taking photographs far too close to a bull buffalo, had met his demise, a sobering story to me, who, without the warning of danger on foot, might have met the same fate.

After the park tour, with Bill Andrus of the TR Foundation showing us the Roosevelt Maltese Cross log cabin and other interesting memorabilia, we went on to Medora, where the site supervisor of the Château de Mores, Doug Paulson, met us and opened the twenty-eight room frontier château for our inspection. On our last night in Dickinson, the Beckerts invited us to dinner, to celebrate a successful trip.

By the time we drove east toward Bismarck, the weather had gotten better. We stopped off at Fort Abraham Lincoln, where Breezy Kohls, Administrator of the Foundation, met us and opened the restored General Custer house.

Mandan villages, views along the Missouri and Little Missouri Rivers with their cottonwood stands, ranch houses, windmills, prairies of grain, and the stark, khaki landscape were images resolutely stored in memory.

Yet, with all the related lore and tales of the Dakotas, no one mentioned a silk train. Had I dreamed it, or was it a fact ignored by historians—that in the 1880s, raw silk had been imported from China, loaded on a guarded train in Seattle, and traveled crosscountry through the Badlands to New York, where the cargo had been reloaded on ships bound for Europe? The answer finally came at the North Dakota Heritage Center in Bismarck, as an archivist brought out old railroad logs, written in faded, Spencerian script. And there, in one of them, I found the proof of a silk train, with the route, the grades, the number of auxiliary engines needed to pull the cars over the steepest inclines. I shall be forever grateful to the archivist and his persistence.

I also wish to thank my editor, Elisa Wares, for her encouragement and interest in the story.

Medora, the town founded by a French marquis, who attempted to build a cattle empire in the west, is a tourist attraction in season, with its own hotels and exciting musical drama produced on those soft "Medora Nights" when legend and history blend to portray a time once forgotten.

I hope you enjoy the story.

FRANCES PATTON STATHAM

Chapter 1

Along a stretch of northwestern Pacific coastline,
where water and sky merge into a colorless abyss, Anya
remained hidden under the salt-encrusted tarpaulin
while the longboat slipped quietly toward shore. All
around her, the forlorn, steady bellow of a foghorn resembled the frightened cry of a sea calf separated from
its mother, and its voice served to magnify the sense of
urgency and danger she felt.

She longed to speak, to ask Ashak, the oarsman, how
much longer it would be before they finally reached the
docks at Elliott Bay. But Anya knew that even a whisper,
overheard on the water, could give away her position.

A few minutes later, the sun slowly began its appearance over the seven hills in the distance, and, seeing its
rays, the Aleut quickened his pace, rowing in double
time. Soon, the morning light would penetrate the heavy
layer of mist surrounding the crude wooden warehouses
that had sprung up along the entire wharf of the bustling
inland port.

Despite the tarpaulin's protection, Anya was cold.
For the past hour, she had forced herself to remain still.
But now, the numbing dampness took over, and she be-
gan to shiver.

1

As if sensing her discomfort, Ashak said, "I see the docks now. Five more minutes and we'll be there." Anya's initial relief was marred by his immediate warning, "But people are beginning to mill about. You'll have to be careful."

"Do you see any other women?" she asked.

He hesitated. "A few."

"Good. Then I should not be noticed."

He did not tell her that the ones he saw were leaning out the windows of a brothel and flirting with the stevedores starting their morning work.

Anya tried not to think of all she'd left behind. More important to her was getting to the railway station of the Northern Pacific, for her very life depended on reaching it and leaving Seattle before she was caught and taken back to Sitka.

Igor's spies would be monitoring all ships headed south for San Francisco. They would not suspect that she planned to take the rugged and dangerous rail trip cross-country through the badlands of the Dakota Territory. So, if she could get from the docks to the station without being noticed, then she stood a chance of vanishing without a trace.

Ashak did not share Anya's enthusiasm. He'd noted that her disguise was already wearing thin. The damp salt air had eroded the black Russian tea rinse on her burnished copper hair in the same way that the sea air affected the iron rings of the boat. If she kept on her hat, perhaps few would notice. But there was little she could do to hide the strange color of her eyes—that startling blue-green of an Alaskan inlet once the winter ice had melted. Someone would be sure to remember her. Nevertheless Ashak brought the boat to rest against the nearest wooden piling.

After he'd secured the line, he carefully removed the tarpaulin from his passenger and pointed to the ladder that led to the wharf. He stood watch while she reanchored her hat with a hurried jab of the pearl hat pin, drew the short veil over her face, and began the awkward climb. Then he hoisted Anya's paisley velvet valise so that it landed, with an almost imperceptible thud, at her feet. With a final salute, Ashak took up his oars to row back to the ship.

Anya Winstead Fodorsky was now on her own.

At the expensive Western Empire Hotel, built on one of the hills overlooking the city, an unsteady Matt Bergen stared into his miniscule shaving mirror. He'd drunk entirely too much the night before, and the sun coming through the window hurt his eyes. But the preceding two weeks had been filled with such backbreaking hard work that he didn't mind the hangover. He'd deserved one night of irresponsibility before starting on the long, arduous trip back to Medora. A pity he couldn't remember more of it than he did.

Matt continued shaving until his hand slipped and the straight razor drew blood. With an oath, he dropped the razor and grabbed a towel to press against his chin. But before he could get the bleeding under control, the sound of jingling spurs and a tap at the door announced his foreman's arrival.

"Matt, the silk train's loaded and waitin' to pull out," Lynx called. "Are you ready?"

Still holding the towel to his face, the towering, blond-headed man walked to the door and opened it.

"God, you look awful," Lynx said, staring at his boss.

"Shut up, and come on inside," Matt ordered. "Make yourself useful and throw my clothes together while I finish shaving."

"Is that what you were doin'? I'da swore you were tryin' to butcher yourself instead."

Matt ignored the sarcasm. "Have you seen the new schoolteacher?" he asked.

"No. But the stationmaster said she spent the night at Miss Emma's boardinghouse. And the lumber for the school is already loaded."

"I still don't know why I have to play nursemaid to some female. Why couldn't George have dispatched her on the next passenger train?"

"Because there ain't one till next week on account of the trestle." Fastening the straps of the leather case, Lynx added, "It's not like you need to do much for her, except rustle up some food twice a day, at the most."

"It's not that at all," Matt said. "I just don't want the guards to have their minds on anything but the silk."

"Well, maybe she's plain. Maybe the boys won't be taken by her."

"She wears petticoats, doesn't she?" Considering the discussion of the teacher at an end, he changed the subject. "Does Kwa-ling have all the cooking supplies on board?"

"Yep."

"Then let's go."

In the almost deserted depot, with its two crude benches facing each other, brown-haired Sarah Macauley, unremarkable in looks, sat and waited. But as the minutes ticked away, she began to realize the enormity of what she'd set in motion. Two months previously, her life had seemed so dismal. Then she'd seen the newspaper advertisement.

"Northern Pacific Railway seeking teacher for the town of Medora in Dakota Territory. Must be single, of excellent character, and possess teacher's diploma and certification. Generous room and board."

At first she'd done nothing more than cut out the advertisement and hide it in her diary. Then, after a week, she'd finally summoned enough courage to reply. She had not expected to get the job. And she probably would not have taken it except for Cousin Lettie, who had opened the acceptance letter.

"So this is what you were doing behind my back, Sarah," she'd said, waving the letter in front of her. "Just like your ungrateful mama, leaving the one who took her in. But remember, your mama didn't last much more than a year out in the wilderness. If you go, you probably won't, either, with all those wild outlaws and Indians."

"But I've been trained as a teacher, Cousin Lettie. Not a house servant."

Her defensive remark had triggered a glazed look, devoid of love. "Then go. But don't expect me to take you in again. Once you leave this hearth, you're on your own."

"Yes, Cousin Lettie."

As Sarah sat and remembered the chilling conversation, the waiting room door creaked open and another woman, valise in hand, entered the station. Sarah immediately brightened. Perhaps she wouldn't have to brave all those lonely miles without companionship, after all.

While Anya walked across the rough-planked flooring to the stationmaster's cage, Sarah watched. She took note of the woman's slender, aristocratic carriage and the well-cut traveling suit. But sometimes, looks were deceiving. Even a town prostitute could hire a good seamstress. It was the speech that always gave one away. So Sarah listened unashamedly to the ensuing conversation.

In a cultured, well-modulated voice, Anya said, "Please, I'd like to buy a one-way ticket on your Eastern route."

"Where to?" the man asked.

"Chicago."

He consulted the schedule pinned to his cage. "Next week. Either Wednesday or Thursday, depending on the repair crew. That'll be—"

"No. That's too late," she protested. "I want a ticket on the train getting ready to pull out now."

"Can't," he said, adjusting his green eyeshade. "That train's not on the regular run. Besides, it don't go all the way to Chicago."

"But can't I purchase a ticket as far as it's going?"

"No. It's a private train with a private cargo. Only the lady over there gets to ride on it. By special permission."

Anya glanced at the bench where Sarah sat and then

back to the stationmaster. "Who would I have to see to get permission, too?"

"The president of the railroad, and he's hundreds of miles away. Now, do you want a ticket for next week or not?"

"I don't think so." With Igor's spies directly behind her, Anya knew she could not afford to spend even one night in Seattle.

With her reply, Wagoner, the stationmaster, returned to his desk.

For a moment, Anya remained by the window, as if uncertain what to do. Then she resolutely picked up her velvet valise, walked to the empty bench opposite a disappointed Sarah, and sat down.

The silence, punctuated at intervals by the metallic click of Morse code keys, was finally broken by Sarah. "I was hoping you were another teacher."

Anya responded, "Is that what you are?"

Sarah nodded. "I'm on my way to Medora. It's a pity you won't be traveling on the same train."

"Yes. I really don't know what I'll do until next week."

"Miss Emma's boardinghouse—across the street—is very nice. I stayed there last night."

Anya's rueful smile indicated her dilemma. "I have only enough money for the railway ticket." Once again, she stared toward the stationmaster. Then she leaned over to retrieve her valise. As she stood, she nodded to Sarah. "I hope you have a safe trip."

"Just a minute. Perhaps if I spoke to Mr. Wagoner . . ."

"Oh, would you?"

"It might not help, but there's no harm trying."

Sarah walked to the window and cleared her throat to gain the stationmaster's attention. "Mr. Wagoner?"

"Yes, ma'am?"

She tried to keep her voice steady. "No doubt you're aware that Mr. Jenkins, the president of this railroad, hired me to teach at Medora."

He merely stared.

"But it's a long and difficult trip over the mountains, especially for a woman traveling alone."

"That it is," he agreed.

"So why can't this other woman ride the train with me? There's plenty of room."

Wagoner immediately became defensive. "Got to think of the cargo. Raw silk's as expensive as gold. Why, she might be a spy in cahoots with outlaws waitin' to rob the train."

"Come now, Mr. Wagoner. Look at her. She's not the type."

"Well, no. Doesn't appear to be," he admitted. "But Ma Berry, who held up the bank last month, didn't look the type, either."

As the train whistle sounded, Wagoner said, "You'd better go ahead and board, Miss Macauley. The train'll be pullin' out any minute." Thinking the conversation at an end, he picked up his lantern.

"Oh, dear. I really don't know what to do. Maybe I'd better wait until next week, too."

Her words caused him a momentary panic. "But they're expecting you and the schoolhouse lumber to arrive at the same time. It's too late to take it off the train."

"Then what do you suggest, Mr. Wagoner?"

He glared at Sarah. He should have known she would upset things at the last minute. It was always the quiet ones you couldn't trust. Stubborn as a mule when it suited them—just like his wife, Martha, who never lost a round when she had that same look in her eye. When the train engine whistled impatiently a second time, he suddenly capitulated. "Oh, all right. Tell the woman to hurry up to the window. But if something bad happens because of her, it's gonna be on your head, Miss Macauley."

Anya, listening to the conversation, responded immediately to Sarah's motioning. Being careful not to reveal the large bag of gold coins, she reached for her smaller purse and hurriedly counted out the money for the ticket.

A few moments later, as the pair set out toward the train that belched large, black puffs of smoke into the air, Anya said, "I'm so grateful to you. I just hope you and the stationmaster won't get into trouble on my account."

Sarah laughed. "I know Mr. Wagoner won't. He stamped your ticket for next week."

By the time the two women boarded the private passenger car that had been attached to the train like an afterthought, a queasy Matthew Bergen was already settled in the first car up front; Lynx had taken his place beside the engineer. Only Kwa-ling, the cook, and Wagoner, the stationmaster, who signaled the train's departure with his lantern, were witnesses to the boarding of the two women.

With armed guards hidden in every boxcar containing the crates of raw silk that had traveled by ship from China to Vancouver and on to Seattle, the silk train began its hazardous journey. For the next five days, it would traverse a large portion of the two thousand miles of track connecting West to East, through mountain wilderness, deep gorges, the badlands, and vast prairies, to its final destination—the filature on the Red River of the North.

Chapter 2

Less than a half hour's journey from Seattle, all traces of civilization vanished. Gone were the saloons, seamen's hotels, and brothels lining the docks, and in their places stood great fir trees, pines, and red cedars that stretched upward toward the gathering clouds. At regular intervals, a sharp northerly wind swept over the iron tracks, dispersing the black cinders spewn from the twin engines' smokestacks and leaving a fresh scent that permeated the passenger car shared by Anya and Sarah.

After an exchange of names and a few impersonal remarks, the two settled into a companionable silence, with Sarah by a window while Anya, alias Anna Ford, sat in the shadows as far from view as possible.

But as the noisy train approached a crystal lake where a flock of wild geese began to take flight, its pristine beauty prompted Sarah to break the silence. "Oh, you must come to the window and look out," she urged. "What a lovely sight."

Anya had no wish to peer out the window where, even with the slightest chance, she might be seen by a passing trapper on his way to Seattle, or spied upon by one of the guards making his periodic checks from the catwalk overhead. But refusing Sarah's attempt at friendliness would be churlish, especially after the woman had gone to such lengths to help her. So, as she reluctantly left her seat, she took a white lace handkerchief from her purse to cover most of her face. "The soot," she said, providing a plausible explanation for her action.

"I suppose I should do the same," Sarah said. "We'll be travel-worn enough as it is, by the time we arrive at our destinations."

The rapidly passing scene showed no curious human face, merely the startled behavior of wildlife whose home had been invaded by a belching iron enemy. So after acknowledging the primeval beauty, a more relaxed Anya sat down immediately opposite Sarah and returned her handkerchief to her purse. Deeming it a safe subject, since Sarah had already mentioned her destination, Anya said, "Tell me about the town of Medora, Miss Macauley. Where is it located?"

Sarah's face, plain in repose, took on a vivacity as she answered. "On the Little Missouri River in the Dakota Territory. A French marquis named it for his wife. Of course, I don't expect to be teaching their daughter. They'll have a private tutor when she's old enough. But there're lots of other ranchers and ranch hands with families. They're the ones I'll be teaching. That is, after the schoolhouse is built."

Over the next miles, the train sped through mountain

gaps, raced down into fertile valleys, and groaned its way back to higher elevations. On the journey, an eager Sarah confessed her hopes and dreams to a sympathetic Anya. Then, realizing that she'd talked far too long, Sarah said, "I'm afraid I've bored you."

"Nonsense. Your plans for the new school are quite fascinating."

"But it's your turn now. You'll find I'm a good listener, too."

Anya tugged at the dark ribbon on her blouse. She was reluctant to talk about herself, despite Sarah's urging. "My story is really quite dull," she began. "I was married early, but now my husband is dead. So I'm on my way to live with relatives."

"In Chicago."

"What?"

"I remember you tried to buy a ticket to Chicago."

"Oh, yes."

A few minutes of silence elapsed, until Sarah prompted her. "Go on."

Far from the more snobbish cities, few rules of etiquette prevailed in the West. To inquire of a man his name and where he came from was considered an invasion of privacy. Yet no such restraint protected a woman. Her entire life's history was important in a territory where only two kinds of women were recognized—virtuous or virtueless—and treated accordingly.

Sarah was sweet and trusting, and that's why Anya hated herself for her deception. But the truth was too dangerous. As she spoke, Anya twisted the large cabochon ruby ring round and round on the finger of her left hand.

"I was an only child—and quite young when my mother died. . . ."

"So was I," Sarah said, feeling a further kinship with Anya.

"Then when I was eight, my father sent me away to school."

"Where?"

Deliberately vague, Anya replied, "Oh, to a private female academy in the East." Then she hurriedly continued, "Until I was seventeen, I studied the usual subjects—music and art, French . . ."

"French?" The eagerness in Sarah's voice was apparent. "Do you speak the language well?"

"Some say I do."

"Then you'd be able to help me. I do so want to be able to converse better in the language, just in case I'm invited— Wait. Let me find the lexicon."

An excited Sarah stood and made her way to the end of the car where her small trunk of books had been stored for the journey. Once again, her enthusiasm had absolved Anya from further lies.

While Anya helped Sarah with her pronunciation, the odor of food cooking invaded the passenger car. "On any other train I would feel insulted," Anya said, "riding behind the dining car."

"Why is that?" Sarah asked.

"Well, it's a little like sitting below the salt at a diplomatic dinner. But I'm so grateful to be on this train, it doesn't really matter."

Sniffing the air, Sarah said, "I see what you mean. I wonder what the cook is preparing."

"Fish," Anya said quickly. "Fried in blubber."

They laughed and returned to the French lesson. It was in this position, with their heads together, that Kwa-ling later found the two.

"Excuse, missees. My name Kwa-ling. I bring tray of food. Sourdough bread, fish, and sweet cherries. Cow's milk, too—cold from icebox."

Without looking up from the book, Anya murmured a quick thank-you, while Sarah was more effusive. Removing her wire-rimmed reading spectacles, she smiled. "You must thank Mr. Bergen as well, Kwa-ling. Now, if you'll just put the tray on the table . . ."

"Yes, missee."

Kwa-ling bowed politely to both women and vanished back to his dining car, where he had set up service for his boss and the men guarding the train.

The Chinese servant had not always been a cook. Like hundreds of his countrymen, he had come to America to work on the railroads. But after several backbreaking years, a terrible accident occurred. Someone had set off a dynamite charge too soon, causing a murderous avalanche. And he had been wrongfully accused of the disaster. If it had not been for Matt, who'd believed in his innocence, he would have been lynched. So in saving him, Matt had received much more than a cook. He was now the recipient of Kwa-ling's total loyalty and devotion.

The guards came in shifts to the dining car. While one group ate, the ones on duty, with their rifles, made

periodic checks, their heavy footsteps resounding overhead along the entire length of the train. Only Anya,
Sarah, the engineer, and firemen had their food brought
to them—the men by necessity, the women by whim of
Matt Bergen, who wanted none of his men to be distracted by a woman, no matter how plain.

After the first group had nearly finished eating, Matt
himself came to the dining car. His hangover was almost gone. Only a remnant of irritability remained to
remind him of his recent indiscretion.

Kwa-ling rushed to serve him. "Fish very fresh," he
said, placing the choicest portion in front of Matt. "I
bought at wharf this morning."

Matt nodded. "You must have gotten there before the
sun came up."

"Is only way to buy," Kwa-ling replied.

He stood quietly by Matt's seat and waited for the
man to taste the fish. Only when Matt pronounced it
good would he continue serving.

"Very nice, Kwa-ling," he said. And then, remembering the woman passenger, he added, "I suppose you've
already seen to the teacher?"

"Yes, Mr. Matt. I fix food for the other missee, too."

"What do you mean? I thought there was only one
woman on board."

"Two missees got on train."

Matt scowled at the news, and Kwa-ling, seeing the
man's displeasure, was sorry that he had mentioned the
second woman. He hurried back to his galley kitchen
for more plates.

By the time Lynx came to sit with Matt, the boss was still scowling. "Kwa-ling tells me there are two women on board. I know one is the teacher. Do you have any idea who the other one is?"

"Haven't a clue. But if you'd like me to go and see—" A grinning Lynx was half out of his chair before Matt stopped him.

"That won't be necessary. We'll find out soon enough. Both are bound to want to get out and stretch their legs tomorrow when we stop to take on more coal and water."

"Then I'll be happy to escort them for you, Matt."

"No. You'll need to keep your mind on the silk. I'll get Kwa-ling to watch over them instead."

A disappointed Lynx said, "You sure are determined to make this a dull trip."

"And you'd better pray that I succeed. Unless you're itching for another shoot-out down the line."

"That's not the kind of excitement I'm lookin' for," Lynx admitted.

Matt soon finished his meal, laid his linen napkin by his plate, and said, "I'll see you later, Lynx." As he walked through the dining car, he stopped to speak with some of the other guards who had come in. Kwa-ling watched through the passageway of the galley kitchen until his boss was out of sight.

That night, while the train sped through the wilderness, Matt, finally alone in his car, leaned over the mahogany desk and finished the paperwork having to do with his latest purchase of Texas steers. Unlike his neighbor, Antoine, he had realized that the early bonanza years were over, with prices for meat steadily going down. The Easterners seemed to prefer, at least for the moment, corn-fed cows over those that grazed on prairie and buffalo grass.

With all of his holdings, Matt could afford to ride out this temporary shift in the public's tastes. But he knew that many of the other ranchers could not. More than the usual number of cowboys would be out of work this coming winter, but not his own hands. It was important for him to keep buying more grazing land and more cattle, to maintain the way of life inherited from his grandfather. But in order to do so, he needed to find new sources of income.

The day he'd seized upon the idea of building a silk filature on the Red River of the North had been a momentous one. For months he'd watched rich cargoes of oriental raw silk speeding regularly across the entire continent on the way to the Eastern ports and the ships sailing to Europe.

Then the thought occurred to him: Why should all the raw silk be sent to France and Belgium? Why not weave the cloth closer to home for the ladies of Chicago and New York to buy? Now Matt realized he'd taken a tremendous gamble, sinking so much money into this new venture. But the gamble was beginning to pay off in a big way.

Satisfied, he closed his ledger and walked to the open platform, where he stood to survey the evening sky. As the train rounded a curve, he noticed the dim light from the chandelier in the last passenger car. Then the rails

straightened and the intervening dining car obscured his
view.

In a berth hidden by red damask draperies, Anya lay
and listened to the steady breathing of a sleeping Sarah.
In the temporary shelter of the moving train, it had been
so easy for her to forget the trouble following her—at
least for brief periods of time. But now, in the dark, all
confidence deserted her. Once she left the silk train,
she'd be more vulnerable than ever. No matter where
she went, Igor would eventually find her, destroying
both her and the papers she had confiscated. All she
could realistically hope for was some place to hide from
him for a time. But where?

Igor had been on her mind all evening. She'd seen his
handsome, cruel face as she'd gone through the motions
of washing away the day's dirt and grime from her person
and smoothing her wrinkled traveling suit across the back
of an empty seat. Her fear, that he might appear at any
moment, had even compelled her to keep on her underwear, like some poor soul poised for flight, rather than
putting on her gown in privacy as Sarah had done.

Lulled by the steady, monotonous clack of train wheels
on rigid iron tracks, an exhausted Anya finally closed her
eyes. Her troubled thoughts took flight like the geese
earlier that day, and she drifted into an uneasy sleep.

With each shifting grade of the terrain, the flickering
brass chandelier swung like an erratic pendulum. Long before morning, when all oil was spent, the second passenger car attached to the silk train plunged into total
darkness.

Chapter 3

Anya awoke with cold steel pressed to her temple.

Completely disoriented in the dark, she began to struggle against an unknown assailant. But as her arms flailed the air, hitting nothing, she realized that no one was about. The small pistol under her pillow had merely slipped from its hiding place during her restless sleep.

"Is something the matter?" a sleepy Sarah called out from the adjacent berth.

"No. I'm sorry I disturbed you. I was having a bad dream," Anya replied.

"It must have been that strange dish we had for supper. Kwa-ling could benefit from a few cooking lessons."

"Yes, it was probably the food," Anya agreed. "Well, good night again."

"Good night," Sarah murmured, quickly going back to sleep.

Anya was not so lucky. She stayed awake for a long time, sitting up, with her hand cradling the pistol. But as the minutes multiplied, she realized it would be insane to spend the remainder of the night in that rigid position. She put the weapon beneath the pillow and lay down, willing her body to take in even, long breaths of air until a calmness soothed her mind and she slipped once again into needed slumber.

As the sun came up, igniting the vast landscape, Matt had already begun his day. He was aware that the silk train was now winding its way through the sacred land of Tall Tree, the Heyoka medicine man who had long ago befriended Matt Bergen's father, saving him with his herbs. He was now Matt's friend, treating the injuries of his cowboys when no doctor was about.

But Matt did not see the land that morning with the same vision as the Indian. Tall Tree's ancient heights, where only eagles could soar and kindred spirits could converse in language known only by those who remembered their primitive dreams, had been subdued, the faces of the mountains blown off by dynamite and the voices in the wind merely the hum of telegraph wires.

Instead of beauty, Matt was aware of danger—in the low supply of water and fuel, in the rapidly rising elevation that would be too strenuous for the train to continue unaided, relying instead on auxiliary engines waiting to pull the cars over the vast mountain. He would feel a lot better once they'd gotten through the tunnel.

Inside the engine, where he'd spent the latter part of the night, a frustrated Lynx, his face half blackened from coal dust, was also uneasy. For nearly fifteen years he'd followed Matt to hell and back, breaking in mustangs, chasing outlaws, going on Texas drives, riding the range. But it had all been done in the saddle. It just wasn't natural for a cowman to be riding an engine instead of a horse. And he couldn't understand why Matt would want to get into something so foreign to his nature.

It certainly wasn't as if he'd been cut out of the herd, like an old bull buffalo, destined to spend the rest of his life alone on the plain, ignored by his kind until a mountain lion brought him down. Matt had a lot of friends, including some highfalutin ones—Mr. Roosevelt from New York, and that foreign kettle of fish, the Marquis de Mores. But maybe that was the trouble. He'd listened to too many of the marquis's wild schemes.

Maybe this was the right time for Lynx to move on, to have a life of his own. He'd laid by enough money for a small spread. But a ranch needed a woman—a wife.

Lynx's foul mood softened as he thought of the teacher riding on the train. Not many of her sort ever came to places like Medora. A lot of men would want to court her. Even though he'd pretended indifference, he knew that, to stand a chance with her, he needed to get the jump on all the other bachelors before the train reached the town. Despite Matt, he'd make sure he met her that morning, as soon as the train stopped.

The sudden action of the engineer brought Lynx out of his daydreaming. "What's the matter, Joe?"

"The track ahead. Look!"

"My God! We'll all be killed!"

The abrupt action of the engineer stopping the train brought a massive jolt, a protesting cry of steel against steel affecting each car, one after the other, until, in the last passenger car, a sleeping Anya and Sarah were dumped unceremoniously out of their berths. Landing on the red Persian carpet runner in the aisle, they stared at each other in surprise.

The fear that Igor had caught up with them and had, somehow, stopped the train, was Anya's first thought. But no, that wasn't logical. He would not have had time. "There must be something on the tracks," she said, slowly getting to her feet. Holding out her hand to help Sarah, she asked, "Are you all right?"

"I think so."

"Then, we'd better hurry and dress," Anya suggested. "We might be stopped for quite a while."

"I hope it's no more serious than a fallen tree blocking the tracks."

A spine-tingling howl, the neighing of horses, and the sound of shots exchanged, indicated a much worse situation. Hearing the noise, Sarah turned pale. "It sounds as if we're being attacked."

"Yes." Anya hurried to the berth to retrieve her purse from under the pillow.

"My mother was scalped by Indians—"

"It might be outlaws instead," Anya said, remembering the stationmaster's words.

"I think I'd rather be captured by outlaws than Indians," Sarah said.

"No one is going to capture us," Anya assured her. "Whoever is out there is much more interested in the silk. But if anybody gets past the guards, I have a gun to protect us."

"Maybe if we're quiet and stay out of sight, no one will even know we're on the train."

Outside, the gunfire continued. An angry Matt, defending his cargo from the open windows of the dining car, was not fooled by the war paint. He would recognize that scoundrel, Driscoll, anywhere—by the way he sat his horse. It didn't matter whether he used a saddle or rode bareback, as he did now. But he was a clever one, as most scoundrels were, sprinkling a few renegade half-breeds among his band of outlaws, so that the poor Indians would be blamed. He should have strung him up three years ago in the arroyo when he'd caught him branding some of Matt's calves as his own.

"God, I wish I had a horse under me," Lynx complained at Matt's side. "If we ever get out of this, I'll never—"

"I don't like being pinned down any more than you do," Matt interrupted. "So stop bellyaching and shoot that bastard coming up on your left."

In the passenger car, Anya listened to the raging battle without seeing anything, for the blinds were still drawn at the windows and she didn't dare open them to see.

For her, the experience was similar to being hidden the previous day under the longboat's tarpaulin, with each minute stretched into an interminable time period, ungoverned by the clock. But now there was no Ashak to tell her how many guards were on board, who the enemies were, and who was winning. She would have to wait, yet be prepared to defend both Sarah and herself.

At the sound of broken glass and a scuffle on the platform outside their car, Sarah whispered, "Oh, I'm so scared. I think somebody's coming in here."

"Whatever happens, Sarah, stay hidden behind the seat." Anya tightened her hold on her gun and waited, while the breached door slowly opened, revealing the outline of a half-naked man.

At his approach, Sarah forgot Anya's admonition. Her only thought was to get away, to run from the ferocious-looking Indian, who had stepped from her childhood nightmares into the present and was coming to get her as he had gotten her mother. She stood, poised for flight, her movement in the semidarkness of the passenger car attracting the man's attention.

He fired into the shadows, barely missing Anya, who immediately returned his fire. For a split second he remained upright, then he slumped to the floor.

"I think I shot him," a surprised Anya said, not taking her eyes from the man's body. Cautiously, with the gun still in her hands, she left her place behind the Pullman seat and crept toward him, to make certain he was dead.

He was a large man, and, in the dim light, she studied his coarse features, the heavy stubble of beard, disguised by red paint. From that she knew that he was not an Indian, after all. But he was still a man, and she had killed him.

Anya could not afford to panic, to allow remorse to overcome her. What was done was done. But the Dakota Territory, unlike lawless Alaska, had judges and courts of inquiry. In her precarious position, she could not afford to be questioned, to have her name listed in official documents, no matter the certainty of the decision. It would be much better if no one suspected he'd been shot inside the passenger car.

Forcing herself to think of the outlaw as an Eskimo might think of a seal he had just harpooned, she took hold of his feet and tried to drag him outside to the platform. But he was much too heavy for her to accomplish the deed alone.

"Sarah, I'm afraid you'll have to help me," she called. "We need to get him out of the car."

There was no response.

"Sarah?"

Anya walked back to the seat where she and Sarah had hidden. Seeing the unresponsive woman lying on the floor, Anya decided that Sarah had fainted from fright. She knelt beside her and touched her shoulder to try to rouse her. But her hand came in contact with a wet, sticky substance instead. In alarm, she saw the large bloody stain that had spread across the woman's white blouse. Her unseeing eyes stared upward, and there was no sign of life.

"Sarah!" she cried, taking the woman's limp body in her arms. "Please don't be dead, Sarah." The tears that Anya had not shed for herself now flowed for a young woman she had met a mere twenty-four hours earlier. But in that brief time, Anya had come to know Sarah's sweet, loving spirit, her eagerness, her enthusiasm. "Don't let *your* dreams die, too, Sarah Macauley."

Outside, the battle started anew, but Anya paid little attention. She sat on the floor and held Sarah, her thoughts on the unfairness of life. If anyone had to die, it should have been Anya Fodorsky, for her fate had been sealed from the moment she'd left Sitka.

She looked down at the small opal on Sarah's finger, and then to the ruby and diamonds encircling her own ring finger. Despite the differences in price, each had the same value, for both had been given in love—the ruby by Anya's father, the opal by Sarah's mother.

She didn't know why she did it, exchanging the rings for a moment. She only remembered thinking what a joke on Igor, if their personal effects became mixed up—and he thought that Anya was dead instead of Sarah. But, of course, she could never give up her ring, the possession that was dearest to her heart.

Yet the idea, once planted, refused to go away. What if she switched identities with Sarah? No one on the train had seen them, except Kwa-ling. And not a single person in the town, by Sarah's own admission, knew her by sight. But life as a teacher—? Could Anya manage? Helping Father Ambrose at the mission school was not the same as being responsible for the education of an entire town. But she'd had a classical education. Her father had seen to that. And with Sarah's trunk, full of books and lessons, surely she could manage it—at least for a while, until she could arrange something else.

Anya did not have the luxury of time to weigh her decision. A blond giant of a man came crashing through the opposite door at that moment, shouting, "Miss Macauley, where are you? Are you safe?"

She only had time to pick up the wire-rimmed glasses and peer myopically toward him. "I'm here," Anya an-

swered. "But a terrible tragedy has occurred. This
woman is dead."

Chapter 4

Matt Bergen knelt down beside the dead woman and
felt for a pulse in her throat. "She had no business being on this train," he barked. "Who is she? And how
did it happen?"

Through Sarah's glasses, the scowling man beside her
looked formidable. "Anya, the Princess Fodorsky. At
least that's who she said she was."

"And is this her gun?"

"Yes."

"Did she shoot herself?"

"Of course not," Anya answered, his condescending
tone causing an angry flush to spread across her cheeks.
"The Indian shot her."

"What Indian?"

"The one who—You'll find his body at the end of the
aisle."

Anya had not expected such a verbal bombardment
from an overbearing stranger. She needed to be alone to
think, to decide whether she was actually doing the right
thing or not. Turning the situation to her advantage, she
said, "Excuse me, please. I think I'm going to be ill."

She fled toward the water closet, leaving Matt alone with Sarah and the dead outlaw.

When Anya returned, the outlaw had been removed from the car and Matt's attention now focused on the tragedy of Sarah. "We'll have to bury her," Matt said, "and send her things back to her nearest of kin. Which is her valise?"

Anya noticed the treasured ruby ring already in the man's hand. Her money, her clothes—all her things, even her gun—would be sent back to Igor. She regretted the loss of her ring most of all. Yet, she realized, it was necessary if her husband were to believe that she was truly dead. He knew how much it meant to her. But what a pity that she'd had no time to retrieve at least a few gold coins, since Sarah had confided her financial impoverishment.

Anya hesitated, but the lie concerning her identity had gone too far for her to retract. "The one over there," she finally replied, pointing to her own paisley valise.

Not far from the rails, with the morning sun casting an eerie glow over the wild, desolate landscape, Sarah, as the Princess Fodorsky, was laid to rest beyond the site selected for the five dead outlaws and one guard. The large pile of rocks that had been placed on the tracks to wreck the train was put to better use, protecting the grave.

Matt presided personally over the woman's burial. But feeling the inadequacy of the service, he turned to the stricken Anya, standing beside him. "Would you like to say a few words on her behalf?"

How ironic that he was actually asking her to participate in her own funeral. When she did not answer immediately, he added, "After all, you knew her better than anyone else on the train."

"Yes," she replied in a soft voice. But as she gathered her thoughts, she tried not to remember herself, but Sarah. Saying a few words over her grave was the least she could do in exchange for being given a new chance.

"I did not know the Princess Fodorsky for long," she began. "A mere twenty-four hours. Yet in that brief time, her kindness and sweetness, her zest for life, were apparent. She marveled in the quieter things—the beauty of words, the majesty of the mountain lakes we passed, the flight of the wild geese from the still waters. Today, she, too, has taken flight to the heavens . . ." Anya's voice broke in a small sob. Then she quickly continued, "We on earth wish her the pleasantest of journeys. . . ."

The guards stopped their work and listened, strangely affected by Anya's eulogy. "She's a fine teacher," one whispered. "You can tell."

"Yes. The children in Medora will be lucky to have her."

Lynx, with his face still blackened from coal dust, overheard their comments. His chest swelled with pride. They were talking about the woman he had selected to marry. Only Miss Sarah Macauley didn't know it yet.

* * *

Like a wail, the train's whistle announced that sufficient steam had built up and it was time to continue the journey.

"You will, of course, ride in my private car for the rest of the day, Miss Macauley," Matt stated.

Being with the man was the last thing that Anya wanted. "Thank you, but I really prefer to remain where I am."

"What you prefer has nothing to do with it. The next few miles are going to be extremely hazardous. You're in my care, like it or not, and I intend to see you safely delivered to Medora."

"I'm not your cargo of silk, Mr. Bergen."

Her show of spirit irritated him. "If only you were, then I could lock you up in a boxcar and forget about you."

His hand on her elbow was firm, guiding her to his private car. There was nothing she could do about it for now, but it was imperative for her to go through Sarah's trunk, her books, her correspondence. If she were to be successful in the charade that had so unexpectedly landed at her feet, then she would have to be well versed in the life of Sarah Macauley before reaching Medora.

A quick glance around the private car indicated that Matt liked to travel in comfort. Far more luxurious than the other car, the surroundings resembled an opulent suite, with seats of plush mohair and furniture of the best red mahogany. Indicating a chair, Matt sat down at his desk, his attention on the report he needed to write.

Deliberately choosing another seat as far away from the desk as possible, so that she might remove the glasses that had begun to give her a headache, Anya sat in silence, with her hands clasped together. She made no effort to converse.

Finally speaking, Matt said, "We'll be passing through a tunnel any minute. Don't be alarmed at the blackness."

Anya did not look up. She merely nodded and continued her silence.

Matt had not expected this reaction. He'd been prepared for constant interruption. Instead, the young woman seemed self-contained, not looking to him for anything beyond her forced shelter. Rather than being relieved, he felt oddly disappointed.

He gave up trying to draft his report of the attempted train robbery. Without being too obvious, he watched the still figure at the end of the car. For someone who'd been through such a harrowing experience, Sarah Macauley was remarkably calm. Too calm, in his estimation. Then it dawned on him. She was still in shock. That was why she was so silent, why she seemed oblivious to the bloody stains on her traveling suit.

He set aside his paper and pen and walked to the seat opposite her. "We'll be going through the tunnel any moment now."

Startled at his voice so near, she did not have time to put on the wire-rimmed glasses. She stared at him, the magnificent color of her eyes undisguised. And as she did so, some strange emotion he could not put a name to overwhelmed him. The sudden jolt through his entire body made him remember when he'd been thrown by his horse during a violent summer storm. Mercifully, for Matt, the passenger car roared into the tunnel.

The clacking wheels reverberated, keeping time to the rapid beating of his heart. His senses heightened, each nuance of sound magnified by the blackness. He was aware of the woman nearby, so close, in fact, that he had to force himself not to reach out to touch her. The feeling was foreign to him, unbidden and unwelcome, and he struggled against it.

Once the passenger car emerged into the light again, Matt had regained his aplomb. Continuing his conversation as if the experience had never occurred, he said, "I'm sorry you've had no food this morning. And I'm afraid it will be longer still, since Kwa-ling won't be able to cook until we get through the pass."

"I'm really not hungry," Anya said, her glasses back in place on the bridge of her nose. Then, feeling as if Sarah would not have been so abrupt, she smiled and said, "Is it true that nine engines are waiting to pull the train over the mountains?"

"Yes, it's true. But if you're afraid of heights, you'd better not look over the precipice. You'll think you're falling off the mountain any minute."

"I'm only afraid of what I can't see, Mr. Bergen."

"Then you'll have to change your attitude, if you're to survive in the Dakota Territory."

Anya pressed her lips tightly together, to keep from retorting. What a greenhorn he must think her. She would love to tell him that anyone who'd survived half a lifetime in Alaska would have no trouble in Dakota. But she knew she must not be angered into giving herself away. She was no longer the headstrong, proud Anya. For her, the past was dead. The sooner she began to think of herself as Sarah Macauley, teacher, the safer she would be.

"Miss Macauley?"

"Yes?"

"Your first name is Sarah, is it not?"

Anya nodded.

"And mine is Matt. Only my enemies call me Mr. Bergen."

From that, Anya gathered that they were now on a first-name basis.

The train began to slow again, indicating that they were finally approaching the first wilderness way station. Matt stood and said, "When the train stops, it's best if you remain here, Sarah."

"How long will it be, Mr."—she quickly caught herself—"Matt?"

"Only a few minutes."

Once he'd left, Anya looked out the window. The way station in the middle of nowhere was a surprise. Yet it should not have been. Additional supplies for the Northwest railroad were every bit as important to survival as the crude Alaskan huts spread throughout the tundra. Many a trapper or traveler caught in a sudden blizzard had been saved by one, with its store of food and firewood. If her own father had been able to crawl a few hundred yards more in the snow, he, too, would have been saved. At least that's what Igor had told her. Back then she had believed him. The mistrust came later, after they were married. Perhaps he had lied to her about her father's death, too.

Outside, everyone seemed to be busy. She saw Kwa-ling hurrying toward the water tank with his twin iron kettles. And two guards, with rifles, disappeared into the brush. The shots that rang out alarmed her, until she saw the two returning with deer over their shoulders— probably their dinner for that night.

For the past several hours, Anya had longed for the opportunity to return to the other passenger car. True, she would have to pass through the dining car to get there, but seeing Kwa-ling outside, Anya felt safe enough. And watching Matt scale the water tower, she realized she could easily be back in her seat before he missed her.

"It's not fair, Matt."

"What are you complaining about now, Lynx?" he asked, looking down from the tower, where he was adjusting the pouring spout.

"What all the men are grumblin' about. That they haven't had a chance to be near the new schoolteacher or talk with her."

Matt laughed as the water began to flow into the open tank behind the engine. Raising his voice over the noise, he teased, "And what makes you think she'd take notice of any of you sorry good-for-nothings? Especially you, Lynx."

"Well, now, I'm not such a bad-lookin' fellow."

"Have you looked at yourself lately?"

"What's the matter?"

"You resemble a chimney sweep, with all that coal dust on your face."

A surprised Lynx took the palm of his hand, rubbed

his chin, and then stared down at the black residue. "Damn it, Matt. Why didn't you tell me sooner?"

"I didn't know you were in the courting mood."

"Well, I am. And the least you can do is invite Miss Macauley to have dinner in the dining car tonight."

"When you're there?"

"Me and some of the other fellows, I reckon."

"Consider it done, Lynx. Far be it from me to stand in the way of true love."

With the tank filled, Lynx closed the iron lid while Matt reanchored the chain to the pouring spout and began to climb down the tower ladder.

"You'll really invite her?"

"I said I would, didn't I? Now round up the rest of the men. It's past time to go."

In the passenger car that she'd shared with Sarah, Anya hurriedly went through the battered trunk, looking for the teaching contract and subsequent correspondence. She had not realized that the trunk was locked, and she chided herself that she'd lost valuable time retracing her steps back to the second car for the key in Sarah's purse.

She'd not only found the key, but Sarah's money as well. It was far worse than she'd imagined—a few measly coins knotted in the corner of a white linen handkerchief.

Now, gathering the papers she'd been looking for, Anya closed the trunk lid and returned to the other car. But her uneasiness remained. What if the teaching position did not work out and she had to leave Medora in a hurry? How was she to survive without her own money?

Taking her seat, Anya stared across the aisle at the shelf where Matt had put her paisley valise, with the purse inside. Did she dare take some of her own money?

Anya could still hear the men loading supplies. If she were going to do it, this would probably be her only opportunity. Without further hesitation, she rose, opened the valise, and retrieved the purse.

With one gold coin in her hand, Anya glanced over her shoulder. Matt stood in the doorway, a strange expression on his face. She had no idea how long he'd been there, silently watching her.

Chapter 5

"I found a gold piece in the aisle," Anya explained. "Since it must have belonged to the princess, I was putting it back in her purse." Reluctantly she handed the coin to Matt, who now faced her.

"You could have kept it," he said, "and no one would have been the wiser."

"If you had found it, would you have done so, Mr. Bergen?"

"I may be guilty of a few things in my life that I'm not proud of," Matt responded, "but stealing from a dead person isn't one of them."

The censure in his voice was apparent. From his tone,

she knew he did not believe her. And why should he? She'd been caught red-handed.

He took the coin and the heavy purse from Anya. "I didn't realize the woman was carrying so much money. I should have put her effects in the safe immediately."

Anya sat down. Shuffling Sarah's papers, she ignored Matt as he unlocked the safe, deposited her purse with the bag of gold coins, and then relocked the door. But a moment later, he again stood before her.

"We have a good supply of water on board now. If you'd like, I'll escort you to the other car so that you can freshen up." He stared pointedly at her bloodstained traveling suit.

"Yes, thank you. I do need to change."

"Here, I'll take your papers and put them on my desk until you get back. Your spectacles, too."

Anya sighed. Protesting would only cause more suspicion.

The two left Matt's private car, his firm hand on her arm making certain that she did not slip as she jumped across the coupling linking it with the dining car. Seeing Matt approach, Kwa-ling smiled and said, "You like cup of coffee, boss?"

"In a minute," he answered. "First, Miss Macauley needs the kettle of hot water. Is it ready?"

Kwa-ling openly stared at the woman. "Is on stove. I carry it for her."

For the past hour or so, Anya had felt like a prisoner. So it was with great relief that, once she was safe in her own car, Matt jumped onto the other platform, while Kwa-ling helped her with the water. But a quick glance through the open door of the dining car showed Matt settling down for his coffee a mere stone's throw away.

The contents of Sarah's valise offered few dresses from which to choose. Selecting a dull gray one with a pathetic little collar of yellowed lace, Anya set it aside and searched for fresh underwear. The quality of the clothes mattered less to her than their fit. All during her bath, she'd worried, remembering the two senile aunts of her friend, Elaina, and the morning when the eldest had appeared at breakfast, inadvertently dressed in the other sister's clothes.

"I don't know *what* has happened to my wardrobe," the woman had lamented, tugging at the drooping dress and attempting to push back the sleeves that covered her hands. "I'll just have to get the dressmaker to come and alter it."

"*Tía*, that isn't your dress," Elaina had said, attempting to hold back the laughter.

Now, staring at Sarah's dress, Anya wondered if Matt might say the same—that the garment did not belong to her. She could not put off the moment of truth any longer. She slipped the dress over her head, buttoned it, and then looked in the mirror.

What she had feared was evident. Although she and Sarah were almost identical in height, their bodies were quite different; the dress was too large. But perhaps the man would not notice, she thought, especially if she wrapped a shawl around her shoulders. Much could be hidden under a shawl.

Anya looked at her discarded traveling suit. She

would never be able to wear it again because of the stains. But unlike Matt's reaction to it, the sight of Sarah's blood did not repulse her. To Anya, it had a more symbolic meaning—like the smeared lintels that had protected the ancient Hebrews from the angel of death. She did not pretend to understand its full implications. She only knew that she would keep the suit to serve as a reminder of the day she had been given a new life. Folding it, she placed it in the shabby valise and searched for a shawl to wear.

At last, perching a small gray hat on her hair, which she had drawn tightly into a knot on the top of her head, Anya reexamined her image. She looked much more like Sarah now. Satisfied, she patted the stolen papers that she'd sewn into her petticoat and left the passenger car.

When she reappeared, Kwa-ling was waiting to help her across the divide. The bare flicker of surprise at her appearance quickly vanished from Kwa-ling's black eyes. Once inside, he said, "Mr. Matt gone now. But he say you sit down and have cup of coffee. Pretty soon, we start over mountain. Good view through dining car."

She noticed that the adjacent windows all around her had been pulled down and locked, a sure indication that the train was embarking on a more hazardous journey, as Matt had warned. Taking a seat with a good view, a hungry Anya said, "The coffee smells delicious, Kwa-ling."

"Fire put out. Fix food later."

She took a sip of the strong coffee and tried to ignore the rumblings of her empty stomach.

She was soon distracted by the commotion outside—

the switching of engines from the side track to the main line, the shifting and realignment of the train. Lanterns spoke in a language of color, reds and greens and yellow, making it unnecessary for the participants to speak aloud. It would be difficult to be heard anyway, Anya thought, over all the clang and clamor of metal against metal. But finally the signal to move was given. Anya felt the sudden lunge of the dining car. They were now leaving the way station behind.

On the route over the mountains, the tremendous power that all nine engines generated was desperately needed, the titans of steam warring in a constant battle against the titans of nature. At times it seemed that the mountains might win. One slight shift, one slight miscalculation, and the train, with its valuable cargo, could easily disappear into the swirling mist of the bottomless Valhalla directly below.

Like liquid smoke, the clouds surrounded the windows, obscuring Anya's view and giving her a sense of weightlessness, as if the train were no longer anchored to iron railings, but climbing some vaporous trail upward to the heavens.

Unable to see outside, she turned her thoughts inward, the images of childhood imprinting themselves on her mind in brilliant colors, a trick she had used during the interminable days and nights of the midnight sun, when the landscape was painted in harsh, jagged brush strokes of nothing but white—the noncolor of cold, treachery, and danger.

The silk train vanished. She became a child again, the

brilliant colors surrounding her in warmth, until she finally exhausted the palette in her mind and her world became a blinding white again.

"A candle, Papa. Motah won't light a candle for me."

"Anya can see perfectly well without a candle. It's a waste of money."

But Papa understood her fear. "Light a candle for the little one, Motah. It's such a small thing to give her comfort."

The sound of a pan, a dish in the galley kitchen sliding across the floor, suddenly forced Anya back into the present, where Kwa-ling was fighting his own battle to maintain order and stability in his domain.

Shaken by the intensity of her childhood memories, as if she had actually traveled backward in time, Anya chided herself. She looked around her, at the dining tables with their linen covers, at the empty coffee cup in her hands. She touched the nearby window with her fingers, tracing the droplets of moisture gathering in the top left corner. It was not good to become so immersed in the past, as she had. She would be much better served by remaining aware of what was happening in the present.

No one was more aware of the present, of the ongoing clash between nature and man, than Matt Bergen, riding in the lead engine. Neither he nor the chief engineer spoke. However superstitious it might strike others, the same feeling was shared by both—that the added weight of a single word in the air could tax the engines unnecessarily.

Inside each boxcar, the guards were silent, too. They carefully watched the roped crates that had been lashed down to keep them from shifting. No sudden movement on their part, no idle conversation, put them at risk. The men listened to the strain of the engines and held their collective breath when it seemed that the train was in danger of stopping its escalation and sliding backward to destruction. Then a sigh of relief would indicate when that particular peril had passed.

But once the silk train reached the heights, the danger was not over, as Anya had hoped, for the downward trip out of the clouds, equally hazardous, equally challenging, began. And so, for the major portion of the afternoon, the defiance against nature continued.

In the dining car, Anya watched for glimpses of snowcapped peaks and jumped when branches of green slapped at the window. Yet the brief occurrences did not take Anya's mind from the constant squeal of brakes and the fire sparks of the wheels. She was exhausted from the noise, her body stiff from sitting, but even if she had wanted to do so, she could not return to either passenger car. If she attempted it, one misstep could assign her to a wilderness grave.

Finally, when Anya's admiration of nature had worn thin and she'd begun to question the sanity of all involved in the mammoth undertaking, the descent from the heights suddenly ended with a smooth gliding of the engines into another way station.

A great roar of men's voices erupted, resembling the

sounds of a successfully completed Texas cattle drive. Understanding its exuberance, Matt regretted his promise to allow Miss Sarah Macauley to have dinner in the dining car that night.

"I'm sorry about your glasses, Sarah," Matt said, picking up the frames that had been smashed by the paperweight from his desk.

"It wasn't your fault, Matt."

"Oh, but it was. And I'll have them repaired for you. That is, if you feel you really need them."

What was Matt saying? That he'd found her out? That sometime during the day he'd discovered she wasn't Sarah, after all? "What are you talking about? Of course I need them."

"No, you don't. I've seen how you stumble when you wear them. And I watched you peering over them to read." His mouth curved into a knowing smile. "They're just a prop, aren't they? Who do they really belong to, Sarah? Your cousin Lettie?"

Anya tried to look appropriately guilty, but relief was all she felt. "They belonged to—to my mother."

"And did that hat and dress belong to your mother, too?"

"What's wrong with them?"

"Stop playing games with me, Sarah. I won't allow it. Just as I won't allow you to go into dinner looking like you do now. The men have had a difficult day, but they've gone to a great deal of trouble getting ready for tonight, since they know you're coming. So take off

that monstrous hat and comb your hair the way it was."
He pointed to the mirror at the other end of the car.

A few minutes later, she faced him again. "Well? Do
I meet with your approval?"

"Much better," he acknowledged. "Still . . ." Matt
walked to the velvet valise and opened it. Pulling out a
red cashmere shawl embroidered with yellow roses, he
said, "Wear this."

"I seem to remember your words about stealing from
the—"

He didn't let her finish. "You won't keep it," he said.
"You're borrowing it just for tonight. If the husband
didn't mind his wife traveling alone, he certainly won't
object to your wearing her shawl for a few hours."

The mention of Igor effectively stopped further retort.

"Now let's go on to the dining car. We're celebrating
with venison tonight."

It was just as well that Anya had no idea of the commotion she'd caused among the guards. That evening,
as Matt brought her into the dining car to eat, she
merely saw an eager assemblage of cowboys slicked
down, faces clean. Standing awkwardly, they waited for
her to take her seat. She was not aware that some had
given up their entire month's salary for a chance to get
a clearer view of her for even a short time.

As Matt's foreman, Lynx had been the one who'd
thought up the lottery, since only half the guards could
leave the cargo at one time. Matt didn't know it, but
he'd even sold off the other two places at the same table
to the highest bidders. Of course, the money Lynx made

would change hands at cards several times before the train reached Medora. He was as certain of that as he was that the two ugliest ones would bid the highest for the seats. And they had. With Matt not sitting at the table, it meant he'd have the best chance to make a good impression.

"Miss Macauley, may I present my foreman, Lynx Mulligan."

"Mr. Mulligan."

The sandy-haired Lynx, with a clean blue bandanna around his neck and his spurs making a jangling sound, stepped forward. With his arm extended, he said, "A pleasure to meet you, ma'am. I'll escort you to your table."

Surprised, she looked at Matt, who nodded his assent. Anya had no recourse but to take Lynx's arm, since Matt had evidently abandoned her. Directly in front of her was the gauntlet of men, poised on each side of the aisle.

She knew how Sarah would have reacted to the situation—a little embarrassed, with her eyes cast down in modesty. And she might have tried to act the same way, if Matt had not taken such perverse pleasure in throwing her to the wolves, so to speak. But they did not intimidate her since, heaven knows, she'd had enough practice running a gauntlet of stiff-necked, overbearing minor royalty and consuls. So she lifted her head, smiled, and nodded to each man as she walked to the waiting table. In turn, she was rewarded with bashful smiles and looks of appreciation.

But seeing two of the ugliest men she'd ever seen in

her life—waiting for her to sit down beside them—almost unnerved her. Not knowing that it was Lynx, instead of Matt, who had arranged these other dinner partners, she began to make immediate plans to repay him.

Taking her seat, she said, "Hello. I'm Sarah Macauley."

"The new schoolteacher for Medora," Lynx added in a possessive manner, as if he were already well acquainted with her. "This here's Travis, and this one's Snake Man."

"Howdy do, ma'am," they chorused.

"And do you both live in Medora?" she asked.

"Well, me, I live closer to Dickinson, when I'm not ridin' the line," Travis answered.

"The rail line?"

Lynx laughed. "No, ma'am. Ridin' the line means the same as ridin' the range. We all work for Matt. But me, I been thinkin' recently of startin' my own spread."

"I never knew that, Lynx," a surprised Snake Man responded. "Have you talked to Matt about it?"

"Not yet. I'd like to keep it under my hat for a while longer."

Kwa-ling appeared with the plates piled high with venison and gravy. Lynx, who'd gotten in some practice that day because of the close calls, offered to pray over the food, too. Women expected that sort of thing.

He was not the only one at the table who intended to impress the new schoolteacher with his gentlemanly behavior and knowledge. Travis and Snake Man had also planned a few things of their own. They merely waited for Lynx to exhaust his meager repertoire.

Chapter 6

"Never let a snake get so close that he can see the glint of sun in your eye, Miss Sarah."

"Is that what happened to you?" she asked, acknowledging for the first time the black patch Snake Man wore.

"Yes, ma'am."

"He lost an eye and gained a nickname," Travis explained. "All on the same day."

"But I can still down a buffalo with one shot, good as any other man," Snake Man insisted.

"I don't doubt that."

"The next time I go huntin', I'll get one for you. A buffalo robe is mighty warm. You'll be needin' one this comin' winter."

"How kind of you. I appreciate that very much. I understand all of General Custer's troops were issued buffalo coats when they enlisted."

"Didn't help *them* much," Lynx said, out of sorts that Snake Man had thought of the gift first.

"But Lynx, Miss Sarah ain't goin' to be out fightin' Indians," Travis reminded him. "She's goin' to be in that snug schoolhouse we're all gonna raise for 'er."

"That's right," Lynx said, smiling again. "Since I'm

47

in charge, as Matt's foreman, I'll see to it that it's the finest schoolhouse this side of Bismarck."

"I got two leaded-glass windows I been savin' for a long time," the smitten, pockmarked Travis confessed. "I reckon your livin' quarters on the back could use 'em."

Anya became distressed at such generosity. "No, Travis," she said. "You mustn't sacrifice your glass windows. Wooden shutters will be fine."

"Won't be a sacrifice. If you don't mind me bein' so bold, I ain't never seen eyes the color of yours before. They need to be took care of, with good light for your readin'."

"I hate to break up the party," Matt's voice interrupted from the entrance of the dining car. "But the other guards want to eat, too. So on your way, boys."

A reluctant Snake Man looked at Anya. "Thank you, ma'am, for lettin' us sit at the table with you."

"It sure was a pleasure, Miss Sarah," Travis said, getting up, too. "If you ever need anything, just call on old Travis here."

Anya smiled. "Thank you both. And you, too, Lynx."

Lynx remained at the table with Anya until the men had all dispersed. "I'll escort you back to your quarters now. I know how tired you must be."

But as they began to walk, Anya hesitated. "Aren't we going in the wrong direction?"

"No, ma'am."

"But the passenger car I shared . . ."

"Didn't Matt tell you? It's gone. He left it on the side track before we started over the mountains."

"But the trunk's in it, with all my books ... my clothes ..."

"Matt put the trunk in the boxcar with the lumber. Guess you'll have to ask him what he did with your clothes."

When they reached the platform, Matt nodded to Lynx. "Better get on up to the engine."

"Sure thing, Matt. Well, good night, Miss Sarah."

"Good night, Lynx. And thank you for a lovely evening."

She watched him swing up the ladder and disappear, as surefooted as a mountain goat, along the catwalk of the silk train.

"Did you enjoy your venison, Sarah?"

She ignored Matt's question. "Why did you uncouple the other passenger car? Where am I to sleep? Here, on the open platform?"

"This is hardly the night for that—with the storm brewing." As if to give emphasis to his prediction, a lightning bolt lit up the evening sky. But instead of thunder, a jangle of spurs all along the catwalk of the train followed. "We'd better go inside to discuss it. I wouldn't want you to be caught in the stampede."

Anya barely had time to get out of the way before the second wave of hungry guards swung downward and raced for seats in the dining car.

Inside his private Pullman, Matt said, "There're several berths to choose from. Take your pick, Sarah."

"You mean ... in here with you?"

"Think of this as just another Pullman on the train."

"But it isn't. It's yours," she protested.

"Once you draw the draperies, it shouldn't matter."

"It matters to me. I don't see why you suddenly decided to take off the other car."

He began to show his irritation. "Think back over the day, Sarah. Weren't there moments when you questioned whether the train was going to make it through the mountains or not?"

"Yes, a few times," she confessed, grudgingly.

"So then you understand why I had to do it. The silk shipment was unusually large this trip, and the lumber for the schoolhouse added to the weight. An extra Pullman car would have been disastrous."

"Why didn't you come to that conclusion before we left Seattle?"

"I did. But I won't debate the issue any further."

Suddenly seeing how tired he looked, Anya's anger subsided. "I'm sorry, Matt. Rather than complain, I should thank you. At least you were kind enough to give your two passengers twenty-four hours of luxurious privacy."

"Don't attribute any kindness to me!" Matt snapped, his irritation showing again. "I got one of you killed."

"It wasn't your fault."

"Everything that happens on this train is my fault," he shot back. "But what was that other woman doing on the train, anyway?" he repeated, his question having gone unanswered all day. "Who let her on?"

"That was *my* fault, I'm afraid. I persuaded Mr. Wagoner to sell her a ticket since she seemed so desperate. I think she was running away from her husband."

Matt nodded. "I suspected as much."

Anya removed the red shawl, folded it, and walked to the valise that had been hers. With her back turned, she said, "Is her husband the one you'll send her belongings to?"

"Yes. I'll attend to it as soon as I deliver the silk to my factory outside Fargo."

"How long will that take?"

"Another few days. I'll send a letter ahead, and then ship her things to Sitka next month from Seattle."

With the other shawl across her shoulders, a relieved Anya took a seat and closed her eyes. The tragic news, and all her belongings, would get to Igor before the ice began to block the waterways in August. If he believed that she was truly dead—and he would have no reason not to—he would call off his spies, and she could spend an entire winter in safety. But she knew Igor well. His suspicious mind would be at work all winter. Once the ice began to break in late spring, she would have to move on.

A clap of thunder gave Anya a start and she opened her eyes. Matt stood directly over her. "I was just going to wake you. But I see the thunder did that for me."

"I didn't realize I had dozed."

"The sound of the train wheels becomes very hypnotic, especially at night. But I think you'll be more comfortable in a berth. Choose the one you want, and draw the draperies." He began to walk away. "I'm going to check with Kwa-ling about tomorrow."

So he had the presence of mind to leave the car long enough for her to get ready for bed. That, at least, was in his favor. As she stood, she saw Sarah's shabby valise at her feet.

Once in bed, she fought against going to sleep. Her bad dreams had wakened Sarah the evening before. She could not afford for the same thing to happen that night. But added to her other burden was the realization that she was an interloper who had usurped another woman's name, her mission, and even her nightgown.

She was still awake when Matt returned, and later, she heard him climb into the berth directly opposite. Remaining quiet, she listened to the sounds around her. Far into the night, the lonely wail of the train's whistle vied with the cry of nocturnal animals foraging for sustenance. But in the end, with a slight snore coming from the other berth, Anya fell asleep, too.

Matt's insistent voice woke her. "Sarah, are you awake? Kwa-ling has brought your breakfast."

A sleepy Anya yawned and stretched. Then she sat up quickly. Was it morning already? Had she slept the entire night through, without disturbance?

"Yes, I'm awake," she answered, brushing her hair out of her eyes. "Tell Kwa-ling to leave the coffee by the chair."

"I'll do better than that," Matt answered. "Here it is."

Before Anya knew what had happened, she was staring into Matt's face. "Your breakfast, ma'am," he said in a teasing manner, offering her the bamboo tray from the partially opened drapery.

Her reaction to seeing a man so early in the morning was far different from what he expected. She made no startled move. She merely smiled and took the tray, as if she were used to being served in bed, used to seeing a man when she first awoke.

Matt quickly closed the drapery again. "Kwa-ling will be bringing hot water for your bath a little later. I'll be with Lynx for the remainder of the morning, so you'll have the car to yourself."

His voice had changed, a coldness replacing the teasing warmth. Had she done something unknowingly to cause it? Igor had been that way, too, changing moods without warning. Anya shrugged and picked up the steaming cup of coffee. Perhaps all men were like that—Matt included.

So Medora's new teacher was not quite so innocent as she pretended, Matt thought, walking rapidly toward the dining car. She'd made no move to cover herself as any modest young woman would do. In fact, she was probably quite aware of the enticing picture she made—with her soft, angelic face framed by the long tousled hair, and those enormous sleepy eyes staring at him. She'd behaved as if she were the Princess Fodorsky herself, rather than the penniless young Sarah Macauley. Well, that was the last time he would ever do anything like bringing her a morning tray. She could fend for herself the rest of the trip.

Matt sat down in the empty car and waited for Lynx. But he still could not get the woman out of his mind. His thoughts turned to her behavior the evening before in the dining car. Oh, still rather prim and proper, he admitted, but ingratiating herself with half the men on board.

Now he realized what her game must be in coming to the Territory. She was looking for a husband—and to think he'd almost fallen into the trap himself!

" 'Mornin', Matt. Did Miss Sarah sleep well last night?" Lynx asked, sliding into the seat opposite him.

"How should *I* know?"

"Well, you don't have to bite my head off this early in the day, just for askin' a civil question."

"I've got more important things on my mind. You heard the rain, I suppose?"

"All night."

The first group of guards began to swagger into the dining car, good-natured laughter and camaraderie evident in their behavior. Some stopped off at the table where Matt and Lynx sat. But it was the foreman they wanted to see.

" 'Mornin'. When does the biddin' begin, Lynx?"

Lynx's eyes flashed a sudden warning. "Later, boys. I'll talk to you later. Me and Matt are havin' a conference right now."

"What was that about?" Matt asked.

"Oh, the boys are havin' a little raffle, to keep their spirits up."

But then the truth became apparent when two other men stopped. "Snake Man and Travis haven't quit talkin' about last night," the one called Gus said. "Travis allowed if he had any more money, he wouldn't mind payin' *two* months' salary just to get to sit with Miss Macauley again."

"Yeah," the second cowboy added. "But I told him it was *our* turn tonight."

"Sorry to disappoint you," Matt responded. "Miss Macauley won't be eating in the dining car for the rest of the trip. She'll take her meals in the Pullman."

"That's not fair, Matt."

"I didn't say it was. But that's the way it's going to be."

The two men groaned and walked on, realizing their boss would not change his mind.

"All right, Lynx, explain yourself. Did you charge Snake Man and Travis for last night?"

An uncomfortable Lynx hedged. "You heard Gus. They were more than willin' to pay."

"Give them their money back."

"You shouldn't be so hard on everybody, Matt. You can't imagine how much it means to the men to be around a fine woman, even for an hour."

"You greatly exaggerate the experience, Lynx."

"That's easy for you to say, since you now have Miss Sarah all to yourself."

Chapter 7

"Idiot! You let her get away."

"She had help, my prince," the servant, Torzhok,

said, cowering before Igor. "But she is being followed. Soon the princess will be persuaded to come home."

Igor laughed at the man's choice of words. "The only persuasion that will work with her is a rope around her pretty neck."

"If that is what you wish, my prince."

"But she is to come to no harm," he insisted. "I want the pleasure of punishing her myself. You can have Ashak to do with as you will."

Dismissing Torzhok with a haughty nod, Igor began to pace back and forth. His long strides resembled those of a caged snow leopard, his sculptured face in quiet, dangerous contemplation.

He looked around him, aware of the room, its fine furnishings, and its former owner, William Winstead. The American and his daughter, Anya, had been quite useful. Because of the two, Igor had been able to remain in Alaska until the sea otter trade had been depleted.

Igor's plan had always been to make enough money so that he could eventually go back to St. Petersburg and enter the society his name assured him. He'd had one without the other for so long—a name, but no fortune, not even enough rubles to repair the roof of the family dacha. And now that he had accumulated a fortune, it was Anya who threatened to destroy the other. He had to get the incriminating papers back and silence her forever.

A pity, though, that it had turned out this way. The first time he'd seen young Anya Winstead riding in the sleigh past the embassy, he'd been captivated by her looks, especially the mane of burnished copper hair, spilling out in riotous curls from her fox fur hood. From that day, he'd watched her grow up, taking her place at her father's side, serving as hostess for his diplomatic dinners. She was as equally at home in French, the polite language of Russian nobility, as she was in the more guttural Aleut, quietly spoken to the servants. Yet Igor's attention to her accomplishments was always diverted by her looks. He remembered thinking one evening that only a whore or a princess would have the audacity to be born with hair that color. After he'd arranged her father's death, he could have made her either one. But thinking of his eventual triumphant return to Russia, he'd chosen to marry her.

Since she'd been so young, he'd even kept Nutee for the times his unusual sexual appetite demanded assuaging. It was better, he'd thought, not to frighten Anya at first. There would be plenty of time later to introduce her to what he liked most.

Now, by running away from him, Anya had lost any consideration he might have allowed. Once she was in his hands again, she would be used as Nutee had been used. And after a week as his prisoner, she would beg him to strangle her.

Igor felt a perverse excitement begin to stir. His face took on a harsh, cruel mien as he shouted, "Nutee! Come here, woman!"

Trembling at the sound of the cossack devil's voice, Nutee grabbed her parka and ran toward the outside kitchen door. Intent on escape, she bumped into a grinning Torzhok. With an iron grip on her wrist, he said, "Didn't you hear the prince calling you?"

"No. And let me go. I have to get more fuel for the cooking fire."

"It might be wiser for you to humor him. Later, when he's in a better mood, Prince Igor will more likely listen when you beg him to spare your brother's life."

"I don't know what you're talking about."

"I'm talking about Ashak. He helped the princess escape. And you know what happens to people who go against the prince."

Nutee felt a pain in her heart. She was already sick of the prince's cruelty to her people. Her brief show of spirit vanished; a great sadness replaced it.

"That's more like it," Torzhok said, relaxing his hold. "Go, now. The prince is waiting for you."

Far away, in the private Pullman of the silk train, Anya sat at the mahogany desk and read the correspondence belonging to Sarah.

"You are indeed fortunate that Amelia Chaboillez has agreed to provide room and board for you until the schoolhouse is built and your living quarters are ready," the letter began. "Her ranch is twenty miles south of Medora, and although she has no grandchildren to benefit from the school, she is still willing to help support it.

"So I advise you to be circumspect in all endeavors, doing nothing to antagonize her in any way. Her late husband was a descendant of one of Dakota's first settlers, and she wields a powerful influence in the Territory. Look to her for guidance, and you will not go wrong."

An uneasiness gripped Anya. Had the Chaboillez woman and Sarah exchanged letters? Quickly shuffling through the papers, she looked for the Chaboillez signature. But it seemed that the only correspondence Sarah had received had been written by the superintendent of schools, with accompanying forms to be filled out regularly, and the one letter from the president of the railroad, outlining her salary—twenty dollars a month.

Anya thought of the few nice clothes she'd been able to bring with her. She'd spent more than twice that amount on one outfit alone. And she couldn't even keep it because of Matt. Actually that wasn't entirely true. It was because of Igor that she'd been forced to give up her valise and the money she would have used to purchase what she needed. A warm winter coat and fur-lined boots were necessities in a land of long, snow-filled winters.

Recalling the thinness of Sarah's coat, folded in the top of the shabby trunk, Anya became downhearted. What irony, if she escaped Igor only to die from the winter's cold. At that moment, Snake Man's promise of a buffalo hide took on much more importance. Anya was glad that, on the previous evening, she had not visibly recoiled from his outward appearance.

If she had learned only one lesson from her cruel husband, it had been that a person's face did not always reveal the heart. Igor had been so charming, and it had been such an easy thing to fall in love with him. She remembered the first time he'd appeared at dinner, a guest of her father's. Through the parlor window, she and her friend, Elaina, had watched his arrival on the spirited white stallion adorned in jeweled, ornate-tooled leather bridle and saddle, with white plumes at the horse's head.

"Look, Elaina," she'd exclaimed. "Isn't he spectacular?"

Elaina giggled. "Are you speaking of the horse or the man?"

"The prince, of course. Just look at how magnificent he is in his uniform."

Igor's coat and trousers, of formfitting red and blue, were decorated with gold. His sweeping dark cape, thrown jauntily over one shoulder, cascaded to his fine polished black boots. Watching him alight, Anya immediately attributed to the Russian prince all the chivalric qualities she'd dreamed of in a fantasy lover. Later, she would discover his flaws and his heinous sins. But that night, she saw only the facade, felt only the magnetism of his charm.

"Papa says he's a friend of the Grand Duke Alexis—and was invited to accompany him and General Custer on a hunting safari in America."

"Then he must be awfully old, Anya," Elaina replied. "At least in his thirties."

"Papa is in his fifties, and I don't think of *him* as old," she responded. Hearing Nutee open the massive front door, Anya became silent and held her finger to her lips to make sure Elaina did the same. But Elaina had already forgotten the prince. Her attention was directed toward the approaching carriage belonging to the Marques d'Oro.

"Prince Igor, may I present my daughter, Anya, and her friend, Elaina de Cascais."

"*Enchanté,* mam'selles," Igor replied, nodding first to Elaina before taking Anya's trembling hand into his own and staring boldly into her eyes.

In despair, a bitter and wiser Anya refused to dredge up further memories from the past. She lay her head on Matt's desk and closed her eyes, seeking to gain absolution from her conscience for the sham she had embarked upon.

A half hour later, Matt found her in the same position, sound asleep. "Sarah, I hate to wake you," he said. "But we're coming to a stop. You'll have to leave the train."

"Are we in Medora already?"

"No."

"Then why do I have to leave the train?" she asked.

"We've come to the damaged trestle," he explained. "Each car will have to be loaded on the ferry and taken across the river."

Anya stood up and reached for Sarah's shawl, which she'd draped across the back of the chair.

"You'll ride in the skiff with Prairie Dog," Matt said. "He'll watch over you while we get the train to the track on the other side."

"Prairie Dog? What sort of name is that?"

"One that was earned by a lot of hard work. But he's

rather sensitive about it. So you'd better not make fun of it in his presence."

"I'm not in the habit of making fun of a person's name. I was merely interested in its derivation."

"Maybe he'll tell you how he came by it, if he likes you. But leave your schoolteacher vocabulary for your pupils. He won't understand."

"Thank you for the advice."

"That's what school board members are for," Matt replied, suddenly smiling.

His words, spoken in a teasing manner, brought a sudden chill. She had not realized that Matt Bergen was one of the officials she would have to answer to.

The high bridge over the gorge looked as secure as any cornstalk bridge Anya had ever seen, but evidently the floodwaters had damaged the underpinnings. As she stood and stared at it, Matt said, "Last week the work train fell into the river. If you look carefully, you can see the break in the tracks."

"Were there any survivors?" Anya inquired.

"No."

He guided her toward the edge of the riverbank, where one of the men she'd seen the previous day, going hunting, waited. "Take good care of her, Prairie Dog," he said, leaving her with the man.

"Here, let me give you a hand, ma'am. The bank is awful steep and slippery."

A few minutes later, Anya was safely in the skiff, headed to the other side of the river, where a large stand of cottonwoods grew. The wind swept along the path of the river, its gusts threatening to tear the shawl from Anya's shoulders. Quickly she grabbed the woolen material and anchored it more securely.

"How long will it take?" Anya asked, thinking of the mammoth operation of getting the two engines and all the boxcars across the river.

"Hard to say," Prairie Dog replied, noncommittally.

"Has it ever been done before?"

"Sure. All the time, before the trestle was finished. Matt knows how to do it."

"That's good to hear. It would be such a shame for him to get the raw silk this far, and then lose it in the river."

Prairie Dog nodded. Rowing harder now against the wind, he turned all his attention to the problem of getting the skiff safely to the other side. Anya, respecting his efforts, did not burden him with further conversation.

At times he rested, allowing the boat to drift with the current. Then his efforts began again, with the ultimate goal still a distance away. He steered between large boulders that jutted from the water, their tops visible despite the high level of the river.

When they were halfway across, storm clouds began to gather, great masses of white changing to gray, and then to an ominous black.

"Looks like we're in for a downpour," Prairie Dog warned.

He had no more than uttered the words when the rain began. Quickly Anya threw the shawl over her head and prayed that the water would not strip the remaining vestiges of the dark tea rinse from her copper-colored hair.

Chapter 8

Seeking cover under a giant cottonwood tree on the other side of the river, Anya watched the seemingly impossible maneuver begin. Strong ropes coupled the first engine to a team of mules. With a shout from the mule master, the team began to strain forward, pulling the engine down the gradual slope to the waiting ferry. "The rain isn't going to help, is it, Prairie Dog?" she said.

"No. A pity it couldn't have waited till tonight."

"How long do you think it will take for the entire train to get across?"

"Probably the rest of the day."

"And you're supposed to sit here with me while all this work is going on?"

"Yes, ma'am."

"If you were alone, what would you be doing right now?"

Prairie Dog hesitated. "Huntin' for game for the men's supper. Tastes mighty good, cooked out in the open like this."

"Then why can't you?"

"Matt would have my hide, Miss Sarah. Watchin' after you was the job he gave me."

"But if *I* decided to go hunting, you'd have to follow me, would you not?"

Prairie Dog grinned. "If you was a shootin' woman, like the marquis's wife, Miss Medora." His face became sober again. "But accordin' to Matt, you're not. So we might as well make ourselves as comfortable as possible."

"Can you keep a secret, Prairie Dog?"

"As good as most men, I guess."

"Matt Bergen doesn't know me well at all. Give me a gun and I'll match you, deer for deer, grouse for grouse. But you musn't tell a soul. Is it a deal?" She held out her hand and waited for him to seal the bargain.

He stared at the proffered hand, small and slender, indecision causing his weathered brow to wrinkle beneath the wide brim of his hat. Then his rough hand reached out. "A deal," he finally said, pumping her hand up and down. "But you'll need more than a gun. Here, take my hat to keep the rain off your face."

"I couldn't take your hat, Prairie Dog."

He was equally stubborn. "Then the deal's off."

"Oh, all right. Give me the hat," Anya said, removing the wet shawl from her head and replacing it with the cowboy's hat. "But wait. Let me drape my shawl around this tree stump. If Matt looks this way, he'll think I'm still huddled under the tree canopy for shelter."

When she had finished, Prairie Dog said, "I know I

don't need to tell you about wild animals, but I consider it my duty, anyway. Some, like deer, run away when they see a human comin', but others stand their ground and charge. Once we're huntin', there'll be no talkin' and you won't go off on your own. You'll stay right beside me."

"Agreed. Now which gun do I get?"

"Which do you want? The pistol or the rifle?"

"The Winchester," she answered.

He loaded it and gave it to her. "Do you have any questions before we start out?"

"No."

"Then let's go."

Anya followed the man in the direction of the far clump of bushes on the rise of land beyond the river bottom. Despite her long skirts, wet and heavy from the rain, she kept up the pace he set. When Prairie Dog stopped the first time, she did the same, her eyes following the slight movement in the grass ahead, as a snake slithered across their path and was gone. Then they continued their silent journey through the tall grass. A few minutes later, they stood before the entrance of the copse.

Motioning for her to find a comfortable spot, Prairie Dog and Anya took cover and waited. The rain came down in steady sheets, bathing Prairie Dog's weathered, unprotected face and dripping from the brim of his hat, which Anya was wearing. For both, getting soaked was of little concern. Keeping the weapons dry was more important.

After what seemed an interminable time, the rain finally subsided. Gradually the sun came out, giving brilliance to the small rain droplets that clung tenaciously to the leafy vegetation.

For Anya, it was difficult, at first, to see the young buck, camouflaged as he was against the landscape of brown and green. But with Prairie Dog's prompting, she saw a slight movement, a toss of the head that gave away the animal's position. Pointing to herself, as if to say, This one is mine, Anya slowly raised the Winchester to her shoulder.

Prairie Dog did not expect Anya to be successful, especially on the first try—with an unfamiliar weapon. But it was early enough so that, even if she scared away most of the animals by a missed shot, he could still gather sufficient game for their supper.

The sound of the shot reverberated downriver, putting to flight a covey of startled birds feeding on wild grain. Matt and Lynx paused a moment from their work, eyes seeking the direction from which the rifle shot had come.

"That's Prairie Dog's Winchester," Lynx said. "I'd recognize its sound anywhere."

Matt nodded. "He probably shot a snake getting a little too close to the schoolmarm." The joking tone disguised his initial alarm at the sound.

Lynx understood, and, like Matt, he waited, listening for returning fire. When it did not come, both relaxed and went back to work.

"I'd be proud to claim that shot, Miss Sarah," an impressed Prairie Dog said, helping Anya up from the ground, where the recoil of the rifle had knocked her. "I just hope you won't have too big a bruise from it."

"I should have remembered how hard they kick."

"Yes, ma'am. Just like a mule. But you rest awhile here. I'll go and get the buck."

"How many more deer do we need?"

"One more. Then I'll send word for Kwa-ling to come across. He can butcher them and start a roastin' fire, while we go huntin' for some birds."

An hour later, Prairie Dog had downed the second deer. Making a travois with two young saplings, he began to drag the carcasses back toward the river. "When we pass the tree stump, you can get your shawl and I'll take my hat back."

A little later, as they sat on the riverbank and guarded the two deer while they waited for Kwa-ling, Anya said, "All day, Prairie Dog, I've been curious about one thing."

"What's that, ma'am?"

"How did you get your name?"

Prairie Dog laughed, then quickly became serious. "Well, several years ago, my horse stepped in a prairie dog hole and went down, trappin' me under him. The horse had to be shot because of his broken leg. At first, I was sorry that Matt didn't shoot me, too, my leg was hurt so bad. But then, after I got well enough, I declared war on every prairie dog town I could find. There's a government bounty on their tails, you know—three cents apiece.

"Now, what happened later, I ain't real proud of. But you'll hear the story sooner or later, anyway. I woke up in the Dickinson saloon on a Sunday mornin' in the middle of a Methodist service, with a collection plate poked in my belly. I'd lost all my money the night before and the church ladies were starin' at me. So I pulled out a few gopher tails from my pocket and put them in the plate. The preacher cashed them in, and pretty soon, other people were doin' the same. That's the story, Miss Sarah, and that's how I got my name."

"Thank you for telling me." Anya did not ask any further questions. She waited the rest of the time in silence, until she saw Kwa-ling, loaded down with his knives and black pots, alight from the ferry. She went to meet him while Prairie Dog remained with their future meal. One moment of inattention and their entire supper could be carried off by predators.

Seeing the smiling Anya coming toward him, with the sun framing her, Kwa-ling gave no indication that he was surprised at her changed appearance, at her hair that was now completely stripped of its disguise. For, in truth, he had been aware of the disguise from the first. China, during its rebellions, had not been kind to white-skinned, light-haired foreigners. They had done the same thing as this woman, resorting to dyes for the hair and the skin in order to survive. But in the end it had not saved them from massacre.

The second time he had seen her—in the passenger car—he had wondered what she was running from. But it was no business of his, just as it was not up to him to mention to anyone—even Matt—how she had arrived in Seattle.

Seeing Kwa-ling loaded down with his wares, like an itinerant tinker, Anya said, "Here, Kwa-ling. Let me help you with some of those pots."

"Missee needs to get dry," he said, handing her several pots to carry. "Not good to stay in wet clothes. I build fire right away."

"That's awfully kind of you," she said, acknowledging his concern. "As soon as you pick out a spot, Prairie Dog and I will gather the wood. He's already shot the game for our supper."

A distance away from the continuing rails, where the silk train had begun to take shape again, car by car, Kwa-ling set up his wilderness kitchen, clearing the land of the surrounding grass, and, with the help of Prairie Dog, he dug a roasting pit.

Using small sticks and grass, the Chinese servant coaxed a fire into being, feeding it then with larger pieces of wood until it flamed upward. Anya, standing close and holding out her hands to the flames, basked not only in its warmth, but in a feeling that she had almost forgotten. But then she jerked her hands back, as if she had been burned. She must not allow herself this weakness. She did not belong to this camaraderie, this circle of beings who took for granted, despite the petty bickerings, a supreme loyalty to one another. She was alone, with no one except herself to depend on for survival.

Anya deliberately walked away from the fire, and Kwa-ling, puzzling why her obvious joy had vanished in an instant, decided that she must have suffered a great loss. He had seen the same bleak look in Matt's eyes when he thought no one was observing him.

For the first time in months, Kwa-ling became hopeful. Could not sorrow shared, as well as joy, bring a man and a woman together? Perhaps the fates had sent this woman with sun-kissed hair to this time and place for a purpose. He would be interested to see what happened next.

Around the fire, pungent with the aroma of venison and grouse, Matt and Lynx, Snake Man and Travis, Prairie Dog and Anya sat, finishing the meal that Kwa-ling had prepared. The others had returned to the silk train, now intact on the rails. Hovering like clouds in the cool breeze, the steam from the twin engines signaled the end of the brief rest. Now it was time to continue the journey.

Seeing Anya beginning to shiver, Matt got up. "I'll walk to the train with Sarah," he said. "The rest of you help Kwa-ling put out the fire and carry the utensils." He looked at Prairie Dog, with his hat pulled low over his face. "You did yourself proud, Prairie Dog. The grouse were especially good."

"But I—" Anya's warning look made him remember his pact with her. "Thanks, Matt," he said, uncomfortable at taking all the credit for the bountiful meal.

On their way back to the passenger car, Matt suddenly reached out to stop Anya as an elk, on its way to the river to drink, bounded across their path. His hand on her sore shoulder caused Anya to wince.

"I didn't mean to hurt you," Matt apologized, once

the animal had gone. "I just wanted to make sure you didn't collide with the elk. Guess I was a little too rough."

"No harm's done," she answered, continuing on her way.

"I do want to thank you, Sarah, for staying out of the men's way while they got their work done today. It couldn't have been much fun for you, sitting and waiting all that time."

"Oh, I was busy, too, in my own way," she answered. "I had lots to think about."

"No doubt. You probably planned the entire school year."

"Well, not the *whole* year."

Anya walked inside the car while Matt remained on the ground and watched for the ones who'd been left at the campfire. A few minutes later, with everyone accounted for, Matt gave the signal to Lynx in the first engine, and, as the train began moving, he hopped aboard the platform of the Pullman.

Anya had her back to him as he entered the car. Under the lighted chandelier, the full impact of her copper-colored hair hit him. So that was what was so different about her appearance—that and the shrinkage of her dress from the rain. Feeling an urgent need to see her at closer range, he strode toward her. "Is your shoulder feeling better?"

At the sound of his voice, she turned, almost bumping into him. Surprised that he was so close, she stammered, "It—it's fine."

But then he saw the discoloration that had begun to

spread upward from her collarbone. A look of dismay marred his handsome features at the sight of the ugly bruise. "Did I do that?"

"No, Matt. I stumbled on a tree stump."

Examining the discoloration more fully, he said, "You're lying."

"Can you prove it?"

"I don't have to. A man would be blind not to recognize the effects of a rifle kick. You were the one using Prairie Dog's Winchester today, weren't you?"

She did not deny it.

Chapter 9

That night, an angry Matt, unable to sleep, lay in his berth and stared at the vertical line of light edging the drawn drapery. He could not get the woman out of his mind. Her appearance, her actions, had changed from one day to the next. Or had it been his perception of her that had changed instead? At that moment, he wasn't sure of anything, except that Sarah Macauley was a thorn in his side, forcing him to feel emotions that he thought he had buried for good.

Damn her eyes, he couldn't even trust her to tell him the truth. If she had lied about shooting a gun, she could have lied about other things, too. Thinking the worst of her made him suddenly feel better. She was not a bit like Mellie, whom he'd adored.

With a guilty start, he realized that he had not thought of Mellie for a long time. Like her letters, tied with faded ribbon and relegated to an attic trunk, her memory had also been gathering dust in the back of his mind. But that night, with his emotions in such turmoil, Matt knew he must resurrect his picture of the perfect, sweet Mellie. She was the only weapon he had against the imperfect, flesh-and-blood woman who had invaded his private car and threatened to invade his empty heart.

It had not been easy courting Mellie Chaboillez, with the feud between the Bergens and Chaboillezes as strong as on the day it had started three generations previously. It was past time to put the feud to rest, especially since no one could remember why it had started in the first place. But Mellie had thrived on the intrigue of secret messages, stolen moments, secret trysts. For her, the feud heightened her feeling of kinship with other thwarted lovers.

Thinking of their last secret meeting, Matt set the scene in his mind: the tall cottonwood tree by the arroyo; the two horses that came from opposite directions, with trails of dust serving as a reminder that it had not rained for a long time.

Slung over the pommel of his saddle was the Winchester that he carried everywhere with him. And folded in his saddlebag was the urgent message she'd sent him.

As if he were an impersonal observer standing on the nearby butte, colored in shades of rose and purple by the late afternoon sun, Matt watched the two lovers dismount from their horses and rush to meet each other.

"What's wrong, Mellie?"

She smiled that endearing smile, her face showing none of the urgency indicated by her message. "Nothing's wrong, Matt. I just suddenly had the answer and wanted to tell you."

"You've talked with your father?"

"No. It wouldn't do any good. But listen to my plan. If we eloped, then our problems would be solved."

A disappointed Matt shook his head. "That would only add to them, Mellie. I'd rather try to work things out with your family."

Mellie was displeased with his reaction. He could tell by the way her mouth turned into a pout. "By the time your father and mine settle their differences, we'll be too old to get married. Matt, I'm tired of waiting. If you don't want to marry me, tell me now, and we can stop seeing each other."

"You know I could never live without you. It would tear me apart to think of you as some other man's wife."

The smile returned to Mellie's lips. "I hear there's a Methodist preacher in Dickinson now. I'll send you word when I can get away."

"You don't think Amelia will be suspicious?"

"My mother's always suspicious. But she's always busy, too. I'll be gone before she misses me. Now here's what we'll do. . . ."

He listened as she unfolded her plans, his silence taken for agreement.

* * *

In the berth, Matt broke into a sweat. Recalling that last encounter so long ago, he knew he should have put his foot down. But he'd been afraid that he might lose the woman he loved, if he did. In the end, that's exactly what happened.

Always unheedful of the vagaries of nature, she had sent word to him just as threatening clouds and a banshee wind whipped over the plains from the north. It was a dangerous time to meet in the arroyo, long dry from the drought. For if it began to rain in earnest, flash floods could easily spread, rapidly filling up the old creek bed and trapping any living thing. Even though she would never understand, Matt knew he had to stop her from meeting him there. He headed immediately for the forbidden Chaboillez ranch, eluding the hostile ranch hands guarding the property boundaries. By the time he arrived, the rain had already begun. . . .

"Get off this property, Matt Bergen. You're not welcome here." Amelia Chaboillez stood before him with her rifle raised.

He had no doubt that she would pull the trigger if she so desired. And she was an excellent shot. "Put the gun down, Amelia, and see to your daughter."

"What are you talking about?"

"Where is Mellie?"

"She's in her room, but that's no concern of yours."

"Find her. Make sure she's safe."

Amelia lowered the rifle. "Keep an eye on him, Diego, while I go inside."

A bolt of lightning and the resulting crack of thunder brought terror to Matt's skittish horse. "Steady, boy, steady," he cautioned, holding on to the reins while he waited for Amelia to come back and tell him that her daughter was safe inside the house.

Amelia reappeared. "She's gone. But you knew it all along, didn't you, Matt? Where is she? I demand to know."

Matt had already remounted his horse. "She must be on her way to the arroyo. We've got to stop her, Amelia."

As he left the ranch, he heard Amelia shouting for her horse. Feud or no feud, he had to admire the woman. She knew the danger, even if her daughter didn't. It was up to the two of them to save the headstrong, stubborn Mellie Chaboillez from the flash flood that was certain to come.

Within a few minutes, Amelia had caught up with Matt. Together they rode across Chaboillez land toward the Bergen ranch, their vision obscured by the steady downpour. At the line shack, they headed north, tracing the route along the divide, the deceptive gully lined with sagebrush.

Before they reached the cottonwood tree, the designated place of rendezvous, Matt heard a dreadful roar of water racing down the gully, with no deterrent powerful enough to withstand its onslaught. "Mellie!" he shouted, his heart pounding in rhythm to his horse's hoofbeats.

"Mellie!" Amelia's anguished voice echoed.

From the vantage point of higher ground, Amelia and Matt looked down and saw the swift current run, taking with it twigs, limbs, and a small calf caught in its whirling eddy. Barely visible in the distance was the top portion of the cottonwood tree.

Then a saddlebag, hanging on a broken limb, drifted by. Matt groaned and raced his horse dangerously near to the water's edge. There was no doubt of its owner. Mellie's initials had been branded into the leather.

"Go back, Amelia," Matt shouted. "I'm going on to find her."

But Amelia, also recognizing the saddlebag, said, "There's no need, Matt. My heart has turned to stone. I know she's already gone."

"No! She could still be alive," a frantic Matt answered, urging his horse forward.

Two hours later, when the rains had ceased, an exhausted Matt saw a telltale bit of lace caught between two limbs. It was barely visible above the debris that had come to rest against the bank. He plunged his horse into the water to rescue it.

That day the arroyo was witness to his grief. His cry traveled along the path made by the flood and echoed across the land as he lifted Mellie's limp form from its watery grave.

But as soon as he reached the bank, the body was torn from his arms by Henri Chaboillez, who had arrived home only an hour before from Fargo. "Give her to me, you murderer," he said, a look of lasting hatred combined with a father's grief.

Matt had watched while Amelia and Henri set homeward, the pace of their horses slow and measured, as if one small misstep would bring discomfort to their beloved daughter.

He had not been allowed to attend the private funeral, or place flowers on Mellie's grave, for she had been buried on Chaboillez property. When both Henri Chaboillez and Matt's father, Edward, died two years later, Matt had hoped that he could finally make his peace with Amelia. But she was not interested.

Now, lying in his berth and thinking of the tragedy that had occurred five years previously, Matt realized that a reexamination of the sad events had not served any good purpose. In fact, it had done the opposite, forcing him to see the participants of the drama in a new light and to face what his heart had known—that despite her charm, Mellie had always been impulsive and determined to have her own way. But regardless, he still accepted the blame for what had happened to her.

At least Mellie had been consistent in her nature, not at all like the woman across from him, who kept him off-balance by her erratic behavior, the chameleon change from prude to hoyden and back again. She had also shown no respect for his position or money or power. He knew of no other woman who would be so careless.

Angry at her for turning his five-year memory of Mellie's perfection to ashes within the space of a few hours—and seducing him by some hidden witchery—he whispered, "Sarah, what have you done to me?"

He did not expect an answer, and he received none.

Chapter 10

During the night, the landscape changed, the lushness of trees vanishing into a wide prairie covered in blue-green sagebrush. Where the sagebrush ended, strange plumes of smoke rose from the bowels of the earth, where layers of coal had been struck by lightning years before and continued to burn, the smoke escaping as if from mounded earth lodges of a prehistoric people.

To strangers, this terrain would appear formidable and frightening. But to Matt, taking measure of the arid vastness in the early morning light, the scene brought a sense of wonder, the feeling as equally strong as the first time, when he had traveled with his father to the Indian village where the Heyoka medicine man lived. Matt had been fourteen years old at the time—still young enough to be awed by the burning land, and yet old enough to realize the seriousness of the journey. If Tall Tree could not heal his father's arm, poisoned by the rusty plow, then he would die. In the wilderness, it was as simple as that.

Now, years later, Matt Bergen stood on the platform of the moving train and stretched his large frame, his muscles still feeling the effects of yesterday's labor. But the worst was behind him. Unless something unforeseen occurred, the train would be pulling into Medora by late afternoon. Once he was rid of his female passenger and the schoolhouse lumber, and had a good meal and bath, he could resume his trip to Fargo in peace, with no troubling thoughts to plague him. Smiling, he hopped across the divide to the dining car, where Lynx was waiting to eat breakfast with him.

The day was a long one for Anya, left alone in the Pullman, with only Kwa-ling making a brief appearance with food. That morning, she had glanced ruefully at her hair in the small mirror and realized why Matt had looked at her so strangely the evening before.

She would not have chosen the timing, but perhaps it was just as well that the rain had removed the mousy color before she reached Medora. It would have been extremely hard to maintain the disguise throughout the winter.

With time to herself, Anya reread Sarah's correspondence. She was still uneasy about Amelia Chaboillez, the wealthy ranchwoman who had volunteered to take her in for the rest of the summer. She would like to have asked Matt about her but no good could come of it. Anya would only make him angry again, since everything she said or did seemed to bring out the worst in him.

Yet it would be nice if she knew whether someone were to meet her at the train station, or whether she was expected to arrange transportation to the ranch herself. With so little money, she had to be careful not to squander a penny.

Sitting in the easy chair, Anya heard a sound behind her. She quickly turned, seeing Matt appear.

"Is your shoulder better today?" he inquired, as if he didn't care one way or the other.

"Fine, thank you." Changing the subject, she asked, "How much longer will it be before we reach Medora?"

"About twenty more minutes. That's what I came to tell you. But since we're a day late, I don't expect Amelia will have anybody meeting you."

"Then I'll hire a carriage."

"The Sweet Grass Ranch is too far out for you to get there before dark. I'd advise you to spend the night at one of the local hotels and start first thing in the morning."

Anya had not planned on the double cost, but she did not argue. Instead she said, "This Amelia Chaboillez . . . Do you know her?"

"We're acquainted."

"Is there anything special that I should know about her?"

"Not particularly. She's a strong, stubborn woman, so you two should get along quite well."

Anya's face quickly masked her hurt at the barb. Her interest in the woman had caused her to forget caution. But his words silenced her. If she needed further information, she would ask one of the others instead. Ignoring Matt, Anya rose from her chair to retrieve the shabby valise.

"She lives alone," Matt finally said. "The rest of her family is dead."

Anya turned around, her soft blue-green eyes meeting

his apologetic gaze. "Thank you for telling me," she said. "It makes a difference."

Matt cleared his throat. "I have a message for you from Kwa-ling."

"Oh?"

"He said, 'May the ghosts of your ancestors always walk before you with a brightly lit lantern.' I suppose that's his way of giving you his Chinese blessing."

Anya smiled. "Thank him for me, Matt, and tell him in return that I wish for him *une mille mers*—" Anya quickly stopped. "That's all right. I'll tell him myself when the train stops."

"I probably would not have remembered it anyway."

Caught off-guard, Anya had almost given herself away. Sarah Macauley would never have used an Aleut hunting blessing. Only the Princess Fodorsky would have known it. So close. She had come so close to spoiling everything because of a few kind words from Matt's cook.

But one thing Sarah certainly would have done. Using a more serious, formal voice, Anya said, "I want to thank you, Matt, for your care and consideration these past four days. I know how disruptive it's been for you having me on board. But I'm most appreciative."

Matt stared at the woman. She had certainly used the right word—disruptive. She had disrupted his thoughts, his memories, and his sleep. But he would never let her know that. He nodded. "At least you're here, safe and sound."

The train began to slow, and Matt disappeared, leaving Anya alone in the Pullman. Cautiously she watched from the window as the train rolled into the Medora station.

Much like the other wooden depots built along the Western rail lines, the building was rustic gray, with a sharp-pitched roof to keep winter snow from accumulating on its shingles. It was set slightly apart from the town in the distance.

From the window, Anya strained to see the twenty-eight-room château that, according to her conversation with Sarah, the Marquis de Mores had built high on a hill overlooking the town. But the only landmark she saw was the smoking brick obelisk of a chimney from the marquis's slaughterhouse.

The train continued at a slow pace, past the station and much farther down the track. When it finally came to a stop on one of the side tracks, a new group of noisy cowboys hurried from the train station toward the boxcars. Anya stepped back from the window. Her reticence in leaving the car that had served as a temporary haven was compounded by the sudden appearance of these unfamiliar faces. So she waited, taking her time to gather her few belongings.

"Sarah, I don't want to rush you," Matt's voice called from the door a few minutes later. "But all the men off-duty are waiting to tell you good-bye before they go over to the saloon. And they're a mighty thirsty bunch."

"I'm sorry. I didn't realize . . ."

". . . that you've turned the heads of nearly all my men on this train?"

"No. That they were waiting. I'll come immediately."

As she debarked from the private car and began to

walk back toward the station, Anya saw the men standing and waiting, their hats in hand—Travis, Snake Man, Prairie Dog, Lynx, and all the others. With the porch as her destination, a smiling Anya acknowledged each cowboy as she passed by.

"Godspeed to ya', Miss Sarah."

"Bless you, Miss Sarah."

"Thank you," she replied. "I'll never forget your kindness."

"I'll bring you the buffalo hide before winter," Snake Man promised.

"And you'll have those leaded-glass windows before fall," Travis added.

Lynx, not to be outdone, said, "I'm comin' back in an hour, to make sure the lumber's unloaded carefullike."

"Thank you, Lynx."

Prairie Dog was last. As Anya approached, he leaned over and whispered, "A single woman needs a good gun around these parts." He winked and said, "I'll see what I can do."

Before she could reply, he was off.

"Looks like Amelia didn't send anyone for you," Matt said, glancing around at the now deserted station. "If you care to wait, I'll give you a ride to the hotel where I'm going."

"You have a carriage coming?"

"Yes. From the livery stable."

"What about your silk cargo? Is it safe for you to go off and leave it?"

"Other guards are already in place. As soon as fresh

supplies are loaded and I've had a good meal and bath at the hotel, I'll be off again."

Cyrus, the eleven-year-old, freckle-faced son of Tom Meacham, the livery stable owner, raced toward the station with his pa's carriage. He wasn't happy at the news that a schoolteacher had arrived in the town. School was for babies, not for boys like him. He was big for his age and could fight, shoot, ride, and spit as good as any grown man. But his ma had told him that, come fall, he was going to school, to learn how to read and write. Well, he would just see about that. If his ma forced him to go, then he would make life so miserable, the teacher would leave before the year was out.

Feeling better just thinking of his plan, Cyrus whistled at the horse, urging him to trot faster. As soon as he reached the station, Cyrus jumped from the carriage. "Afternoon, Mr. Matt. My pa sent the carriage for that mealymouthed teacher, like you asked. Where is he? Inside the station?"

Matt laughed as Anya turned around. Watching them assess each other, he said, "Miss Sarah, may I present one of your first pupils, Cyrus Meacham. I hope you're not too disappointed, Cyrus, that Miss Macauley is not a man."

Staring at the overgrown, insolent boy, Anya had a sinking feeling. He was exactly like one of the boys at Father Ambrose's school. She remembered what hell the kindly man had gone through. Poor, sweet Sarah, with her starry eyes and high hopes. Was this to have been her lot, too, if she had lived? Plagued by some bully at every turn? Anya was almost glad that Sarah would never know such misery. The only drawback was that she, Anya, would have to deal with the boy herself.

Unable to think of a reply to Matt's comment, Cyrus turned red. Hell, he sure had put his foot in it this time!

Anya did not help him out, or attempt to relieve him of his embarrassment. In a firm voice, she said, "My trunk is over there, Cyrus. Will you be able to lift it by yourself?"

"If it ain't got lead in it."

"No. Just books that you'll be studying this fall."

As soon as he'd left, Matt said, "You know the trunk's much too heavy for the boy, Sarah."

She put her hand on his arm as he started to follow Cyrus. "Yes, I know. But wait for him to find out."

Matt grinned. "You're going to be a hard teacher, Sarah Macauley. I can see it coming."

The two watched while Cyrus tugged at the trunk, to no avail. He glared at Sarah as she finally signaled for Matt to help him.

"The damned trunk's *heavier* than lead," Cyrus complained to Matt, picking up one end of the trunk.

"I couldn't have lifted it by myself, either. Sometimes, it takes teamwork to get a thing done."

"Ain't that the damned truth."

"Cyrus, better watch your language around Miss Macauley."

Riding toward the town, Anya realized she had taken a chance with the boy. Only time would tell whether she had made the situation better or worse.

"Medora is a thriving little town," Matt explained,

"even though most of the people live on ranches outside. But we have a dry goods store, several saloons, Tom's livery stable, and five hotels. The marquis has various endeavors, as well. Besides his cattle ranch, he has a refrigerated rail car company and a meat-packing plant. As soon as the schoolhouse goes up, Medora will begin to attract even more families."

"Where do you live, Matt?" Anya inquired.

"About twenty miles down the Little Missouri."

Cyrus, listening to the conversation, suddenly remembered the message his pa had sent. "I forgot to tell you, Mr. Matt. Pa said to let you know Old Four-Eyes is back."

"Is that an outlaw?" Anya inquired.

Cyrus smirked. The teacher didn't know anything worthwhile.

"No, Sarah," Matt answered. "That's the name people around here call Mr. Theodore Roosevelt from New York. He owns a ranch not far from here. You'll probably meet him at the château. The Marquise de Mores is also from New York."

Remembering what Sarah had said, Anya laughed. "I had assumed she was French, too. I was even brushing up on my pronunciation so I could converse with her easily."

"Actually, she's of German descent. Her father is Baron von Hoffman, a financier on Wall Street. But I daresay she'll appreciate your efforts."

"She might not be here much longer, either," Cyrus said, enjoying the way the conversation had turned.

"Especially if the sheriff arrests the marquis for murder—"

"Here we are at the hotel," Matt cut in quickly. "Cyrus, I'll stay with the horse while you go inside and find someone to take Miss Macauley's trunk upstairs."

Anya looked around her, at the seemingly peaceful little town, the impressive two-story hotel with the brands of neighboring ranches seared into its wooden sides near the front door. She could understand Cyrus's hostility, his evident lack of tact concerning the length of her stay in Medora.

What she could not understand was Matt Bergen's secrecy during the entire four days she'd spent on the silk train. He had deliberately kept her in the dark about the town, its residents, and its troubling intrigues.

What other disturbing facts would she uncover in the days to come?

Chapter 11

At Sweet Grass Ranch, Amelia Chaboillez rode alongside her foreman, Stretch Hawkins, their two horses keeping up a steady pace despite the wide sweep of land they'd searched, looking for the lost calves.

Stretch glanced covertly at the woman he worked for. Tall and erect in the saddle, Amelia wore the same brown leather hat, the same chaps and gloves she'd worn for twenty years. Most people wouldn't notice that her hair had grown a little whiter this past year, her face a little more weathered from the sun. Regardless, she was still a fine-looking woman.

There'd been a time there, soon after Henri had died, when he thought he might be lucky enough to marry her, despite their difference in age. It didn't mean that much to him, her being older. But it had mattered to Amelia.

"You know what people will say, Stretch," she'd told him. "They'll think I'm robbing the cradle, and that you're marrying me for my money."

"To hell with what people think, Amelia. We know it isn't true."

"Yes. But we've got enough strife and gossip in this territory. Besides, I need a foreman much more than I need a husband."

So in the end, he had remained as Chaboillez foreman on the Sweet Grass Ranch, with not a soul knowing he'd ever had other aspirations.

Riding beside her now, Stretch wondered if she'd ever regretted her decision. She would never tell him, but she must be getting a little lonely living by herself. That would explain her sudden whim of allowing the new schoolteacher to spend the summer at the ranch. She'd never done that before—inviting an outsider to the grand old house with its turret wing facing the east.

"Let's go back, Stretch," Amelia said. "I may have a message from Miss Macauley."

"Too bad the train didn't get to Medora yesterday,

when it was supposed to," Stretch replied. "It was a big waste of time, goin' into town."

Amelia laughed. "Stop pretending, Stretch. You know you enjoyed it. Got you out of a lot of work here."

"That's just it. I should have finished fixin' the fence around the wheat fields by now."

"Well, you and the boys can do that tomorrow."

Amelia set her horse to a gallop, wheeling into the yard where the wind bent the heads of the yellow flowers planted near the doorstep. She didn't wait for help. Instead she slid from the saddle, and, with her hat pushed back, she ran up the steps to the porch, calling to her servant as she went.

"Clara, were there any messages today?"

"One, Miss Amelia. Miss Effie's boy rode by. Said she's havin' a quiltin' bee next Saturday, for the schoolteacher's housewarmin'. Said bring as many scraps of cloth as you can manage, and some sewin' thread."

"But there was no message from the teacher herself?"

"No, ma'am."

A disappointed Amelia retraced her steps to attend to her horse, but Stretch had already taken the mare to the barn.

In his hotel room, Matt Bergen sat cross-legged in the large tin tub and smoked a cigar while he waited for Ruby to pour more hot water. When she'd finished, he said, "Ruby, you might as well scrub my back while you're here."

The fat, elderly Ruby giggled, wiped her wet hands on her apron, and picked up the bristle brush. Running it over the cake of soap, she said, "I hear you've had an excitin' trip so far."

"I wouldn't call it exciting. Aggravating is more like it."

"I don't wonder. You're lucky the outlaws didn't try to steal *her* instead of the silk."

"You're talking about the teacher?"

"Yes. She's a pretty little thing, even if she is too skinny. Lem said they were already squabblin' over her at the bar."

"Then I hope she's taking a tray in her room, instead of eating downstairs."

"She's not doin' either one. Said she wasn't hungry. Just wanted a bath."

Matt frowned. He was ravenously hungry, especially with the aroma of beefsteaks seeping up from the kitchen. Sarah had to be hungry, too. But maybe she was running short of money.

"That'll do, Ruby. Hand me a towel, and then I want you to take care of something else for me."

In another room farther down the hall, a well-scrubbed Anya put on Sarah's white linen nightgown and climbed into bed. By the dim light of a kerosene lamp on the bedside table she began to read. But her mind was not on the book. Rather, it was on her vulnerable situation, alone in a strange hotel, with no gun at her side for protection.

She listened uneasily to the sound of men's voices coming from downstairs. There was no telling who might be talking to Matt or his ranch hands at that very moment—even someone working for Igor.

An unexpected knock at the door startled Anya. She tightened her fingers around the book and held her breath, hoping that when she didn't answer, the person would go away. But the knock was persistent.

"Miss Macauley, this is Ruby. May I come in?"

Still, Anya was hesitant.

"Miss Macauley, I hope you're not already asleep. I have something for you."

Thinking it might be a message from the Chaboillez ranch, Anya said, "Just a moment." She climbed out of bed, put the gray shawl around her shoulders, and walked to the door to unlatch it. Still wary, she called out, "Are you alone?"

"Yes, ma'am."

As she partially opened the door, she saw a heavy tray of steaming food in Ruby's arms. "I'm afraid there's been some mistake. I didn't order supper."

"But somebody else did for you."

"Who?"

"Matt Bergen."

"Then you may take it to *his* room."

"He's already eaten and left the hotel. So step aside and let me put it down. The tray's too heavy for me to be holdin' forever."

"Then come in." Anya realized that the cost of the bountiful meal would put a dent in her meager allowance, but it couldn't be helped. "Just add the food to my bill."

"No need to. Matt's already paid for it."

"That was kind of him." Not wanting Ruby to misunderstand, she added, "Does he make a habit of buying supper for strangers?"

"No. Not females, anyway. Guess he's taken a likin' to you, or else he thinks you're a mite skinny." Ruby set the tray on the bedside table. "When you're finished, you can put it outside your door. I'll send one of the kitchen boys to get it later."

When Anya tried to give Ruby a few pennies for her trouble, the woman shook her head. "He's already took care of that, too."

Moments later, Anya began her meal. Earlier, she had resigned herself to a hungry evening, but now, she savored each bite of beefsteak, each chunk of sourdough bread. To do otherwise, or to refuse to eat what had been cooked, would be a sin, for food was too important to waste. The starving of entire villages cut off from the rest of the world during winter was one of Alaska's legacies, a tragedy pressed into her memory as surely as the small purple flower pressed into her prayer book.

While she ate, Anya heard the whistle of the silk train in the distance. Despite his benevolence, she was relieved that Matt Bergen was leaving Medora behind. It had been difficult assuming another's identity, especially under Matt's surveillance. She'd made mistakes, done and said things to cause him to look at her in a questioning manner. Now he would put her out of mind, and she could begin a new life.

Finally wrapping an extra piece of bread in a napkin for her breakfast the next morning, Anya took the empty tray and set it on the floor outside her room. Then she hurriedly latched the door and ran back to bed.

During the night, Anya slept soundly, neither waking when the supper tray was removed from the hallway nor later, when a large rat carried off the hoarded bread to a cubbyhole in the wall.

But Matt, with his private Pullman to himself as the silk train sped toward the Red River of the North, slept little. Handing over the personal effects of the Princess Fodorsky to the dispatcher to send on the next westbound train, and leaving Sarah Macauley to Amelia, should have put an end to his sense of responsibility. Yet something about the two women bothered him, and he had the uneasy feeling that he was not free of either one.

The next morning, Anya prepared to leave the hotel. Paying for her night's stay at the front desk, she said, "I need to hire a carriage to take me to the Chaboillez ranch. Do you have someone who can go over to the livery stable and see about it?" She did not look forward to seeing Cyrus again.

"Ain't necessary, Miss Macauley," Lem, the proprietor, said, glancing through the window. "Miss Amelia's foreman just drove up. Reckon he's come into town to fetch you."

Anya looked in the same direction, seeing a tall, pleasant-looking man jump from a vehicle and loop the horses' reins to a hitching post. She hurriedly walked to the staircase to get her valise.

"You're just in time, Stretch," Lem said as the door opened. "Miss Macauley's ready and waitin'."

"Went over to the station," Stretch commented. "Heard the train came in last evening."

"That's right. They had a little trouble along the way, but here she is, safe and sound."

"Howdy, ma'am. You got anything else?" he asked, taking the shabby valise from her.

"Yes. A trunk. It's still upstairs."

Within a few minutes, Anya was settled in the carriage, with the trunk lashed to the back. As they left town and headed south toward Sweet Grass Ranch, they passed a stagecoach coming into town.

"I didn't realize there was a coach line into Medora," a wary Anya said, shading her face from view.

"Yep. From Deadwood. But it won't last long, like a lot of other things the marquis has started."

"Why is that?"

"Because he's an outsider—and a foreigner, to boot."

"But isn't everyone an outsider to begin with?"

Stretch laughed. "I reckon so. Only they don't go around with a title hangin' around their necks, like the marquis. 'Reverend' is about the only title men around here don't resent, though even that makes us a little uncomfortable."

Anya didn't comment. She was thinking of Igor and his tremendous pride in being a prince. He would never willingly give up that title. For his entire life, his estimation of himself had revolved around the Fodorsky name and heritage.

"Do you smell that odor coming from the chimney of the abattoir?"

"Yes."

"That's the marquis's, too. It's lucky for you that the schoolhouse will be built upwind from it."

Changing the subject, Anya said, "Tell me about Sweet Grass Ranch, Stretch. Since I'll be spending the rest of the summer there, I'd like to know a little about it."

"Well, it's one of the largest spreads around these parts. When Henri Chaboillez was alive, he raised beef cattle and enough crops to make the ranch self-sufficient. But several years ago, Amelia decided to enclose some of the land and start raising wheat, like they do farther east. With two crops a year, it's been profitable, so far."

"And the house? Tell me about the house."

"Well, now, I'm not much good at describin' things." Stretch was silent a moment. "I guess you could say it's large and comfortable, with fireplaces even in the bedrooms. Henri's grandfather built the house, but it's been added to, a wing here, a porch there.

"When their little girl grew up, Amelia had Henri build a two-story turret at the front. But once Mellie died, it was closed up, with nobody allowed to go inside, not even Clara to clean it. Last week, all that changed. I understand that's where you'll be stayin'."

"What happened to Mellie?"

"She drowned when she was seventeen."

"What a tragedy."

A sympathetic Anya became quiet, preferring to

watch the large bald eagle overhead, swooping and gliding on the strong currents of the wind. A few minutes
later, Stretch suddenly said, "You don't believe in
ghosts, do you, Miss Sarah?"

Surprised at the question, she replied, "I've never
seen one. I hear they're every bit as elusive as a yeti."

Chapter 12

"What's a yeti?" Stretch asked.

"It's what the Sherpas in Tibet call an abominable
snowman. They've seen large tracks in the snow that
supposedly belong to him, but few, if any, have seen
what's made them."

Impressed, Stretch said, "Amelia sure is going to enjoy havin' a schoolteacher around."

Anya laughed. "I also hope the children are going to
enjoy coming to school, to this outsider."

"You won't be an outsider for long, once the word
gets around that you're at the Chaboillez ranch for the
summer. All the women around here look up to
Amelia."

"Is that why she's invited me to stay with her until
the schoolhouse is built? To make sure I'm accepted?"

"Well, that could be one of the reasons, I guess."

Anya did not inquire further. Stretch's explanation

was sufficient to give her an uneasy feeling. If things went awry, then Amelia Chaboillez could suffer, too. It had not occurred to her that others would be affected by her subterfuge.

During the silence that followed, Anya mulled over the conversation with Stretch. What had made him bring up the subject of ghosts when he talked about Amelia and her daughter, Mellie? "Stretch," she inquired, "is the Chaboillez house supposed to be haunted?"

The foreman coughed and took his time, wiping his face with his bandanna. "I only know that Clara, the housekeeper, claims to've heard strange noises comin' from the turret at night."

"And she thinks it's Mellie's ghost?"

"Yep."

"There could be another explanation, too. Lots of houses creak and groan at night," Anya commented.

"That's what I told Clara."

The carriage traveled at a steady pace along a dusty road that disappeared at times, then reappeared beyond large outcroppings of rock. Attempting to bring the conversation back to a safer subject, Stretch pointed to a formation just off the road and said, "You see that bright red layer of rock? That's scoria, in case you've never seen it before."

"And what is the black layer below it?" Anya asked.

"Coal. You can see where people have chipped it out to use for fuel. There's an old man back in the hills who built his house over a large deposit of coal. In the wintertime, all he has to do is go down in his cellar with his pick. In a few minutes, he has enough fuel to last the rest of the day. It makes sense, when a blizzard comes and you can't get out for days at a time."

"Does that happen often?"

"We always have more than enough snow, but some winters are worse than others."

A gusty breeze flapped at Anya's hat, and, if it had not been for the hat pin, she would have lost it. She put her hand on the crown to straighten it. "The wind feels cold already," she ventured.

"We'll have an early fall and winter, more than likely. At least that's what Tall Tree says, and he's almost never wrong."

"I heard someone else mention his name."

"Was it Matt Bergen?"

"It could have been. Or maybe it was Matt's cook, Kwa-ling."

Stretch hesitated. "Guess while I'm warnin' you about things, I might as well warn you not to talk about Matt in Amelia's house."

"I gathered they're not the best of friends. What happened?"

"Well, it's an ongoin' feud that started a long time ago. That's all I can tell you."

"And are there any other subjects that are taboo with Amelia?" a frustrated Anya asked. "Mellie, for instance?"

"If she wants to talk about her daughter, she will. But she'll have to get to know you first."

"How long have you been foreman at the ranch?" Anya inquired.

"Fifteen years."

"Which means you're probably a friend, too."

"Yep. There's nothing I wouldn't do for Amelia or the ranch."

"She's lucky to have you.'

Stretch grinned. "That's what I keep tellin' her."

A thoughtful Anya stared into the distance and drew her shawl closer around her. At that moment, she thought of Ashak. He was much like Stretch, dependable and loyal. But if Igor ever found out that the Aleut had been the one to help her to escape, then his life would be worth little.

The trail turned sharply and began to parallel the tributary of the river, visible through the cottonwood trees. The horses snorted in anticipation and picked up speed. Stretch laughed. "They know they'll be fed soon. In a minute or so, you'll see the house come into view just over that ridge."

Anya was not prepared for the magnificence of the house, set like a lonely sentinel against the clouded sky. It was white, with dark green shutters and a steep-pitched roof. A comfortable, wraparound porch connected one side of the two-story house to the turret wing. Atop the tall turret, a copper weather vane moved in rhythm to the strong northeasterly wind.

"It's beautiful," Anya commented, admiring the design. "But I'm surprised that the house is so far from the barns."

"You're only lookin' at what's above ground. There're underground passageways to the other buildings."

Seeing the carriage approach, a young boy, sitting on the fence railing, jumped down and opened the gate that led into the front meadow. He stared at Anya, who smiled back at him. Then when the carriage had passed, he relocked the gate and ran to catch up with the moving vehicle.

"There's Amelia now," Stretch said, nodding in the direction of the porch. "My God, she's got on a dress."

"Is that unusual?"

"You betcha."

Anya watched the woman walk down the steps to meet the carriage. Amelia Chaboillez was almost as she had pictured her in her mind—sunburned and slender, with white hair. But there was an added dimension to her, too—a magnetism that drew Anya to her immediately.

"Miss Macauley, I'm so glad you've finally arrived. Welcome to Sweet Grass Ranch."

"Thank you, Mrs. Chaboillez. I'm happy to be here."

"Come inside. We'll have a glass of lemonade in the parlor, while the boys put your luggage in your room."

At Stretch's guffaw, Amelia glared at him good-naturedly, as if they shared a secret joke, and then continued, "Lunch will be ready soon. I hope you brought a good appetite with you."

Anya smiled. "I certainly did."

Amelia turned again to Stretch. "You're welcome to eat lunch with us."

"If it's all the same to you, Amelia, I'll have a bite with the hands and then get on with my chores."

"Suit yourself." Returning her attention to Anya, she

led her up the steps and to the screened door, where the housekeeper stood, watching. "Miss Macauley, this is Clara. She's indispensable. If you need anything, she's the one to ask."

"Hello, Clara."

"Afternoon, ma'am. Guess you'll be wantin' a washup after the long trip. I'll show you where."

When Anya hesitated, Amelia said, "She'll bring you back to the parlor. I'll just check on the lemonade."

The gray-haired, middle-aged Clara looked so sensible that Anya had difficulty reconciling Stretch's story of ghosts with her outward appearance. Following the woman to the back of the house, a curious Anya noted the fine old pieces of furniture, visible from the hallway.

"That was my grandson," Clara said. "The one who waited at the gate for you. He's goin' to be one of your pupils when the new school opens."

"He's a fine-looking little boy. What's his name?"

"Purdy. Jamie Purdy. He's my son's child."

Clara opened the door to a large closet where a washbasin, towels, and other necessaries waited. "There's a nice big mirror hangin' on the wall, in case you want to take off your hat and smooth your hair."

"It certainly needs it. The wind was quite strong."

A few minutes later, a refreshed Anya walked with Clara toward the parlor. Seated in a cushioned wooden chair before the stone fireplace, with a pitcher of lemonade on the tray beside her, the white-haired Amelia motioned for Anya to take a seat opposite her. "I don't usually drink lemonade," Amelia confided. "That's why Stretch laughed. He knows sherry is more to my liking, at my age."

"Then by all means, have your glass of sherry."

Amelia smiled. "Lemonade is a better thirst-quencher for a young woman. Since you've just ridden over the dusty prairie, I'll be polite for once and drink a glass with you."

Amelia took one of the leaded crystal goblets, poured a full measure, and handed it to Anya. A thirsty Anya waited for Amelia to fill her own goblet before taking a sip.

By the time lunch was served, the older woman had made up her mind about Anya. Despite her ill-fitting clothes, she liked what she saw, what she heard. She was glad that she had invited Sarah Macauley to stay at the ranch. "You know I'm not much on formal names," Amelia said, leaning toward Anya. "And I hope you're not, either."

Anya smiled, remembering the same conversation with Matt. "Call me Sarah."

"And you can call me Amelia. I keep looking around for my mother-in-law when you say 'Mrs. Chaboillez.' And I've had on this dress long enough, too," she added. "It's time to get back into my work clothes."

With lunch over, both rose from the table. "Make yourself at home, Sarah. And I'll see you at supper. We usually eat around dusk."

Later, Anya looked out from the window of the up-stairs turret room and saw Amelia riding off into the distance. She was now alone in the house, for Clara had also left as soon as lunch was over and she'd shown Anya to the quarters that would be her home for the next several months.

She had been pleased with the arrangement of the downstairs sitting room, with a desk in the corner and winding steps upward to the large, round bedroom. In it, a faint odor of lavender permeated the air, and Anya sensed a quiet, waiting feeling, as if the doors had been closed for too long and the room yearned for new laughter, new dreams, new joy.

She could not reconcile this warm, welcoming feeling with the warning Stretch had given her. Would things change when the room filled with evening shadows and the sun no longer shone?

Anya dismissed that possibility. Much more to her detriment was the longing for stability, the regret for times past, when she was safe, protected. She had been running for so long, and she was tired, an easy prey in this stronghold of lace and girlish innocence. She must maintain her vigilance, even as she rested for a short while, like a hunted animal gathering strength for the continuation of the hunt.

Anya turned her thoughts deliberately to the chore at hand, the unpacking of Sarah's valise and trunk. She hung up the two dresses, the two white blouses and long, dark skirts, shook out the thin winter coat, and placed it, along with the extra pair of shoes, inside the closet. But the bloodstained traveling costume was gone.

Anya tried to remember the last time she'd seen it.

Had someone deliberately taken it from the valise, or had it merely been lost with all the moving back and forth on the train? Puzzled at its disappearance, Anya continued to think about it while she finished unpacking, taking Sarah's school supplies and books down the winding stairs to the sitting room below. Then she finally sat down to rest. Soon her eyelids became heavy; her relaxed body sought the comfortable contour of the cushioned settee, and she began to dream.

Over the ridge, where the wheat fields separated part of the range from the river, a satisfied Amelia stood beside Stretch as the last of the new railings went into place.

"There, that should do it," she said, surveying the repaired fence.

Stretch waited for the ranch hands to roll up the remaining barbed wire, load it on the wagon, and leave before he commented, "You're a mighty stubborn woman, Amelia."

"Well, it's my land," she said. "And I have the right to plant wheat wherever I choose."

"You know it and I know it," Stretch conceded. "But the steers don't understand."

"They'll understand soon enough, with the barbed-wire fence around it," she answered, remounting her horse.

"I hope you're right," he said, not at all sure the animals wouldn't break it down again to follow the old cattle drive path to the river.

Stretch and Amelia rode side by side as usual, taking

their time since the work for the day had ended. "What did you think of Sarah Macauley?" Stretch asked.

"I like her, Stretch. You can tell she's poor, by her shabby clothes. But she's well-bred. A cut above what I was expecting."

Stretch nodded. "If I'm any judge, she'll make a good teacher."

"For this year, anyway. Some man's going to snatch her up for a wife. I just hope it isn't Matt Bergen."

"Say the word, Amelia, and I'll make certain he doesn't get his hands on her."

Amelia laughed. "If you're entertaining anything underhanded, forget it, Stretch. Matt's far too smart to fall into a trap." In a teasing manner, she added, "Of course, you could always marry her yourself."

Chapter 13

The silk train sped across the prairie, making up for lost time, crossing the bridge at Bismarck, steaming past the vast wheat fields that provided bread to a growing nation. Silos replaced the tall buttes in the West, the sun's reflection striking the cone-shaped, metal roofs where the grain was stored until it was loaded into boxcars and shipped to flour mills on the eastbound run.

A more relaxed Matt Bergen set his mind to the filature, to the voracious power looms that waited for the new shipment of raw silk. He realized he'd been particularly lucky on his trip to France eighteen months previously. It was there that he had hired Jean Bonneau, an expert in the throwing of silk, the weaving, the dyeing. For three generations, the Bonneau family had been involved in the silk industry. And no one could have persuaded Jean to leave Lyons, if it had not been for the duel.

"Monsieur, I entrust my youngest son to you," the elder Bonneau had said, wiping the tears from his eyes. "He is a hot-blooded young man when it comes to *l'amour*, but in all other things he is trustworthy. Take him with you, and I promise that you will not be sorry."

Matt had not been sorry a single day. As manager, Jean had overseen the building of the factory, the importing of dyes, and the installation of the needed equipment. Now, with the operation in full production a scant six months, it looked as if Matt and Jean had launched a new venture that could only prosper—at least as long as Jean's whereabouts remained undiscovered by the family of the man he'd dueled to the death.

"Hey, Matt," Lynx called out, walking into the private car. "You think I could hop on the next westbound train from Fargo with the others, instead of waitin' around for you? I been away a mighty long time."

"That's a good idea, Lynx," Matt said. "I know you've been chomping at the bit to get started on the schoolhouse."

"Well, I was aimin' to check on the ranch first."

"Good. You might check on Tall Tree, too, while

you're at it. Make sure Driscoll hasn't burned the old man's shack down."

"You're sure it was Driscoll who tried to rob the train?"

"Ninety percent certain."

"Then it's a shame we didn't hang 'im last year."

"He'll hang himself, one of these days. Just a matter of time. But he can still hurt a lot of people in the meantime."

"Well, at least Miss Sarah is safe. She came through all the goings-on just fine, didn't she, Matt?"

"That she did," he agreed, not eager to talk about the woman he'd tried to put out of his mind.

"She's—"

"Lynx," Matt interrupted. "Was there anything else you wanted to ask me?"

"Reckon that was all."

"Then don't you think you'd better get a bite to eat while you have the chance?"

"You comin', Matt?"

"No. Tell Kwa-ling I'll be in later."

"You're in a right foul mood. Hope this ain't goin' to become a habit."

Matt glared at his foreman. "And I hope your infernal harping on 'Miss Sarah' isn't going to become a habit, either."

Lynx laughed. "So the love bug's bit you, too."

"Get out of here, Lynx."

"Yes, boss."

* * *

Deep within the Dakota hills, Tall Tree took some sacred tobacco from his pouch and sprinkled it on the ground next to the mother plant, where he had pulled up a medicinal root. Wrapping it carefully and placing it in the basket with the others, he walked on, closer to the water.

He was ancient, having lived far beyond the time allotted to most mortals. Yet his erect posture, his piercing eyes, belied that fact. Only the deep-rutted wrinkles carved into his face like the age rings of a cedar broadcast his advanced years.

To most, he seemed a harmless old Indian, rendered powerless by the military and homeless by the division of land among the settlers. That was exactly the picture he wished others to see. In reality, he was quite different. As a medicine man, he could go to ground as easily as a gopher in times of danger—could call on power from the four winds when necessary. But today, he had no other thoughts than the gathering of his healing herbs.

Tall Tree continued the search for a particular plant growing along the riverbank. He felt its movement, its trembling, long before he saw it. In exhortation, he raised his voice, thanking the Great Spirit for placing it in his path. Then he plucked several stems, being careful not to be greedy. Leaving the main plant behind, with the gift of a kernel of corn, he walked on.

The old man seemed unaware that he was being tracked. Without hurrying, he attended to his quest, replenishing the low supply of herbs that hung from the overhead beam of his log shack, wrapping each one, then placing it in his basket. But all the time, he was quietly leading his predator farther and farther afield. The shack was his power place, hidden and separate from his quarters on the nearby reservation. It would not do for someone who exuded such malevolence to stumble upon it.

In the draw, Driscoll's horse whinnied, its sound causing the outlaw a momentary caution. But Tall Tree didn't seem to notice. Just to make sure, the man waited a few moments for the Indian to get ahead. Then he urged his horse up the slant and toward the rocks, his eyes searching the landscape for the figure dressed in old brown trousers and buckskin vest.

"Now where did that damn Indian go?" Driscoll muttered. Tall Tree had vanished, almost from under his very eyes. But he couldn't have gone far, maybe just between the rocks.

Finally forgetting caution, Driscoll rode directly toward the rocks. He didn't care now whether the Indian saw him or not. He'd sworn to get even for the fiasco concerning the silk shipment. The thing that would hurt Matt the most was for something to happen to the old man. It was safer, too, than challenging Matt directly. The authorities wouldn't bother to investigate what had happened to one more Indian.

"Tall Tree, I know you're hidin' from me," he shouted. "But it ain't no use. You might as well come on out."

Left and right Driscoll rode, investigating the rocks from every side, but he saw nothing except a rattlesnake, coiled in the sun.

*   *   *

At the shack, Tall Tree, busy with tying his herbs to the rafter, listened to the sound of shots in the distance. With a *ping*, they reverberated against the rocks, their sheer number broadcasting the frustration of the interloper.

With no more than a diffident acknowledgment of the sound, Tall Tree completed his task and then sat in the broken-down chair near the door to enjoy his pipe.

On the rail spur linking the grounds of the filature with the main line, the boxcars came to a stop. The trip had been successful; the raw silk was now in the hands of Jean and the factory workers.

From the safe, Matt brought out the guards' payroll. "I hope some of this gets back to Medora," he said.

"Well, it might be redistributed on the way. . . ."

"Yeah. Out of one pocket and into another."

The men joked, walking one by one to pick up the envelopes with their extra wages. Within a few minutes, the only two left were Matt and Kwa-ling. "Don't you want to ride back with the other men?" Matt asked.

"If all same to you, I stay. Cook for you."

Matt knew that, although Kwa-ling liked to gamble, he was sending as much money as he could back to his family in China. He had probably lost all the money he could afford and wasn't eager to lose any more. "Suit yourself," he said, "but I won't need you until tomorrow. I'm spending tonight at Bonneau's house."

Kwa-ling nodded. He tucked his pay envelope into his blue jacket and walked back to the dining car.

Shortly afterward, Matt left the train and made his way to the filature, where Jean was waiting for him. He was a small man, dark, with an elegant mustache that matched his long wavy hair. Over his paisley vest, white shirt, and dark worsted trousers, he wore a black apron for protection.

"How did the new dye turn out?" Matt asked.

Jean smiled. "Come and see for yourself, Matt. The women are packing the bolts now for shipment."

In the large shipping room, the elegant silk was being carefully wrapped in muslin, the women in their white gloves treating each bolt in the special manner it deserved.

Nodding to one of the women to unwrap several lengths of one particular bolt, Jean waited for Matt to recognize its unusual beauty.

"Even more spectacular than I expected," a satisfied Matt said. "What color do you call that?"

"Aubergine, with a tracery of gold. Since the combination has turned out so well, we will have to use it again soon."

The woman began to rewrap the silk, but Matt intervened. "Just a minute. I think I'll buy that bolt myself."

Jean laughed. "And who is this woman who deserves such an expensive gift?" he asked in a lilting, teasing accent.

"You have the wrong idea, Jean. It's a housewarming gift for the new schoolteacher I just delivered to Medora. Her best dress was ruined on the train, and I feel responsible."

Jean's eyes danced. "She has golden hair?"

"No. More like copper." Matt quickly caught himself. "But that's of no concern."

"Nevertheless, the color will look magnificent on her. Marianne, wrap that bolt for monsieur. We will not ship it to Chicago."

"Yes, sir."

"Just deliver it to Kwa-ling on the train," Matt instructed. In a hurry to put the episode behind him, he said, "Well, Jean, let's get on with the tour."

Outside, in the rail yard, the unloading of the boxcars continued, the crates carefully removed and taken inside the filature. The cowpunchers, who had guarded it on the final leg of the trip, left the Fargo station for the ride back home. Used to sleeping on the range in all types of weather, with only a bedroll for cover, a saddle for a pillow, each was eager to return to the wide open spaces. The trip from Medora had been too tame for them. That was evident as they listened to Lynx, who regaled them with the particulars of the hazardous journey through the mountains and the badlands. With each mile traveled, Lynx felt compelled to embroider the events, so that by the time they all reached Medora, the story had passed from truth into legend, destined to be repeated around campfires and chuck wagons for years to come.

"Out here, Sarah, the only law is the six-shooter," Amelia explained. "And the sooner you become an expert with one, the better off you'll be."

The two sat on the front steps of the ranch house,

catching as much of the sun as they could before the raw afternoon winds drove them back inside.

"But I understood there was a sheriff—and a jail for lawbreakers."

Amelia laughed. "One hundred and fifty miles away."

"So that's why I saw everyone armed to the teeth in Medora!"

"Yes. It will take more than a railroad to bring civilization to the Dakota Territory. The lawless element operates at will around here."

"But the new school should help some, don't you think?"

"If it's allowed to open."

"What do you mean, Amelia?"

"You've got a hard task ahead of you, child. I'm sure no one's told you, but you're the second teacher the railroad's hired."

"What happened to the first?"

"There was a welcoming committee that met the young man at the depot. Shot off his hat the minute he stepped from the train. The last anybody saw of him, he was running down the track. That's why *you* didn't come on a regular run."

Neither spoke of Matt Bergen, but for the first time, Anya understood why Sarah Macauley had been given a seat on the silk train. Perhaps, too, that was why the cowboys had lined up to tell her good-bye at the station. It was their way of protecting her from the same fate.

"Now don't take this to heart too much, Sarah. By

the time school starts, Stretch and I will have you well on the way to handling any emergency."

Anya looked at Amelia, her face exuding confidence. How she wished she could feel the same.

Chapter 14

The indoctrination of Anya to the frontier began on a pleasant July morning, shortly before the sun rose. A knock at the bedroom door awakened her. "Come in," she said, her voice husky from sleep.

Rather than the housekeeper bringing her a hot cup of tea, it was Amelia, herself, who walked into the bedroom, with a lighted lamp in one hand and a riding outfit similar to her own in the other.

"Here, you're to wear this today," Amelia said. "It was Mellie's. You'll find some boots in the closet. As soon as you've dressed, meet me in the parlor."

She draped the clothes over a nearby chair and lit the lamp on the table beside the bed. Without waiting for either protest or confirmation, Amelia then left the room.

Anya did not know whether to be irritated or grateful that the woman had put her plan into action so fast. Anya had stayed up extremely late the night before, studying and reading. She was always her best at night, the mornings merely the time of day to be gotten through, until her brain began to work and she really came alive. Ever since she'd left Alaska, she'd had trouble adjusting to early meals, early bedtimes, and early awakenings. She had no clock to check the time, but the hour had to be worse than usual. Even the rooster had not yet crowed to awaken the hens to their duty in the barnyard.

The water in the ewer was icy cold, causing her a momentary shock as she bathed her face. For a brief moment, she longed for the recent pampering of Kwa-ling, who had heated her bathwater on the dining car stove.

Quickly Anya slipped out of her nightgown and into the borrowed clothes that smelled of leather and laven-der. Surprisingly the buckskin divided skirt and jacket fit her much better than Sarah's clothes.

The boots were not hard to find, the three pairs, custom-made and of varying shades of leather, visible on a shelf at the back of the closet. The only problem was in choosing which to wear. She deliberately took the pair that had seen the most wear.

Carrying them into the sitting room, Anya sat down and pulled and tugged until the boots slipped on, a firm fit with no room to spare. Then, with the lamp search-ing out the shadows on the way, she proceeded into the parlor, where Amelia was waiting.

When she appeared, the woman's eyes silently ap-proved Anya's appearance. But with the approval, Anya thought she saw a momentary look of sadness, quickly dispelled by a smile. "We'll have breakfast on the range," Amelia announced, "in case you're wondering."

"How long will we be gone from the house?"

"It all depends on how apt a pupil the teacher is," a teasing male voice announced from the door. " 'Mornin', Amelia. 'Mornin', Sarah."

" 'Morning, Stretch. Are the horses saddled up?"

"Yep. Ready to go?"

Amelia nodded. She left the parlor, and Anya followed.

Directly outside, at the base of the steps, the horses waited for their riders. One was smaller than the other two, a speckled red sorrel with flaxen mane and tail. "This here's a nice little Indian pony," Stretch said. "Bought him from a fellow comin' from the gold fields at Coeur d'Alene."

"Who probably stole him from some Grosventres Indian in the Killdeer Mountains," Amelia added.

"Well, I got a bill of sale. That's all that matters."

"What's his name?" Anya asked.

"Ain't had time to name 'im. Reckon one will do well as another."

"Why don't you name him?" Amelia suggested.

Anya slowly reached out her hand and stroked the animal's head in a soothing manner. The ears twitched, and the intelligent eyes gazed back at her, watching and waiting. Surveying the animal, Anya was oblivious to Stretch as he held his hand for Amelia's boot.

"We got a few miles to ride," Stretch said, regaining Anya's attention. "That is, if you're up to it. His name can wait."

Anya allowed Stretch to give her a boost into the saddle the same way he'd helped Amelia. The pony, with an unfamiliar rider on his back, whinnied and sidled to the right, but Anya quickly brought him under control.

"Well, look at that, Amelia," Stretch said, pretending surprise. "I think the lady can ride."

"I expect she'll surprise us in a lot of things, Stretch," an amused Amelia retorted.

Out of the small fenced meadow, the three rode to the east, with the sun coming up beyond the river. Following its curve, they headed north, past the stand of cottonwoods, past the wheat fields and the rolling plateau that changed from green to blue and back to green again. Toward the west, the sun's rays explored the eroded buttes, cast in light and shadow, in shades of scoria and lignite, a palette of earthy colors far different from the glacial blue of the ice mountains on Anya's own Alaskan landscape.

They skirted a deep canyon, its approach announced by a marking of elk antlers and rocks, arranged like a shrine to the wild spirits that inhabited it. Anya could tell that the pony sensed danger as they trotted along the rim.

Soon, a young antelope bounded in front of them, paying no heed to the humans or the horses. It disappeared into the tall prairie grass, catching up with another antelope. The two disappeared as Stretch pointed out a mountain lion, standing on a butte, its presence the cause of the antelopes' sudden flight to safer ground.

"Are we still on your property, Amelia?" Anya finally asked.

"Yes. Then the free range extends for another twenty miles. Raising cattle takes a lot of land and a lot of grass."

"When is your roundup?"

Amelia looked to Stretch, waiting for him to answer. "We just finished the spring roundup in June. That was to cut out the calves and brand them. Then we have another in the fall, when we send the cattle to market."

"That's why school won't start until after the fall roundup," Amelia explained. "Everybody with a pair of hands is needed."

"So now is the lull between the two busy seasons," Anya said.

"You might say that," Stretch agreed. "But we're still busy makin' repairs."

"When I was on the train, I saw some sheep. Do you raise any?"

"Ain't none around here," Stretch said, his voice sounding angry. "Those animals eat the grass right down to the roots, ruinin' the grazin' for the cattle. We shoot sheep and sheepherders."

"Cattle rustlers, too," Amelia said, sounding just as angry. "I've lost a lot of cattle and a lot of horses this past year."

After that short conversation, Anya decided it would be best not to ask any more questions for a while. Instead she set her mind to choosing a name for the sorrel pony.

* * *

Farther to the west, other minds were on the cattle rustlers and thieves that had invaded the Territory and threatened to turn neighbor against neighbor. Even the Marquis de Mores had become a victim, with his cattle stolen, his brands changed by a hot frying pan and then sold back to him at a substantial profit by the thieves. No one knew who to trust. Many dared not complain to the authorities, since they might be the very ones involved in the profitable scheme.

Lately the thieves had become even bolder, murdering a rancher and his two cowboys and driving his entire herd into eastern Montana to resell at a later date.

Because of this lawlessness, the entire Territory was at risk. Something had to be done before the honest settlers and ranchers were driven out by the desperadoes and misfits that had gone mainly unchallenged.

There was only one way to rid the Territory of the rustlers—a group of reliable ranchers appointing a sheriff of their own and riding with him to clean up the mess.

This was the scheduled secret meeting that brought Matt back from his filature on the Red River of the North.

So that morning, while Anya rode beside Amelia and Stretch to the place where she was to hone her skills with a six-shooter, Matt was riding his horse forty miles away, along an old trail that had gone back to the wild, with its steep ravines treacherous from the previous day's rain.

He, too, had started out long before the sun was up,

and now he had finally reached the agreed-upon rendezvous point—a small log cabin with dirt floor and dirt roof resembling a hogan. It was hidden from view on three sides by craggy buttes. Yet its view toward the east was spectacular, sweeping toward the creek where the early morning mist rose to meet the rising sun.

He was late. The others' horses were in the corral; the meeting had probably already begun.

"Glad to see you, Matt," Ed Baynes said, stepping out from his hiding place and lowering his rifle.

"Sorry to be late."

"That's all right. Crawley just got here, too. Now we're all accounted for." Giving a nod to his son to continue guarding the approach, he followed Matt inside the cabin.

Matt's eyes quickly adjusted to the darkness; he recognized the other seven, including Roosevelt, who had just returned from New York. He was wearing his new fringed buckskin suit and a wide sombrero that nearly all newcomers succumbed to. But despite his dress, his Eastern accent, he had shown his mettle a number of times, gaining the respect of each man in the room.

Noticeably absent was the marquis, for although he was honest, one of his own men, whom he trusted, was suspected. If that man alerted his cronies to the planned raid, then it would be a failure.

"Now that we're all here," Shaun Drayton began, "the first order of business is electing a sheriff."

"This is more formal than the Cattleman's Association," one rancher voiced. "I thought we'd all decided on C. J. for that."

"We got to have it done all legal and proper, Rufus. Do you want to nominate him?"

"I reckon I do."

"All in favor of C. J., say aye."

"Aye." Every man's voice rose in accord.

"Any opposed?"

"You just heard us all say aye," another rancher complained.

"Hearing no opposition, C. J. has just been duly elected as sheriff. Now it's his turn to speak."

Shaun sat down and waited for C. J. to present his plans for ridding the Territory of the rustlers and murderers.

Well-educated, with a gentle appearance, C. J. did not resemble the typical lawman of the plains. Although he was one of the youngest there, he had a quick mind, capable of formulating an immediate plan of action.

"Gentlemen, you know the seriousness of this endeavor," he began. "And you know, too, that the element of surprise is our best weapon. That's why the whole thing must be kept an absolute secret, with only you in this room aware of the details."

"That's not a fair battle, C. J.," one man complained. "Eight law-abidin' citizens against at least seventy-five desperadoes."

"You're right, Gunther. That's why we have to have some of your best men join us. Matt, why don't you start? How many cowpunchers do you have that you would trust with your own life?"

"Well, I've got Lynx, my foreman. Then Travis,

Snake Man, and Prairie Dog. Some of the others are 'maybes.' "

"Matt's a lucky devil," Henry said. "Me, I don't have but about two I'm absolutely sure of."

"I have two, also," Roosevelt spoke up.

By the time the rest in the room anteed up their reliables, it was evident that the battle would still be one-sided, with the lawless outnumbering the posse nearly three to one.

"What about Amelia's foreman?" Gunther asked.

"He has a big mouth," Henry complained.

"Then we'd better not say anything to him," C. J. decided.

Matt visibly relaxed. There was something about Stretch that he didn't like. But if he had spoken against him, the others would have thought it was because of the long-standing feud between the Bergens and the Chaboillezes.

"We've still got a major problem," C. J. said. "Finding their hideouts. It would be much better if we had somebody with us who knew every inch of ground, every place the outlaws could be hiding."

"I could probably persuade Tall Tree to ride with us as scout," Matt offered. "If anyone knows that treacherous land, it's Tall Tree. But don't expect him to do anything except guide us." A murmur of approval filled the room at Matt's suggestion.

As soon as the timing of the raid had been decided upon, the eight men left the secret meeting, fanning out in different directions and heading for their own ranches to the east, the north, the west, and the south—to the valleys bordering the Little Missouri, the Heart and its tributaries—some riding along the old Custer Trail of '76, strewn with memories of Little Bighorn.

This time, they could not afford another massacre.

Chapter 15

A shot rang out, hitting its intended target.

Impressed, Stretch said, "Let's see if that was an accident, Sarah." He set another can on the fence post and then walked back to her side. "All right, try again."

This time, Anya missed, her bullet ricocheting against the barbed wire instead. "Sorry."

"That's all right. You've got a good eye. You just need practice," Amelia said encouragingly. "Aim a little higher next time."

"Now bring the gun up slow," Stretch said. "And act like that tin can yonder is your worst enemy, determined to do you in."

The image of Igor, laughing and mocking her, was not difficult to dredge up. Squinting her eyes against the sun, Anya took aim, spending the four remaining bullets in rapid succession, hitting the can, knocking it from the post, and then shooting it as it lay on the ground.

"Whoa, Sarah," Stretch cautioned. "That'll do. Whoever he was, he's dead."

An embarrassed Anya became aware of the two staring at her. "Who was your villain, Sarah?" Amelia asked sympathetically.

"The man responsible for my father's death."

The woman suddenly looked old. "I think you've practiced enough for one day." In an effort to lighten the pall that had settled over them, Amelia said, "I'm starving. I'll race you both to the chuck wagon in the north pasture."

Soon the two larger horses were in a gallop, side by side, with the Indian pony, whom Anya had named "Dreamer," not far behind.

In the northern latitudes, where the short summer blossomed with riotous color, a beaten and heartsick Ashak lay manacled to the iron rung in the floor of a shed in Sitka. He had drifted in and out of consciousness, tortured in body and tortured in mind. He could neither remember how long he'd lain there, nor what information Igor and Torzhok had forced from him. His greatest fear was that he had given Anya away.

In the darkness, he heard someone working with the lock, and then, through half-closed eyes, he saw a shaft of light as the metal door was pushed open. He groaned, for he knew that he had reached the point where he could no longer endure the torture.

"Ashak?" a voice whispered. "Are you in there?"

His heart gave a leap. It was not Torzhok, after all. The voice sounded like that of his sister. "Nutee? Is that you, Nutee?"

"Oh, Ashak. Thank God I've found you. Father Ambrose and I have been looking everywhere for you."

"Go, Nutee," he warned. "Torzhok will be back any minute."

"But I've come to help you escape. Father Ambrose has a boat. He can take us to one of the islands in the north."

"It's too late for me," Ashak said. "No, you must save yourself, while there's still time."

"I can't go without you."

"You'll have to. My legs are shattered, and I'm dying. I need only a knife. Did you bring one with you?"

"Yes."

"Then give it to me."

Nutee knelt beside her brother, her warm tears falling onto his swollen face. Seeing his broken body, she reluctantly placed the knife in his hands. Quietly she began to sing the grieving song of her people when they had lost a loved one. But he stopped her.

"Sing for my soul when you are safe," he urged.

She touched his cheek and then fled, carefully locking the metal door behind her, so that no one would know she had found her brother.

Less than a half hour later, Torzhok returned to the shed with Igor. "Ashak cannot hold out much longer," Torzhok crowed. "In the next few minutes, we will learn from him where the Princess Anya is hiding."

But that was not to be. Ashak lay still on the crude

wooden floor, a knife in his heart and a peaceful smile on his face.

"The bastard is dead!" Igor shouted. He glared at his companion. "Did you kill him, Torzhok?"

The servant saw the dangerous eyes gleaming at him in the semidarkness. "No, my prince. He must have killed himself."

"How did he get the knife?"

Torzhok shrugged. "Perhaps it was in the shed all along."

"Or someone could have brought it to him."

"Then he would have been rescued, would he not? As you saw, the door was still locked."

"This makes me angry, Torzhok."

"I know, my prince, how disappointed you are," he soothed. "But we will find her yet. It will only take a little longer."

"If we do not find her before winter," Igor warned, "then your services to me will no longer be required."

A fleeting sense of fear caused Torzhok to back away. But then he remembered. Igor could never do without him. They were linked together, past and present. Without him, Igor had no future. "I am sorry to hear that, Prince. I shall try to do better."

Slightly mollified by Torzhok's show of subservience, Igor pointed to Ashak. "Bury him," he ordered. "Then return to the compound."

The prince left the isolated shed beyond the docks and returned to his tethered horse. In the bay, a packet ship from Seattle rode at anchor. Igor took little notice as he galloped away to the house that had once belonged to Anya's father.

An hour later, Torzhok brought Igor the mail that had arrived on the packet. Totally consumed by his own disappointment over Ashak, and the absence of Nutee, the prince waved his servant away, continuing to pace up and down in the study.

Torzhok knew better than to challenge his master's wishes, even though the letter from Seattle looked interesting. Shrugging, he placed the unopened mail on a silver tray in the hallway and went to see why no smoke rose from the kitchen chimney.

Asleep in the corner of the kitchen, an ancient Eskimo woman snored. "Wake up, Crone," Torzhok ordered, shaking her so hard that her few remaining teeth rattled. "You've let the cooking fire go out, and you know the prince is having guests for dinner tonight."

Her inscrutable dark eyes looked through him, as if he were of no more substance than the dust motes suspended in the air. She had never cringed before him like the younger Nutee, no matter how fiercely he spoke. Perhaps it was because of her age, the fact that she was hanging on to life by a thread—and she didn't seem to care when that thread unraveled. It was difficult to put fear in a person who had already made friends with death.

"Once the fires are going again," he said, "get out the linen and china. Nutee will need help."

"What makes you think she will come back?"

"What are you talking about, Crone? Where is she?"

The woman laughed, the mirthful sound disintegrating into a cough. "Gone. Forever, like the good spirits from this house."

He reached out to shake her again, but something in her eyes made him think better of it. If what she said was true, then he would have to cook the dinner, and Crone would have to serve it. The prince could not risk the humiliation, after the whisperings about Anya, that his servants had left him, too.

Several hours later, Torzhok raced from kitchen to front door, changing livery coats when appropriate. He knew that the Russian members of the Alaskan-American Trading Company never looked closely at servants. By changing coats with regularity, he would be taken for the full retinue the house had enjoyed before Anya disappeared.

But with Crone, he was not so sure. He had scrubbed her face and hands himself, and dressed her in Nutee's serving outfit. But she still resembled a wrinkled apple doll hidden amid white embroidered cap, red apron, and blue dress that tended to slide off one shoulder.

"Stand up straight, Crone," he ordered, placing a large tray in her unsteady hands. He motioned for her to follow him into the dining room, where the guests were already seated.

As Crone shuffled in, with her mukluks barely hidden under the long skirt, Igor stared in horror. A questioning glance at Torzhok confirmed his worst suspicions. His dinner party was in danger of total disaster. From deep within, he summoned his charm, deliberately taking his guests' minds from the service.

Through one course to the next, the dinner continued, each potential disaster narrowly averted by Torzhok's watchfulness. A fish course, the serving of moose meat, the summer vegetables and fruit, were all washed down by appropriate wines, liberally poured by Torzhok, returning to the dining room in a steward's coat, different in color from his other serving coat.

But when dinner was almost over, and Igor felt he could at last relax, Crone reappeared. Torzhok, pouring the last wine, was too far away to help when the tray of cheeses and crackers tipped and some of the crackers slid to the floor. In horror, both he and Igor saw the old woman stoop down, pick up the crackers, and begin to brush them off before returning them to the serving tray.

Quickly Igor diverted his guests' attention. In lilting French, he spoke to the woman at his right, the aristocratic wife of one of the officials of the trading company. "Madame, you are a vision tonight," he said. "You must tell me the name of your dressmaker, so that I may order Anya a dress of similar style."

"By all means, Prince Igor," she replied in a pleased voice. "I have missed Anya, as I'm sure you have, too. Will she be coming home soon?"

"I think perhaps she will be away until spring."

"It's strange that you have not heard from her, Igor," Stanislaus, the woman's husband, said, his voice filled with concern. "If one did not know better, people would think you had done away with her."

"Yes," the other partner, cousin to the grand duke, teased. "I have heard rumors to that effect in the street."

Torzhok, seeing his master's temper ready to explode, leaned over and whispered in his ear.

Igor, in control again, smiled. "Ah, my servant has just informed me that a letter arrived today on the packet ship. I have not had time to read it."

"Then tell your servant to bring it into the dining room immediately," Tatiana urged. "All of us want to hear what Anya has to say."

"Madame, you are my guests," he answered. "I would not presume to bore you this evening with domestic matters."

The insistence to produce the letter was too great. In the end, there was nothing Igor could do but to have it brought to him.

Torzhok carried the small tray to the table and set it beside his master. From the handwriting on the envelope, Igor could see that it was not from Anya. But he was determined to see the farce through. Opening it, he looked down at what was written:

My dear Prince Igor:

I regret to inform you that your wife, the Princess Anya, was killed on July 8 by outlaws in their robbery attempt on a Northern Pacific Railroad train bound from Seattle to Fargo in the Dakota Territory. She was given a Christian burial in the wilderness, and her personal effects will be shipped to you in the near future. . . .

"Read it to us, Igor. Don't keep it to yourself."

A shaken Igor looked up, remembering that he had guests. "I'm afraid it's bad news," he said. "My beloved Anya is dead."

"That can't be."

"Who is the letter from?"

"What does it say?"

"Are you sure it's genuine?"

Stanislaus stood up, walked to Igor's side, and took the letter from his hand. He read it aloud, with the rest of the party gasping at the unfortunate news. He then turned it over to look at the postmark, the address of the sender. "The letter appears to be genuine. It's from the president of a silk import firm, who was on the train."

"Oh, my poor prince," Tatiana said. "What a tragedy."

The cousin to the grand duke frowned. "But Igor, what was she doing on the train? I thought you said she had gone by ship."

"Don't bother him with such questions," his stately wife, Catherine, scolded. "Can't you see the man is devastated? Come, we must all go and let Igor grieve in solitude."

Torzhok did not have time to change livery coats. He raced to the entrance hall, handed over each fur, each woolen shawl, until all were gone.

"A total disaster," Igor complained. "And the letter was the worst of all. I don't believe a word of it. Anya had someone write it for her. As if I would be fool enough to believe it."

"It *could* be true, my prince," an exhausted Torzhok said.

"Only when I see her bones; only when I have back everything she's stolen from me—only then will I believe it."

"But the letter has served its purpose, has it not?"

"What do you mean?"

"No one can kill a woman who is already dead."

Igor smiled. "I see what you mean. Yes, it might not have been such a bad thing, opening the letter at the table tonight. By morning, the entire society of Sitka will no longer be gossiping behind my back. Instead, they'll be sympathizing with me in the loss of my beautiful Anya."

Chapter 16

In a small grove of cottonwoods, beyond the saloons and hotels of Medora, Lynx and the volunteers of the town began the building of the local schoolhouse. The sketchy plans called for two rooms, one with a potbellied stove and space for the pupils and their seats, and the other room, slightly smaller, for the teacher's living quarters, with a stone hearth for a fire, a black iron stove for cooking, and a loft for sleeping.

"Now, we can't forget the outhouses," Travis said.

"You aimin' to put windows in them, too?" Snake Man asked, looking at the two leaded-glass windows the cowpuncher was hovering over.

Travis grinned. "Crescent moons will do just fine." Then he said, "Well, I'm keepin' my promise to Miss Sarah. But looks like yours will be a little harder."

"If you're speakin' of the buffalo robe, time ain't run out yet. I'll shoot me a buffalo before the house-warmin', just wait and see."

Lynx, listening to the sparring of the two, said, "Shut up your bickerin' and hoist those timbers. We got only three days to finish up."

"It would be nice for Miss Sarah to see it before it's finished, in case she wants to change somethin'."

"That's a good idea, Travis."

"I'll be happy to ride over to where she's stayin'," a pleased Travis offered.

Snake Man laughed. "You'd be shot dead by Amelia's men before you set foot on the porch."

"He's right. We'd better send Cyrus instead," Lynx replied. "Prairie Dog, hop on your horse and trot over to the stable. Tell Cyrus to go let Miss Sarah know we'd be pleased to have her inspect the buildin' tomorrow, if she can get here."

Prairie Dog, who never had much to say, merely nodded. He limped to his horse and set off. As soon as he'd gone, Lynx walked over to the water bucket and drank from the tin dipper. Eyeing the two men from Crawley's Diamond Bar Ranch, Deke and Sam, working at the other end, he said in a low voice to Travis, "Did you hear what happened at Mr. Roosevelt's new ranch the other day?"

"What?"

"The marquis's men paid a little visit. Said they didn't much like Roosevelt buildin' there, even though he's claimed more'n his share of public land. They were right threatenin', but Sewall told me when the men saw Roosevelt wasn't goin' to be intimidated, they sort of backed off. 'Course it didn't hurt none for Sewall to have his gun at the ready."

"Four-Eyes is a feisty fellow," Snake Man said approvingly. "He's not afraid of anybody. And he's got the same kind workin' for 'im."

"Too bad more ranchers ain't like that," Lynx said. "I hear some of the smaller ones are bein' burned out, and when they leave, their land is bein' gobbled up by some secret land-hungry group."

As Deke and Sam quit to get a drink of water, Lynx smiled and said, "How you comin' along with the windowsills in the back?"

"Ought to have the glass in by late afternoon."

"Good."

A half hour after they'd all gone back to work, Prairie Dog returned in a mule wagon, with Cyrus beside him and his horse tied to the back.

"Whatcha got there, Prairie Dog?" Lynx asked, peering at the covered object in the back of the wagon.

"Got us a bell," he said. "Every schoolhouse I seen had a bell. Reckon Miss Sarah can use one, too."

"Where'd you get it?"

Prairie Dog acted as if he hadn't heard the question.

He untied his horse and said to the workmen, "Help me get the bell out, so Cyrus can be on his way to the ranch."

Lynx understood. He motioned to the other men to lift it down while he talked with Cyrus. "Now, you know what to tell Miss Sarah?"

"Yep. Be here tomorrow if you want to see the schoolhouse."

"That ain't quite it, Cyrus. You're to be more polite. Ask Miss Sarah kindly if she can take the time to come and inspect the schoolhouse tomorrow. Now you got that?"

"Yep."

"Then on your way."

As soon as the wagon had disappeared, Lynx asked again, "Where did you get it?"

Prairie Dog looked a little sheepish. His eyes moved from one man to the other before he spoke. "This ain't for the newspaper," he announced. "Or for loudmouthed kids like Cyrus to know."

As Lynx removed the cover, he recognized a train engine's bell. He changed his question. "Where did you steal it?"

"I ain't no bell rustler," Prairie Dog snorted. "I salvaged it—from that wrecked engine they brought up from the river."

Before the afternoon was ended, a pole had been set deep in the ground near the front door, and at its top, the bell had been installed. Since the railroad had provided the lumber for the school, it was only proper that it had also provided a bell. At least that was the consensus of the cowboys.

That evening, in the twenty-eight-room château of Antoine, the Marquis de Mores, and his wife, Medora, the couple, finishing a glass of imported French wine, finally left the elegant dining room and went into the parlor, where the servants had laid a fire.

Settling back on the comfortable chaise with its fur lap robe, Antoine said, "Play for me, Medora." His hand indicated the beautiful Kurtz piano that had been shipped by rail from New York.

"What would you like to hear, Antoine?" she asked, rising from her chair and walking toward the piano.

"Perhaps something from one of the new Italian operas," he suggested.

Antoine loved this part of the evening, when little Athenais was in bed, the business of the day behind him. He loved to watch his beautiful wife, her graceful hands so accomplished, equally at home with playing the most difficult opera scores, painting a pastoral scene in watercolor, or handling a hunting gun in the wild. Not many men could boast of such a wife—one who had beauty and brains, was charming to be with, and was extremely rich, too.

Of course, he had brought much to the marriage as well. He was descended from royalty, and if it had not been for the unfortunate Revolution, he might have been king of France. It was still a possibility—but a dream that he kept to himself. Others might not appreciate his grandiose plans.

But it was not beyond the realm of imagination that he could develop an empire in the American West—and make such immense wealth that he could return to France, and, from his position of power, demand the crown that should have been his.

"I have the new score of Puccini's *Gianni Schicci*," Medora said, breaking into his reverie. "There's a beautiful aria in it. Would you like to hear that?"

"Yes, *chérie*. But play the overture first, so that I can get a sense of all the melodies in the opera."

Medora opened the new score, pressed the pages open with the palm of her hand, and began to play. To the side of the piano hung her portrait, Antoine's favorite. Tonight she was in blue, in a dress quite similar to the one in the portrait, so that he had two views of her at the same time—the living, vital one in profile; the painted one staring at him like an angel from the gilt frame on the wall.

Antoine shut his eyes and listened to the music in earnest. Too soon, Medora stopped, closing the opera score and coming to sit near the fire.

"That was beautiful, Medora. *Merci*."

She smiled at her husband, the man she had fallen in love with on the French Riviera, when she had been on holiday with her father, Baron von Hoffman. "How much longer will we be here, Antoine?" she inquired, listening to the wind roar outside.

"For several more months, I think. Why? Are you missing the social life you left behind?"

"A little."

"Then if you wish, as soon as it's feasible, we can leave. Where would you like to spend the winter?"

"I think I would like to open the house in Sardinia after the baby is born. It will be so much warmer there for the children."

Antoine nodded. "But I must get in a little shooting before we go." Medora was an even better shot than he, but in the early stages of pregnancy, she had to be careful. The traveling wagon in which she usually slept was luxurious, with a bed, chest, and space for her hunting weapon. But the bumpy and wild terrain on a horse was too dangerous for one in her condition. Seeing the brief flicker of disappointment, he was sympathetic. "I'm sorry that you won't be able to go with me this time."

She suddenly smiled. "I know what we can do. We'll plan a party here for a weekend soon. While you and your friends go shooting, the women can stay with me in the château. A dinner party for the first evening," she said, thinking aloud. "Then you and the men can leave early the next morning. And when the hunt is over, we'll celebrate your return with another dinner party."

"What a capital idea," he said. "Now whom would you like to invite?"

Medora hesitated. "We will have to be very proper, Antoine," she cautioned. "Because of Papa and New York, we must invite Theodore." Seeing the look of dislike on his face, she quickly added, "I know you have differences with him at the moment, but he's a gentleman. Besides, that will give him the opportunity to return the latest book you lent him."

Antoine laughed, his good humor restored. "I'd like

Matt Bergen to come, even though I know you'd like to have Amelia, too."

"Yes. But I'll make sure to seat them at opposite ends of the dinner table. Having the Crawleys, the Bayneses, and the Draytons will help. And C. J., of course."

"I understand Mrs. Drayton has gone back East."

"Then I suppose we'll have to invite the new schoolteacher who's staying at Amelia's ranch." Medora did not sound enthusiastic. But she needed an even number. And it was always nice to have another young woman. Even though Sarah Macauley was penniless, with no obvious background, at least she was better educated than most of the other women.

"I'll leave that entirely up to you," Antoine said, lighting his pipe for a final smoke before retiring to his bedroom.

The next day, in the early part of the afternoon, Anya and Amelia rode into Medora, with Diego at their side.

The Mexican's service to the Chaboillez ranch had been a long one, going back to a Texas cattle drive made by Henri, when he was still a young man. Lately the years seemed to be catching up with Diego, and Amelia, noticing it, had brought him in from the line, from the dampness of the cold nights on the range. For although he'd never mentioned it, she'd seen how his hands were becoming misshapen from rheumatism. Now she assigned other jobs to him, so that he could keep his pride, but at the same time, sleep in a dry bunk each night.

Today he rode proudly, his rifle slung across his saddle and his sombrero shading his wary eyes from the sun. His dark mustache was every bit as magnificent as the marquis's, except that he let his own droop naturally, instead of waxing it upward into fine points.

"Now be civil, Diego," Amelia warned him, even before they reached the schoolhouse. "Matt's men are in charge of the building. We are on common ground."

"Doesn't matter. If they make a false move, I shoot."

"Stubborn as a Texas longhorn," Amelia complained to Anya. "Don't know why I keep him on."

Diego grinned. Amelia still afforded him no slack, and he was happy.

Anya, with her loyalty divided, felt uneasy. The time spent on the silk train had forged a bond between her and the cowboys who had served as guards. She was truly eager to see the work they'd done on the school. But she was grateful to Amelia, too, for giving her a place to live for the summer. Her uneasiness was magnified by a feeling of vulnerability in leaving the safety and obscurity of the ranch.

Seeing them as they arrived, Lynx came forward. "Afternoon, Miss Amelia. Afternoon, Miss Sarah."

"Hello, Lynx," Anya said.

"Thought you might like to see how the buildin' is progressin'. It's still not too late to change somethin' you might not like."

"From what I can see, it looks wonderful." Anya slipped from the pony. "Are you coming inside, Amelia?"

"No, Sarah. I'll ride on to the dry goods store. There

are a few items I need. Take your time, and I'll be back as soon as I've finished."

Diego started to follow Amelia, but she stopped him. "Wait here, Diego. You can take care of Sarah's pony while I'm gone."

The Mexican was clearly unhappy, but he obeyed Amelia nevertheless.

Lynx led Anya toward the building, pointing out the bell. Prairie Dog, suddenly finding something to take care of inside, smiled at the teacher's enthusiasm.

Like a welcoming committee, Travis and Snake Man came to stand beside Prairie Dog. "We hope you're pleased so far, Miss Sarah," they said, speaking as if they had rehearsed it several times.

"Oh, it's beautiful," she said.

"Wait till you see the windows in the next room. They're much larger than these," Travis said, indicating the smaller ones provided for the school.

"Now, boys, don't brag so much," a voice exclaimed from the open door. "Give her time to make an adequate inspection."

Anya looked in the direction of the voice. Surrounded by a halo of sun, Matt Bergen's tall frame took up the entire doorway.

"Hello, Sarah. How have you been?"

In a nervous gesture, Anya quickly smoothed her windblown hair. "Fine, Matt," she replied politely. "And you?"

Chapter 17

Lynx was even less pleased to see his boss than Anya was. He'd known Matt was coming, but to Lynx's way of thinking, the boss had chosen a mighty poor time. Why couldn't Matt have waited another day, so that he could have had Miss Sarah to himself?

"Thought you were still at the filature, Matt," Lynx said, frowning.

"I came back sooner than I'd planned," he replied. "But don't let me stop you from what you were doing."

"Miss Sarah came to inspect the schoolhouse, since it's nigh about finished. Thought, if she wants anything different, now's the time to talk about it."

"Then by all means, show her around."

Lynx was gratified that Matt didn't seem interested in walking with them. Instead, after a brief glance around the main room, he went outside.

"Now this is where you'll be holdin' class," Lynx said, his attention returning to Anya. "The desks can go either way, facin' the door, or facin' the wall."

Anya nodded, thinking of the mission school and visualizing its seating arrangement. She remembered how cold it was in winter and how Father Ambrose had gathered his students as closely as possible around the stove. "I think we might divide the room—the little ones over here," she said, "and the larger students over there. That way, no one will be too far from the stove, or from my desk."

"That's a good idea," Lynx said. "Hadn't thought of that."

"The place is wonderful. By the time you put up some pegs for the coats, and a cupboard of shelves for the slates, the room will be perfect."

"We're plannin' on doin' that tomorrow," Lynx replied, unwilling to let her think he'd forgotten something that important.

"Then let's go to the next room," Anya suggested. "There's nothing else needed in the classroom."

"We're puttin' a door through here," Travis interrupted, "so you can get back and forth to your livin' quarters without gettin' snowed or rained on."

"Thank you."

Snake Man was determined not to be outdone. He added, "And we're buildin' a shed so the wood can stay dry. It's easier to start a fire with some kindlin'. The lignite takes an awful long time to catch."

"But where will we get the coal?" Anya asked.

"Oh, that's already taken care of," Lynx informed her. "You don't have to worry about fuel."

From the moment Anya stepped inside the room that would serve as her home, she thought of Sarah and of how much she would have loved it. Although completely devoid of furniture, the room already possessed a charming warmth. She felt it in the stone hearth of rock, its timbered cottonwood slab of a mantel, in the stairs that led to the open loft, and in the two large leaded-glass windows that had been placed on each side of the hearth.

She walked to one of the windows, touching the pane of glass. Anya could visualize sitting before the fire in a rocking chair and reading from the light that poured through the windows. Turning around, she said, "Oh, I'm so pleased with absolutely everything. It's perfect."

"Not quite," a dissenting voice replied. "That is, if you don't want to carry water all the way from the river."

Lynx struck his left hand with his fist as he realized what Matt was talking about. "The well. We completely forgot about diggin' a well."

Anya, seeing the crestfallen look on the cowpunchers' faces, felt obligated to defend them against Matt Bergen. "But Lynx, I thought your job was to oversee the building of the schoolhouse. How can you be expected to do everything else, too?"

"A good point, Sarah," Matt replied. "I'll see to the well, personally, before the housewarming."

"Housewarming?"

"Nobody's told you? The community will be furnishing what you need in the way of furniture, bedding, and cooking pots. The people are planning a big welcome party for you before school begins."

Hearing those words, Anya suddenly realized that she, the proud and wealthy Princess Anya Winstead Fodorsky, was now a destitute unknown, forced to rely on the largesse of strangers for even the barest of necessities. For a moment, she struggled with her pride. She wanted to scream at Matthew Bergen, "Do you not realize who I am? Can you not see that I've been surrounded by wealth all my life?" She didn't know who made her angrier—her husband Igor, for having put her in this position, or Matt, for reminding her of it in no uncertain terms.

"That's very kind of them," she finally replied, swallowing her anger and pride.

"Well, I'll see you fellows back at the ranch," Matt said. "Good afternoon, Sarah."

"Good-bye," she replied, saving her smile for the men who had worked so hard to please her.

Matt's brief consultation with Lynx, out of her hearing, left Anya alone with the other cowboys. In chatting with the three, she tried to ignore a scowling Diego peering at them through the window. It seemed that he was more concerned with watching over her than the pony. But perhaps that was what Amelia had in mind all along.

"Once you finish up here, I have another job for you," Matt informed Lynx. "But this one is to be kept secret. It's dangerous, but has to be done."

"It ain't on no darn train, is it?"

"No. You'll be on your horse."

"Good. Tramp needs a long run before he forgets what he's for. And so do I."

"Then finish up here by tomorrow and get the men back to the ranch."

"Are those three goin', too?"

"Yes. But they're not to know where until the last minute."

"I hear you, Matt."

Seeing Amelia returning from the dry goods store, Matt left, riding in the opposite direction.

An unusually pleased Amelia rejoined Diego and waited for Anya. Watching the young woman stride out of the school and wave to her as she walked to the pony, Amelia tightened her hands on the reins. From a distance, she looked so much like Mellie, or what Amelia had envisioned Mellie would look like if she had lived. But perhaps it was the riding clothes, after all, instead of the physical appearance. For once she got close enough, Sarah's copper-colored hair, her blue-green eyes, broadcast her uniqueness, not to be confused with her own daughter. Yet Amelia's heart responded.

"Do you like the school, Sarah?" Amelia inquired.

"Oh, yes. It's far nicer than I expected. Do you have time to take a look inside?"

"I'll see it another day. We need to hurry back to Sweet Grass before dark."

Anya understood. She mounted her pony, leaving behind the town, the biting horseflies, and the odor rising from the chimney of the marquis's meat-packing plant.

Swatting at a persistent horsefly, Amelia took a quick mental note. She must make sure that Sarah received a proper gauze netting for her bed at the housewarming.

Two days later, in the predawn hours, Matt and his men, Gil Crawley, Shaun Drayton, Ed Baynes, and the new chief of police, C. J., joined the others at the draw and waited for Tall Tree to appear.

"You're sure he's coming?" C. J. asked.

"Yes," Matt replied. "He said he would."

"One day that old man is goin' to disappoint you, Matt," Crawley said, "and not show up. I'd hate to be around you then."

In the darkness, Crawley couldn't see Matt's face. He merely heard the irony in his voice. "Let's get one thing straight, Gil. Tall Tree is his own man, and I respect him for it. Sometimes when I've asked for his help, he's refused. That's his prerogative as a medicine man. But once he gives his word, he doesn't renege like some people I know."

"If you're talking about my promise of two men, I can't help it that I thought better of it after the meeting. You wouldn't want to risk the outlaws gettin' word ahead of time, would you?"

"Listen," a voice broke in. "I hear somebody comin'."

They all quieted down and peered into the darkness. Only Matt was aware that Tall Tree's pony was already beside him. Sitting erect on the saddle blanket, the old man was dressed in the same brown trousers, the familiar buckskin vest, with a badger skin upon his head.

The badger's eyes seemed to be staring straight ahead, looking for its prey. The small group left the draw and rode toward Driscoll's hideout.

One of the first things that Matt remembered as a boy was Tall Tree's explanation of the hunter and the hunted.

"Look at the eyes of a deer," he'd explained. "They are not placed like a mountain lion's. Instead, they're on the sides of the head. Now rabbit or hawk. Which is the hunter?" he'd asked. "Which is the hunted? Remember the position of the eyes."

Matt smiled, recalling that early lesson. He glanced at the Indian riding beside him. Something primeval, deep within, was glad that the badger was staring straight ahead.

Later that morning, after Amelia had left the ranch to attend the second quilting party, a bored Anya saddled her pony, Dreamer, to take him for a gallop.

"You sure you won't get lost?" Ward, one of the dubious cowpunchers at the barn, asked her.

She shook her head. "Don't worry. I'm only going to ride where I've ridden before."

"I wish Stretch was here. Or Diego," he said. "Somebody ought to ride with you. Miss Amelia would be awfully put out if she thought we wasn't lookin' out for you."

Anya looked toward the gate where Jamie Purdy was sitting, chewing on a blade of prairie grass. "Does Jamie ride?" she inquired.

"Like a little Injun."

"Then maybe he'll ride with me," Anya suggested.

Ward whistled between his teeth, the shrill sound catching Jamie's attention. With a motioning of the hand, he signaled for the boy.

Jumping from the fence, Jamie began running toward the barn. "What's wrong, Ward?" he asked.

"Not a thing. How'd you like to go for a nice ride with Miss Sarah?"

His eyes lit up. "Can I ride the new mustang?"

"No. He ain't completely broke yet. I'll saddle up little Betsy for ya."

Jamie shrugged. He really hadn't expected Ward to say yes. He was satisfied enough to go riding with his new teacher—without having somebody else trailing along.

Within minutes, the two, woman and boy, left the stable and headed in the direction of the wheat fields, following the meandering stream and enjoying the circling of the eagles overhead.

Toward the west, a few large white clouds had begun to form, creating a patchwork in the blue sky. But to Anya, they did not look threatening.

To make conversation, Jamie said, "You ever hear about the day Mellie was drowned?"

"No, Jamie."

"Well, it was right after I was born. But my grandma said it started out with just one little cloud, like that one over there, I expect."

Anya looked in the direction the child was pointing. The small cloud was different from the others, its color an angry gray, like a wolf among a fleecy white flock of sheep.

"Then what happened?" Anya prompted.

"It started rainin' something dreadful. Mellie got swept away in the flood. That's why my grandma said never to ride near that arroyo unless the sky is blue as a bluebottle fly."

"Then we won't go anywhere near it," Anya agreed.

"Would you like to hear how it happened?"

Anya hesitated. "Only if you want to tell me."

"Well, you know it was Matt Bergen's fault that she died. They were running away to get married."

"Oh?"

"Yep. Nearly everybody on the ranch was here then—Stretch, Diego. But not Ward. He was hired afterward. My pa was here that day, too. But he never talks to me about it. Only Grandma, sometimes."

"I think we've talked enough about the past, Jamie," she said gently, a sadness marring the day. "Come on. Let's ride."

Chapter 18

Anya was not prepared for the fierceness of the storm, coming so suddenly as it did, with only one gray cloud for warning. Even then she could have managed with the downpour of rain. But caught on the open prairie, with lightning cracking like a whip in every direction, she was just as vulnerable as if she'd been caught in a kayak on the open sea. To make it worse, Jamie was with her. It was not good for him to get so wet and chilled.

"Is there a line shack nearby?" she shouted over the deafening noise of the storm.

"There's a little place over there," he answered, pointing slightly to the northwest.

"Then let's head for it."

The nervous ponies plunged across the open range, their hooves kicking up clods of dark gumbo mud. A flash of lightning immediately in front of them caused the ponies to swerve to the left, their riders needing no coaxing to urge them onward.

"How much farther?" Anya asked, anxious only to reach shelter as soon as possible.

"Just over that hill," Jamie said, ducking his head as an avalanche of rain slapped at his face.

The land grew wilder, more craggy, with scrub pines replacing the prairie grass, with large rocks rising like chimneys, their tops smoothed and leveled by the continuous erosion of wind and rain through the centuries. Then downhill they rode, forced to ford the small stream already forming in one of the dry gulches, in order to get to the higher elevation beyond.

The rustic building, finally coming into view, was a welcome sight to Anya, with its shingled roof and logged sides. She did not question the fence on each side that seemed to divide the front section of the cabin from the back half. She saw only a promised haven from the storm for Jamie and a shelter for the ponies.

She and the boy stopped under the protruding roof, supported by crude, vertical logs spaced three to four feet apart. Sliding down from the saddle, Anya tied her pony's reins to the wooden post near the chinked log wall. She waited for Jamie to do the same.

As Anya started to knock at the closed door, Jamie said, "Nobody lives here. We can go in."

The door creaked when she opened it; a scurry of feet echoed across the floor as some animal fled in the darkness. Anya's hand reached for the six-shooter that she wore. Then she thought better of it. "It's probably a gopher," she said, more to reassure herself than Jamie.

"Just so it's not a rattlesnake," he said. "I hate rattlesnakes."

They both stood immediately inside the open door, waiting for their eyes to adjust to the darkness. A flash of lightning, illuminating the room, was sufficient for Anya to see that its wild occupant had disappeared, presenting no danger to them.

"Do you think we might find a lantern or lamp to light?" Anya asked.

"There was one the last time I was here," Jamie replied. "I put it back in the cupboard."

The child seemed to be well acquainted with the cabin. Soon he'd brought out a lantern and matches. "Do you come here often?" she inquired, helping him to light it.

Jamie hesitated. "Promise you can keep a secret?"

In silence, she crossed her heart with her fingers.

"I'm not supposed to. But I like it here. Sometimes, I pretend it's mine."

Anya smiled. "Then I'll pretend it's yours, too. Thank you, Jamie, for having such a nice place to wait out the storm. Now let's see about making a fire."

"Oh, I can start the fire by myself," he insisted, walking toward the hearth. "I'll bet when you see how good a fire I can make, you'll want me to do it every mornin' at the schoolhouse."

"I wouldn't expect you to get to school that early. But you could certainly help keep it going during the day."

"I wouldn't mind. Pa's store's just a hop, skip, and a jump from the school."

"Thank you for offering, Jamie. But that's something we can talk about later."

He was so proud, building the fire from the dry sticks already in the fireplace. She watched him, a child small for his age, his arms and legs far too thin. But Clara, his grandmother, had been encouraged at his progress, at the improvement in his color.

"I'm keepin' him—the poor, motherless child—for the summer," she'd confided to Anya. "My son, Randall, is hopin' that farm life will help put some meat on his bones. And he's happier, too, away from town and that bully, Cyrus."

The sticks caught fire, and soon the two hugged the hearth, turning themselves before it like sheep on a roasting spit so that their clothes would dry. Jamie's eyes sparkled. He was enjoying the afternoon, enjoying Anya's total attention, despite the fury of the storm.

Finally Anya left the hearth to explore the rest of the room. It was strange that only a small window slid open, a shutter really, revealing another room, similar in appearance, on the other side, yet with no door to connect the two.

"That's unusual," Anya said, peering into the other room. "I wonder why no one saw fit to put a door here."

Again Jamie was the purveyor of information. " 'Cause that side belongs to Matt. This side belongs to Miss Amelia."

The concept, accepted so readily by Jamie, was confusing to Anya. But she was not privy to the nuances of the feud that had divided the two families. She only knew that Matt was not welcome on the Sweet Grass Ranch. She supposed, though, that the Bergens and the Chaboillezes would have need of some common ground, some sanctuary in which to meet, to discuss whatever neighbors had to settle—water rights or grazing land, cattle or fences. Though it made her uneasy, she realized that she would have to get used to this ill feeling between the two wealthy ranch families. But at the moment, she had more important things on her mind.

The storm that had forced Anya to seek shelter slowed down the search party for the rustlers. But Matt and the other men had come much too far to turn around and go home. Momentarily holding up under a clump of trees, they waited for Tall Tree to return from his scouting.

Wet and chilled, Shaun Drayton rubbed his hands. "Guess it's just as well that the marquis didn't come along this time," he said to Matt. "But his hunting wagon sure would come in handy about now."

"I'd settle for his huntin' coach," Crawley said, joining in the conversation.

An equally wet and chilled Matt smiled, remembering the latter vehicle the marquis had commissioned in Paris, patterning it after the one Napoléon had used in his Moscow campaign, with its backseat capable of being made into a bed.

"The noise of either one of those vehicles would be enough to wake the dead. If you fellows haven't forgotten, this is supposed to be a surprise strike and then a race for home."

Farther away, Lynx had his own cadre of followers, sheltering themselves under another stand of trees. The cowhands' thoughts were not so much on the dampness and cold, than on the uneven fight ahead.

"Tall Tree's been gone a mighty long time," Deke said, tightening the cinch around his horse's belly. "What's to keep him from ridin' on and maybe settin' a trap for us?" He looked from Travis to Snake Man to Prairie Dog, as if they would have firsthand information on the Indian who was their boss's friend.

Lynx had always felt uneasy around Tall Tree, himself. But as he saw the uncertainty cloud the men's eyes, he knew he'd have to do something to stop it. "What's to keep him from runnin' away and joinin' the Wild West show? I'll tell you why. Because Buffalo Bill's already got Sitting Bull with him, and he don't need another medicine man."

The men laughed, their uneasiness vanishing under Lynx's humor.

Soon Tall Tree reappeared, and, from a distance, the cowhands watched the conference taking place with Matt and C. J. Then, when Matt motioned for them, Lynx and the others remounted their horses and left the leafy shelter.

With the rain still pouring and the lightning flashing, with the quick bolts of light answered by a thunderous voice reverberating over the countryside, another rider swept in from the opposite direction and headed for the secret hiding place to warn Driscoll and his men.

Their makeshift corral, built beyond one of the ravines, held a number of beef cattle with various range brands. Because of the wind and rain that kept putting out the branding fire, the animals had been given a temporary reprieve. Leaving one man to guard the cattle, the rest had gone back to the dirt cabin to wait out the storm.

Almost impossible to spot, the sod roof had been planted with prairie grass, and, from a distance, there were no telltale signs that would indicate a living soul for miles around. Feeling secure in their hideaway, the men began to play cards to pass the time.

"Won't take long to change the marquis's brand," one said, dealing the cards.

"Yeah. I wonder when it's finally goin' to occur to him that we're stealin' his herds and then resellin' them back to him."

"Not for quite a while," a swaggering Driscoll responded, "especially with Loy on our side."

"Yep. Wish Stretch was as dependable," the third poker player commented.

"I can't quite figure that guy out. Why's he in this game, anyway?"

Driscoll smiled. "He has big stakes—the Chaboillez ranch. That's what his game is. Only he ain't got quite enough money yet to buy Amelia out."

"As long as she's alive, she won't sell. Everybody knows that."

"She might, if it got unhealthy enough for 'er," Driscoll said, acting as if he knew something the others didn't.

"Well, one thing for sure, she'd soon as rot in hell as sell the ranch to Matt Bergen."

Driscoll suddenly held up his hand. The men around him became quiet and reached for their guns as they monitored the noise outside.

By the time the knock sounded, they were all in position. "Driscoll," the voice called from the other side of the door. "I got a message for ya."

Driscoll motioned for his men to cover him. "Wait. I'll come outside," he answered.

"Don't go. It could be a trick," Bart warned.

"If it is, you'll find out soon enough from the shot."

As Driscoll slowly opened the door, his men were thinking what a fine, unselfish leader he was, willing to take major risks, himself. They waited, listening, ready to begin shooting. But then, in less than a minute, Driscoll walked back inside.

"Who was it? What'd he want?"

"There's trouble brewin' farther north. Got to go see

about it. Bart, you're to ride with me. Cougar, I'm puttin' you in charge here. Jus' as soon as the rain stops, finish changin' the brands, then drive the herd on to the cattle station."

Driscoll wasted no time in leaving. In a way, he was sorry that he'd had to sacrifice Cougar and the other men to the vigilantes. If they'd had a chance to finish rebranding the cattle, things would have been different. But the stolen cattle served as a death warrant for them all. Better for him and Bart to escape the noose than for all of them to be hanged. The only way he could buy enough time for that was for Cougar and the other men to put up a good fight with the vigilantes. They would never know that he had double-crossed them. But that was the price they had to pay for not finishing their work before the rain started.

Bart, wearing a feather in his hat and an Indian blanket as a poncho against the rain, galloped steadily beside Driscoll. The messenger had disappeared in another direction. Down in the valley behind them, a shot rang out, followed by a barrage of other shots. Hearing the noise of battle, Bart gazed with questioning dark eyes at the man beside him, but waited for his boss to speak.

"Sounds like trouble," Driscoll said. "Good thing we left when we did."

Bart made no comment. The two raced their horses faster, a sense of urgency punctuated by shots that echoed from dark ravine to rain-soaked mountains. Finally the shots stopped, replaced by the steady whine of a rising wind, the raucous cry of fighting magpies, and the constant dripping of rain. Bart's only thought was that if Driscoll had not ordered him to leave, he would probably be swinging, at that moment, from a cotton-wood tree in the valley below.

Matt's distaste for the necessary chore was in part offset by the discovery of the stolen cattle.

"The way I look at it," a voice beside him said, "you wouldn't think twice about shootin' a wildcat that's killin' your newborn calves on the range."

He looked over at Lynx, his foreman. "A wildcat doesn't know right from wrong," Matt refuted. "He's merely doing what nature intended for him. But a man, now. He's different. He should know better."

"Well, I know a few who won't ever be doin' this again," a philosophical Lynx replied. "But it's too bad Driscoll got away. I wonder who warned him."

"I have my ideas," Matt said, loud enough for only Lynx to hear.

At Sweet Grass Ranch, the rain stopped, leaving a rainbow for Anya and Jamie to follow home.

"Miss Sarah, do you think anybody's ever been lucky enough to find a pot of gold? If I knew it was at the end of the rainbow, I'd spend the rest of my life lookin' for it."

Anya hesitated. "I don't know of anyone. But there might be something even better for you to have, Jamie."

"What?"

"A dream. If you follow that dream, there's no telling what you'll find at the end."

"Oh, I've already got the dream. But I need money for it."

Anya sighed. It seemed she wasn't the only one hampered by a lack of money.

"You know what it is? My dream?"

"Does it have to do with the cabin we were in?"

"Yes. One day, I want to buy it. For Papa and Grandma."

Over the mountain, Matt and the other ranchers began their solemn return. Standing on a hill was Tall Tree, who had removed his badger skin and now looked like any other ancient Indian on his spotted pony. He waved to Matt, then disappeared.

The cowpunchers were kept busy, herding the stolen cattle before them. Snake Man, Prairie Dog, Travis, and the others were much more at home dealing with recalcitrant animals than with lawless men. Most of them had learned early in life that the land was wild and life was harsh and short. They took each day as it came, and then disappointment did not gnaw at them.

Lynx thought he'd given up his dreams long ago, until Sarah Macauley came into his life. Deep down, he knew he didn't stand much of a chance with her. But something had inspired him to go through the motions, to prove, if only to himself, that he could do more with his life than sit on a fence and measure how far he could spit.

"Look! A buffalo," Snake Man suddenly called out, cutting into Lynx's thoughts. "Fellows, he's mine!" he shouted.

No one had seen a buffalo for months. Now, an old shaggy male, ostracized from his herd, grazed on the newly washed prairie grass. At the sound of the cattle, the animal looked up and then veered off in a gallop. Snake Man veered at the same time, close behind.

This was the opportunity he'd been waiting for. If he were successful, Miss Sarah Macauley would be presented her promised buffalo robe at the housewarming.

Chapter 19

Matt saw the bull buffalo take off in a run across the prairie, with Snake Man far behind. Aware of his cowpuncher's wish to present a warm winter fur to Sarah, he, also, left the main group and began to gallop in the same direction.

It had been a number of weeks since he'd seen a single buffalo. Most of them had already been slaughtered by the thousands of dudes coming in on the trains, with their egos even bigger than their weapons. And once they'd had their sport, they'd boarded the next train East, leaving the carcasses to rot in the sun.

Matt was not against hunting. He'd spent his entire life relying on the land to provide food, to provide clothing for winter, basic necessities in a harsh climate that could freeze a man's unprotected body in a matter of minutes. But he was against the wholesale killing of animals merely for the sake of killing, or as he suspected, for the purpose of eliminating the main food supply of the Indians.

He saw Snake Man's pony stumble, then right itself, an unfortunate happening when a few seconds one way or the other could spell the difference between success or failure. Wanting Snake Man to succeed, Matt spurred his own horse, galloping in a wide sweep to reach the cutoff to the west before the buffalo could escape into the coulee.

He was barely in time. The buffalo, seeing the second rider blocking his way, changed course, veering again to the north. Then, seeing his escape in that direction thwarted by the bluff, he turned east. But that path was challenged by Snake Man.

The two, Matt and Snake Man, used to working together on the range with stubborn longhorns prone to stampede, were a congenial team, wheeling inward and outward, playing the same life-threatening game that each was born to, tiring the bull buffalo until, at last, he was cornered, his rage showing in a snort from his nostrils, the pawing of a hoof against the ground.

This was the time of ultimate danger. Matt had seen many a man, not familiar with the animals, relax, thinking that the chase was over. But true to the ways of a two-thousand-pound behemoth, the buffalo charged, heading directly toward Snake Man and his pony. The challenge now was between Snake Man and the bull. Regardless of the outcome, it would not be sporting for Matt to interfere.

With a primal howl that swept over the harsh terrain, Snake Man urged his pony forward in direct confrontation. He had only one chance to pierce the buffalo's humped shoulder beneath the collar blade, the entrance of death, similar to an Achilles' heel, and then to avoid fatal collision as the animal passed by, still with the momentum of the run.

Snake Man urged his pony onward, making sure that the buffalo would be to his right. To most hunters, it would make no difference which side the animal passed. But at almost the last second, the wily buffalo, as if sensing some flaw in the hunter, charged on Snake Man's blind side.

Caught in a dilemma that gave no time for redress, Snake Man turned his head and shot, the breath of the animal blasting him square in the face, his pony rearing in fright at the close encounter.

From his position a short distance away, Matt saw the disastrous confrontation, the merging of the two uneven forces. For a moment it seemed the buffalo had brought Snake Man down. But then Matt saw Snake Man righting himself and regaining control of his pony.

The old bull lumbered away, to the vast disappointment of Snake Man. Matt, too, was disappointed, but the fact that his cowpuncher was still alive softened his regret.

"He came up on my blind side," Snake Man cried in frustration. "I didn't have time to change course."

Matt, ready to commiserate with him, searched the uneven terrain to catch a last glimpse of the animal. But still within eye view, the buffalo finally slowed and fell to earth, his legs giving way under the weight of his body.

"Look, Snake Man," he said, pointing. "I think you got him, after all."

"What did ya say, Matt?"

Matt grinned and shouted, "You got him. Congratulations!"

A surprised cowboy turned, looking in the direction that his boss had pointed. He began to race toward the downed buffalo, with Matt not far behind. A few minutes later, the two men examined the buffalo, admiring its shaggy, thick fur.

"I'll go back over the hill and get some of the men to help you," Matt said. "He's one of the biggest I've ever seen."

"Yes," a happy Snake Man responded. "Kwa-ling can cook us some steaks tonight. And Miss Sarah can have the fur robe I promised. Too bad old Tall Tree left. I woulda let him have the tongue and some of the meat for his people."

"That is a good idea, Snake Man," a voice responded. "My people thank you."

"Where'd you come from? I thought you was long gone," Snake Man said, surprised at seeing the Indian on his pony.

"The spirit of the buffalo called. I make ceremony to celebrate his brave warrior heart."

Matt and Snake Man looked at each other, remembering the cowardly rustlers who had not died nearly so bravely as the buffalo. Matt wondered if Driscoll, who had left his men to the mercy of the posse, would stop long enough to mourn their passing into the next world.

That evening, after the rustled cattle were secretly claimed by their owners, Matt and his most trusted men, Lynx, Travis, Prairie Dog, and Snake Man, set out for the Bergen ranch. Returning with the buffalo to show for their long day, no one at the ranch would connect their hunting trip to the discovery of the dead rustlers.

Two days later, Matt and Kwa-ling drove a ranch wagon into Medora for supplies. Turning over the reins to his servant, Matt said, "Kwa-ling, I'm going over to the post office to pick up my mail. As soon as you're done at the store, meet me at the saloon."

"Is all right if I get new washtub?"

"I thought I bought a new one last month."

"No good. Full of holes."

"What happened?"

"Somebody use for target practice."

Matt frowned. "Then get another one. But you'll have to find a safer place to keep it."

Kwa-ling nodded. "I hide it, for sure."

Matt jumped down from the wagon and crossed the road, walking in the direction of the post office.

"Hey, Matt," a voice called out as he passed the horse trough. "You seen that fancy draft horse the marquis shipped in yesterday?"

"No."

"C. J. says it's a Percheron. You ever hear of that brand before?"

Matt nodded. "French," he said. "Like the marquis."

"Well, I hope it's broke in better than those stage-coach horses the marquis bought from Eben," another said, laughing. "You shoulda seen the driver leavin' here this mornin' for Deadwood. With the first taste of bits in their mouths, the horses was runnin' like bats outa hell. Felt sorta sorry for the two passengers."

"I feel sorry for the marquis having to do business with the likes of you," Matt said, his humor containing a slight sting. "Lucky for all of you he's a gentleman and takes you at your word."

The two who had spoken looked slightly sheepish. "What else are we gonna do to have some fun around here?" one asked.

"Yeah. He sure ain't one of us, sittin' on that high hill, with his twenty servants and a rich wife, and all his fancy friends a-comin' and a-goin'."

"Let's hope he never catches you shortchanging him," Matt warned. "He might speak with an accent, but I've never seen a man more expert with weapons."

One of the men shifted uneasily. "There's a rumor goin' around that he was responsible for that necktie party several days ago. You know anything about it, Matt?"

"Only what I read in the paper," he replied, leaving the small group of men.

Behind the desk, Caulk, the stout, middle-aged postal clerk, gathered Matt's mail, which had accumulated in the appropriate pigeonhole. Like most of the ranchers, Matt usually came into town once a week. But sometimes he was far too busy, waiting for several weeks at a time.

"Well, I see you got one, too," the clerk said. "Guess you'll be brushin' up your best bib and tucker for it."

Matt smiled. If anyone around knew what was going on, it was Caulk. Some had even accused him of reading their mail. Matt didn't know about that, but he did know that his journals and magazines were dog-eared by the time they finally appeared in his box. Looking at the expensive envelope on the top of the pile, Matt said, "What is it?"

"An invitation to the château. You might as well open it now, since there's a reply card inside. You can fill it out and I'll put it in the marquis's slot."

While Matt tore the seal, Caulk went on. "Now, if Mr. Roosevelt and Miss Amelia would come pick up their mail, then the whole affair would be settled."

Matt read the invitation. Caulk, as usual, was right. Matt inquired curiously, "Did Miss Macauley happen to get an invitation, too?"

"Yep. It's in with Miss Amelia's mail. Once Miss Macauley moves into the schoolhouse, I'll give her a slot of her own."

Matt moved to the end of the counter, where the inkstand rested. Caulk waited for Matt to finish, then took the envelope. "Oh, and you might want to open that other letter, too, while you're here. Come all the way from Alaska."

Instead, Matt bundled the unopened mail together and slipped it under his arm. "Kwa-ling's waiting for me," he said. "See you next week."

A disappointed Caulk watched Matt go. The envelope had been too thick for him to see through, even holding it over the lantern. He knew it didn't have anything to do with the silk shipments, though. It was a shame that Matt was in too much of a hurry to open it.

As Matt walked down the street, the odor of the abattoir hung over the town, for the meat-packing plant was in full production. Antoine had brought in a number of butchers from Chicago and his Northern Pacific refrigerator cars were iced up, waiting for the fresh meat to be loaded.

Medora had sprung up almost overnight. Its small community was a welcome change from Little Missouri, the notorious settlement across the river. Antoine had even built his wife a little brick church, and his rich in-laws a brick house to stay in when they visited from New York. With the advent of the new school, other families would be moving in soon. The railroad had seen to that, allowing passengers going West to ride for free.

Why then did Matt not have a good feeling about it? Perhaps it was because so many of the settlers looked upon the titled Frenchman as an outsider, not one of them. If something could be done to turn this around, Antoine could bring good things to the Territory. But even down to the lowliest horse thief, nearly everyone seemed to be against him.

Matt slapped at a stinging fly as he entered the saloon. He searched for Kwa-ling, finally finding him sitting in the shadows. He placed the mail on the table and said, "Have you had a drink yet, Kwa-ling?"

"Yes, boss. At the store."

"I mean something stronger than water."

"No, boss. I wait for you."

"What'll you have, Matt?" the bartender called to the blond giant.

"A bottle of whiskey and two glasses."

The bartender brought the order, setting the two glasses down in front of Matt. The bartender looked at Kwa-ling, but said nothing. Pretending he had not noticed, Matt set one glass before Kwa-ling and poured his servant a drink.

"Coolies ought to stick with their own kind," a man at the bar mumbled.

"If you value your life, stranger, you won't say that loud enough for anybody else to hear," the bartender warned.

"Why? What's so special about him?"

"It's not the Chinaman. It's the man sittin' with him. As far as we're concerned, Matt's one of the most powerful men in the Territory."

The stranger drank in silence, his eyes shifting occasionally to the table in the far corner. By the time Matt and Kwa-ling left, he had gotten a clear view. From now on, the stranger would be able to recognize Matt Bergen anywhere.

Chapter 20

The Bergen ranch was an empire in itself, spreading for miles over the prairie, with its large weathered house of ponderosa and stone set on a slight elevation that overlooked the river. It was sheltered from the strong winter winds by a chain of hills in the distance.

Long before the Territory had been settled by other emigrants, Matt's grandfather, Bjorn Bergen, with his two Norwegian elkhounds, had left the northern fur trapping trails and headed in a westerly direction, where he'd finally found his idea of paradise—open land and water that reminded him of his native Norway.

As Matt and Kwa-ling approached the ranch gate at sunset, two elkhounds, descendants of the original dogs, left the porch, and bounded across the open terrain to meet Matt. With their tails wagging, they escorted the ranch wagon to the side yard, where it came to a stop.

"Get some of the fellows to help you unload, Kwa-ling," Matt said. "I'll start the fire in the kitchen."

"I fix you good dinner tonight," Kwa-ling promised.

Matt nodded and hopped down from the wagon. Talking to the dogs following him, he stepped onto the side porch and used the bootjack to rid himself of his muddy boots. The elkhounds sniffed the boots in curiosity, their eyes resembling those of petulant children who had not been allowed to share an adventure.

"No, boys. I didn't go hunting," he assured them. "Maybe we'll go tomorrow."

Leaving the boots on the porch, Matt walked inside with the dogs at his heels. The large room he entered was a masculine domain, with rawhide chairs, deep-cushioned sofas set before the stone fireplace, and a large desk in the corner. This was where he did most of his work. He seldom went into the more formal part of the house, rarely used the massive front doors, with supporting columns on each side and adorned with carved symbols of Norwegian myth.

He dropped the mail on his desk and walked toward the kitchen to start a fire in the cooking stove. When that was done, he returned to his den and lighted the lamps.

Matt took up the rest of his mail, opening the letter Caulk had been so curious about. At the post office, he'd known that it was an answer to his own letter to Fodorsky. But he had not been eager to read the response of a distraught husband, perhaps to be blamed for the death of the man's wife. Some things, Matt did not like to share.

His eyes scanned the letter, the elegant and exact formings of the sentences indicating that English was not the primary language of the writer. Strangely devoid of blame, the letter was merely the prince's plea for a meeting with Matt the next time he was in Seattle, to discuss his wife's final hours and to be given precise directions to the grave of his beloved Anya.

Matt could relate to that. The family plot on the hillside contained not only the remains of those who'd died on the Dakota prairie, but also the reinterred bones of his uncle, who had been killed on a Texas cattle trail. His father had not rested until he'd found the grave and brought his younger brother home.

Matt set aside the letter and began to peruse a Chicago newspaper. It didn't matter that the paper was more than a week old. It still contained valuable information that the Dickinson and Mandan papers did not print.

His eyes were drawn to an advertisement of a new shipment of French silk available—his own. He smiled. Jean Bonneau was doing a good marketing job. Of course, it didn't hurt any to have some of the society matrons photographed in their finished ensembles. Staring at the photograph, he saw that no dress looked any better than the one Kwa-ling had made for Sarah from the bolt of aubergine-and-gold silk that he had brought from the factory. With the French pattern provided by Jean, and the stained traveling suit to go by for size, the new outfit would be an elegant addition to Sarah's meager wardrobe.

He was glad that the housewarming had been set before the weekend party at the château. That way, he could give the present to Sarah without arousing idle talk. It would help her tremendously with the people of Medora if she wore such an appropriate ensemble that first evening.

"Boss, supper is ready," Kwa-ling called, standing in the doorway.

In surprise, Matt looked up. It had seemed just a few minutes since he'd lighted the fire. "Coming," he said, getting up from the rawhide chair and heading for the washbasin stand in the hall before taking his place in the dining alcove off the kitchen.

In a small hotel in Chicago, Jean Bonneau lay contentedly beside the beautiful and voluptuous Reneé du Guys. He was a passionate man who loved the shape, the silken feel of a worldly woman with her arms and legs wrapped about his body. No young virgins for him. Give him a skillful woman who had nothing to cry over but her passion for him.

Of course, his penchant for married women was what had gotten him into trouble in the first place, forcing him to flee from France. How he had missed the expert lovemaking, the little nothings spoken into the ear of one who understood his native language of love. Having to translate diminished his ardor considerably.

Closing his eyes, he replayed the entire encounter in his mind, savoring his first sight of Reneé at the exclusive shop where he'd gone to take orders for the next shipment of silk.

Partially hidden behind the curtain, Jean had noticed her immediately, coming in on the arm of the stout foreigner. From their conversation with the head seamstress, he soon realized that the dark-haired beauty from New Orleans had entered into an alliance, traveling with the wealthy man on his American tour. But as usual in these cases, she was destined to remain behind when he returned to Europe and his wife.

"Will you be all right, *Liebchen*?" the foreigner inquired. "You can find your way back to the hotel when you've finished?"

"*Oui*, Karl. Go on to your tailor."

He took out his gold pocket watch, glanced at it, and then resumed his conversation. "I will see you back at the hotel by six." Turning to the seamstress, he said, "She is to have as many clothes as you can make in a week, including a shooting costume. Send the bill to me at my hotel."

"Yes, sir. And thank you for your patronage." The woman gave a slight nod, her words at odds with her manner. The man did not seem to notice, but the amused Jean was well aware of the turmoil of the corseted puritan seamstress. She needed the business, but she also needed the business of the society matron whose appointment was less than twenty minutes away. And it would not do for the two to meet face-to-face.

After the foreigner closed the door, Jean walked into view. "Madame, I have a suggestion," he said to the seamstress. "Since you're pressed for time, why don't you take the young lady's measurements, and I will accompany her back to her hotel with the samples of material. She would be able to take the entire afternoon to choose, if she so wished."

"She might not agree, Mr. Bonneau."

"On the contrary," Reneé said, staring boldly at the handsome Jean. "I think it's a splendid idea." The arrangement appealed to her much more than spending the afternoon at the small shop.

"Madame, Jean Bonneau at your service." He smiled, and like a courtier, he bent over her hand with a flourish.

Her dark eyes danced. "Reneé du Guys."

"*Enchanté.*"

At the hotel suite—it took Reneé little time to choose what she wanted—an afternoon of love with Jean. "You make me tremble with desire, *chéri*," she said, willing for the Frenchman to help her out of her confining clothes.

He made a ritual of unbuttoning a few buttons of her dress and pressing his lips against her throat. He then unbuttoned three more buttons and slid his hand into the widened opening, his wonder at the hidden softness causing his stomach muscles to tighten and his manhood to react.

Slowly, creatively, he worked, his expertise driving Reneé almost to the edge. "Hurry, *chéri*," she whispered. "I can't stand it much longer."

Jean smiled, turning his attention to removing his own clothes, to give her time to cool her passion somewhat. Then he lifted her on to the bed, where he held her in his arms. Disappointed by his sudden restraint— not at all like Karl, who leapt on her quickly and less than a minute later rolled over to sleep—she opened her eyes to peer at his body. Reassured that he had not lost his ardor, she lay back in his arms and waited.

Like animals in heat they played, linked together in

body and desire, arms and legs entangled, mouths coupled, his manhood seeking her innermost recesses time and again with teasing, strong thrusts. Each time his partial withdrawal seemed like a tremendous threat, a tremendous loss for one who had never experienced this type of lovemaking before.

Then, with all the heightened sensations that bound male to female throughout eternity, the primal body finally took over, forgetting plan and purpose and time, and rushing on to boundless ecstasy.

Jean's return to reality came suddenly, with heavy footsteps up the hallway, a key turning in the lock, and the sound of a knock at the bedroom door.

"*Liebchen*, are you back?" Karl inquired. "I finished earlier than I thought."

Jean saw Reneé glance wildly at the rumpled bed, the cold tea tray, and his half-naked body. "He will kill us both," Reneé whispered. "Quick, take your clothes and go."

"Where?"

"In there," she said, pointing to the adjoining sitting room. "And take the tray with you. I'll try to stall him as long as I can."

Juggling his clothes and the clattering tea tray, Jean rushed from the room, leaving Reneé to deal as best she could with her stout lover.

"*Liebchen?*"

"Just a moment, Karl," Reneé called out, her voice sounding far steadier than she felt. Hurriedly she made up the bed, smoothing the wrinkles, and then put on a long, flowing robe before she finally unlocked the bedroom door.

"What were you doing with my own bedroom door locked against me?" Karl inquired, his stout face red with anger.

"I did not know you would be back so early," she said, flustered at his suspicious look.

In the small salon adjoining the bedroom, the hastily dressed Jean was trapped. The door into the hallway was locked, with no key in view. There was only one way he could think of to get out of this compromising situation in one piece. Calmly he sat down in a chair and picked up a cup of disgustingly cold tea.

The door burst open; a hostile Karl said, "Aha!" at the discovery of someone else in the suite.

Behind Karl, Reneé stared at the foppish man seated in the chair and holding the teacup in an affected manner. For a second, she did not recognize Jean. He had slicked his hair back, twisted his mustache into rattails, and put on the most awful eyeglasses. Even his clothes had taken on another personality, with his shoulders considerably narrowed.

"Good afternoon," Jean lisped. "Has Madame finished choosing the material?"

"Who are you?" Karl bellowed.

"He's the man from the seamstress's shop," Reneé said quickly, drawing the folds of her robe together. "I had a headache, and he was kind enough to bring the materials to the hotel. That was the reason I had the door locked, Karl. I was draping the silk around me to see if the colors suited."

Looking again at Jean, Karl relaxed. He had nothing to fear from this effete ninny. Heaven knows he'd seen enough of his kind in Paris and Vienna to realize they were all harmless to women.

Karl leaned over and picked up a sample of the aubergine and gold that Jean had planned to show Madame. "Did you select this one?" he inquired.

"Do you like it, Karl?"

"Very much. In fact, I think I would like to buy an extra bolt to take home as well."

Jean forced himself to appear happy. "Madame will be very pleased," he said, lisping again.

"Well, *Liebchen*, I think I'll go downstairs for a beer. Send the man on his way when you're finished, and I'll be back in time to dress for dinner."

"*Oui*, Karl," Reneé replied, her eyes flirting with him as he left.

Once they were alone, Jean took out his handkerchief and mopped his brow. "That was too close, *chérie*," he said in his normal voice.

Reneé laughed. "Have you ever played the *Folies*?"

"No."

"Then perhaps you should. Your theatrics are quite amazing."

Jean frowned, gesturing to the hallway. Nodding, Reneé said in a loud voice, "Well, thank you, monsieur, for being such a help. Now, you will make sure to give the seamstress my selections?"

"At once." Jean stood up, gathered his satchel of

samples, and walked through the suite. *"Au revoir,"* he said, snapping his heels together in an exaggerated manner.

"Au revoir."

With his case in hand, Jean minced his way down the long hall, past the tall palm where Karl stood, as if checking for something in his waistcoat. *"Au revoir, monsieur,"* Jean said as he passed by.

Karl did not bother to answer the little fop. Instead he walked down the flight of stairs as Jean Bonneau waited for the elevator.

On his carriage ride back to his own hotel, Jean repaired his appearance while he thought of his near disaster. Matt Bergen would not be pleased that the same silk he'd chosen for his ladylove would also grace a little demimondaine from New Orleans. One good thing about it, though, was that Matt need never know.

Chapter 21

"Where are we going, Amelia?" a suspicious Anya inquired, climbing into the carriage beside the white-haired woman. "You've been secretive all day."

"We're going to a hoedown in Medora," she answered.

"And we need to take extra clothes for that?"

"Yes. It'll be too late to drive home afterward. We'll spend the night at the hotel and come back to the ranch in the morning."

As if that brief explanation were sufficient, Amelia chastened Diego, who was loading a large supply of food into another carriage. "Be careful, Diego. Clara will have your hide if you mess up her cakes."

"That was the ham, Miss Amelia. I'm saving a place for the cakes on top."

"Well, just make sure they don't break into pieces on the way."

"Or have a few of 'em disappear," an amused Stretch said, ready to drive the first carriage out of the yard.

As soon as Stretch took the carriage past the gate, Clara and Jamie hurried from the kitchen and climbed into the second carriage with the food. "You were a good boy, Jamie," she said, "keepin' tonight's house-warmin' a secret from Miss Sarah."

"It was about the hardest thing I ever had to do," Jamie confessed.

"Well, I'm proud of you. And I know your pa is, too."

But others in the town and on nearby ranches had not kept the timing so secret that Driscoll, the outlaw, had not been apprised of it. Still smarting from his close escape from the vigilante group of cattlemen—and the loss of the rustled cattle and some of his men—he felt particularly vengeful, waiting for an appropriate time to strike back. He could not have asked for a more ideal evening, when many of the ranchers, their families, and their hands would be in town, leaving only a skeleton crew to guard their homes.

From his vantage point at a fork in the road, he settled down between the rocks and waited for Matt Bergen to pass by on his way to town. Driscoll was certain Matt would be attending, since he was a member of the school board. And if Driscoll were lucky, Matt would have taken along his foreman and the hands who'd helped to build the schoolhouse.

"I declare, you look like a fancy shoat dressed up for the killin'," Prairie Dog said, teasing Matt as he stepped onto the porch.

Matt grinned. "If you like the coat so well, I might just let you wear it one day."

"I fancy the vest even more."

"Then I'll give it to you for offering to stay behind."

"I don't mind, Matt, watchin' over things while you're gone. All I'd do anyway is gawk at Miss Sarah all evenin'. I sure couldn't ask 'er to dance, with this gimp leg. But I'd like ya to do me a favor."

"What's that?"

"Take this little package with you and hide it somewhere safe for 'er."

Matt balanced the wrapped package in his hands. Feeling its weight and shape through the coarse floursack material, he said, "A gun? You're giving her a six-shooter?"

"Yep. She needs one if she's gonna stay alone in that little schoolhouse at night."

"You think she can use it as well as she did your Winchester?"

Prairie Dog grinned. "If she can't, it won't take her long to learn. Will you do it, Matt?"

"Sure."

"Hey, Matt," Lynx called. "You comin'?"

"Right away." Matt left the porch with the wrapped silk dress and Prairie Dog's gift. He supposed it would be a good idea to lock both in the clothespress he'd taken to the school earlier, so Sarah could open them later, without curious eyes watching.

He and Snake Man had checked the schoolhouse the previous day, noting with satisfaction the condition of the living quarters. Already in place were the iron bed and mattress, linen sheets, and the colorful quilts the women had spent the last few weeks sewing together at the bees. In the keeping room, he noticed a black iron skillet and pots, as well as blue enamelware and cutlery that Sam and Deke had salvaged from a deserted shack.

One of the rancher's wives, Maude Applegate, was busy hanging two pairs of blue calico curtains above Travis's leaded-glass windows. "Edna's bringin' a straw broom and a braided rug for the hearth," she informed Matt.

"This is a mighty fine settle," Snake Man said, draping his buffalo robe over it. "Wonder who brought it."

"The newlyweds, Sven and Ingrid," Maude replied. "Guess with six children between them, they thought they'd better give Miss Macauley a comfortable place to sit and rest after school. Sven's boys are all smokin' pistols, accordin' to Ingrid. But to my way of thinkin', her girls are just about as wild."

Glancing around the room, Matt said, "Maude, you've all done a wonderful job. Miss Macauley should be quite pleased."

Brushing the compliment aside, she said, "Well, we still got to decorate the schoolroom. But it won't take that long. We'll just put some tables against one wall to hold the food, and drape a little greenery on the stand for the fiddler."

Matt was thinking of this previous inspection as he and Lynx passed by the rocks outside his ranch. Nothing in the landscape seemed different; he felt no unusual danger lurking. Everything seemed as it should be, with the afternoon sun growing old, casting its elongated shadows along the sides of the trail that led toward Medora.

Farther behind on the trail were the carriages holding Amelia, Stretch, and Anya in one, and Jamie and Clara in the other. Diego, riding shotgun, paced his horse steadily and kept a sharp lookout to the rear.

Feeling particularly at peace, Amelia glanced at Anya. The young woman possessed a quiet elegance, her hair soft about her face, her borrowed gray-blue dress, devoid of the girlish lace that Mellie had worn, calling attention to her marvelous eyes. Although this Sarah Macauley could never take the place of her Mellie, Amelia found to her surprise that her heart had made room for her as well. She was proud of her and of what she would be able to accomplish, if given a fair chance.

They continued their journey, stopping several times to rest the horses, with Amelia giving almost the entire population of the town and the surrounding countryside time enough to take their places. Shortly before dark, the Chaboillez carriage arrived in Medora.

A boy who had been keeping watch for Amelia's coach suddenly slid down from his perch in a tree and began to run toward the school. "The teacher's comin'!" he shouted. "I just saw her."

"Then ring the bell, Josie," Gil Crawley, a member of the school committee, ordered. "We want Miss Macauley to be welcomed in a proper way."

"Listen, Amelia. That sounds like the school bell."

The woman smiled at Anya. "Yes. I suppose now you've guessed who the party's for."

It had not occurred to Anya that the housewarming Matt had so casually mentioned would be an important social event. Seeing all the horses and carriages, she said, "Is the entire town gathered at the school?"

Aware of the stricken look on Anya's face, Amelia said, "It won't be so bad, I assure you. All you have to do is pay attention to the children, compliment the women on their cooking and sewing, and dance sedately with their husbands. That's not an impossible order, is it?"

Anya struggled to regain her composure. "I suppose not. Only I wish you'd told me sooner, Amelia."

"Then it wouldn't have been a surprise," Stretch commented.

"I suppose you were in on it, too, Stretch."

"Yep."

"So was Jamie," Amelia said.

Anya forced herself to laugh. "And he never said a word to me."

"Good for him."

The welcoming committee stood before the school as the Chaboillez carriage came to a stop. Anya had little time to smooth her hair and her dress before hands reached out to help her from the carriage. "Well, Amelia, you're right on time," a man's voice boomed. "Welcome to the new school, Miss Macauley. I'm Gil Crawley, a member of the school board. The others are waiting inside to greet you."

"How do you do, Mr. Crawley."

"And this is my daughter, Josie. She's going to be one of your pupils."

Josie curtsied, and, in a proud voice said, "I hope you're hungry, Miss Macauley. Mama's made the most mouth-watering pies for us to eat tonight."

Anya, remembering Amelia's admonition, smiled at the child. "I'll look forward to a piece," she assured her, walking toward the door. Inside, the fiddler had already begun to tune up for the festivities.

Farther away, at the edge of town, a train with several special cars attached stopped at the almost deserted depot. Inside were members of a European hunting club, including Karl Schultz, with their guns, luggage, and assorted servants, on their way to Montana and Wyoming.

A bored Reneé du Guys, waiting for the train to be unloaded, leaned out the open window and listened to the music floating through the air. Her foot started tapping to the captivating rhythm, her spirits suddenly lifted by the lighthearted music.

She called out to the man carrying a lantern past the palace car: "Monsieur, what is happening? Where is that music coming from?"

"From the school," he replied. "It's a housewarmin' for the new teacher."

"Reneé," a stern voice chided. "Stop hanging out the window. Go back to your seat."

Reneé sighed. "*Oui*, Karl."

At the schoolhouse, a proud Maude Applegate had been selected to take Sarah Macauley on an intimate tour of her living quarters. Following nearby were the other women, the men having been forced to remain by the cider bowl or the pump outside.

As Anya glanced around the keeping room, murmuring appropriate thanks to each woman who had stationed herself before her own gifts, she thought of the real Sarah and of how much this display of affection would have meant to her. But standing before the settle, with the luxuriant buffalo fur robe as evidence of Snake Man's promise, Anya did not feel quite so guilty. Perhaps she had engendered a little affection and respect on her own, despite the masquerade.

"Now let's go to the loft," Maude suggested, leading the way up the narrow stairs to the open space that overlooked the keeping room below.

"This quilt on the bed is the wedding ring pattern," Maude said, smiling. "We decided at the quilting bee that you can take it with you later, when you get married."

"Oh, teachers are not allowed to marry," Anya quickly responded. "But it's so beautiful." She looked at all the proud women gathered around the quilt. "Thank you very much."

"Maude," a voice called from the doorway. "Are you ladies finished? Everybody's hungry."

"Coming, Gil," she said. Maude turned again to Anya. "Put this around your neck," she added. "It's the key to the clothespress. You can open it later."

Anya, Amelia, Maude, and all the other women left the schoolteacher's quarters and joined the men and children waiting to eat. With great ceremony, the preacher from Dickinson blessed the food, the building, the children, the town, and the teacher. Once the long prayer had ended, the eating began. Out of the corner of her eye, Anya saw Matt and Lynx—both watching her. She nodded to them, acknowledging their presence, silently thanking them for the soundness of the building they'd built for the children of Medora.

Thinking of the children, Anya suddenly realized that she had not seen Jamie all evening. Setting her plate down, she left Amelia and walked to the door, searching into the darkness for some sign of the child in the yard. "Jamie," she called, but there was no answer.

"Are you looking for someone, Sarah?" Matt asked, coming from the shadows behind her.

"Yes. Little Jamie Purdy. I hope nothing's happened to him." Then she saw a flickering lantern at the end of the path to the boys' outhouse. "Is that Cyrus leaning against the door?"

"Looks like it. You go back inside. I'll find Jamie."

"Cyrus, what are you doing?" Matt inquired.

"Oh, just standin' guard for a friend," he answered.

"Jamie, are you in there?"

"Yes, sir."

"Have you finished?"

"A long time ago."

"Then let him out, Cyrus."

Cyrus smiled the peculiar smile he always wore when he'd been caught doing something he shouldn't. "It was all a joke," he explained to Matt.

"Well, the joke's over." He opened the door. "Come on, Jamie. Wash your hands at the pump, then let's go back to the party. I expect you're hungry."

"I am. I just hope some of Grandma's pound cake is still on the table."

A few minutes later, Anya saw Matt with Jamie, who began to heap his plate with food, starting with dessert. Although their eyes met only briefly, the exchange between Anya and Matt was significant enough for the protective Amelia to notice. But using a flimsy excuse, Maude soon drew Amelia away from Anya's side.

Matt took that opportunity to walk toward Anya. "I don't want to rush you," he said, "but everyone is waiting for the chairman of the school board to claim the first dance. May I?"

"And the party would be ruined if I refused?"

"Precisely."

Anya stood up. "Then for protocol's sake, I accept."

The fiddler changed his music to a waltz, with Matt sweeping a graceful Anya around the empty floor. As they danced, images from a winter festival flitted across her mind, blurs of lights and greenery, the feel of her father's arms, his handsome face smiling down at her. She was so happy. Then the fiddler abruptly changed his music, causing Anya to stiffen in Matt's arms.

Only Matt seemed to notice the sadness in Anya's eyes. By that time, nearly everyone had begun to dance, even the boys and girls at the edge of the dance floor.

"You've danced with our teacher long enough, Matt," Gil Crawley said, tapping him on the shoulder. Reluctantly Matt gave her up, but Crawley was soon replaced by other members of the board.

From their vantage point, Travis and Snake Man watched the dancing from the open door, storing up the events of the evening to tell Prairie Dog and Gus. Only Lynx, the foreman, eventually got up enough nerve to ask Sarah to dance.

The toe-tapping, old-fashioned reels went on for several more hours, with occasional trips to the punch bowl or pump trough for something a little stronger. Few were openly anxious about the dangers of the prairie or the outlaws who might be afoot that night.

Chapter 22

"My, that was *some* shindig, wasn't it, Matt?" Lynx said as they started home late that night.

"That it was, Lynx," he agreed. "But I'm glad it's over. Maybe now, with the school built, we can get a little work done around the ranch."

"I was talkin' with Drayton, private-like. He said Driscoll keeps turnin' up like a bad penny. Somebody spotted him and a few of his men several days ago not far up the canyon. He was a mite uneasy about it."

"We'll all be uneasy until he's caught, Lynx."

"Well, I hope he hasn't got wind of how few hands we have right now at the Double B Ranch."

"Gus and the boys should be back in another week."

"Yeah. If they don't run into bad weather on the trail. You remember that awful sleet storm we got caught in 'bout four years ago this side of Abilene?"

"What's this with the gloom and doom, Lynx?"

"Well, I guess I been tryin' to decide if it's time to get my own spread, Matt. I been with you a powerful long time. Now don't get me wrong. I've enjoyed working for you. But lately, I've had a hankerin' for a house of my own and a few cattle to run . . ."

". . . and a wife named Sarah Macauley, no doubt."

"Well now, what's wrong with that?" Lynx's voice sounded defensive. "I can't say it ain't occurred to me."

"To you, and at least a dozen others."

Travis, who had been traveling with Snake Man farther ahead, suddenly galloped back toward the carriage. "Matt, there's a fire in the distance," he shouted. "Looks like it might be comin' from the ranch."

Alarmed, Matt said, "Then you and Snake Man ride on ahead. We'll be right behind." Within moments, he and Lynx had freed the horses from their harness and abandoned the carriage. Without saddles, they rode bareback, Indian-style, their hands holding on to the manes as they raced to catch up with the other two cowpunchers.

Forgotten was Lynx's surprising confession; forgotten was the housewarming for the new school. All Matt's thoughts were on reaching the ranch that his grandfather had built in time to save it from destruction.

"Whatever happens, Kwa-ling, don't leave the house unguarded," Prairie Dog had told the servant at the first sign of trouble. Now, kneeling in the darkness, with one of Matt's rifles pointed through an open window, Kwa-ling muttered all the swear words he'd learned on the rail work crew. Going from one window to another, in the hope that no one would suspect he was the house's only occupant, he shot at random into the moving shadows.

Out toward the corral, he heard a barrage of gunfire, answered by the neighing of frightened horses. But he had no idea how many riders had come in the night to plunder and steal. He kept to his own station, willing to defend Matt's home with his life, while Prairie Dog did the same for the barn and the animals penned in the corral.

But soon a burning arrow, like a comet crossing the sky, landed in the upper-level opening of the large barn, setting fire to the grain that Matt had harvested for the winter. It did not take long for the fire to grow, filling the barn with smoke. Kwa-ling heard the animals, trapped inside the stalls, begin to whinny and kick in terror. What should he do? Should he go to Prairie Dog's aid to try to free the animals and save the barn? Before he could decide, he saw another kerosene-soaked arrow flying through the air. But this one was directed toward the house. Holding his breath, he tried to keep it in sight. If it landed on the roof, then the house would be in just as much danger as the barn. But the arrow fell short, landing on the porch instead.

Kwa-ling immediately ran to fill a bucket of water from the kitchen pump. Then he ran back through the hall, opened the side door wide, and sloshed the liquid on the smoldering fire, producing a hissing sound.

Two other hands, riding in from the range, had heard the shooting and come to help. But they were outnumbered by the band of outlaws determined to destroy Matt's ranch. Pinned down by their gunfire on the other side of the corral, the three watched helplessly while the barn continued to burn.

"I can't stand to hear those animals screamin'," Prairie Dog said. "I'm gonna ride across the clearin' and let them out. Cover me as best you can."

"That's suicide," one replied. "You'll be shot for sure."

But Prairie Dog was not dissuaded. He leapt on his horse and rushed across the clearing. Shots rang out, answered by a returning volley of shots.

"Did he make it?"

"Must have. I see the animals comin' out."

About that time, Matt, Lynx, Travis, and Snake Man rode in, their guns announcing their arrival. The outlaws, realizing that reinforcements had arrived, fled into the darkness, their mischief cut short by Matt's return.

"Look," Travis said. "They're turnin' tail and runnin'. You want some of us to go after them, Matt?"

"No. We need all the help to save the barn."

When the gunfire had ceased, Kwa-ling rushed from the house, grabbed his new washtub, and took his place at the water pump, filling the large basin. Buckets of water soon passed down the line, from one man to another in steady tempo, the minutes forgotten as each did his share and more to keep the barn and the grain from being totally destroyed.

Gradually the blaze lessened, the squeak of the pump eventually winning over the dry crackle of grain; only a smoldering structure remained, the barn damaged, yet not lost.

With the greater danger over, Matt and his men took a brief rest before beginning the final chore of removing the hay in the loft, subject to flaring into flame again. "Where's Prairie Dog?" he asked.

"Last time I saw 'im," one of the other hands replied, "he went to open the barn door."

"His horse over there," Kwa-ling said, pointing to the brown mustang with an empty saddle.

"Prairie Dog," Matt shouted. "Where are you?"

He combed the entire corral and the area around the barn, but there was still no sign of the man. Fanning out farther, Matt continued calling his name. Finally, in the shadows about thirty yards from the barn, a hoarse whisper responded: "Over here, Matt."

The man lay in an unnatural position, almost identical to the position Matt had found him in some years before when his horse had stepped into a prairie dog hole. "Looks like I'm really done for this time, Matt," he apologized.

"Lynx," Matt called. "Travis, Snake Man, get a large slab and bring it over here quick."

"Did you find him?"

"Yes. But he's been hurt. We've got to get him into the house."

"Ain't no use, Matt," Prairie Dog whispered. "I been shot up too bad, lost too much blood. Just let me lie out here where I can see the stars."

"How are you going to wear this vest I promised you, if you won't let us tend to your wounds?"

"I reckon you could bury me in it."

Prairie Dog already had the look of death on his face. Moving him, Matt realized, would only hasten the short time left. So if his friend wanted to remain outside for a few minutes longer, Matt would not challenge this last wish. He knelt beside him.

"Did Miss Sarah like the six-shooter?" Prairie Dog rasped.

As far as he knew, Sarah had not unlocked the clothespress. But Matt lied for his friend's sake. "Yes. She asked me to tell you how much she appreciates it."

Prairie Dog smiled. In a fading voice, he said, "I got a little money hid in a jar under the bunkhouse floor." Matt leaned closer to hear. "After you buy some whiskey for the boys, I want her to have what's left. Will you see that she gets it?"

Matt did not argue. "Yes."

Prairie Dog stopped talking. His eyes stared up at the stars. By the time the men came with the wooden slab, he was still staring at the stars. But Prairie Dog was dead.

"We'll take him into the house now," a solemn Matt said, the men following Kwa-ling, who held a lantern to light their way.

"Sounds as if we're not going to get much sleep tonight," Amelia commented, "with all that ruckus going on below."

Anya looked over at Amelia, taking her nightgown from her small valise. "Europeans always eat late," she said, "even when they're going to get up early the next day." Seeing the strangers at the hotel had alarmed Anya, causing her to avert her face as she and Amelia had entered.

"Well, I don't know why I'm complaining. Just habit, I guess. I never get much sleep these days. But it doesn't have anything to do with noise. Just old age."

"You're not old, Amelia."

"Tell that to my back on a stiff morning." Amelia smiled. "But tonight, at the housewarming, I didn't feel old."

"You didn't look it, either. You danced even more than I did."

Amelia's eyes sparkled, as if she suddenly had an idea. "Are you sleepy, Sarah?"

Anya hesitated. "Not really."

"Then how about a nice little glass of sherry? While we're drinking it, we can watch what's going on."

"I'd prefer not going downstairs, Amelia."

"Oh, we wouldn't have to go downstairs. Lem has a private little spot behind the curtains on the balcony. We could see the people below, but they couldn't see us."

"How do we get there?"

Amelia laughed. "By ringing for Ruby. She can tell us if it's being used or not."

A few minutes later, Amelia and Anya sat on the balcony and sipped their late night toddy. "Take a look, Sarah," Amelia urged, pushing back the curtain a fraction of an inch. "You see that woman over there?"

"The one in the beautiful dress?" Anya stared at the woman who was attired in aubergine silk with gold tracery.

"Yes, with the fat foreigner. I've seen dozens like her—young women who go from one lover to another, yet are destined to be abandoned eventually." Amelia sighed. "They never seem to learn."

"Then why do they do it?"

"For as many reasons as stars in the universe. Some

from boredom, others from greed—a few because they've reached the end of their ropes—the same reasons men come West." As if it had just occurred to her, Amelia suddenly asked, "Why did you come West, Sarah Macauley?"

Caught momentarily off-guard, Anya stared at Amelia. "The latter reason, I think," she finally confessed.

"Well, at least you've chosen an honorable profession. Don't be in a hurry to give it up for someone's empty promises."

"Are you warning me, Amelia?"

"Perhaps." She picked up her glass. "But this is neither the time nor the place for that."

The conversation soon changed, with Amelia reminiscing about the days when Henri was still alive. "I remember the first time he ever took me hunting with him. We went into Montana Territory to shoot wild mountain sheep. Of course we didn't have the luxuries of these people," she said, staring down at the members of the hunting party. "We went by horseback, with a few pack mules carrying our supplies. Those were simple days, Sarah, and I miss them more as each year goes by."

A faraway look invaded Anya's eyes. "Yes. Once they're lost, you can never recapture them."

"Sometimes, though, it helps to talk about the days we were happiest. When you're ready, Sarah, I'll be a good listener."

"Thank you, Amelia."

"Now drink up. We'd better get off to bed. We'll have an early start to the ranch in the morning."

Feeling the key to the locked clothespress around her neck, Anya remembered she'd had no time that evening to see what was hidden inside the piece of furniture. Curious because of her brief conversation with Matt, she said, "Do you think we could stop at the school for a few minutes before we leave Medora? I need to check on something."

"We'll make time," Amelia assured her. "Right after we pick up Clara and Jamie."

The two women walked back to the room they shared. Soon both were ready for bed. Smiling at Amelia, who had plaited her white hair into a long pigtail, similar to Kwa-ling's, Anya blew out the lamp and climbed onto her side of the large bed.

"Good night, Amelia."

"Good night." With a laugh, Amelia added, "If I happen to snore, Sarah, just wake me up."

"You won't bother me. Once I go to sleep, almost nothing can disturb me."

Chapter 23

A strong wind blew over the vast prairie that night, a lonely wail of sound unhindered for miles, its voice a forewarning that summer was almost over. Its message swept south past the buttes, the coulees, and draws— past crude, sod-roofed shacks, rich bonanza farms of wheat to the east, and grazing pastures to the west. Gaining momentum with each mile, the wind followed the muddied lanes of small, upstart towns that had been built all along the rail line to attract newly arrived immigrants. Medora was no different.

Listening to the howling sound of the wind about the eaves of the hotel, Anya lay quietly beside the sleeping Amelia and thought of the laughing men and women below. It seemed a century ago that she had been equally carefree, equally elegant, albeit in a different way. So many things had changed in the past weeks. She had taken for granted the beautiful clothes and the personal comforts that money could buy for so long. But that was not the case now. Yet, what good were these things without a sense of inner peace, a knowledge that she was out of harm's way?

Anya'had no reassurances of either. Each time a stranger suddenly appeared, her composure was sorely tested. True, that night at the housewarming she finally realized she was among friends, not enemies. She was touched by the displays of community warmth and acceptance that had nothing to do with wealth or family background, or the lack of it.

But the housewarming was over, and now she had a new danger with which to cope—the invitation to the château for the coming weekend. The party would involve another group of people, and the possibility that some titled, international friend of the marquis's might recognize her was born anew.

Anya yawned and closed her eyes. The wind subsided, and she finally went to sleep, Amelia's dainty snore of little consequence.

Early the next morning, Anya watched from the upstairs window as the hunting party departed with guides, wagons, and horses. The men were dressed quite differently from the previous evening. Polished leather boots, sombreros, colorful neckerchiefs, and fringed suits of buckskin had replaced their elegant black-and-white evening clothes. The few women whom Anya saw were also in shooting costumes. One was mounted on a sidesaddle, but the others, including the woman Anya had particularly noticed the evening before, sat in one of the wagons.

"Do you see our carriage, Sarah?" Amelia inquired.

"Not yet. The hunting party is leaving."

A few minutes later, after the hubbub had subsided, the Chaboillez carriage appeared before the hotel. The two women walked downstairs, where Lem, the proprietor, was waiting to see them off. "Don't stay away so long next time, Amelia," he urged.

"I'll be back only when you buy some decent sherry," she said teasingly.

By the time Amelia pulled the carriage up to the dry goods store around the corner where Randall Purdy clerked, Clara and Jamie were waiting.

"Pa gave me four peppermint sticks," a proud Jamie

said immediately as he climbed inside the carriage. "It's a good thing Stretch went home last night."

Clara smiled. "What he's sayin' is that we each get a whole stick. Good mornin', Amelia. 'Mornin', Sarah."

Moving over to make room for Jamie, Anya said to the boy, "That's awfully nice of you, to share your candy with us."

Clutching the small bag, Jamie looked up at her. "Pa told me we should wait till we get out of town, so the flies won't stick to it, like they do to the flypaper in the store."

"That's a good idea," Amelia agreed, trying to sound serious. "Right after Sarah stops at the school for a moment, we'll be on our way."

"Did you forget something last night?" Clara inquired.

"Yes. The cards from several of the gifts. I want to write all the thank-you notes within the next day or so."

"Some of the people won't be able to read," Clara offered.

"But I'm going to learn to read, ain't I, Miss Sarah?"

She did not correct the child's grammar. There would be plenty of time for that. "You certainly are, Jamie," she assured him.

At the schoolhouse, Anya went inside, while Amelia and Clara elected to remain in the shade, and Jamie ran to the pump to get a drink of water.

Once she had walked from the large, empty room to her future living quarters, Anya stood in the middle of the floor and surveyed every angle, seeing it differently from the previous night, when so many had crowded into it. Then, taking the key from the chain around her neck, Anya walked to the clothespress and unlocked it.

Two packages were inside—one small, the other a little larger. Aware that Amelia was waiting, she hurriedly opened the small sack. A six-shooter, well-used, but polished so that it caught the rays of the sun coming in from the windows, took her by surprise. Yet it shouldn't have, for the little piece of paper with a crude drawing of a prairie dog indicated the giver. She smiled, remembering Prairie Dog's comment that a woman alone should have a gun. She carefully rewrapped it in the sack and returned it to the shelf. It should be safe, locked away, until she moved to the schoolhouse.

The second package was much more elegantly wrapped, with a white envelope attached to the outside. The message read:

> The promised replacement for the ruined traveling suit. This silk is from a special limited run from the filature. Matt.

Unwrapping it, Anya struggled with her feelings. She was not certain she wanted this gift from Matt. Yet the material could solve the problem of what to wear that first evening at the château. If Amelia had a proper pattern she could borrow, and if she worked rapidly, Anya could have the dress finished in time.

But instead of a bolt of material, the silk had been finished into an elegant two-piece dress. Anya frowned. Matt should have known that personal clothing was far too intimate for a man to give a woman who was neither his wife nor lover. Nevertheless her hand stroked the beautiful material of aubergine and gold as she walked to the settle to shake out the dress and get a better look. Draped across the settle, the dress's unusual color and cut seemed familiar. Of course! The fancy woman at the hotel— She had worn one exactly like it. What connection did she have to Matt? Had she been one of his women before he'd grown tired of her and handed her over to the foreigner?

Thinking about the two dresses, Anya became furious. Igor had done the same thing, buying identical capes for her and his illicit love, knowing full well that they would meet each other in the street. Anya decided that Matt was no better than Igor, only he had not banked on being caught.

Limited run, indeed! How many more women were wearing the same dress made from the same pattern? Well, she would not be one of them. Still, she held the dress up to her body, measuring it. It did not make her feel better that it seemed to fit. Anya finally refolded the dress, put it back into the clothespress, locked it, and then walked out of the school.

Once the carriage cleared the town and the air became fresh again, Jamie opened his paper bag to share the sticks of peppermint candy.

Over the vast prairie, where no tree obscured the view, a mirage suddenly appeared, an elongated image of an Indian and his pony, the vision several stories high, like some colossal statue caught between heaven and earth.

"Look at the mirage," Amelia said, pointing in the distance with her peppermint stick. "He must be at least seven miles away."

"Do you mean he's actually there?" Anya asked.

"Yes. He's real, all right. Only not of such giant proportions. Henri told me once that it has to do with the bending of light across the plain. People who've never seen one think it's just a Dakota tall tale."

"Last year, I was visitin' my cousin on a wheat farm outside Casselton," Clara said, joining in. "And I saw the entire town in the sky. It was pretty amazin'."

Amelia nodded. "They grow Number 1 hard in Casselton. That's the same wheat I planted. We should have it harvested by next week, if the weather holds out."

Several hours later, the carriage arrived at Sweet Grass Ranch. They were met by Stretch and Diego, who had seen them from the corral. As Anya climbed down, Diego said, "Miss Sarah, a message came for you an hour ago. It's on the hall table inside."

Anya's hand went to her throat. Who would be sending her a message? "I have no idea who it could be from," she said to Amelia.

"Maybe it's from the school superintendent," the woman responded. "But there's only one way to find out."

Anya rushed inside and picked up the envelope. She recognized Matt Bergen's writing. What could he possibly want from her less than twenty-four hours after she'd seen him? Feeling guilty about opening the letter in Amelia's house, she read it quickly.

"No! Not Prairie Dog!"

"Bad news, Sarah?"

"I'm afraid so, Amelia. One of the men guarding the silk train was killed by rustlers last night. It seems he had a last request concerning me. I don't quite know what to do."

"Let me see." Amelia took the letter, read it, and returned it to Anya without mentioning Matt. "You'd better honor a dying man's wish, Sarah. It would be bad luck not to."

"You don't mind?"

"That doesn't matter. Tomorrow morning I'll get Diego to ride with you as far as the cabin on the property line."

Jamie, walking by on his way to the kitchen, looked back at Anya when he heard Amelia mention the cabin. A wary expression crossed his face.

"That's most kind of you, Amelia."

Hearing Anya's answer, Jamie sighed in relief and vanished down the hall.

Early the next morning, Anya, dressed in the borrowed riding clothes and boots, set out on Dreamer with Diego leading the way. The last time she'd ridden in the direction of the cabin, she had been seeking shelter from a storm. Today she was retracing the same route to attend the funeral of a man who had befriended her in his own rough way. It was for Prairie Dog, and not Matt, that she was going.

Glad that Diego was guiding her, since there were few landmarks that she remembered once she'd left the ranch buildings behind, Anya tried to think of Prairie Dog and that day at the ferry when she'd gone hunting with him. But Matt's face kept intruding in her thoughts, demanding that she come to terms with her hostile feelings concerning him. Would he be equally hostile once he saw her dressed in Mellie's clothes? Or would he even recognize them?

At the cabin, Matt had put his horse in the shade of the lean-to and found a seat for himself on the nearby outcropping of rocks. He wasn't sure that Sarah would come, but for Prairie Dog's sake, he'd decided to wait a few minutes more before riding back to the Double B Ranch.

He finally saw two riders a distance away. Shading his eyes against the morning sun, he stood and watched. He recognized Diego, but gazing at the woman in the sidesaddle, he took a step forward. If he had not known better, he would have sworn that it was Mellie. But then the wind swept her hat to her back, revealing Sarah Macauley's copper hair. So Amelia was still playing her little games with him.

Shortly before Anya reached the cabin, Diego held up. He waited until Anya waved to him, then he vanished.

"Good morning, Sarah."

A serious Anya nodded to Matt. "How do I get to the other side?"

"You either jump the fence . . . or ride several miles down the line."

The challenge irritated Anya, bringing out all the hostile feelings she'd tried to keep in check. She trotted her pony down the line, as if she were going to ride the entire distance. But a few moments later, she whirled Dreamer around and headed straight for the fence— while a surprised Matt yelled, "Stop, Sarah. I didn't mean it!"

Chapter 24

Matt stood by helplessly, not daring to move, not daring to call out again, for fear that he might distract the pony. In the split second before Anya reached the fence, he realized that he had gone too far. He had goaded her into this dangerous situation because Sarah was using Mellie's saddle—the one that he'd rescued from the arroyo—and wearing Mellie's boots and riding clothes. Like a fool, he'd taken the bait, as Amelia probably had planned. But his reaction had not harmed either Amelia or himself. It was Sarah Macauley who had been placed in danger.

He held his breath as the woman gave a final kick, urging the pony to jump. Dreamer's hooves left the ground, the pony barely clearing the split-rail fence, for one of his hind legs knocked the top railing from its groove as she jumped.

Stumbling and almost going down on the other side,

the pony was saved from disaster by Anya's quick recovery. Pulling the reins to bring the pony's head upward, she averted the spill that Matt had been certain would occur.

"Don't ever do that again."

With glacial eyes, Anya gazed at the man blocking her way. "I'll do what I please, Matt. I'm not Mellie."

He stared hard at her, then finally answered, "No, you're not. But does Amelia know that?"

"Evidently so, since she didn't object to my coming this morning."

Her comment momentarily silenced him. He went back to get his horse while she waited. Then the two rode toward his house on the Double B Ranch.

Kwa-ling, keeping vigil on the porch, was pleased to see the woman arrive with Matt. He had already aired and dusted the front parlor and the guest bedroom, in anticipation of her coming. After Prairie Dog's funeral, he would prepare a nice meal for her before she left to go back to the Chaboillez ranch.

"Good morning, Kwa-ling," she greeted him as she slipped from the pony.

"How are you, missee?"

"Quite sad."

"We all sad," Kwa-ling replied. "But come. I show you where you freshen up and rest before funeral."

"I expect she's thirsty, too, Kwa-ling," Matt said.

"Yes, I am," Anya admitted.

"I'll be back for you in a few minutes," Matt said to

Anya, then rode out of the yard, taking her pony with him.

Anya followed the servant into the house, luxurious by prairie standards. She could see the Scandinavian influence in the decorative geometric designs, the painted furniture, the fine old lace at the parlor windows. Recalling one of the colorful Russian houses in Sitka, her throat began to ache. Despite her resolve, tears sprang to her eyes, but when Kwa-ling returned with a pitcher of water and a glass, he pretended not to notice.

A few minutes later, after she'd washed her face and recombed her hair, she walked from the bedroom into the parlor. Through the lace at the window, she saw a number of cowpunchers ride into the yard and take their places quietly beside a buckboard with a pine box resting in the back.

"Missee, you ready?" Kwa-ling asked, coming to the parlor door.

"Yes."

The procession was slow, with Kwa-ling driving the buckboard. Directly behind it, where the next of kin would have ridden, were Matt and Anya. Next came the men who had worked with Prairie Dog—Travis and Snake Man, Lynx, and a few others from neighboring ranches. No minister was with them, for in the heat, they could not wait for one to arrive.

A short distance above the ranch house and the blackened barn where the tragedy had occurred, an iron fence protected a plot of land, covered in yellow daisies and pink roses entwined through the grass. Seven headstones stood in a row, some of the older ones slanting in the direction of the wind. At the far edge, another grave had been dug.

Matt had given Anya warning that she would be expected to say something at the service. So, for the second time that summer, she grieved over a person that she'd known only a short time. They listened and again approved of her eulogy.

Then leaving the men to their final duty with their shovels, Matt put his hand on Anya's arm and directed her to her pony, tied to the fence. "Kwa-ling is expecting you to stay for lunch. I hope you can eat something."

Anya hesitated. "Are the others coming, too?"

"No. They'll be eating at the chuck wagon."

She did not want to be alone with Matt. "Then why don't we eat with them?"

"Because they'll be drinking to Prairie Dog's memory for the rest of the day. And I can't vouch for their behavior when they're drunk."

While Kwa-ling put the finishing touches to the midday meal, Matt brought a box holding Prairie Dog's legacy into the parlor and set it on a table before Anya.

"What's this?"

"Prairie Dog's worldly goods. He wanted you to have them."

"But his next of kin . . . ?"

"He has none."

Matt watched as Anya opened the wooden box that held the jar of money and a few personal items. Prairie Dog had never been able to save much, so Matt had secretly added to the jar. But she seemed to be much more interested in the trinkets than in the money.

Picking up an old medal, she stared at it. "He must have been in the war, Matt."

"More than likely. A Rebel, judging from the inscription. But he never talked about his earlier life, and nobody ever inquired."

"Excuse, but food is on table," Kwa-ling announced.

The composure that Anya had struggled to maintain with Matt that day, out of respect for Prairie Dog, was quite fragile at the dining table. Although she was determined not to mention his housewarming gift, he gave her several opportunities to do so.

"I suppose you're getting ready for the weekend at the château," he said.

"No. I haven't thought too much about it," she replied. "But I *am* looking forward to meeting Mr. Roosevelt."

Matt nodded. "He's a rich young widower now. Lost his wife and his mother on the same day. I'm sure many a female is praying that he'll notice her."

Anya ignored the pointed remark. She smiled and said, "I hope he'll have time to talk about the legislative process to the schoolchildren, especially since I understand he's just returned from the political convention in Chicago."

"More peas, Miss Macauley?" Kwa-ling asked, hastening to her side with the vegetable bowl.

"No, thank you, Kwa-ling. Everything is delicious, but I'll need to be going in a few minutes."

"Then I bring fruit soon. Boss ordered limb of bananas and basket of oranges from Duluth."

"I haven't had an orange since last Christmas, when I found one in my stocking," a wistful Anya replied.

"Cousin Lettie, no doubt?" Matt prompted.

"Who?" Anya quickly recovered. "Oh, yes. Cousin Lettie."

Kwa-ling cleared the table, taking the tray of dishes back to the kitchen. After he'd disappeared, Matt said, "How is your cousin Lettie?"

"I haven't heard from her."

"Caulk, at the post office, says you haven't received *any* mail since you've been here." In a half-teasing tone, he added, "If I didn't know better, I'd think *you* were the one running away on the silk train, instead of the Princess Fodorsky."

A nervous Anya almost turned over her water goblet as she reached for it. Righting it with her other hand, she picked it up and took a sip just as Kwa-ling returned with the dessert plates and fruit bowl. After he'd disappeared again, she took her time, cutting the orange with a sharp knife. Then she wiped her hands, sighed, and looked directly into Matt's face, confessing what Sarah had confessed to her.

"You might as well know, Matt. I won't be hearing from Cousin Lettie. We're estranged, because I accepted this teaching position. My mother and father are both dead. So, you see, I have much in common with Prairie Dog."

She looked so sad at that moment, that Matt could have kicked himself for adding to her pain.

* * *

Matt rode back to the line cabin with her, where Diego's horse was tethered. Returning the box to her, Matt removed a short section—the width of a carriage—from the split-rail fence, so that Dreamer could pass through.

In low tones, so as not to be overheard by Diego, Matt said, "It must have been difficult for you today, Sarah, for a number of reasons. But I'm especially sorry that you had to bear the brunt of a feud that should have been resolved long ago."

Somehow, looking into his eyes, she did not feel the same animosity toward him. Something had changed, subtly but surely. She merely said, "Good-bye, Matt," for in truth, she did not trust herself to say more.

He rode to a rise on his land, to a large outcropping of rock, where he stopped and watched Sarah Macauley galloping back with Diego toward Sweet Grass Ranch. The late afternoon sun painted the prairie in pinks and gold, framing rider and pony in a brilliant aura. Seeing her disappear, Matt knew that she was his future, just as surely as Mellie was his past.

Chapter 25

On the day they were expected at the château, Amelia and Anya set out early in the well-sprung Chaboillez carriage, with Amelia's favorite horse tied to the back. For the trip, the older woman wore her familiar divided skirt, jacket, boots, and sombrero. She had lived too long on the prairie to waste her time trying to impress anyone. Her clothes, of ancient vintage, suited her fine. But as a sop to the special occasion, she had packed three dresses and a few good pieces of jewelry that Henri had given her years before.

Anya, too, had packed three dresses, which she'd altered to fit her better, but she was completely without jewelry of any kind. Sarah's opal ring had served its purpose, and now it lay wrapped in a handkerchief in the trunk. She could not bring herself to wear it any longer.

Seated beside Amelia, Anya looked up at the sky, suddenly darkened by great flocks of migrating sandhill cranes. "It looks as if winter might come early this year," she said. Despite Sarah's coat, and the shawl wrapped around her head, Anya shivered from the cutting wind.

"Yes," Amelia responded. "But I hope we don't have

nearly so much snow as last year. All the ranchers I know lost quite a number of calves and yearlings on the range. And the Draytons lost their handyman, too."

"What happened to him?"

"He drank a little too much and couldn't find his way back to the ranch in the blizzard. He froze to death."

"How sad."

Anya grew silent again, her thoughts on Alaska, its weather equally devastating. She remembered the unfortunate ships of previous years, which had become stranded from late summer until the following spring because of early ice floes, and the near starvation of their entire crews. Although she did not wish ill of anyone, she nevertheless hoped for an early winter in Sitka, since it would keep Igor caged for a while longer.

On that same day, from ranches all along the Little Missouri, the marquis's guests came, bringing with them their hunting rifles, buffalo guns, and six-shooters. Matt Bergen brought his two elkhounds as well. The dogs were used to going along on hunts with Matt and Antoine. Tonight they would sleep, as usual, in the carriage house below the main one.

While Matt was still on the road, some distance below the town, he heard a voice calling out to him. "Bergen, wait up." Turning his head, he saw Roosevelt, urging his horse into a gallop.

"By Godfrey, I'm glad to see you," Theodore said, finally catching up with Matt. He took his glasses off and wiped the dust from them with his bandanna. "I've never seen so many suspicious-looking characters for the past five miles."

"Did you recognize any of them?"

"No. Probably a new bunch that Driscoll has brought in." Breaking into a canter beside Matt, Theodore continued: "I presume we're going to the same place."

Matt nodded. "To the château."

Theodore grinned. "I have a Tolstoy novel in my saddlebag. Antoine will be gratified that I finished it and am finally returning it."

Still thinking of the outlaws, Matt said, "It's too bad those two rustlers getting on the train the other day never learned to read."

Theodore chuckled. "My foreman was talking about that this morning as I was leaving. But I didn't hear the particulars. What actually happened, Matt?"

"Well, you know, C. J. has a habit of printing the obituaries of the hanged outlaws and posting them in the office window, so everybody in town can see. But this time, he slipped up. He was so sure Rorke and Skutta had been caught and hanged in the latest raid, that he went ahead and printed their names."

Matt continued: "But the next day, the two men came around the corner, alive as he was. C. J. said he held his breath when he saw them stop and look at the paper. But then they walked on and boarded the train. If they'd been able to read, they would have seen the law was after them and vanished. Instead, they walked straight into the posse."

* * *

Heading north above Deadwood, in a carriage with a large trunk lashed to the back, an irritated Gil Crawley glared at his determined wife. "I told you, Emma, we ain't goin' to no palace. They might call it a château, but it's just a big, old ramblin' farmhouse painted gray, with red shingles."

"I don't care what you say, Mr. Crawley, or how much you complain. Mama said a lady should be dressed suitably for all occasions."

"But that don't mean you have to take along every stitch of clothin' you own. It's hard on the horses to be carryin' such a load."

"Mama says—"

"Emma," he interrupted, "on this trip, I don't want to hear another damn thing your mama said."

"Well," Emma replied in an obvious huff, "I'm glad she's in Boston and can't hear you talking this way."

"That makes two of us," Gil answered, signaling the horses to trot faster. He'd made a mistake, bringing Emma to this godforsaken part of the world. Her constant harping on how things were so much better in Boston had given him a bad taste in his mouth. He'd lost good companionship, too, because of her. The boys never came to the house anymore, and he couldn't blame them. If he wanted to drink or play cards, he'd had to slip out to the bunkhouse.

But nothing could spoil his anticipation of the scheduled hunt for that weekend. He would be in his element with the men, while Emma, to her delight, would be hobnobbing with the marquise and storing up every detail to write her snobbish mother and sisters in Boston.

* * *

From the west, closer to the Yellowstone River, Ed Baynes and his wife, Conchita, rode in the carriage that had belonged to her family and was part of a dowry she'd brought to the marriage from Texas seven years previously. They conversed in Spanish, for Conchita was still not at home in English.

Ed was twenty years older than Conchita, his second wife. That day he'd gone to buy cattle from her father, he'd no idea he'd be finding something of much greater value. At first he had not suspected it, for in face she'd been plain, with dark eyebrows, her hair drawn tightly in a bun and hidden by the black mantilla. Back then she resembled an awkward young crow, dressed in black from head to toe. But she was still in mourning for her mother, recently dead.

It was on the next trip that her father, Manuel, had seen to it that she ate at the dinner table with them. His pointed remarks about his daughter's eligibility had embarrassed her. Ed had seen it in her dark eyes, and he'd felt sorry for her. But not sorry enough to change his life—until later that evening, when the two had been thrown together and left alone in the salon.

"You do not have to waste the rest of your evening with me, Mr. Baynes," she said quietly. "A few minutes more, and then you will be free to leave. My father will be angry only with me."

"Why, Conchita?"

"Because I do not have sufficient beauty to attract you. And he will not marry again until I am settled elsewhere."

A startled Ed stared at Conchita. Few women would have been so frank. But then he grew angry—why, he didn't know. "Who told you that you're not beautiful?"

"My mother, my father, my tutors—"

"Well, they're wrong. All wrong. When you smile at me, I think you're beautiful."

"You do?"

"Yes. Now smile, Conchita." He settled down in the chair. "And you can pour me some more sangria. I think I'll stay awhile."

Driving along, with Conchita beside him, Ed remembered the whirlwind events that had surrounded his marriage. To the surprise of his friends in the Dakotas, he'd brought back from Manuel's hacienda not only a fine head of cattle, but a wife, too. Looking at her, sitting so proudly beside him, he realized his concern for her had grown into a love he'd never experienced before. She'd given him a son and daughter, too. So now he had a family again, to take the place of the one he'd lost.

"I understand the schoolteacher will be at the château, Conchita," he said. "That should please you because of little Esteban."

"*Sí.* It's very important for him to begin his education," she said. "Even though I shall miss him this winter."

"But we couldn't have found a better place for him to board than with Maude Applegate. And we'll still have Edwina at home."

"She doesn't understand why she can't go, too."

Ed laughed. "Our little headstrong daughter doesn't understand why she can't ride the range with the cowboys, either. I think we're going to have trouble with that one later on."

"She's so like you," Conchita said.

"And Esteban is like you."

Conchita sighed. "For his sake, sometimes I wish it were not so, my husband."

"He's perfect the way he is," Ed assured her.

At the *Badlands Cowboy* newspaper office, C. J. shut down the presses and walked upstairs to his living quarters. His hands were black with print, and so he began the time-consuming business of scrubbing them clean with strong soap. Ever since the invitation had come, he had been impatient for the day to arrive. The hunt mattered little to him. It was the charming and intelligent Medora de Mores that excited him—the exchange of ideas with her, her wit, her talent. He was secretly in love with her, but because she was a faithful married woman, he could never reveal how he adored her.

If any of his colleagues at Harvard had told him that he would leave the comforts of the East to go West and run a small newspaper in a raw, lawless territory, he would have laughed in their faces. But here he was, without a wife, without the Brahmin coterie surrounding him, without any ambition except to rid the country of its dangerous elements and make it a safer place for the woman he could never possess.

Yet he knew that time was running out. The baron was growing tired of losing money in his son-in-law's ventures. His stagecoach line to Deadwood had lost the bid for the mail route. And his abattoir was doing badly.

C. J. finished getting ready, packing his bag and checking his hunting equipment. Still, it was too early to leave, for it wouldn't take him long to get to the château. Nevertheless he locked the door behind him and started toward the livery stable for his horse.

"Take your time, Cyrus," he said, watching the boy immediately lift a saddle from its block. "I'm in no hurry."

"That's good to hear, C. J.," Shaun Drayton said, leading his tired and dusty horse into the stable. "Come have a drink with me over at the saloon, while my horse gets a good rubdown."

"All right, Shaun." C. J. turned to Cyrus. "Put my saddle down and tend to Mr. Drayton's horse. We'll be back here in about an hour."

With a few expletives renting the air, Cyrus did as he was told.

"One day, son, your mouth is going to land you in trouble," C. J. predicted.

"Yeah. In just about three weeks," an amused Shaun agreed. "Isn't that when school starts, Cyrus?"

The two men left the livery stable, laughing at Cyrus's reaction to their teasing. "Sarah Macauley's got her task cut out for her in that one," C. J. said.

"You think we ought to warn her?"

"I expect she's already been warned."

A few minutes later, C. J. and Shaun sat at a table, where the newsman deliberately nursed his whiskey glass as Shaun poured a second drink. "Felt I needed a little something stronger after the long ride," the slightly stout, balding Shaun confessed. "I hear Antoine only serves his fine French wine for dinner."

C. J. nodded. "Has his own sommelier. He sets great store in his cellar."

Watching Shaun pour yet another glass, the fastidious C. J. was concerned. He didn't want his friend to be drunk by the time they arrived at the château. "Don't you think you've had enough for now?"

"You think I'm getting drunk, C. J.?"

"You're well on the way. What's the matter? You don't usually drink this much so early in the day."

The spirits had relaxed Shaun's tongue. "It's worryin' about Addie, I guess. She's been gone such a long time."

"Several months isn't really that long to visit one's family in Wisconsin."

"But I don't think she's coming back. I think she's left me for good."

"I'm sorry, Shaun."

"But keep it under your hat. Wouldn't want anybody else to know till I'm sure."

"Let's go and get some fresh air," C. J. suggested, taking the whiskey bottle from the table and returning it to the saloonkeeper. "Put my name on it, John, and save it for me," he said, paying for the bottle before leaving the saloon with Shaun.

By late afternoon, when Amelia and Anya drew up to the door of the château, the marquis's servants were busy removing a large trunk from another carriage.

"I see we're not the first to arrive," Amelia said. "Judging from the size of that trunk, Emma Crawley's already gotten here."

Anya was not interested in the trunk—for a familiar rider with two dogs at his side was disappearing down the slope in the direction of the carriage house.

Chapter 26

Medora stood inside the door, greeting Amelia as she and Anya entered. "I'm so glad you could come, Amelia. And this must be Miss Macauley?"

"Yes, Medora. Sarah Macauley." She turned to Anya. "May I present the Marquise de Mores."

"Madame," Anya said, acknowledging the introduction. "Thank you for inviting me."

"Yes. Well, we needed an even number," she answered, hardly looking at Anya. "Amelia, Isabelle will show you both to your room. You'll have time for a bath and nice rest before dinner. We'll be gathering at half past seven in the salon."

As Anya followed Amelia and the servant up the stairs, she smiled ironically. Medora was typical of those born to a certain wealth and style—charming and sure of herself, yet a little distant with anyone she did

not consider to be on the same social footing. But
Anya, as the Princess Fodorsky, outranked Medora in
the titled hierarchy, so it was rather amusing to be dismissed at a glance.

But Anya could not fault Medora for her behavior. In
Sitka, Anya had been guilty of the same thing. It was
only in assuming Sarah Macauley's identity that Anya
had begun to change, to react to people as Sarah would
have reacted. And that had brought her untold riches in
getting to know people like Prairie Dog, Snake Man,
Travis, and all the others.

Still, a part of her was sorry that she had not brought
the new silk dress to wear that evening. But then she remembered who'd given it to her, and that made her feel
better about not wearing it.

"This will be your bedroom for the weekend," Isabelle said, stopping before the room at the end of the
long upstairs hall. "There's fresh water in the pitcher
for you to drink, and I'll start bringing some hot
bathwater right away. If you would like anything
pressed, Sybil will be happy to do it."

A tin hip tub sat at the foot of each twin bed. Gauze
netting to ward off the insects had been drawn to the
sides of the beds, and a small boudoir chair stood before a mirrored vanity table. "Well, what do you think
of the château, Sarah?" Amelia asked, once Isabelle had
disappeared.

Anya closed the door before answering. "It's very
nice," she hedged. "At least what I've seen. But why
are the bedrooms so small and the hallway so large?"

"I'm told that the hallway is set up for mass when the priest visits. It's also used much like an upstairs parlor."

Anya and Amelia both began to unpack their valises, shaking out the dresses that had been folded. "I suppose it would be best to have this pressed," Anya said, holding up a wrinkled, dark blue dress that she had altered. Although she had added to the fullness of the sleeves, the dress still looked quite plain.

"Then I'll have this old faithful pressed, too," Amelia said.

The buckets of hot water soon arrived, two at a time, until the hip tubs were filled. With a screen giving privacy, both women bathed, then put on their nightgowns and climbed into bed for a rest.

While they napped, Isabelle and Sybil attended to their dresses and then returned them without disturbing the room's occupants.

Up and down the hall, other servants did the same, with one of the guests a little disgruntled. "I had a bath day before yesterday," Gil Crawley complained. "It ain't good for a man to take a bath more than once a week."

Emma, his wife, started to quote her mother on the subject of cleanliness, but her husband's warning glance kept her silent.

A child's crying in the next room awoke Anya. She sat up, pushed back the netting, and looked at the small French clock. But before she could see what time it was, chimes rang out. "Amelia," she called. "We'd better get up and dress for dinner."

Amelia sat up. "Heavens," she said, yawning. "I never doze during the day. I must be getting old."

"We had a long trip," Anya replied.

Later, the mirror in the bedroom reflected two images, one completely devoid of ornamentation. Amelia, noticing this, turned and said, "Let me see how you look, Sarah."

Anya faced Amelia, whose diamond jewels sparkled in the final rays of the sun coming through the window. The older woman did not care for the drab dark dress on the schoolteacher, despite its recent alteration. The dullness took away the vitality of Sarah's magnificent eyes and made the copper of her hair seem a little too flamboyant.

"Well?" Anya prompted.

"I think the dress needs something," Amelia answered. "Did you bring any jewelry with you?"

"No, Amelia."

"Then you must wear some of mine." The woman rummaged in her jewel case until she came across an heirloom blue-topaz-and-filigreed-silver brooch with matching earrings. "Here, put these on."

"Really, Amelia—"

"Stop protesting and do as I say."

Reluctantly Anya pinned the brooch at her throat and put on the earrings. The addition completely changed her appearance, accenting the color of her eyes, with the dress taking on an elegance that it did not possess without the jewelry.

"Much better," Amelia said, satisfied at the transformation. "Now let's go and meet the others."

Downstairs, a handsome, tall Matt Bergen, dressed in evening clothes, joined Antoine, C. J., and some of the other men. Although he politely entered into the conversation, he also listened for the sound of footsteps coming down the hallway. He saw Amelia appear through the threshold first, followed by Anya. Waiting until the introductions had taken place, he steered Anya away from Amelia and the other men.

In low tones, so as not to be overheard, he scolded, "Kwa-ling will be most disappointed that you did not wear the aubergine-and-gold silk tonight."

Reacting to the disapproval in Matt's voice, Anya said, "What does he have to do with the dress?"

"He was the tailor."

Surprised, she asked, "Did he also make the one for that other woman?"

Now it was Matt's turn to act surprised. "What are you talking about? What other woman?"

"There's no need to pretend with me, Matt. I saw her at the Medora hotel a few days ago. In a similar dress, the identical silk. I suppose that was a little payoff before you gave her up to the other man."

"I don't know what you're talking about, Sarah. You're the only one—"

"Good evening, Matt. May I join in the conversation?"

Matt looked up to see Roosevelt standing at his elbow and waiting to be introduced to Sarah. There was nothing he could do except to be civil. But before the evening was over, he would make sure to get to the bottom of this baffling conversation. "Sarah, may I present Mr. Theodore Roosevelt of New York. . . ."

Anya began to discuss the political convention with the aristocratic politician who had turned rancher. Matt withdrew, joining another group. But he still kept a possessive eye on the woman engaged in animated conversation.

A half hour later, after the entire group had gathered, a servant announced dinner. The formal dining room was festive, with blue-and-white Meissen china, sparkling crystal goblets, and heavy silver flatware at each place. Above the table hung a gas chandelier of brass and crystal, turned low, so that the romantic atmosphere of lighted candles on the table would not be spoiled.

"I believe you're seated here, Sarah," Matt said, indicating a place halfway down the table. Flanked by Theodore, he walked on to a place of honor near Medora, while Amelia was seated at the opposite end near Antoine and the slightly inebriated Shaun. With C. J. and Amelia's attention diverted to the unhappy man, the marquis had no recourse but to be attentive to Emma. In her best blue-blood demeanor, she signaled her satisfaction at being placed so near the marquis, leaving her husband, Sarah Macauley, Ed, and Conchita, across from each other in the center, not sufficiently near either end to join in the more intimate conversations.

Aware of the silence among the four, Ed apologized to Sarah. "My wife does not speak much English."

"Is she Spanish?" Anya inquired.

"Yes."

"Then we should have no trouble conversing," she said, smiling at Conchita. "I speak that language, too."

"Well, I got enough Spanish on me to get along on cattle drives," Gil offered. "Reckon if I clean it up a bit, I can hold my own."

In Sitka, Anya would have better manners than to speak in one language that would deliberately exclude others from the dinner conversation. But at the end of each table that night, in the middle of the Dakota plains, the guests seemed to be engrossed, paying little attention to what was going on in the center. Conchita, who had been so ill at ease, sparkled under Anya's kindness and understanding, and the four held their own animated small talk in Spanish, occasionally interrupted by either Medora or Antoine in an effort to include all their guests.

As the dinner progressed, it seemed only natural to Anya to lapse into French in speaking with the foreign servant, back to Spanish for Conchita, and then into English for Gil when his Spanish was not sufficient. She had done this at her father's diplomatic table, and she thought little about it. But a sudden quietness, a turning of heads at the joviality of their conversation, and Antoine's amusing repartee as he joined in, suddenly made her feel self-conscious.

"You seem to speak a lot of languages, Miss Macauley," a displeased Emma, having lost the marquis's attention, said. "Do you happen to speak Swedish, too?"

"No, I don't."

"A pity," Emma replied. "Mr. Crawley has just hired a Swedish woman to help me in the kitchen, and she doesn't speak a word of English. It's really quite a chore to get her to understand what I want." She smiled toward Medora. "You're so fortunate to be able to converse with your servants."

"My wife speaks seven languages," Antoine said, dismissing Emma's comment. "How many do you speak, Miss Macauley?"

"Only five," Anya answered, quickly omitting the native Aleut dialect, for Sarah Macauley would have no explanation for knowing that language.

"Then you must come again," Medora added, as if seeing her for the first time. "Especially when we have guests from Europe."

"Thank you, madame," Anya murmured uncomfortably, eager to escape Matt's questioning eyes.

Once dinner was over, the women retired from the dining room, leaving the men to their after-dinner drinks and their plans for the next day's hunting trip. But before Anya disappeared, Matt stopped her. "You're not going to get off so lightly," he whispered. "We'll finish our conversation later tonight."

Anya shook her head. "There's nothing to discuss." Seeing an interested Emma watching them, Anya smiled and said, "Well, good night, Mr. Bergen. I hope you have excellent hunting tomorrow." She quickly rejoined Conchita and began to walk toward the salon.

Amelia, standing at the doorway, announced, "Remember, Antoine, I'm going hunting tomorrow, too. So be sure to have one of your servants wake me in time."

"Your guns and supplies are already in the hunting wagon, Amelia," he assured her. "We won't leave without you."

"Then I'll say good night to everyone."

Knowing that the men needed to get to bed at a reasonable hour, Medora did not entertain the three women for long in the salon. A demitasse of coffee and a little polite conversation were all that were offered. Music and cards could wait for the next day, when the women would be by themselves. So as soon as she heard the scraping of chairs in the dining room and the sound of footsteps on the stairs, Medora tactfully put an end to the evening.

With Isabelle guiding them by lamplight, Emma, Conchita, and Anya went to their rooms, where the bed linen had been turned down and the gauze netting put into place to ward off the flies and mosquitoes. All along the upstairs hallway, doors opened and closed as the château's occupants settled down for the night.

In the bedroom she shared with Amelia, Anya heard a steady breathing, indicating that the older woman was already asleep. Tiptoeing quietly, so as not to disturb her, Anya removed the borrowed brooch and earrings, put them back in the jewelry box on the vanity table, and started to unbutton her dress. But a knock at the door stopped her.

"Who is it?" she whispered.

"Matt. I have to see you."

"No. It's far too late."

She turned from the door, but a persistent Matt knocked again. Opening it a few inches, she peered into the shadows. "You're going to wake Amelia."

"Then come outside. I won't go to bed until you explain your strange behavior."

"*My* strange behavior?"

"Careful. You'll wake Amelia."

In exasperation, Anya stepped into the hallway. With a few lights still visible beneath the bedroom doors, Matt took Anya's hand and led her down the back stairs and onto the covered porch that held a winter sleigh, similar to the familiar Russian droshky. He helped her into the sleigh and sat down beside her.

"Now we'll finish our conversation."

Chapter 27

"Tell me about this other woman who was wearing your dress."

"I'm sure you know much more about her than I do."

"Sarah, I can't conjure up a person I've probably never seen," Matt said. "You'll have to help me, if I'm to find out why you're so angry with me."

"In the first place, a man does not usually provide expensive clothes for a complete stranger."

"But you're no stranger. I was merely replacing the suit that was ruined on the train."

"I wasn't speaking of myself. I was speaking of the woman at the hotel. In your note, you said the silk was an exclusive design. You didn't have to lie about that to me, Matt."

"But it's true. I took the only bolt. And Kwa-ling made the dress from it, by a pattern that Jean—" All at once, Matt stopped.

"Go on."

Thinking of Jean Bonneau and his romantic escapades, Matt realized that the manager of his silk filature could easily be at the bottom of the mystery. It was not impossible that the woman Sarah had seen was one of Jean's amours.

"Was this woman with a Frenchman, rather slight and dapper, with a black mustache?"

"No. He was either German or Swiss—a large man. Why?"

The disappointment showed in Matt's voice. "I thought she might have been with my filature manager. But evidently not."

A period of silence followed, until Anya said, "This Frenchman you were speaking of . . ."

"Jean. Jean Bonneau."

"He gave the pattern to Kwa-ling?"

"No. To me."

"But he had access to the same silk material?"

"Only if he decided to run another bolt after I left the filature. It was far too expensive to make it a standard run."

His bafflement over the entire episode was obvious. Anya might have been too quick to blame him. Of all people, she should know that things were not always as they appeared. "Matt, I'm sorry. It seems I may have misjudged you."

Her apology made him angry. "So thinking the worst of me, you decided to flaunt your poverty by wearing this hand-me-down that guaranteed Emma Crawley a place of honor beside the marquis, instead of you."

"If the marquis had ever dined at *my* table," she snapped, forgetting herself, "he would have found himself in the seat *I* occupied, and not because of the cut of his clothes."

Once the words were out, Anya knew she'd made a dreadful mistake. Hurriedly she added, "Nevertheless, I had a perfectly good time where I was."

"So I noticed. Conchita must have been quite grateful that you could speak her language."

"She was."

The harshness in his voice, and the implied criticism, were not warranted. He had longed to be beside Sarah, sharing in the lively dinner conversation, just as C. J. had, more than likely, wished he'd been closer to Medora.

Sitting beside Matt in the dark, Anya was not aware of his feelings. She was fighting her own battle against the same strong magnetism that had drawn her to him from the first moment they'd met. Her sense of danger was heightened by the knowledge that she was where she had no business being—in a nocturnal rendezvous with Matt while the other guests in the château were already asleep.

Attempting to break the spell, Anya stood. "Well, now that the misunderstanding is cleared up, I'll say good night."

She waited to be helped from the sleigh. But Matt's hand drew her to him instead. "What shall I tell Kwaling?" he whispered.

"A thank-you should be sufficient, don't you think?"

"Perhaps for him. But not for me." Surprised, she felt his lips on hers, demanding for himself what she would not willingly offer to him on her own.

"Matt, please."

Her voice and her body were at odds, her innate response much more powerful than her words. He took his time, his lips moving to her throat and then back to her willing mouth. Abruptly he stopped. Helping her from the sleigh, he said, "Go on to bed, Sarah Macauley."

With only the moonlight to guide her, Anya took flight in the dark, wending her way from the open porch to the stairs leading to the long hallway. She should never have come to the château, should never have allowed herself to fall in love with Matt Bergen. It could only lead to more grief, for if she had a future, it did not lie in this town, which a marquis had named for his wife.

With her husband sound asleep, Emma listened at the partially opened door. She heard Anya's footsteps, followed a few minutes later by heavier footfall. First one door opened and closed, then another at the opposite end of the hall. Although it was too dark to make out any more than fleeting shadows, Emma was almost certain she knew who had met. She could hardly wait to tell Mr. Crawley the next morning.

Long before Emma awoke, Amelia and the men set out for the hunting grounds. The hunting wagon and the chuck wagon had already been sent ahead, leaving spare horses and pack mules, supplies, and a second contingent of servants to form a winding procession that traveled along the river and turned westward toward Montana. Matt's two elkhounds, frolicking and sniffing, followed their master, fanned out to explore, and then returned at regular intervals.

A repentant Shaun rode beside Amelia. "I'm sorry about last night, Amelia," he said. "C. J. told me this morning how you watched over me at the dinner table so I wouldn't disgrace myself."

"Henri used to get a little drunk, too, when he was hurting," she answered.

"So you know my wife's gone for good."

"Yes. And I know how much you must miss her."

"Does it get any better as the years go by, Amelia?"

"The pain's still there, but somehow you finally come to grips with it. But Shaun, Addie isn't dead . . . like my Mellie and Henri. There's always the possibility that she might have a change of heart and come back."

"That's what tears me up. There're days I get to thinkin' she might be comin' over the hill. I wait all day, until sundown, but she never comes. Sometimes I think I'd be better off if she'd died instead of gone to Wisconsin—then my innards wouldn't be pulled back and forth like a piece of taffy candy."

Amelia offered no more words to comfort the man. She had problems of her own.

The steady trek into the wilderness continued. The excitement of the hunt was ingrained in each person, aroused by the smell of leather, the cedar fragrance on the wind, the flight of birds. Their feelings were prompted by ancient, ancestral instincts handed down from one generation to another as surely as the color of hair or eyes, or the strength of muscle and sinew.

Only their accoutrements were different—bows and arrows had been replaced by rifles; a piece of meat dried in the sun gave way to luxurious supplies carried in wagons and tended by servants. Yet for all the modern conveniences at hand, the veneer of civilization could vanish in an instant at the first kill. Matt had seen this happen time and again: a visitor reveled in the blood of a downed buffalo while he cut off the tail for a souvenir, his actions as primitive as a Neanderthal celebrating the ritual of victory and death. But those present in this hunting party had already shown a basic regard for the balance of nature, rather than reveling in a rampant, wholesale slaughter for trophies. This day would be no different.

They continued to ride until the hunting party reached the scheduled camp that Antoine had chosen. Several tents had been set up, and the servants were busy gathering firewood and water, putting up a serving table and chairs. "By the time the sun begins to go down, we should all be back here for our evening meal," Antoine said.

Assigned certain hunting territories, each hunter, armed with guns, ammunition, and a piercing whistle to summon a wagon after a kill, left the base camp.

"Amelia, will you be all right by yourself?"

"Perfectly all right, Antoine."

"If it's like the last hunt," C. J. commented, "she'll probably be the first to bag her game."

They rode off in various directions, leaving the camp behind.

Back at the château, Anya awoke slowly, her fingers tracing the outline of her lips, begging them to remember the intensity of Matt's kisses. It must have been the wine at dinner that had made her so vulnerable. She should have abstained after the first glass. Yet, she told herself, nothing would be gained by dredging up the events of the previous evening. So dismissing the lingering awareness, she rose to get ready for the day.

She should have felt safer with Matt away on the hunt, but with Amelia gone also, Anya was uneasy about spending the entire day in the company of the other women. To be back at Amelia's ranch, or even in her quarters at the schoolhouse, would suit her much better. Although she dreaded her first teaching day, she knew she would be better off living on her own. Through Prairie Dog's generosity, she was not nearly so destitute for money. But she would have to watch over it carefully, so that, at a moment's notice, she could vanish.

Dressing in the gray dress with gray matching shawl,

Anya left the bedroom and made her way downstairs shortly before Emma and Conchita arrived.

Breakfast was served in the less formal breakfast room, with its red chairs and gray table covered in cotton damask. As the three women entered, Medora greeted them over the fretful cries of little Athenais, seated in the high chair beside her mother. The child was dark-haired, with natural ringlets bound with a blue ribbon that matched the dress under the little white pinafore. Her pink rosebud mouth was turned downward in a pout.

"Good morning," Medora said. "I'm afraid I must apologize for my daughter's behavior. Her governess took ill during the night, and nothing suits the child this morning."

Murmurs of sympathy from Emma and Conchita were greeted by another wail. But as Anya held her hands together to make a shadowed figure on the nearby wall, Athenais's attention was diverted. "Do you see the bird, Athenais?" Anya asked.

"She speaks only French, Sarah. Antoine and I decided it was too confusing to her to speak in more than one language for now. She will learn English later on."

Anya smiled. *"L'oiseau,"* she said, looking at the little girl.

"L'oiseau," the child repeated, wriggling her hands in an attempt to imitate Anya.

Distracted, Athenais obediently opened her mouth to be fed, while Anya continued forming shapes of animals in shadows on the wall.

"You have a way with children, I see," a relieved Medora said, complimenting her. "Now you must eat your own breakfast before it gets cold."

Emma, who had never been very good with children, even her own, did not like the way the morning was going. She had looked forward to a day of gossip and chatter, interspersed with a few games of cards. But she had brought her needlepoint with her, too, for those quiet times when they would be sitting on the porch, perhaps, sipping lemonade and discussing the more intimate things that women confided when their menfolk were not around. But having a squawking child in their midst put a decided damper on things, she thought.

"Did any of you hear someone get up and go downstairs during the night?" Emma asked, eager to see the impact on Anya. "I think perhaps someone was meeting in secret."

Medora smiled. "It must have been my governess, coming downstairs to let me know she was ill."

"Oh, how disappointing. I had hoped a little intrigue was taking place at the château," Emma replied.

"If you're interested in that sort of thing, Emma," Anya suggested, "there's a new novel that's just been published in New York—*The Winfields of Boudoin Castle.*"

"What a coincidence. My mother sent it to me last week. It's in the library," Medora said. "Perhaps you'd like to read it while you're here."

"Why that's very nice of you, Medora," Emma replied.

Medora quickly translated for Conchita. Emma, feel-

ing left out of the Spanish conversation understood by
the other three, begun to sulk.

In a more domesticated environment, which Amelia
would have found too confining, the day passed un-
eventfully, except for Medora's gradual warming to
Sarah, who provided welcome relief by entertaining
Athenais. It had not taken her long to realize what a
gem Sarah was to the town. Long before nightfall,
Medora had made up her mind. To assure the success of
the school, she, herself, would provide the next year's
funding for the teacher's salary. She would not miss the
money, which would come from her additional private
income of ninety thousand dollars a year, which her father had set aside for her to spend on baubles.

That evening, after Athenais had been put to bed, the
four women gathered for dinner, with the promise of a
more enjoyable night spent with music and cards, while
in the wilderness, the hungry hunters returned, one by
one, to an equally fine table of food and wine.

"Has anyone seen Amelia?" Matt inquired.

"No," C. J. answered. "But I just got here a few minutes ago myself. Theodore, is Amelia Chaboillez in
camp?"

"I haven't seen her. Will, the wagon boy, said she's
the only one who didn't bag anything today."

"That's most unusual, since she's about the best shot
around."

A worried Antoine listened to the comments. "Perhaps that's the reason she's late."

"Yeah. The sun ain't all the way down yet. She'll get here soon, mark my words. We'll see her draggin' in her own deer or elk in a few minutes," Gil predicted.

Despite Gil's optimism, an uneasiness settled around the camp. "Maybe we'd better start eating," Shaun suggested. "Just in case we have to get a search party going later."

"A good idea," Antoine replied. He picked up a glass of wine. "Gentlemen, to your health."

"And to Amelia's, God be willin'," Shaun said under his breath.

With one eye out for the approach of the stubborn ranchwoman, the men wolfed down their food. But hearing a horse galloping toward camp, they visibly relaxed.

"That's Amelia now," Shaun said. "I'd recognize the sound of her mount anywhere."

As the last vestiges of the sun disappeared over the horizon, a riderless horse swept into camp, passing by the men on its way to the makeshift corral where the other horses and mules were feeding.

"My God, Amelia's not on the horse. Something must have happened to her."

Matt stood up immediately. "Come on, we'll have to find her before a wild animal does."

"But how are we going to find her in the dark?"

"The dogs. We'll use the dogs to pick up her scent," he answered.

The men grabbed their guns and raced to the corral, while Antoine shouted for the servants to saddle up their horses. With every available lantern taken, the men rode out of camp. A leather glove, stuffed into Amelia's saddlebag, provided the only scent for the dogs. But in looking for it, Matt had also seen blood on the saddle. Its discovery was not encouraging.

Chapter 28

High in the hills, where night spread like a velvet blanket, covering the rugged terrain, a hungry mountain lion stood, sniffed the air, and listened to the sounds coming from the rocks in the distance. Cautiously he left his lookout and began to track the scent of his warm-blooded prey.

A wounded Amelia, conscious of the dangerous situation surrounding her, moved carefully, attempting to reposition her body. Her arm ached, despite the sling she'd made from the bandanna around her neck. But far greater than the pain was her anger, directed not only toward her unknown assailant, but at herself for being such an open target.

It had all happened so quickly—the shot that had hit her in the arm, her horse's sudden rearing, the subsequent avalanche of rocks. In an instant, she'd found herself on the ground, minus her rifle, her whistle, and with her left foot pinned under the rocks.

Stunned, she lay where she'd fallen, her brain trying

to make sense of what had happened to her body. It had been an accident, she told herself, another in the hunting party mistaking her horse for an elk. Unable to speak, she waited for the hunter to investigate or claim his prize. She even sensed another horse nearby. But when the rider rode away, leaving her, she realized that the shot had been deliberate. Someone had wanted her killed, and the hunt was an ideal cover for the perpetrator.

Now, hours later, she waited for that same perpetrator to come back under the guise of finding her body, for they would all be out looking for her. No one but the culprit would be able to find her at night, partially hidden as she was under the rocks. And when he found her still alive, what then? Would he finish the job before he hauled her body back to camp?

In the valley below, the lanterns spread out as the riders searched for Amelia Chaboillez. Matt, leaving the other riders behind, followed the two dogs as they headed into the hills. From each quadrant, Matt could hear the whistles of the other men, keeping in touch with each other and hoping for an answer from Amelia.

"What's wrong, boy? Have you lost the scent?" Matt called out to one of his dogs, who seemed to dart back and forth without direction. This happened at times when the strong, gamy odor of animals crossed the path and threw them off the delicate scent of the one hunted. Dismounting from his horse, Matt once again allowed the dog to sniff the glove he'd found in Amelia's saddlebag. Then, as if his memory had been prompted, the dog set off again.

The mountain lion crept closer now, a caution engendered by the moving lantern lights below. But the caution was combined with a determination to reach his quarry before it was snatched away by other predators. The animal moved stealthily, stopping at the least change in the wind and surveying the terrain with his feral yellow eyes. Then he moved on in a lithe, sinuous stride, the soft pads of his feet cushioning the sound of his large body as he jumped onto the group of rocks directly above Amelia. There he stood, his tail twitching back and forth in anticipation of the kill.

"Amelia, where are you? Can you hear me?"

Her heart sank at the sound of Matt's voice. With her land always coveted by the Bergens, she was not surprised that he was nearby. The feud between families had lasted so long that only she and Matt were left, with her land up for grabs when she died without an heir. If she answered Matt now, then he would know she was still alive.

But, in the end, it didn't matter. The dogs had found her.

All at once, the elkhounds began to growl and snarl. She watched Matt by the lantern light as he lifted his rifle and aimed toward her. She closed her eyes for the fatal bullet. But when the gun went off and she felt nothing, she shouted, "You missed." Her voice reverberated over the hills, echoing into the valley below.

"No, Amelia. I didn't. The mountain lion is dead. Now let's get you out of this mess. How badly are you hurt?"

"I've been shot, as if you didn't know. My foot is caught under this pile of rocks." She was still wary of him as he dismounted, blew his whistle for anyone close enough to hear, and brought the lantern to peer closer at her. Surprised, she watched him as he examined her arm.

"Lucky for you that the bullet didn't break the bone," he pronounced. Then he began to examine the boulders holding her captive. "This is going to be a tricky operation, Amelia, especially in the dark. The top boulder is much too heavy for me to move by myself. So I'll have to use Sidewinder. If you begin to feel any pressure, let me know."

"Don't worry. I will." She was at his mercy—and despite her antagonism, she knew it. And so did he.

He took his time tying his rope around the boulder. Making sure it was fastened securely, he looped the other end of the rope to the saddle's pommel. Guiding Sidewinder, he inched the boulder from its position, calling back to Amelia each time the boulder moved. Although the night wind possessed a decided chill, Matt broke into a sweat. One misstep, one miscalculation, could crush the woman rather than save her.

With all his energies directed toward his task, he did not hear Shaun Drayton, who'd responded to Matt's whistle signal. The Irishman rode up just in time to see the boulder dislodged. Holding his flickering lantern high, he said, "Did you find her, Matt?"

"Yes."

"And you can help him get me out from under these rocks," Amelia said, her spirit undaunted by her ordeal.

Staring at her, Shaun reverted to his native accent. "Saints preserved, Amelia. How did ye ever get into such a fix?"

"Somebody shot me and left me for dead."

"Looks like they tried to bury you, too."

"She's lost a lot of blood, Shaun, so let's not waste time in chitchat," Matt said. "Let's get to work."

"And what are ye goin' to do with that large cat?"

"You can have him," Matt replied, "unless Amelia wants him."

"I just want a good stiff drink," she said.

The hunting wagon, in which Amelia would have slept that night on the cot, became the ambulance to take her back to the château. Antoine, insistent on breaking camp in the middle of the night and returning with her, was dissuaded by an adamant Amelia.

"I will not spoil your hunting trip, Antoine, any more than I have already. The rest of you stay and enjoy it. But you must promise to bag at least one wild boar for me."

"I promise, Amelia."

The men and servants watched as Matt and Shaun left, their horses tied behind the hunting wagon that held the white-haired Amelia, whose flesh wound had already begun to swell from the lead poison of the bullet. She had declined Matt's offer to dig the bullet out.

* * *

At the château that morning, after breakfast, the women sat on the porch overlooking the bluff. It was a pastoral scene, filled with quiet pursuits: Medora, with her watercolors, painting the vista before her; Emma, working on her needlepoint; Conchita, her quilting; while Anya read aloud to them all from the novel that had been discussed the evening before. At times she translated small passages for Conchita, then lapsed back into English. Off in the distance, the governess, now recovered, pulled a contented Athenais in a small red wagon.

The scene was soon disrupted by the arrival of the hunting wagon, which rolled noisily up the cobblestone drive and into the yard. Medora set down her paints and rushed to meet it, with Anya not far behind.

"What's wrong? Has something happened to Antoine?" a white-faced Medora inquired.

"No," Matt answered. "It's Amelia Chaboillez. She's been shot."

Anya gave a cry, rushed to the wagon, and opened the door. "Amelia?"

"Don't be alarmed, Sarah," the older woman called out. "I'm too tough to kill."

"But your arm—"

"I'll see to it, once I get home. I'd appreciate it if you could pack my valise immediately."

"Amelia, you're not fit to ride another mile today," Matt protested. Shaun agreed with him, but Amelia was determined to leave as soon as her carriage and horses were brought up from the stables.

In the end, no one could dissuade her. With the other

women standing on the porch and watching, Amelia climbed into her carriage and turned the reins over to Anya. Matt, no longer interested in returning to the hunt with Shaun, left also, riding ahead of the Chaboillez carriage.

Stopping off at the post office, Matt was greeted by a surprised Caulk. "Thought you'd still be at the shindig on the hill."

He didn't bother to explain. "Caulk, do you know the whereabouts of the doctor?"

"What's wrong? Somebody hurt?"

"Just answer my question."

"Well, he's miles away. That German fellow hired him to go on the hunt for the next two weeks. Seems he didn't bring his personal physician with him, like some of the foreigners do. Paid him a lot of money, so he just up and left."

"Thanks."

"Hey, don't you want your mail?"

"I'll get it later."

Caulk watched Matt mount his horse and disappear down the dirt street.

The way Amelia had behaved, acting as if the entire accident were his fault, had made Matt extremely irritable. It would suit her right for him just to ride on to his own ranch and forget about her. But he remembered the episode with his father too well. Stubborn and vengeful as Amelia was, he could not abandon her to lead poisoning.

It had been over twelve hours. The only one who

could do her any good now was Tall Tree. But the Indian never offered his expertise. People had to seek him out, and even then, he might decline to help. There was nothing left but to persuade Amelia to ask for his healing powers. Making up his mind, Matt galloped out of town toward the main road, with his dogs racing after him.

Anya glanced anxiously at the woman riding beside her. Despite the sombrero that shaded her face, Amelia looked flushed, with patches of pink on her cheeks. "Would you like to stop and rest, Amelia?"

"No. Let's keep going. I want to be in my own house, my own bed." She slowly shifted her aching arm. "Damn him for disabling me. He should have killed me when he had the chance."

"You mean you know who shot you?"

"I have my suspicions. That's all I'm going to say."

"I thought it was an accident."

"No. I'm sure it was deliberate." Her eyes held such a feverish intensity, Anya wondered if the woman were delirious. With each mile, she began to get more and more worried over Amelia's deteriorating condition. Then suddenly Matt reappeared.

"The doctor's away, Amelia," he began. "I checked with Caulk at the post office. But Tall Tree might treat you, if you ask for his help."

When Amelia did not respond, Anya did. "Who's he?"

"A Heyoka medicine man. He saved my father years ago."

"Is this Tall Tree far away?" she asked.

"Another eight miles."

Anya quickly made up her mind. "Then lead us to him, Matt."

He indicated the next fork in the road, where a pile of rocks stood, one upon the other, like a stone totem carved by rain and wind. A black magpie flew in front of the carriage and landed on the top rock, while a prairie dog on its hind legs sniffed the air, then, seeing the dogs, disappeared into its hole.

At first the landscape was the same that it had been for miles—rugged, with buttes and prairie grass, sage and scrub cedars spreading out and clinging to the upper sides of the hills. Then the trail dwindled and finally vanished in a strange new undergrowth, the demarcation eliciting a mystical feeling that this was no ordinary world they were entering, but one transported out of time and place.

"Wait here," Matt instructed Anya. "I'll see if he's around."

He rode on ahead, detouring in a zigzag pattern until he was within calling distance. From his throat came a strange call, more animal than human, much like the greeting of Eskimos in the far north. Then he rode on, without receiving a response in kind.

A few minutes later, Matt returned. "He's here." Matt motioned for Anya to turn the carriage around and hide it out of sight beyond the rocks. "I'll have to carry her the rest of the way. Stay with the horses, Sarah, until I come back."

"You're not carrying me anywhere, Matt Bergen."

He ignored the woman's petulant outburst, picking her up as if she were a child. "Hush, Amelia, and close your eyes."

Anya stood guard by the carriage. She should have been frightened, but she wasn't. There was something very powerful and peaceful about this place. Feeling safe, she relaxed and dozed in the sun.

Chapter 29

"It is good to have a worthy opponent in life," Tall Tree said to Amelia once Matt had left the shack. "But you must not allow the conflict to poison your heart, as the bullet has poisoned your flesh."

"There's nothing wrong with my heart, Tall Tree. So let's get on with removing the bullet from my arm."

His silence as he gazed at her spoke more loudly than words. But he did not reproach her, even as she felt a little ashamed of her answer. Instead he walked over to the hearth, picked up a pipe decorated with feathers, lighted it, and said, "Here, smoke this. It will help you forget."

She did as she was told, taking one long, slow draft, then another, while Tall Tree went about his preparations; steeping his herbs in water on the small stove; removing the ceremonial knife from its wrapping. His brief glance toward Amelia told him what he needed to know, that she was beginning to relax, her eyelids drooping in near sleep. The time was right to remove the bullet.

Later, when Tall Tree reappeared on the porch, Matt rose from the broken-down chair. "Is it over?"

"Yes. I have done what I can. The healing is up to the woman. You may take her with you now."

Matt walked inside. In the darkened cabin, the pungent odor of herbs was still strong. Propped up on a cot in the corner, a sleepy Amelia sat, her injured arm now wrapped in a cocoon of cloth. She made no protest as Matt helped her up and supported her while she walked outside.

No mention was made of payment. But both Tall Tree and Amelia knew that, within the next several days, provisions of staples, tobacco, and fresh meat would suddenly appear on the front porch of Tall Tree's official cabin on the reservation. His power place would remain a secret.

A snapping noise, like a twig broken in two by a boot, startled Anya from her dozing. Immediately alert, she listened, her hand reaching for the six-shooter that Prairie Dog had given her.

Suddenly appearing from another direction with Amelia, Matt asked, "What's the matter?"

"I heard something beyond those rocks."

"Probably an animal."

"A very heavy-footed animal, judging from the sound," she commented. Then, addressing Amelia, she asked, "Are you all right?"

"No, I'm not. Tall Tree cauterized the wound after he took out the bullet. My arm is on fire."

Matt smiled. "I see the effect of the smoke is wearing off. You're becoming your ornery self again, Amelia."

She made ready to reply, but another sound of crackling twigs alerted them all. "Quick, Sarah," Matt said in a low tone. "Drive out of here immediately. I'll follow at a distance. Do you think you can find your way back to the road?"

"I think so." With Amelia at her side, Sarah turned the carriage around and hurried from the hiding place, while Matt remained behind. Leading his horse, Matt investigated in the direction from where the sounds had come.

Driscoll did not see him. The outlaw was too busy spying on the Chaboillez carriage, which had suddenly reappeared. Matt watched as the man got on his horse and began to track the carriage.

What reason could Driscoll possibly have for following the two women? Did he suspect where they'd been? Had he seen Matt taking Amelia to Tall Tree's secret cabin? Or had hiding the carriage served to throw the man off? One thing was clear: Driscoll was up to no good, as usual. But Matt was too near Tall Tree's cabin to challenge him. He wanted no more attention directed to the area. So Matt decided he would merely keep an eye on Driscoll, quietly following him to make sure that no harm came to the women.

* * *

By the time Anya reached the totem of stones, Amelia said, "Now the horses can find their own way home, Sarah."

"I'm glad. I thought for a moment back there—when I made a wrong turn and we were going around in circles—that we were lost for good."

"At least we confused whoever was following us," she answered. "Especially with all our luggage tied to the back."

"But I'm sorry for having wasted so much time in getting you home."

"Well, we just put off Clara's wailing when she sees what happened to me. She keeps telling me I should give up hunting and act like a woman my age."

"Would you actually consider doing that, Amelia?" a skeptical Anya asked.

"No. I plan to live in the saddle and die in the saddle. When it's my time to leave this earth, there's not a thing I can do about it. So I won't pay a bit more attention to Clara today than any other day."

Anya had never known a woman so stubborn, so sure of herself, so unafraid as Amelia Chaboillez. Even with her flaws, she was endearing. Because of her, the summer had been a unique experience. But within three weeks, school was scheduled to start. Anya hoped that Amelia would be recovered enough by then for her to leave without feeling guilty.

True to Amelia's prediction, Clara was alarmed when the carriage returned from the house party two days early. Seeing Amelia's arm wrapped in bandages made her dismay even worse.

"Stop jumping around like a ruffled grouse, Clara," Amelia ordered. "If you want to do something for me, you can help me up the stairs. I'm going to bed for the rest of the day."

"And you're going to stay there for the next week," Clara said.

"We'll just see about that."

Trying to diffuse the argument, Anya said, "I'll get Diego to help bring in the luggage, Amelia. And Clara, we could both use some broth, once Amelia's in bed."

"If you happen to see Stretch, Sarah," Amelia added, "tell him I need to talk with him as soon as possible."

"I don't think he's back yet," Clara said.

"Where did he go?" Amelia asked.

"Well, he said something about rounding up a herd of wild mustangs. He left soon after you did—and took the new men he'd hired."

Amelia frowned. Stretch had no business hiring anybody without her consent, even though it was mostly a formality. But the other was more serious. She had specifically asked him to stay close by while she was away. She would have to talk with him about that, but she could not afford to alienate him so near to roundup time. Now that she was incapacitated, she needed him more than ever.

Late that afternoon, Stretch rode in. Hearing the news of Amelia's accident, he rushed into the house and bounded up the stairs, the sound of his jingling spurs announcing his arrival. He tapped on the bedroom door and walked in.

Seeing her awake, he said, "Amelia, I just talked to Diego. He said you'd been shot. Is that true?"

"I'm afraid so."

"But you're going to be all right?"

"Of course."

"How did it happen? Did you see who did it?"

She didn't know why she was suddenly cautious. "Everything happened so fast, Stretch. One minute I was on my horse, and the next thing I knew, I was on the ground. But I really don't want to discuss that now. Tell me about these new men you hired."

"Well, officially, I know I wasn't supposed to do that. But we'll be needin' help with the roundup soon. Since many of the best workers have been hired to harvest wheat and barley farther east, I thought I'd better nab the few good cowpokes while I could. I hope you approve, Amelia."

"It's all right for this once, Stretch."

"Then I'll get on with the chores. Just rest, Amelia, and I'll take care of things."

Amelia's recovery was slow at first. Clara hovered over her, doing all the things that Tall Tree had instructed for the care of the wound—fixing a poultice of herbs and cooking various greens and meat to help build new blood. The angry red swelling subsided, and, with it, the pain. At the end of two weeks, Amelia began riding her horse again. But for the first time in years, the roundup went on without her full participation.

Over the vast range, for nearly a hundred miles, the ranchers banded together to seek out their wandering herds—especially the cows, their unbranded calves, and the yearlings that had fed off the land for the entire summer. Retinues followed—the cooks with their chuck wagons and supplies; the pack mules carrying pots, pans, bedding, and branding irons; the cutting horses and the hunting dogs. Hidden from view was an assortment of mouth harps, banjos, and well-rehearsed tall tales to be used by lonely men whiling away the long evening hours around the campfires.

From the Sweet Grass Ranch, Stretch set out with the seasoned cowpokes and the new men he'd just hired. A saddened Diego watched them leave. Stretch had made it plain to him that he was no longer useful.

"If it was up to me, Diego, I'da given you your walkin' papers long ago. But Amelia won't hear of it. Me, though, I'm tougher. When a man can't do a day's work, then he don't deserve a day's pay."

Stretch's words lingered in the air, like some malevolent chill that reached into his arthritic bones. But the pain went much deeper—straight to his heart.

"Well, Diego," Amelia said, coming up behind him to inspect the swirl of dust left by the procession. "Looks like we're about the only two left at the ranch. I hope you're not sad about staying behind."

"A man's always sad when he outlives his usefulness."

"What are you talking about? Just because I told Stretch I needed you here more than chasing down some steer—"

"You mean, you asked for me to stay behind?"

"Yes. I didn't tell Stretch, but you're about the only one I can trust these days. And if you think you've outlived your usefulness, you'd better forget that in a hurry. For the next two weeks, you're going to be working harder than ever."

Diego straightened his shoulders, his pain almost forgotten.

"I want you to be making plans to harvest the wheat," Amelia went on. "With Crocker selling out, I'll have to find someone else who's willing to rent me his reapers."

"I hear Widow Johnson bought three new reapers. I bet she'd be willing to rent them out . . . just as soon as she finishes on her own farm."

"Good. Then ride over and ask her this afternoon."

"You don't mind staying by yourself?"

"I'm not totally helpless, Diego," Amelia said. "Remember, I've shot my share of outlaws and thieves in my lifetime. And I'm not too old to do it again. Besides, Sarah, Clara, and Jamie will keep me company."

Early on the same day, from the Double B Ranch, Matt, his foreman Lynx, Travis, Snake Man, and Gus set out with their own entourage, including Kwa-ling with his chuck wagon. Matt had left behind a few more men than usual to guard the ranch, to make sure that some of Driscoll's band didn't come back and burn the new barn. C. J. had been successful in ridding the countryside of many of them, but lately it seemed that two outlaws took the place of every one the posses hanged.

As Matt and Lynx rode along together, the foreman looked at his boss. "Matt, I got my eye on takin' over Wood Cumberland's spread by next spring. Thought you should know this is more than likely my last roundup as your foreman."

"I'm not surprised, Lynx. I knew Sarah had really spurred you hard. But have you spoken to her about your intentions?"

"No need to, Matt. I seen which way the wind was blowin'."

"What do you mean?"

"At Prairie Dog's funeral. We all seen how you two felt about each other that day. So wouldn't be any need for me to ask her for myself. She'd only say no." He hastened to add, "But she made me want to settle down. I'll find somebody, even if I have to go back East to do it. Sewall went to New Hampshire for his bride."

Matt ignored Lynx's assessment. Instead he said, "Sewall runs some of Roosevelt's cattle. How'd you like to do the same for me?"

Matt's suggestion caught Lynx by surprise. He thought for a few minutes before he answered. "It'd be a fine way of gettin' started, Matt. I sure would appreciate it."

"We'd divide the calves and work out the other details. Be thinking of your own brand, Lynx—something that would be hard to alter."

"I already got it picked out—a circle with an *x* in the middle. I'd call the ranch Circle X."

They rode along in companionable silence. Offering help was the least he could do, Matt decided, since Lynx had been such a good foreman, such a good friend, all these years. It was too bad that the woman had come between them, but from the moment he'd seen her, Matt had known Sarah would be trouble.

A group of young strays herded together in the ravine below caught Matt's attention. "C'mon, boys!" he shouted. "Let's cut 'em out and head 'em down the road."

In a rip-roaring manner, they swept into the ravine after the animals. The fall roundup had begun.

In the middle of the roundup, when the early morning chill in the air foretold of winter, Amelia rode alongside the carriage to the ranch gate. In the vehicle were all the possessions that Sarah Macauley had brought with her, plus a few others that Amelia had insisted Anya take from the ranch. Seated beside Anya was little Jamie Purdy, the visit with his grandmother over. Now it was time to return to his father in Medora, so that he might attend school.

"I really hate to leave you, Amelia," Anya said. "Especially with so many of the hands busy with the roundup."

"I appreciate your concern, Sarah, but I'm not helpless. Besides, you're going to be equally busy this week—arranging the desks, seeing to the slates and books. Then, there's the wood for the stove—"

"But I could come back to the ranch for the weekend. That is, if it's all right."

"Of course it is. You know you're always welcome," Amelia answered.

"May I come, too?" Jamie asked.

The woman nodded. "If your papa doesn't mind."

"Oh, he won't mind."

Anya smiled. "Then we'll both see you on Friday."

The woman stopped at the gate and watched the carriage disappear. A sense of loss washed over Amelia. Sarah Macauley had filled a place in her heart that had been vacant since Mellie's death.

That night, while Amelia had dinner alone on the ranch, Anya sat in the rocking chair before the stone hearth of her living quarters. She had drawn the calico curtains at the leaded-glass windows as it had grown dark. Now the flickering glow from the twin lamps on the mantel gave the only light in the room.

It was strange to be surrounded by the things the community had provided for Sarah Macauley's comfort. But she had elicited a few extra gifts herself—the windows, the buffalo robe, the six-shooter, and the silk dress.

She got up and walked to the clothespress. Again she took out the magnificent silk dress that Kwa-ling had made for her. Looking at it, she realized her attitude toward Matt had changed. Perhaps she had needed some excuse to find fault with him—and the woman at the hotel had provided that. Carefully she refolded the dress. One day she would wear it. But it would have to be a very special occasion.

Still restless, Anya paced the length of the room and finally opened the door into the schoolroom, where she had already arranged the new desks. Staring into the darkness, she imagined the faces of her students staring back at her. How well would she be able to take Sarah's place in the classroom? What if she were a disaster at teaching? But wouldn't Sarah have had the same misgivings? After all, this would have been her first year of teaching, too.

Carefully Anya closed the door and slid the bolt into place. With nothing else to do, she got ready for bed. But somehow, she was loath to climb the narrow stairs to the loft. She sat before the embers awhile longer, wrapped in the warm buffalo robe. Gazing into the fire, she thought how easy it would be to become a part of this Dakota community. But that could never be. She must remember that she was fleeing for her life. The time spent here would be a brief sojourn, nothing more. She could never start over, as so many other people had done, leaving their troubles behind. She was still linked to the past.

Finally Anya blew out one lamp. Taking the other, she climbed the narrow stairs to the loft. With the six-shooter under her pillow, she pulled the newly pieced quilt up to her chin and closed her eyes.

The cool, crisp air held the night sounds of Medora— the laughter coming from the saloons; the lowing of the marquis's cattle penned in the railroad corrals; the forlorn whistle of a train as it arrived at the station.

Chapter 30

Shortly before Amelia's cowhands were due to return to the Sweet Grass Ranch, Amelia and Diego took one last inspection tour along the line. It was the day that she and Stretch usually rode together. She remembered how her foreman had teased her about its regularity. "I declare, Amelia, if anybody ever wanted to know where you were at four o'clock on Wednesdays, I wouldn't even have to think. 'Why, she's ridin' the line,' I'd say, and I'd be a hundred percent right."

"You make it sound like a sin, Stretch," she'd replied. "But I think it's good common sense to have a schedule. Otherwise, things wouldn't get done around here."

"Well, you're right about that. Just knowin' you're comin' at a certain time keeps the men on their toes. But I'll tell you one thing. They work a lot harder on Tuesdays than they do on Thursdays," he'd said, with a laugh.

Remembering the conversation, Amelia also smiled. She turned to Diego. "Too bad Stretch isn't here, Diego. He always teases me about following such a rigid schedule. I wonder what he'd say about my starting out late today."

"He'd probably say, 'That Diego. He's so slow he spoiled Miss Amelia's perfect record.' "

"But I'm the one responsible, not you," she said, correcting him gently. "And I don't aim to stay out as long, either. I hate to admit it, but my arm has been paining me some today."

"Then let's go home," Diego suggested. "You've already done too much, helping in the barn."

"Let's check the cabin first. Then we'll head for home."

As Diego and Amelia wheeled their horses in the direction of the cabin, a plume of pungent black smoke began to spiral its way into the sky. "Diego, look! Something's burning!" Amelia shouted.

Diego had seen it, too. "It's too far west to be the house," Diego answered. "Must be the wheat field."

The two raced toward the smoke, with Amelia completely forgetting the nagging pain in her arm. As they got closer, she saw two men at work with torches. "The bastards!" Amelia cried, removing her rifle from across her saddle.

With guns blazing, Diego and Amelia rode in. The two culprits, realizing they had been discovered, quickly abandoned their perfidy, throwing down their torches and running for their horses to flee the scene. But they had done their damage. The entire crop of wheat was already going up in flames, and there was nothing either Amelia or Diego could do about it, except to watch it burn all the way to the river.

* * *

"There's no need to rent the reapers now," a sad Amelia finally said, noting the charred stubble.

"Not this year, anyway. But we could have lost much more than the wheat if the wind had been blowing in the other direction," Diego added philosophically.

"Or if we hadn't arrived back when we did. There's no telling what they would have tried to burn next. I wonder who they were. Did you get a good look at the men, Diego?"

"No. Only the strange, ugly markings on one of the horses."

"One thing's for sure. If either you or I ever see that animal again, we'll know who was responsible for ruining my crop."

From that day on, until the cowboys returned, a vigilant Diego patrolled the area around the ranch to make sure the culprits did not strike again. Inside the house, Amelia and Clara were equally vigilant, taking turns at the top turret window to survey the surrounding landscape.

From this vantage point, late one afternoon, Amelia saw Stretch and the others returning from the roundup. Her sense of relief at their homecoming was marred as they rode into the yard. Searching their faces, she tried to put a name to each one. But few were familiar. What had happened to all the old-timers who had been loyal to both her and Henri? Was this Stretch's doing? Or had the men she knew merely grown old, just as she was growing old? Her uneasiness was soon dispelled when she saw Stretch. Slung across his saddle was a bawling, orphaned calf he was bringing back to save, just like old times.

"Amelia," she said aloud to herself, "you're growing far too suspicious of everybody." She left the turret and walked downstairs to greet her foreman. Just as she would be interested in hearing about the roundup, Stretch would be interested in what had happened to the wheat. But she would not mention the unique markings of the culprit's horse. She and Diego had decided to keep that much to themselves.

Soon after the roundup had ended and the itinerant workers had returned from gathering in the wheat on the large bonanza farms to the east, life in Medora and the surrounding countryside took on a slower pace. Now it was time for school to start, for the children of the Territory to begin their education, while the adults settled down to the lesser chores of winter.

This was the time that Anya had been preparing for and dreading the entire summer. But the waiting had been even worse. Now she was glad that the initial day had finally arrived. For good or for bad, her life, her destiny, could only go forward. There was no returning to the past.

On the first day of school, Anya rose far too early and dressed in Sarah's white blouse and black skirt. She made herself a cup of tea and ate one of the little biscuits she'd found in a tin on the top shelf of the cupboard. She had no appetite for anything more substantial.

With the schoolroom inspected a second time and everything that needed to be done in her living quarters taken care of, Anya sat down in the rocker by the hearth and watched the mantel clock slowly move its hands, minute by minute. Then she gathered her shawl around her and walked into the schoolroom.

With time to spare before starting the fire in the potbellied stove or ringing the school bell, she watched the outside door to the schoolhouse open. Jamie Purdy cautiously stepped inside. "I come to start the fire, Miss Sarah," he announced. He set down his lunch pail and the dog-eared, ancient reading primer that had once belonged to his mother.

"How nice of you, Jamie," she replied. "I've already brought in the kindling and a hod of coal from the pile outside. You can get the matches off my desk."

As the child went about starting the fire, Anya inspected the room one more time. The desks were still in order, some small, some larger. On each one Anya had put a slate, a piece of chalk, and an eraser.

With nothing else to do, Anya stood at the window. The real Sarah had been so thorough in her journal, writing down her plans, including the activities of the first day. But Anya could see Sarah had been idealistic, expecting perfect children, a perfect day, and perfection in herself.

Anya was a little more realistic. She had seen Cyrus in action, so she knew to expect trouble from him, and maybe others as well. Then the weather had not turned out to be perfect, either. Through the window, she saw that angry clouds had begun gathering along the river. If the cold drizzle started in earnest, the children would not be able to go outside. She would have to devise games they could play in the classroom.

"Oh, Lord," she prayed under her breath. "Please don't let this day be a total disaster."

"Did you say something, Miss Sarah?"

"No, Jamie. I was thinking aloud." Anya returned to the stove that had begun to hiss and crackle. She stood for a few moments, warming her hands. Then gazing at Amelia's little watch pinned to her white blouse, she said, "I guess it's time. Let's go and ring the bell, Jamie."

Anya had not expected so many children. They came from every direction, some on ponies, some on foot. The six belonging to Ingrid and Sven came in a wagon. Anya soon realized that the corral Matt had seen to was just as necessary as the desks, the well, and the outhouses.

"Good morning," Anya said, smiling at each child entering. "This is your special card with a number on it. Will you please match it with the same number on a desk?"

"I don't know my numbers," one small child said.

"But I do," another piped up. "I'll help her find where to sit."

A few minutes later, Anya closed the door. Cyrus had not come, after all. She felt guilty at being so relieved, but his absence would make it much easier for her to cope with the other children.

By midmorning, Anya had sorted out the children as to which ones could read and write. It would be difficult, teaching on so many levels, but she knew that she could rely on some of the older ones to help those just getting started.

As she stood beside a desk, checking on one child's first attempt at the alphabet, Josie, the little girl who had attended the housewarming, said, "Miss Sarah, Cyrus is outside. He's been peeking through the window."

"Thank you, Josie." She addressed the class. "All of you remain in your seats and continue working. I'll go and see about Cyrus."

Anya went out the front door, silently closed it, and walked to the side of the building. With his back to her, Cyrus was crouched beneath the window.

"Cyrus, if you'd like to see what's going on in the schoolroom, I suggest you come with me."

He stood and turned around to face her. Anya noticed he had turned a little red at being caught. "I thought I'd just check everything out today. Maybe I'll come tomorrow."

Seeing a lunch pail at his feet, Anya asked, "Do your parents think you're in school this morning?"

He dug his hands into his pockets. "My ma does."

"Then let's not disappoint her. Come inside with me." She motioned for him to pick up his lunch and follow her. Surprisingly he did.

A few minutes later, with a surly Cyrus settled in his desk, Anya took out one of Sarah's storybooks, *The Adventures of Huckleberry Finn*, and began to read to the class. If Scheherazade could keep her head for a thousand days by telling stories, Anya reasoned, then perhaps she would be equally successful. As she began, she ignored the distracting squeaks coming from Cyrus's desk, and as the story progressed, even Cyrus got caught up in the adventures of young Huck, and the noises ceased.

Anya closed the book. "We'll read another chapter tomorrow," she announced.

The day was a long one for Anya, and by its end, she realized she'd used the plans and activities scheduled for the next two days as well. Of course, the rain had been one of the reasons for that. But all in all, the day had gone better than she'd expected.

Sitting before the fire in her own quarters, she felt completely drained of energy. For her, the school day had not ended when the pupils had gone home. There were lessons to prepare for the next day and the next. But now they were done, and she could relax. At that moment, she felt a new respect for Father Ambrose, for all teachers.

With the buffalo robe wrapped around her, Anya closed her eyes, and when she opened them again, it was dark.

By the close of that first week, a routine had been established, both in the classroom and in Anya's life. The assorted snakes and frogs smuggled into class by Cyrus and one of Sven's boys gave Anya the opportunity to turn their pranks into lessons about animals and biology. And the delight in the children's faces, as each slowly learned to read, delighted her as well.

On the weekends when the weather permitted, she went to the ranch to visit Amelia, who had completely recovered from her gunshot wound. Yet, although her friend was now healed, there seemed to be a difference, a new vulnerability, to Amelia.

As for Matt and the others, she saw little of them. But regularly, at her doorstep, she'd found venison and other game. Whoever had left the meat had come and gone without disturbing her. Her only conversation was with an occasional parent, the deliveryman from the store, and Caulk, at the post office, when her first paycheck arrived. Only then did he put her name on one of the pigeonholes.

"When the snows come," Caulk said, "you'll be missin' half your pupils. Last year in Dickinson, the weather got so bad that school shut down in November and didn't open again till spring."

"Do you think we'll have a harsh winter this year, Mr. Caulk?"

"Probably no more so than usual," he replied, "judging from the animals' coats. But sometimes a blizzard sneaks up on your blind side. One I remember especially, several years ago. A little fellow lost his direction between his house and the barn. If he hadn'a froze to death, you'd have had him as a pupil this year."

"How tragic," Anya said, hurrying to leave. The conversation was one she could have done without. But it set her to thinking. She really should buy more staples, now that she had the money.

* * *

One day, far into winter, an uneasy Anya watched the storm clouds gather. An hour previously, the sun had been shining brilliantly. But now the sky held no trace of blue, only swirling clouds that promised a winter snow.

She went back and forth along the rows of desks, checking on the children's work, stopping to help those who seemed to be having trouble. Every few minutes, she glanced out the window.

Snow began to fall, silently at first, in large, beautiful flakes. But then they changed into smaller, more icy ones, peppering the ground. The snowfall continued, and soon the ground was covered and visibility was limited.

What should she do? It was far too early for the school day to be over, but if the children were to get home before dark, she would have to let them leave soon.

Caulk's words the previous month came back to her. What if a child lost his way in the snow? Then she would be responsible. She knew she could not let that happen.

Soon the matter was out of her hands. She could barely see even as far as the corral. She certainly could not send the children home in such weather. They would have to spend the night in the schoolhouse.

"Children," she announced, "because of the snow, I think it's much too dangerous for you to try to get home this afternoon. So you'll all spend the night here at the school."

"Oh, boy," one child said. His enthusiasm was taken up by most of the others.

"But there're certain preparations we'll have to make right now. Cyrus, since you and Andy are the strongest, you'll be in charge of pumping the water. Take the buckets, fill them up, and pour the water into the large black kettle in the keeping room." She turned to Jamie. "Since you'll be in charge of the fires, get Esteban to help you bring in as much coal as you can and pile it on the tarpaulin in the corner. And Josie, you and Eleanor will help me with the cooking later on. Margaret, I'd like you to read to the little ones while I'm outside helping the boys."

Because of the blinding snow, Anya knew she could not risk sending any of the children as far as the corral. She would have to tend to the animals herself—filling their trough with water and spreading the little fodder that was left. After that, the animals would have to fend for themselves.

Knowing that a few children were uneasy, Anya tried to make the experience as festive as possible. All the lamps were lit; all the available covers and quilts brought out. The door between the two quarters was left open, with a fire going in both rooms.

Grateful for the venison that had been delivered several days previously, Anya roasted it on the open hearth, its tantalizing aroma spreading throughout the schoolhouse, filled with hungry boys and girls. When the time came to eat, each child stood in line with his lunch pail. And when the meal was over, each rinsed out his pail and put it back in the allotted place on the school shelf.

Not long after the meal, Jamie came up to Anya and

whispered, "Miss Sarah, Cyrus just used my lunch pail for something bad."

She knew she should have made her announcement sooner. "Then he will have to give you his pail, Jamie," she said, and then proceeded to make her announcement concerning their hygiene. She tried to ignore the titters that followed.

Outside, the snow showed no signs of abatement. Long after the boys had gone to sleep in the schoolroom and the girls in the keeping room, the snow piled up in great drifts, barring both doors. By morning, Anya realized they were all trapped inside.

To bring order to the uncertainty, she held classes as usual. Before the morning was over, she was glad to see that the sun had come out again. Perhaps it would melt the snow enough for the doors to be opened.

It was during the math lesson that she heard the sounds outside, a scraping of shovels and then several voices. She put down her chalk and smiled. "I think we're being rescued," she announced.

Suddenly the front door opened; parents rushed inside to claim their children.

"Mama, we had the best time. Miss Sarah cooked venison for us."

"And five of us slept in her bed under the quilt you helped piece."

"And we told stories and danced."

The childish voices were eager to share their special night. But the parents were just as eager to gather their belongings and take the children home.

Matt, standing aside, silently watched the proceedings, until all were gone. Then he stepped inside to the potbellied stove. "As chairman of the school board, Sarah, I've told the parents there'll be no more school for the rest of this month. So pack your valise. I'm taking you back to the ranch."

"I'm really quite grateful to you, Matt. But I'd rather stay here."

"You can't stay alone. It's not safe. There're too many thieves and cutthroats about."

"Then I'm sure Amelia would—"

"Amelia left for Bismarck day before yesterday to see her lawyer, according to Caulk. There's no telling how long it will take her to get back in this weather."

Anya knew the threat of unsavory characters; she had seen some lurking around the school several times. And even though she had the six-shooter, their presence had stopped her from going outside at night. But the real reason for accepting Matt's offer had to do with Caulk's casual mention that some foreigner had been inquiring earlier about the passengers on the silk train.

"Well?" he prompted.

"All right, Matt. But it will take me a little time to get ready."

Later, with the buffalo robe wrapped around her, Anya left Medora by sleigh. The bells on the horses, the soothing voice of Matt as he called to the animals, prodded her memory and brought tears to her eyes. Closing them to the brightness of the sun, she remembered a happier time when she was not a fugitive, but the adored daughter of a gentle, caring man. Now, that time seemed eons away.

Chapter 31

Despite the sun, the buffalo robe, and the warm mittens and boots, Anya felt the effects of the cold arctic air blowing across the snow-covered plains. Glancing at the man beside her, Anya knew that Matt was no stranger to the vagaries of nature. He understood the treachery of a storm and its aftermath. That was why it was so surprising to Anya that he had come to see about her and the children. Igor would not have risked riding such a distance. He would have remained by a comfortable fire and allowed the one in jeopardy, even his own wife, to fend for herself.

But Anya was still in jeopardy from another direction. For so long she had fought the knowledge that she loved Matt. Now, riding beside him, she could no longer deny the feelings that he evoked in her, even though they were destined to be submerged, never voiced. It would not do for a married woman, even one coupled to a cruel, hateful man, to openly declare her love for someone else. Why could she not have met Matt Bergen first? Why did life have to be so cruel?

"Are you warm enough?" Matt asked, taking his eyes from the road for a moment.

Startled, she looked up at him. "So far," she replied.

"If you get too cold, let me know. There's another ranch several miles ahead, where we can stop and rest by the fire."

"I don't think that will be necessary," Anya replied, trying to keep her emotions in check. "But suit yourself. I'm used to cold weather."

Matt laughed. "A regular snow queen," he said. "But even snow queens are subject to frostbite. Remember that."

The sleigh continued, with the horses' nostrils blowing great white, hoary blasts that mingled with the snowflakes stirring in the wind. Later, as they passed the post signaling the turnoff to the other ranch, Matt again looked at Anya. "Have you changed your mind? Do you want to stop?"

"No."

"Then we'll travel on."

Not long after they had passed the turnoff, the sun's rays, which had shone so brilliantly on the white landscape, bringing tears to the eyes, diminished. A few gathering clouds, floating across the sky, obscured the sun. Watching the sky, Matt said, "I was afraid we wouldn't be clear for long."

"Surely it won't start snowing again before we reach the ranch," Anya argued, remembering the time when she and Jamie had been caught in the thunderstorm.

"It's hard to tell. We'll just have to wait and see." Matt whistled to the horses, urging them faster toward home. Then he became silent, his attention directed to the trail, his eyes seeking the telltale landmarks to guide him. It was not necessary to voice his concern over the rapidly changing weather. Anya felt his uneasiness in the forward bend of his body, in the fingers that gripped the reins more securely, in the face that had hardened like granite, with no smile to soften it.

The few clouds overhead darkened; the dreaded snow began falling in earnest. Neither spoke as a new blanket of white rapidly obliterated the few indentations in the landscape, so that as far as the eye could see, the sleigh was surrounded by a vast ocean of white.

Within a half hour, the situation looked grave. Visibility was now limited to the distance between the sleigh and the horses. "Here, Sarah, hold this compass steady," Matt said, reaching into his coat and pulling out the small instrument. "We should be traveling south by southwest. Let me know if we get off course."

Over the plain, the wind began to howl in a desolate voice. Anya shivered, not only from the cold, but from the eerie sound that reached into her bones, her heart. She swept the snow from the compass face and wondered what they would do if the instrument froze. She felt helpless, almost as if some giant in the sky had suddenly taken over, imprisoning the horses, the sleigh, and the two people in it, in a glass globe, shaking it vigorously in diabolical glee. Compass or no compass, Anya sensed that if the storm kept up with such intensity, they would soon be buried in a great drift.

A short while later, she no longer felt the cold. She was beyond that now. All she wanted to do was close her eyes and sleep. But each time her eyelids drooped,

Matt's angry voice penetrated the white abyss surrounding them. "Wake up, Sarah. You can't go to sleep now. What does the compass read?" he asked, demanding a response from her.

Each time Anya would give a start, tighten her hold on the compass, and try to answer. But the words, like icicles, shattered in midsentence. She no longer cared about anything, whether she lived or died, whether she would ever reach safety. All she wanted to do was sleep.

"We'll never make it to the ranch with all this weight," Matt said. "The horses are getting bogged down. We'll have to leave your trunk and the sleigh here, Sarah, and ride the horses toward the line cabin. That's our only hope."

At the Double B Ranch, Kwa-ling continued to peer out the window of the house. Although he couldn't see past the porch, he had been listening for the sound of bells, straining his ears to decipher them from the other sounds of the storm—the howling wind, the intermittent shifts of snow sliding from the high-pitched roof. For the past hour, he had kept the water simmering on the stove. His boss was not a believer in the old ways, rubbing snow on an already half-frozen body. The sooner the body was brought back to its regular temperature, the less the damage from the cold. So the bathwater was ready and waiting for Matt and the schoolteacher.

Snake Man, Matt's new foreman since Lynx had moved to the other spread, was also listening from his position at the barn. Earlier in the winter, he had strung two strong ropes on poles, one to connect the barn with the bunkhouse and the other to the ranch house, for it was easy to become disoriented when one couldn't see beyond his own face. But the sleigh bells never came. An early darkness began to close in, and a disheartened Snake Man finally left the barn, his hands groping along the rope that led back to the bunkhouse. Matt would have no need of him to help with the horses. Something had happened. He could only pray that Matt and Miss Sarah had found shelter from the storm elsewhere.

Matt and Anya rode through the snow, with their horses linked together by the lariat. Matt's sheer determination pushed them onward. Struggling to find his way, he knew he'd had no right to put the woman riding beside him in such danger. She would have fared much better if he'd allowed her to remain at the school. But he had been selfish, wanting her beside him.

Sarah Macauley was a game one, he had to admit. She had spoken no words of incrimination for their present predicament. Only a few times had she allowed herself to be seduced by the cold. That, in itself, was an accomplishment, as small as she was. Even with his body weight, he'd felt the lure of the snow, like a winter lotus beckoning him into deep sleep and death.

Doubts began to assail him, for he should have reached the cabin before now. Had he taken the wrong direction? The two had been outside much too long, and if they did not find cover before it became completely dark, then all would be over for them.

"Matt, I think I see a portion of roof," Anya suddenly cried out, brushing snow from the scarf covering her face.

The man tried to smile, but his muscles seemed to be frozen. Looking in the direction that Anya was pointing, he said, "It's the cabin. Thank the Lord; we've finally found it."

Within minutes, Matt had a fire going, and Anya, oblivious to the thawing smell of wet wool and fur, drew as close as she could to the hearth. Tenderly Matt removed the wet scarf from around her head and face. "Even your hair is frozen," he said, touching a copper-colored tress.

"And you still have ice on your eyebrows," she responded, taking her hand and lightly brushing it away.

"We're very lucky, you know," he said, staring at her.

"Yes, I know."

They moved away from each other, as if the intimacy were too much to bear. Matt knelt by the hearth, with his back to Anya, while she became busy shaking the great buffalo robe and placing it on the nearby floor to dry.

Without looking at her, Matt said, "There're blankets in the cupboard on my side. Wait at the pass-through and I'll hand them to you. Then, while I see to the horses, you should get out of your wet clothes."

Anya nodded, even though he couldn't see her. She watched him walk out of the cabin—that divided portion owned by Amelia. Why had he not chosen his own side of the cabin to shelter them? Without coming to a logical conclusion, she walked to the pass-through and waited.

Not only did Matt hand her the two blankets, but he also pushed through a supply of wood, one log at the time. "Don't bother with carrying the wood to the hearth," he said. "I'll do that when I come back inside."

She waited for him to close the shutters, and then, standing by the fire, Anya began to remove her clothes. As she hurriedly stripped down to her chemise, she stopped and listened to the noises coming from the other side. Surely Matt wasn't bringing the horses indoors, too! But the sound of hooves on the wooden floor was unmistakable.

Anya smiled. Now she understood. Matt had no intention of allowing his prized horses to brave the elements that night. The animals had saved them both and deserved to be cared for and sheltered, too. Somehow, realizing this, Anya felt a sudden warmth not attributable to the fire on the hearth.

By the time Matt reentered, Anya had her wet clothes draped over a chair beside the fire. Feeling awkward under his scrutiny, she pulled the blanket even closer to her body.

"You still have your boots on," he said. "Here, sit in the other chair and I'll help you get them off."

"I really don't need—"

"Your modesty comes a little late, Sarah. You're already compromised, spending the night alone with me."

Anya was determined not to let him get the best of her. "You forget, Matt. We've already spent the night together—on the silk train. And we have witnesses."

Matt laughed. "So we have. But none of my men will ever tell on us."

"I just hope they'll be every bit as charitable about tonight."

"The only ones who knew where I went today were Kwa-ling and Snake Man. I daresay they'll be so happy to see us tomorrow or the next day, they won't say a word."

"You mean we might be here more than one night?"

"It depends on the storm."

A thoughtful Anya sat down, and Matt, rather than facing her, backed toward the empty chair. "Put your right boot in my hand," he ordered, "and hold on to the chair." When one boot was off, he did the same with the left boot.

While she reached down to remove her stockings, Matt began peeling off his shirt.

"What are you doing?" she inquired.

"I'm getting out of my wet clothes, too," he announced matter-of-factly. "And if you don't want to watch, you can turn your back."

"I'll go to the cupboard and see if I can find something for us to eat."

"Good idea."

Far into the night, the storm showed no signs of abating. With the supply of dry logs dangerously low, Matt had put on only enough wood so that the fire would not go completely out. The heavy clothes and the buffalo robe were still not sufficiently dry to be of any use. And he had blown out the lamp to save the oil for the next day. Even then, he could see Sarah shivering on the small cot next to the hearth. He watched while she arose and walked toward her clothes.

"They're not dry enough for you to put on, Sarah."

"But I'm so cold," she answered, her teeth chattering.

"Then there's only one thing to do," he announced. "I'll keep you warm."

"No, Matt."

"Don't be stubborn, Sarah. Even the animals huddle together to stay warm. What are you worried about? That I'll take advantage of you? I fear too much has happened today for me to be interested in seducing even you."

"I wasn't afraid of that."

"Then don't waste any more energy by arguing."

He came and lay beside her, taking her in his arms. She was stiff at first, until he said, "Relax and go to sleep."

Gradually her body responded to the warmth generated by Matt's body. She closed her eyes. In that period of twilight sleep, when she was most vulnerable, she felt safe. Unknowingly she snuggled closer, unaware of what she was doing to Matt.

"Oh, Sarah," he groaned, knowing that she had drifted into slumber and couldn't hear him. Part of the blanket fell away, and as he attempted to cover her again, his hand brushed against her soft breast. His action brought an immediate response from her body.

"I love you, Sarah," he whispered.

It happened so suddenly. She turned, and the blanket

fell away; her unclothed body was next to his, flesh against flesh.

"Matt," she whispered, making no move to separate from him.

Despite his resolve, he lifted himself on one elbow and stared into her beautiful, sleepy face. Her lips spoke of desire—perhaps his own; he didn't know. He only knew he had to touch them again, to feel his own mouth on hers, the memory of the tryst at Antoine's overwhelming him.

"I love you, Sarah," he repeated. "I've known that for a long time. I want to marry you. So what is happening to us is right."

Anya came awake. "Matt, you must understand. I'm not free—"

"I know that. But I'll get you out of your teaching contract somehow. We belong together—for the rest of our lives. So hush, darling, and let me love you."

Anya did nothing to prevent him. She welcomed him in sadness, not caring about past or future. Her desire had been ignited, and there was no turning back.

Chapter 32

She dressed early, and, at first light, Anya saw that the storm was over. It had done much damage, but its full measure, whether on the open range, or in her heart, could not be assessed until later. But one thing she was sure of. After what had happened, she could not let Matt suspect the true strength of her love for him. Returning to the ranch with him was out of the question. She must take refuge with Amelia.

"Sarah?" a sleepy Matt said. "What are you doing?"

"I'm getting ready to leave, Matt."

"Is the sun out?"

"Yes. The storm seems to be over."

Matt smiled. "So you're eager to get to your new home."

"No, Matt. I'm not going with you."

"What are talking about?"

"I'm going to stay with Amelia for the rest of the month."

Matt rose from the cot, wrapped himself in his blanket, and walked toward the hearth to face Anya. "You can't run away from what's happened, Sarah. I realize I've placed you in an awkward position, but we'll manage to sort things out."

"I've already done that," she replied. "So if you will allow me to borrow one of your horses again, I'll be leaving."

In anger, Matt dropped the blanket and began to pull on his clothes. "Is this your way of saying that you don't believe what I said in the heat of the moment last night? I always stand by my word, Sarah. I said I'd marry you."

"Then I release you from your pledge."

"Woman, what has gotten into you this morning?"

Anya's face was bleak. "A little sense. It would never work, Matt. I can't marry you. So you can forget what happened last night."

"Can you?"

"I will try."

They stood facing each other like two adversaries, when only a few short hours before, they had been lovers. Matt's face hardened. "If you walk out now, I won't ask you again to be my wife."

"I don't expect you to."

Only the crackle and hiss of the last log on the hearth disturbed the silence in the room. Anya turned her back so that Matt would not see the tears forming in her eyes. She could not bear to see the anger, the hurt in his face.

"Will you be able to find your way by yourself? To follow the curl of smoke coming from the ranch?"

"Yes. Jamie and I have ridden back and forth several times."

"Then I'll bring Dorado around as soon as I get on my boots."

"Matt?"

"Yes?" He stopped and waited for her to speak again. But the words were not the ones he'd hoped for.

"If you could rescue my trunk and leave it here by tomorrow, then I can send Diego for it."

"I'll do that. But I also have a favor to ask of you."

Anya turned, but her face, in shadow, was unreadable. Matt watched her while he finished putting on his other boot. Then he spoke. "I would appreciate it if you kept my proposal to yourself. A failed man does not like to be laughed at behind his back."

"No one would ever laugh at you, Matt. But I promise."

He put on his coat and walked out the door. Great beams of sunlight greeted him as he pushed the gate against the remaining snowdrift. Within moments, he had taken the horse and led it back through the opening. Anya came, and, with Matt's help, she mounted the animal.

"You can slap him on his flank, Sarah, as soon as you reach Sweet Grass Ranch. He'll return to me."

"Matt, thank you for—"

He cut her off in midsentence. "You'd better start on. It's still mighty cold out here."

With nothing more to say, a miserable Anya rode from the cabin that still served as a feud symbol between two powerful families. The yearning was strong, but her pride kept her from looking back to take one last glimpse of the man who had held her in his arms.

It was better this way, not looking back. For the tender, caring look that she had cherished had already been replaced with a harsh, accusing mien. She had made Matt Bergen her enemy. "Oh, Dorado," she said, touching the horse's mane. "How I love him. If I could only—" She gave a sob and wiped the tears from her eyes. Once again, she was running away.

When would it ever stop? Heartsick, Anya knew that she could no longer keep the past to herself. It had become too big a burden. As soon as Amelia returned, she would confess all and take the consequences. It no longer mattered whether she lived or died.

Two days after Anya rode into Sweet Grass Ranch, Amelia returned from Bismarck by train. At the livery stable where she'd left her horse, Cyrus had told the woman of the school's postponement, so Amelia was not surprised to see Anya.

"So you've been given an unexpected holiday, I hear," Amelia said, smiling at the sight of Anya, who stood at the front door to welcome her.

"I hope you don't mind that I've come to spend it with you."

"I'd have been miffed if you hadn't," Amelia responded, hurrying inside. "And I hope you and Clara have a nice roaring fire going."

"We do. In the parlor. Your favorite spirits are waiting for you, too."

"Nothing like good sherry to warm your heart and your bones." She glanced at Anya, seeing the drawn face. "You might try a glass, too. Put some color in those pale cheeks of yours."

"Maybe I will," Anya responded. "Perhaps tonight." She needed to keep her wits about her for the rest of the day. Confessions were hard enough, without lulling her brain. Of course, sherry would not be nearly so lethal as Russian vodka, which Igor consumed by the case and had forced her to drink at times, too, when he'd been particularly spiteful.

"Shame on you, Amelia," Clara said, poking her head around the corner. "Tryin' to lead our nice Miss Sarah down your own sinful path. I've already made hot tea for 'er."

"Clara, I don't mind your temperance preaching before the saloons in Medora, but you won't do it in my house," Amelia warned.

"I do everything else in this house for you," Clara replied as she set down the tea tray. "Lookin' after the meals, the cleanin', and the washin' and ironin'. Might as well look after your soul, too."

Anya merely stared at the two women while they argued.

"I've told you a hundred times, Clara. You can hire anybody you want to help you."

"So you think I'm gettin' too old to do my chores, do you?"

"I didn't say that. Now, hush, and go check in the kitchen. I think I smell the bread burning."

As Clara whirled and disappeared, Amelia winked at Anya. "She's an incorrigible old bat. Takes over if you let her. But I guess we've been together too long for me to fire her."

"Did you have a pleasant trip to Bismarck?" Anya asked, not knowing what else to say.

"Not pleasant. Just necessary. Once we're alone, I want to talk to you about it."

"And I have some things I need to discuss with you."

"Fine. What if I come to your sitting room just before supper tonight?"

"All right," Anya said, trying not to show her disappointment at having to wait so long. She knew that

Amelia was tired and that she had other things to attend to concerning the ranch.

The bell rang, indicating that Clara was ready to serve the midday meal. Amelia quickly downed the rest of her sherry, while Anya set her almost full teacup back on the silver tray.

The afternoon passed slowly, with Anya remaining in the turret. From her window, she could see the bleak winter landscape that offered no consolation. From time to time, she turned the pages of a book, without really relating to the story. Her mind was too much on the drama of her own life, which was now more complicated than ever.

Would Amelia understand? Once she confessed, would the older woman be so appalled at her perfidy that she would ask her to leave at once? Because of Prairie Dog's small legacy, Anya could buy a ticket to Chicago. But she thought of the children, who, despite her shaky ability as a teacher, were actually learning. She hated to let them down—especially Jamie and Josie—leaving them in the middle of the year.

And then, how long would she last in a place like Chicago? She would have to earn a living—something she'd never done before. She had no teaching credentials of her own, and she could not picture herself as a seamstress or governess. Her pride would not allow that.

The knock on the door and Amelia's voice calling to her signaled the wait was over. "Come in," she called out, closing the book in her lap and standing up.

As Amelia entered, Anya forced herself to smile. She indicated the comfortable settle while she took the smaller chair beside it. "Did you have a nice rest?" she inquired.

"Yes. It's amazing how refreshed I feel," Amelia replied. "I hope you've had a pleasant afternoon."

Anya was too nervous—and had waited too long—to waste time in pleasantries. What she had to say needed to be said immediately. Looking at her benefactor, she clasped the book against her racing heart and blurted out, "Amelia, I'm not who you think I am."

Amelia's face gave no indication of surprise. For a moment she sat staring at the schoolteacher whom she had sheltered for most of the summer. "I know who you are, Anya," she answered in a quiet voice.

Startled, the copper-haired young woman dropped the book. She made no attempt to pick it up. "You called me Anya," she said.

"Yes. It took me awhile to realize who you actually are—Anya, the Princess Fodorsky—the woman who was supposedly killed on the silk train."

"But how did you find out?" Anya asked, not refuting the truth.

"From the moment we met, you puzzled me. But I think I first started putting things together at the château. I watched you that first evening—saw how at home you were, took note of your aristocratic behavior. Even as the most careful observer, Anya, a mere schoolteacher could not have picked up that manner—the knowledge of languages—in such a short time. You had to be born to it—used to it as a way of life."

"But you said nothing."

"Well, I wasn't completely sure. And remember, I had problems of my own. It was only later that the proof came."

"Proof?" Alarm spread over Anya's face. "What are you talking about?"

"It was the day I'd gone into town to get supplies. Stretch met someone at the saloon who'd been inquiring about Sarah Macauley, the teacher on the silk train. Now, around here, people are close-mouthed, especially when some foreigner is so mule-set on getting a complete description of a person. Lucky that Stretch ushered him out of the saloon and referred him to me at the hotel, where I'd gone to rest.

" 'Is this Sarah Macauley small, with reddish hair and ice-blue eyes?' he demanded.

"His arrogance riled me. I didn't like him. Whatever you'd done didn't bother me nearly as much as he did. So I answered, 'No. She's big-boned and tall, has mousy hair, and a wart on her chin. I tell you, not a single boy or girl is going to get by with anything when that Amazon takes over the school.'

"Then, when he told me he was from Sitka and had come on behalf of Igor, the Prince Fodorsky, to investigate his runaway wife, I began to laugh. 'And you think this awkward country girl might be the princess come back from the dead?' I laughed until the tears rolled down my face. He was so chagrined at his mistake, that he boarded the train and left town."

Amelia's face became serious again. "I think you're

safe now, Anya. Only Stretch and I know who you really are."

"Oh, Amelia, I love you. It's been so difficult pretending to be someone else. I didn't plan it. Really I didn't. But when Sarah died—" The words tumbled out, with Anya confessing everything, except her love for Amelia's enemy, Matt Bergen.

Without realizing it, Anya had moved from the chair and sat down beside Amelia on the settle. Once she'd finished her confession, Amelia hugged her as she would have hugged Mellie.

"I'm glad you told me," Amelia said, "especially before I tell you my own news."

Anya looked up. "I'm sorry. I've been so engrossed in my problems that I'd forgotten you had something else to discuss." Anya wiped her eyes. "So now it's your turn. I only hope I can be as good a listener as you, Amelia."

Amelia stood up and looked out the window, as Anya had done earlier, staring into the white-covered distance. Finally she turned around. "We both have secrets to keep, Sarah." Amelia smiled. "Yes, I'll have to keep on calling you that name to protect you. It's still too dangerous for you to become Anya again."

Anya nodded. She did not prompt Amelia to continue. The woman would tell her what she needed to know in her own good time.

"I went into Bismarck to draw up a new will."

Still Anya waited.

"After I was shot, I had to face up to two things. One, that I wasn't going to live forever. And two, that

Mellie was really dead and I had no heir to leave my property to.

"I've made arrangements for Clara and Diego in their old ages, as well as rewarding Stretch for his years of service as foreman. But I'm leaving Sweet Grass Ranch and all my other assets to you, Sarah Macauley."

Anya's mouth dropped open in surprise. "But why, Amelia? You've known me such a short time. I don't deserve—"

"You deserve a safe haven now, more than ever. Remember, you'll always be in hiding, never be able to marry again until your present husband is dead. Besides, I won't have the property fought over after I'm gone. No telling who might buy it."

Amelia's gaze softened. "You've become a second daughter to me. You love this land; I've seen it in your eyes. And you'll take good care of it."

An eerie sound beyond the closet caused Amelia to smile again. "Clara would say that Mellie's ghost approves of what I've done. Welcome home, Sarah."

The bell from the dining room sounded impatiently. Dinner was ready. The two women left the turret to return to the main part of the house. Anya was still overwhelmed by Amelia's generosity. But as they walked down the hall, past the rooms filled with fine old furniture and the collective memories of three Chaboillez generations, Anya was aware of another house—the one of ponderosa pine, where two Norwegian elkhounds slept by the fire. As much as she longed for the dream, she could never become Matt Bergen's wife. With such animosity between them, they seemed destined to continue the feud that had started so long ago.

Chapter 33

Several days before the month was up, Anya returned to Medora and the schoolhouse. The town seemed indolent, with so many of its residents away for the winter and few activities going on.

Only a skeleton staff had remained at the de Mores château, for Medora and Antoine were spending the winter in New York, where their second child was scheduled to be born. Theodore Roosevelt had also left his Maltese Cross Ranch to return to Albany. The heartsick Shaun Drayton had sold his spread to Matt and followed his wife to Wisconsin.

Although she had not seen him since that fateful day in the cabin, Anya soon learned of Matt's dealings from Caulk, when she went to the post office to pick up her mail—the extra books she'd ordered.

"Don't know what's gotten into Matt," Caulk said. "Seems to be buying up every piece of property that comes on the market. 'Course he's getting a good price, since he can afford to pay cash. His silk business must be doing mighty well for him to sink that much money into land. Nobody's making money in cattle these days." Caulk looked at Anya as if waiting for some appropriate reply to his gossip.

"I understand the silk from his filature is really lovely," she managed to say.

"Yep. Saw an advertisement for it in a newspaper that came recently. Marshall Field is selling dresses made from it."

Anya was anxious to change the subject. "Have you seen Jamie Purdy recently?" she asked.

"Every day since he sent off for that pugilistic stuff from one of his papa's magazines. Told him it was going to take awhile. He'll be mighty pleased that it came in this morning. And none too soon, with that shiner he's sporting."

"Cyrus?"

"Who else? He makes the little fellow's life miserable. But guess you already know that, teaching them both."

Anya nodded. "It's a shame they're not closer to the same size."

"It's a worse shame that Jamie thinks the course he's ordered is going to make a whit of difference."

"Perhaps it will, Mr. Caulk," Anya said. "Especially if someone works with him."

"Got anybody in mind?"

"Yes." She picked up her package from the counter. "Well, good day, Mr. Caulk."

"Good day, ma'am," he said, wondering why she'd suddenly broken off the enjoyable conversation.

* * *

Early on the morning that school began again, Jamie showed up at the schoolhouse to build the fire. But he was too late. Smoke was already rising from the chimney.

"Jamie," Anya said, ignoring the black eye and the disappointed look on his face. "I'm so glad you came early."

"I thought I was going to build the fire."

"We have to spend this short time in a more important way," she explained. "I have something very special to teach you. As soon as you put up your lunch pail, come back into the keeping room."

Puzzled, he obeyed her, quickly placing the pail on the shelf and hanging his overcoat on a peg. He then walked past the schoolroom into the teacher's private quarters.

Anya stood on the soft buffalo robe that she'd placed on the floor a short distance from the hearth. "Close the door, Jamie, and take off your boots."

Through the years, her father had taught Anya many things not considered appropriate for a girl to learn. But Alaska had been a dangerous place, and the day he had thwarted her kidnapping by a band of thugs, he had decided she needed to learn something else. She still remembered nearly every word of that ensuing conversation.

"Anya, my dear, I won't always be around to rescue you from sudden dangers. So you must learn to protect yourself."

"I have the gun you gave me, Father."

"Did you have it with you yesterday, when you and Nutee went to the marketplace?"

"No, Father."

"Then you must also learn a method of defense that will not depend on weapons or superior strength. You must learn to use your brain."

She watched as he motioned for the small Chinese man to enter the library. Barefoot, he was dressed in a white, loose-fitting suit with a colored belt wrapped around his waist. He bowed to her father and then to her.

"This is Wang-chi. He is to be your teacher in the art of oriental self-defense."

Now, ten years later, Anya was the teacher and Jamie, the pupil. She motioned for the boy to join her on the buffalo rug. She then began to explain the first basic moves in much the same way Wang-chi had explained them to her.

But a warning went along with the explanation. "This will be a secret between you and me, Jamie. What you're learning will help you to protect yourself from someone much larger than you. But you must promise never to use it in anger, or to attack another person. It is to be used only when you are attacked by someone else."

"You mean like Cyrus?"

"Yes."

"I promise." The eagerness in Jamie's voice was matched by the width of his smile. At that moment, he loved his teacher even more, if that were possible. The course he'd ordered was too hard for him to read. But looking at the pictures, he'd realized that it would take years, not days, for him to grow strong enough to hold his own with Cyrus.

Now he would come to school each morning as if he were going to build the fire. But instead, he would be learning something very special. Inwardly he vowed to work so hard that Miss Sarah would soon be proud of him.

The next several months passed quickly in the Dakota Territory. At the Double B Ranch, Kwa-ling saw a decided change in Matt Bergen's behavior. The boss worked from dawn to dusk, pushing himself, always on the go, as if he were afraid of a single moment of solitude. Snake Man had noticed it, too, but said nothing until Kwa-ling brought up the subject on the day their boss had ridden over to check on Tall Tree.

"He not been same since he went into town for Miss Sarah," Kwa-ling ventured.

"Wonder what happened between them," Snake Man commented. "They must have had some words, since she didn't come back to the ranch with him, like he thought she would."

"They two headstrong people. Got to expect fireworks sometimes."

"Well, he doesn't act like he's tryin' to patch things up."

"Wrong season. Heart frozen, like ground. Have to wait for spring thaw."

* * *

An impatient Igor was also waiting for spring, when he could leave Sitka for Seattle and the appointment with Matt Bergen. Earlier, he had examined Anya's personal effects thoroughly, but, to his disappointment, the papers she had taken were not in the valise. He had ripped up each dress, each petticoat, seeking the hiding place. But he had not found the papers.

"They must be buried with her," Igor had told Torzhok. And that was why he'd sent his servant, armed with the map of the burial place beside the rails, to dig up the woman's bones and sift through every piece of cloth.

"If you do not find them in the grave," he'd told the servant, "you must go on to Medora to get a good look at the other woman. I would not put it past Anya to have swapped places with her."

"I will find them in the grave, my prince. Little Anya would never give up her ring, or all that gold. You know that."

"Sometimes I think I have never truly known the woman, Torzhok. So do as I say."

"And if all the leads prove to be false, what then?"

Igor's face turned red with anger. "Then I will know that this man, Matthew Bergen, has kept the papers for himself. It would be very convenient for him to offer them back to me for a large sum of money."

"Will you pay it?"

Igor's eyes took on a hooded expression. "What do you think?"

Remembering his conversation with Torzhok, Igor picked up his glass of vodka and stared at it. The papers had not been in the grave, and the schoolteacher had been another woman. He was convinced Matthew Bergen had the papers. Or else, Anya had tricked them all and vanished.

Late in the spring, the rivers became swollen all across the western plains as the snows melted and ran from the higher elevations. Amid the ravines and buttes of the badlands, carcasses of cattle that had not survived the winter became a feast for the birds of prey. By the time of the roundup, the bones had been bleached by the sun.

In a ritual as bonding as the ancient cavemen's search for meat, the ranchers and their cowboys packed bedrolls, supplies, and branding irons for the new calves, then prepared to head out for the range. They all hoped that they could reach the cattle that had survived the decimating cold—before entire herds were rustled by the men working for Driscoll. Despite the war against the wily outlaw, he had still managed to elude the authorities.

On the Double B Ranch, Kwa-ling had packed his cooking pots and supplies in the chuck wagon. When Matt gave the word, he would be ready to move out. That morning, while they waited for Lynx to join them from the other spread, Matt, Snake Man, and Gus were double-checking the pack mules and horses in the corral.

"I'll be sorta sorry not to be ridin' with you on the next silk train, Matt," Snake Man said, "once we get back from the roundup."

"Me, too," Gus agreed.

"It's better this way," Matt replied, "hiring Pinkerton guards for the job. With so much land and cattle to look after, I need all of you here on the ranch."

"Are you really goin' to meet that Russian prince in Seattle, like he requested?" Gus asked.

"Yes. Not that I'm looking forward to it. But I guess he was so devastated by his wife's death, he wants to hear every detail of her last hours. At least I can do that much for him."

"I never trusted a Russky," the insular Snake Man said. "Hear some of 'em are tryin' to buy land east of here. Wish they'd just stay where they belong."

Matt laughed. "Crazy Horse probably felt the same way about us."

A swirl of dust in the distance meant that Lynx and several of his hands were arriving. Matt gave the signal to move out. Amid the whoops and yells, the whinnies and hee-haws, and the creaking of wagon wheels, the spring roundup began.

At the schoolhouse, Anya tried to keep the pupil's minds on their work. It was the last day of school for the year. So many things had been left undone—yet she was proud of each child. Wanting to make the day count, she had pushed them hard all morning.

Anya knew that a few of the older ones, like Cyrus and Andy, were going on the roundup for the first time. It had been hard to keep their interest in the classroom, for they considered it an embarrassment to be with the smaller children. Now she could see their restlessness, the rapid darts of their eyes—hints that they were planning something mischievous to end the day.

But she was also planning something special. That was why she'd wanted them to finish all their work that morning. The afternoon was to be spent in pleasantries, in games and fun. She'd even bought prizes for each child.

She looked down at the watch pinned to her blouse. Smiling, she looked up and said, "Boys and girls, it's now time to clean your slates and store them for the year."

Josie raised her hand. "But Miss Sarah, what are we going to do until it's time to go home?"

"We're going to eat our lunches, and then play games."

"Oh, boy!" one of the children exclaimed. A murmur of excitement swept through the schoolroom.

"As soon as you've finished with your slates," Anya said, "you'll line up for a break. Sophy, you may lead the girls ... Ralph, the boys. I'll be at the pump, waiting for you to wash your hands."

In an orderly manner, they lined up as they had each day since school began. Once the break was over, they came back inside, took their lunch pails from the shelves, and sat down at their desks to eat.

From her own desk, Anya took note of each child, mentally assessing the progress made. But Anya had to admit that she was the one who had learned the most that school year.

It had not been easy for her. Although she had finished what she'd set out to do, and there was a certain

amount of pride in that, she was not enthusiastic about
continuing. Yet what else could she do? She certainly
could not expect Amelia to provide for her. For the moment, there seemed to be no way out.

On the playground, the sun had dried most of the
muddy places. Anya was glad. She wanted all the children to have fun, but she didn't want to send them
home wet and filthy, especially on the last day.

She counted them off for the tug-of-war, separating
them into two groups. Earlier in the year, she'd made
such a mistake—allowing two captains to choose their
own teams. She had seen how the procedure had affected the smaller ones, always being chosen last. Anya
had realized that life would be selective enough later
on. But at least she could do something about it as a
teacher, providing joy and pleasure in their learning
new things, rather than destroying their self-esteem. It
was such a simple thing, finding other ways for the
teams to be chosen, and she was pleased at how some
of the children, a little less able, a little less talented at
the beginning of the year, had lost their dread and actually blossomed and grown.

The tug-of-war began, with Anya as the referee. Back
and forth the rope traveled, one team pulling against the
other, both trying to avoid the demarcation line. But finally the team with Cyrus on its side gained momentum.

"We won! We won!" the team shouted.

"So you did," Anya agreed. She walked to the table
where she had laid out the prizes. "Each member of the

winning team gets a red-and-white peppermint stick," she announced. But then, seeing the disappointment on the other faces, she also announced, "The team who placed second gets green-and-white peppermint sticks."

The children laughed and began to chatter happily. After the peppermint sticks had been eaten, or put away to savor, the games continued, with certain children clear winners. Although some won more than others, Anya made sure that each child received at least one prize.

Finally Anya glanced at her watch. It was almost time to ring the bell. The games were over. She was relieved that nothing unpleasant had happened all afternoon, despite the earlier looks between Cyrus and Andy.

She motioned for all the children to return inside to gather their belongings. Standing at her desk, Anya made her farewell speech. "I want to tell you how much I've enjoyed being your teacher this year. I hope each of you has a pleasant vacation and will return to school in the fall. As soon as I ring the bell, you're dismissed for the summer."

Anya walked past the line of desks, past the front door, and down the path. The bell that had come from the train engine clanged loudly, its sound a familiar one, not only to the pupils but to the people in the town of Medora.

The enthusiastic children swept out of the school. "Good-bye, Miss Sarah," one after the other called to her.

"Good-bye," she answered, smiling. But as she began

to walk back inside, she overheard Cyrus's voice. She had congratulated herself a little too soon.

"Jamie, come here."

"What do you want, Cyrus?"

"You're gonna be a calf on the roundup, and I'm gonna show everybody how to rope and brand you."

"I don't want to play that game, Cyrus."

"Do I have to come and get you?" the larger boy asked, causing the children watching to laugh nervously.

"Yes."

Anya walked toward the group. "That will be enough, Cyrus. You may go on home, now."

Cyrus was not intimidated by Anya's tone. He grinned and shook his head. "School is out, Miss Sarah. Besides, I'm not on the school ground. My pa says when I'm not at school, I can do what I please."

The children gasped. They looked at their teacher and then back to Cyrus, whose attention returned to Jamie, standing defiantly a few feet away.

"Jamie, do I have to come and get you?" he repeated, a little louder this time.

"Yes, Cyrus. But I'd better warn you—"

The boy laughed. "You little pie-eyed runt. For that, I'm gonna smear your face in the mud hole over there."

An upset Sophy came and tugged on Anya's skirt. "Miss Sarah, aren't you going to do something?"

"I'm going to let them fight it out, Sophy."

"But Jamie will get killed."

"Maybe not."

The ponies and wagons remained in the corral. Not a

child moved to go home. They all waited to see Jamie Purdy roped and tied, with his face smeared by mud. Inwardly each boy was thankful that he had not been selected by Cyrus.

With swaggering steps, Cyrus walked up to Jamie to grab his arm. In a lightning move, Jamie twisted his body, freeing himself from the other boy's grip. Surprised, Cyrus looked at Jamie and then at his own empty hand. Cyrus took another step, this time using both hands. But within seconds, he had fallen down.

For the first time, a timid voice piped, "That's the way to go, Jamie."

Like an angry bull, Cyrus picked himself up and lunged for the boy. But Jamie stepped out of the way, and once again, Cyrus found himself on the ground. All around him, the children began to laugh.

Backing away, his steps closer and closer to the mud hole, Jamie watched his confused adversary pick himself up. He did not dare look at his teacher. If he wanted to win—and he desperately wanted that—Jamie knew he had to keep his mind totally on the fight. Otherwise, all the lessons, all the hard work, would be for nothing.

But Cyrus was also determined to win, by any method possible. Taking the lasso from his belt, he began to swing it back and forth. Hitting Jamie in the face with it, he pressed his advantage, closing in for the attack.

What happened next, no one would ever forget. Jamie reached out, took Cyrus's arm, and threw him broadside into the mud hole. He landed with such a thud that the breath was knocked from him and mud spattered in every direction.

As Cyrus lay there, trying to get his breath back, Jamie leaned over and said, "Have you had enough, Cyrus?"

The larger boy merely groaned. He was disgraced. He didn't know what had happened to him, why he'd been so clumsy. He only knew that the children were laughing at him. Pushing himself up, he looked questioningly at Miss Sarah Macauley. Her eyes showed neither triumph nor sorrow.

"Come to the pump, Cyrus. I'll help you get cleaned up." Looking out over the crowd, Anya said, "Go home, children. Your parents are waiting for you."

She did not look at Jamie. He was already surrounded by his admiring classmates. Cyrus was the one who needed her now.

Chapter 34

As soon as the weather changed, bringing the brief display of colorful flowers and summer greenery to the Alaskan landscape, Prince Igor and Torzhok, with two other loyal servants, left Sitka by ship. They traveled much the same route to Vancouver and Seattle that

Anya had traveled, but the conditions were much more favorable.

The handsome and imposing Igor had gotten used to demanding the best—the most comfortable quarters, the finest food and drink, impeccable service—for, after all, he was a prince among riffraff. Some people were born to be served, he believed, while it was the duty of others to serve. And he did not let the captain of the ship forget this for a single moment.

By the time the *Alaskan Queen* finally dropped anchor and the longboats carrying the prince, his servants, and his luggage to shore began to disappear into the mist, the captain was glad to see him go. "Thank the gods that the prince didn't book all the way to San Francisco with us," he said to his first mate, who stood beside him on the bridge. "We would have had a mutiny on our hands."

"Or a burial at sea," the first mate answered. "He never knew how close he came to swimmin' among the sharks at the bottom of the channel."

"Well, we're rid of him now," the captain replied.

"But I feel sorry for whoever comes in contact with him on land," the first mate replied, rubbing his right ear, which the prince had cuffed the day before.

In the lobby of the Western Empire Hotel, a nervous Rucker Pringle waited for the arrival of one of his most prestigious guests. He had sent the best carriage and luggage wagon to the docks, and now, with the uniformed and white-gloved bellmen lined up on each side of the plush red carpet runner, the manager worried for fear that, amid all the preparations, he'd forgotten something.

He was not happy that he'd had to switch his other important guest to a smaller suite. But perhaps Matthew Bergen would understand that the treatment of royalty, especially Russian royalty, demanded precedence over previous arrangements. He only prayed that the two would not arrive at the same time.

Leaving the railway station, Matt Bergen slung his worn leather bag over his shoulder and headed for the hotel. He had staved off the hotel carriage and the little urchins who'd offered to take his luggage, for the long train trip West had been a tedious one, and he needed to stretch his legs after being confined for several days. The bag was a little heavier than usual, for Kwa-ling had insisted that meeting Prince Fodorsky for dinner would require an evening suit. So he'd packed the one Matt had worn that weekend at the château. For himself, Matt would just as soon have left it home.

Walking down the muddy path, he realized this trip to Seattle to arrange for the silk shipment was the first time he'd come alone. Already he missed the company of Lynx and the other cowboys. But the Pinkerton guards made more sense, as he'd explained to his men during the roundup. Lynx had always hated the train trips anyway.

Seeing the hotel's angled roof come into view amid the tall firs, he began to walk faster. A nice bath in his suite and a good meal, which he had not had in a long time, appealed to him. Kwa-ling had done his best, but the chuck wagon food during the roundup had grown stale in a hurry.

At the circular drive, lined with river pebbles, Matt stopped to scrape the mud from his boots, for a special runner had been put down, stretching all the way past the wide front porch to the carriage landing. Before he had finished removing the mud, a carriage approached the landing and stopped. The front doors to the hotel swept open; the manager rushed out, and a curious Matthew watched to see the important visitor who had the entire staff in such a flutter.

"Welcome to our humble hotel, Your Highness," Rucker gushed, signaling for the bellmen. "I am the manager, Rucker Pringle, at your service. We hope your stay with us will be an enjoyable one."

Matt watched as a large man, dressed in a regal Russian uniform with polished black boots, stepped from the carriage. His eyes took an imperial sweep of his surroundings before he finally deigned to nod in the direction of the manager.

So this was the man that he was to have dinner with that evening. Seeing what a bother Rucker was in, a sympathetic Matt waited. The fastidious little man would not take kindly to even a dottle on his carpet runner before the prince had traversed it, much less a muddy footprint. A few minutes later, when things seemed to have quieted down, Matt finally walked inside.

"Good day, Mr. Bergen," the man behind the desk said, greeting him. "I'm sorry, but we didn't see the carriage arrive from the station."

"I walked, Manley," Matt answered. "The key to my suite, please."

Manley coughed. "I hope you don't mind, Mr. Bergen. But we've had to move you to a suite on the second floor."

"Oh?"

"Prince Fodorsky has reserved the entire third floor. I'm afraid we've had to move some of our other guests, too."

"Just give me a key, Manley. I'm tired, and I need a bath. If you have enough hot water, I don't much care where you put me."

Manley smiled. "I knew you'd understand. Some of the other guests, though, are quite unhappy. Especially the gold heiress and her daughter. But they're new rich. Not like you, sir."

Matt laughed. "You'd better watch out, Manley. You're beginning to sound just as snobbish as Rucker."

That afternoon, from his hotel suite that faced the east garden, Matt made arrangements with Pinkerton, setting the time two days later—for the crates of raw silk to be transferred from the warehouse to the special rail cars of the Northern Pacific.

Along with the breeze blowing in from the open doors to the balcony, Matt could also hear the voices from above. Someone was receiving a tongue-lashing. Remembering the unremarkable princess, he was not surprised that she'd chosen to run away. Life with her prince must have been hell for her.

Thinking about that previous trip and trying to remember as much as possible to recount to the husband that evening, Matt walked onto the balcony. Down below, he saw two women, their faces obscured by parasols, walking in the garden. Then they stopped, taking a rest on one of the benches.

"Close your parasol, girl," the mother commanded. "I want the prince to get a good look at your face."

"He probably isn't even aware of us, Mama. Besides, the chambermaid said he was already married."

"He's a widower," Belle Walsh said. "Handsome and rich."

"Papa's rich, too."

"Yes. That's to our advantage. Even with your beauty, Hettie, Prince Igor probably wouldn't be interested in you if you didn't have money, too. I never knew a rich man who couldn't use a bit more money. But it's a shame I didn't name you something a little more exotic. *Hettie* was good enough for your granny, but somehow, it don't seem to suit a princess. What about Theresa? How'd you like it if I started callin' you Theresa, honey?"

"Oh, Mama, let's go back inside. I feel like a pig exhibited at a country fair."

"You're a blue ribbon *lamb*, Hettie," she corrected. "All soft and pink and dewy-eyed. But if you're unhappy, we won't stay out any longer."

As they began to walk down the path toward the French doors to the east gallery, Belle happened to look up and see Matt standing on the second-floor balcony.

"Well, at least you've attracted somebody handsome. Wonder who *he* could be? I wonder if he's rich, too?"

"I'm sure you'll find out before suppertime, Mama," Hettie assured her.

Belle, frankly appraising Matt, who made no move to go back inside, nodded to him, and he politely returned her greeting. "At least he's civil," Belle said. "Not like that snobbish Mr. Watt. I wonder if he might be free for tea tomorrow."

Hettie ignored her mother's machinations. All she wanted to do was go back home to Denver.

That evening, at the appropriate time, Matt followed Igor's servant up the guarded flight of stairs to the third floor. The door into the suite was open for the array of hotel servants bringing in food and drink.

"My prince," Torzhok exclaimed to the seated Igor. "May I present Mr. Matthew Bergen." Torzhok clicked his heels—and in a proud voice, he announced, "His most excellent Highness, Igor, Prince of Fodorsky: liege man to his imperial cousin, the grand duke, and the defender of Minsk and St. Petersburg."

The man was an imposing figure, but Matt was not impressed. He had seen far too many of his kind. Nevertheless, Matt was polite, without being obsequious.

"Do sit down, Mr. Bergen," Igor said, frankly assessing the man before him. "Torzhok, a drink for our guest. What will you have, Mr. Bergen?"

Seeing the bottle of Russian vodka already open, he said, "Vodka will be fine."

Igor was in no hurry to bring up the subject of his

dead wife. He was far more interested in Matt, wondering when he would finally get down to business, offering him the papers.

From one course to another, from fish and venison, caviar and black bread, asparagus and artichokes, potatoes, pudding, and finally fruit and cheese, with the accompanying liqueurs, Matt paced himself, answering unimportant questions and making small talk, all the time watching an intemperate man deny himself nothing.

Finally, when Igor had waved away the trays, the waiters, and his own servants, he stood and poured himself another drink, while Matt chose to sip the one still in his hand. Taking a swallow, Igor said, "Now tell me about my wife, my dear Anya. All you know of her last hours. And leave nothing out. I wish to hear everything."

The hair on Matt's neck began to prickle, the same as it always did when he was in danger. Tall Tree had called it his sixth sense. "Never ignore the feeling, Matt," Tall Tree had said. "It is a sign that the grandparents are trying to warn you."

With an unsteady hand, Matt set down his vodka glass and began to speak. "At first, I did not realize that the princess was on the train. It was only after we had come to a stop because of the rocks the outlaws had put on the tracks—"

An impatient Igor said, "Tell me about the other woman, this Sarah Macauley, the one who survived. Was she beautiful? Did she look like this?" Igor pulled the locket from the small box on the table and opened it, pushing the small miniature closer for Matt to see.

Staring at him was a replica of Sarah Macauley—her copper-colored hair, her flawless white skin, and her overwhelming eyes. Something was wrong. The Russian would never have in his possession an exquisite miniature of an obscure little schoolteacher. This was his wife, Anya. He had set a trap for Matt, trying to cloud his brain with unaccustomed vodka before he grilled him.

"But this is your wife, is it not?" Matt asked.

"Yes," Igor admitted. "Are you certain this is the one you buried?" he demanded.

"I am certain."

Igor still was not satisfied. "What did the other woman look like?" he demanded.

Matt smiled. "A busy man has little time for an ugly woman," he confided. "Especially one with weak eyes. As well as I can remember, she has dark hair."

Matt knew that he had to get out of the suite before he suffocated. His brain was impaired. He could not logically deal with the knowledge that the woman he'd fallen in love with, had saved from the snowstorm, and had asked to marry, was already a married woman. At that moment, he knew he could not be responsible for his behavior if he remained a moment longer in her husband's suite.

"Your Highness," Matt said, swaying as he stood, "I have drunk far too much tonight. If you'll forgive me, I need to go to my room. We'll have to continue this conversation tomorrow."

Igor nodded to Torzhok. "My man will help you."

"Thank you."

With Torzhok holding his arm, Matt lurched toward the door. Taking a tighter grip, Torzhok said, "Steady, Mr. Bergen. I will get you safely downstairs."

A few minutes later, Torzhok returned to his master.

"You saw him to his suite?" Igor inquired.

"Yes, my prince. He barely made it to the chamber pot, where he was sick. But he will sleep off the effects of the vodka tonight, I'm sure. He'll be ready to negotiate tomorrow."

"We must remember not to give him so much liquor next time."

"No. He does not have your capacity," Torzhok said, looking admiringly at the prince.

Igor took it as a compliment. "And now, send the Ferret to the docks, Torzhok," he ordered, speaking of one of the other servants. "I have need of a woman."

"Yes, my prince."

Once in his room, Matt had made a disgusting display, so that Torzhok would leave as soon as possible. With his ear to the door, he had listened until Torzhok's footsteps vanished.

Now he lay in darkness, thinking. Something more was at stake here than a bereaved husband wanting to know about his wife's last hours. Thinking of Sarah—or rather, Anya—Matt felt betrayed. Maybe Igor and Anya deserved each other.

What if next time he told the man that his wife was

very much alive? With visions of Sarah haunting his thoughts, Matt Bergen finally drifted into a troubled sleep—unaware of the muffled scream that came from the suite above.

Chapter 35

By midmorning, Matt felt much better. He had risen early, eaten lightly, and gone for a long walk, preferring fresh air to the smoke-filled club downstairs, where the male guests had gathered to read their newspapers and enjoy their cigars after their bountiful breakfasts in the public dining room.

On returning to the hotel, he saw Manley, the clerk, signaling to him. "Mr. Bergen, I have a message for you." The clerk reached into the pigeonhole and pulled out a stiff white envelope, his name written in a florid script. Stuffing it into his coat pocket, Matt continued to his suite.

He still had not come to a decision concerning Anya. The previous evening, his emotions had been mixed— wanting to protect her, yet feeling betrayed by her. He supposed it was always that way when a man realized he had not been the first to love a certain woman. But what would happen to her if her husband discovered she was still alive? Anya had gone to great lengths to escape him. She must have had a good reason.

Taking the key, he unlocked the suite door and walked inside, where he removed his coat. As he dropped it across a nearby chair, he retrieved the unopened envelope. Certain that it was from the prince, he was in no hurry to read it. Instead he laid it on the desk and turned his attention to financial matters—double-checking the costs of transporting the silk cargo the next day.

A little later, Matt heard a knock at his door. "Come in," he called. "The door's not locked." When he looked up again, he saw Igor's man, Torzhok standing before him. "Yes?"

"I have a message from my prince. He hopes that you have recovered and wishes to know if you would dine with him again this evening at nine o'clock."

Matt remained seated at the desk. "I would prefer it if he would dine with me, instead, at the same hour. Say, here in my suite?"

Torzhok hesitated. That morning, the Ferret had barely escaped by the balcony before the chambermaid walked in to clean Matt's suite. Since the Ferret had found nothing, he planned to come back during dinner that night. But it would be impossible if Matt Bergen were entertaining. "I will convey your wishes to my prince, and let you know within the hour. Thank you, Mr. Bergen."

Once the door had closed, Matt's attention returned to his financial affairs. But then he remembered the unopened envelope. It could not be from Igor, for he had just sent his manservant with a message. Puzzled, Matt slit open the envelope with his pocket knife and began to read.

He smiled when he saw that it was an invitation to tea that afternoon with one very rich Belle Walsh and her eligible daughter, Hettie. He had no misconceptions as to the reason. Invitations like this—from mothers—came along at regular intervals. Ordinarily he declined them all. But the more he thought about this particular invitation, the more appealing it became. He'd seen the young woman with her mother in the garden, and there was no denying that she was a pretty little thing. If he really wanted to get even with Anya, this was the better way to do it. For his purposes, Hettie Walsh would do as well as any other. Quickly making up his mind, he took a piece of stationery and proceeded to write a note of acceptance.

"He's coming," Belle said, smiling as she looked at the reply the bellman had just delivered. "Hettie, you must wear your prettiest frock—blue, I think. Men always like blue. And we'll get Lottie to use the curling tongs on your hair. Now, let's see what we can order for tea. . . . Oh, I think I'll go downstairs immediately and talk with the chef. It's a good thing that I went ahead and reserved the private conservatory off the east gallery yesterday."

Belle gave her daughter no opportunity to disagree with her plans. She left the room immediately. "Lock the door behind me, Hettie."

"Yes, Mama."

* * *

The small conservatory was pleasant, lush with green plants, a fountain in the shape of a boy with fish, and several comfortable benches. Three elaborately carved, wrought-iron chairs flanked the round table covered with a freshly starched linen tablecloth. Farther away stood a tea table, presided over by two waiters.

"I hope the accommodations are to your satisfaction, madame," the rotund chef said, watching Belle lift the mosquito netting from each tray to inspect the food.

"You're sure this is enough?" she inquired.

"Oh, yes, madame. I served twice your number with the same amount of food last week. But, if by any chance you should begin to run low, Rhys here will replenish the trays from the kitchen."

A satisfied Belle nodded, dismissing the chef. "Come, Hettie, and sit on the bench by the fountain. But don't get your dress wet."

"Yes, Mama. Would you like to come and sit with me?"

"No, I'll station myself closer to the door, where I can watch for Mr. Bergen."

Belle did not have long to wait. Matt Bergen showed up promptly at half past three. "Good afternoon, Mrs. Walsh."

"Oh, Mr. Bergen, I'm so pleased that you could join us for tea this afternoon," she greeted him, frankly assessing his entire person. She was already aware of his wealth. But only having seen him from a distance, without her glasses, she was not prepared for such inordinate good looks. Immediately she began to think of the fine-looking blond children Hettie would produce, with Matt as their father. "You must meet my daughter, Hettie. She's just returned from a fancy school in Switzerland that her papa sent her to."

"My pleasure," he murmured between his teeth as he followed the plump, eager woman along the curved brick path to the fountain.

As if she were pushing back the foliage in a jungle for him to get a look at a rare, tropical species, Belle brushed aside the leaves of a potted aspidistra plant beside the bench and said, "Mr. Bergen, may I present my daughter, Hettie. Hettie, this is the Mr. Bergen I was telling you about."

God, what a tedious afternoon this was going to be, Matt thought. Standing before the young woman, with her mother looking on, he felt like a whooping crane being asked to perform a mating dance.

Hettie stood, in all her azure blue splendor, and extended her hand. "How do you do, Mr. Bergen."

He smiled, took her hand, and entered into the game.

In the Dakota Territory, Stretch Hawkins, foreman to Amelia Chaboillez, rode hard to the edge of the ranch boundary. He had been furious ever since he'd eavesdropped on the conversation in the turret between Amelia and the schoolteacher. It had mattered little to him that she was posing as someone else. Many people in the West lived under assumed names. What had rankled him was that Amelia had been taken in by the woman and had changed her will to leave everything to the teacher.

Stretch had worked too many years to allow this to happen. Years ago, he'd thought he might have a chance with Mellie, even though she was interested in Matt. He'd counted on the feud to keep them apart, not knowing until the last minute that they'd decided to elope. Seeing his plans disintegrate, he'd done the only thing possible. With Henri away, and the storm coming up, it had been so easy to arrange the accidental drowning before Matt got to her. Then, with his bad heart, Henri did not present a problem. Stretch only had to wait two more years for the man to drop dead, naturally. But in the meantime, he'd made himself indispensable to Amelia.

Blast the woman for being so obstinate! He would have made her a good husband, if she hadn't been so concerned about the age thing. Now, with her latest actions, she'd left him no choice. Amelia had to go, like her daughter. Then Sarah, or Anya, would be the last one standing in his way.

Stretch drew up to the large mound of rocks and waited for Driscoll, the outlaw. It was past time to put their plans into operation.

Back in Seattle, Belle Walsh was happy. Hettie was getting along famously with Matt Bergen. The tea had been a decided success.

"Does your husband shoot, Mrs. Walsh?" Matt inquired.

"Well, Logan has other interests, too," she hedged, not knowing where the conversation was going.

"Papa is so softhearted," Hettie explained. "He can't stand the sight of bl—"

Belle suddenly nudged her daughter under the table. "Why do you ask, Mr. Bergen?"

"Montana still has wild mountain sheep. I thought if the three of you had time to visit my ranch this summer, then I could arrange a hunting party."

"Logan would absolutely adore that, Mr. Bergen, I can tell you. And Hettie and I would be pleased to see where you live." Belle moved in, as Matt knew she would, pinning him down to a specific time for the visit.

With that taken care of, Matt stood. "I'll write your husband immediately," he said. "Now I must go. But let me tell you how much I've enjoyed getting to know you." He looked at Belle, and then lingeringly at Hettie.

"We'll see you at the end of July, Mr. Bergen," a smiling Belle said, watching the tall, handsome man leave the conservatory. As soon as he was gone, she turned to the waiter. "Oh, Rhys," she said. "Fix me a plate of those sandwiches to take upstairs. I'll be able to eat them better with my corset off."

"Yes, madame."

Belle beamed at her daughter and squeezed her hand without saying anything. The man had wasted no time. He was clearly interested in Hettie. Why else would he have invited them to his ranch? She would have to leave for Denver immediately, so Logan could begin practicing killing things without flinching at the sight of the poor dead creatures.

"Come, Hettie, we have packing to do. We'll be going home tomorrow."

"I'm glad, Mama. I've missed Papa so much."

When Matt returned to his suite late that afternoon, it was in shambles. Someone had thoroughly searched the rooms, going through the drawers and closets, and even slitting the sides of his leather bag. Lucky for him that he had placed his strongbox in the vault downstairs for safekeeping. Otherwise, there would be nothing left to pay the guards or his hotel bill.

He cautiously checked each room to make sure no one was hiding. Noticing the door to the balcony slightly ajar, he closed and locked it before notifying housekeeping that he wished to have his rooms straightened and all linens replaced. But he knew now to be on his guard. Someone wanted something from him. Probably Igor. If he only knew what it was . . .

That evening, Matt prepared for the dinner meeting with the prince. He had chosen much lighter fare and not so many different kinds of liquor. "Changin' liquor in the middle of the evenin' is just like changin' horses in midstream. If you want to be safe, stay with the same one and you won't git throwed." He could hear Prairie Dog now, just as clearly as if he were standing beside him at the bar in the Medora saloon. How he missed the man and his homespun wisdom. But even Prairie Dog had been swoozled by Anya. And that was hard to do.

Several hours later, when dinner was over, a still-wary Matt sat opposite Igor. "I'm sorry I can't tell you any more about your wife. The report of the accident is on file with the Northern Pacific and the territorial governor. The outlaw we think is responsible is still at large, although many of his men have already been hanged."

A strange flicker passed across Igor's face as he narrowed his eyes and waited for Matt to broach the subject of the papers and the sum of money required to get them back. Matt pretended not to notice, choosing instead to wait it out until Igor voiced what he was really after. Matt saw the impatience and ire gradually build, until the prince could contain himself no longer.

"All right, Mr. Bergen. I believe you have something of mine. I am prepared to be generous with you. Shall we begin our bargaining now?"

"I'm afraid I don't understand, sir."

"Of course you do. The papers, man. The ones you found in my wife's luggage and kept for yourself."

Matt's eyes blazed in anger. "You're mistaken. I returned everything that was in your wife's possession," he stated. "There is nothing to bargain."

Seeing Matt's anger—and realizing that he might be telling the truth—Igor softened his attack. "My wife took something very valuable that belonged to me. Imagine yourself in my boots, Mr. Bergen. When the papers were not in her effects, I assumed that she was either still alive, or that someone had stolen them. If I have offended you, then please accept my apology."

Matt nodded, his temper still at a boil. "May I offer you one last drink before you *leave*?"

Torzhok made a choking sound, and Igor's mouth

dropped open. Not since Minsk had anyone been so uncivil to Prince Igor.

"It's late and I must go. Come, Torzhok, and light my way upstairs."

"Yes, my prince." Torzhok grabbed a lamp and followed the Russian. The door reverberated from the slam. Matt, realizing he'd made a formidable enemy, wasted no time in gathering his belongings. Rather than staying at the hotel, he would feel safer spending his remaining night in the silk train.

Chapter 36

After Anya had closed the school for the summer and sent her end-of-the-year report to the superintendent in charge of territorial education, she packed her belongings and moved to Sweet Grass Ranch until fall.

How different this second summer had started. The previous summer and on through the winter, she'd worried for fear that Igor would find her. Now she felt much more relaxed. She would not be surprised if he'd already left Alaska for Russia, thinking that she was no longer a danger to him. And she had Amelia to thank—for sheltering her when she needed it most, sending the inquisitive foreigner on his way without discovering her, and giving her a future. She would never be able to take Mellie's place, but Anya vowed that she would do her utmost to bring comfort to Amelia.

Sitting in her private living room in the turret, she thought of Matt. Her greatest sadness was her alienation from him. Being in his arms had awakened her, making her realize that she was capable of great love. But because she was who she was, Anya would have to forget him, to channel her passion in other directions.

Breaking into Anya's reverie, Amelia called out, "Sarah, are you busy?"

"No. Come in, Amelia."

The woman opened the door. In a pleased voice she said, "Get on your riding outfit. Diego has just brought word that one of the cows on the north range has had twins."

"Isn't that unusual?" Anya asked.

"Yes. If we want to save them, we'll have to bring all three back to the barn."

Anya stood and walked to the closet; Amelia took a seat and waited for the girl to put on her riding clothes.

The same afternoon the two women rode toward the north range in search of the calves, Matt was returning East on the silk train. The Pinkerton men, whom Matt had hired, were guarding the cargo well. No outlaws had sabotaged the tracks thus far, and for the past three days the food in the dining car, cooked by one of the regular chefs, had tasted much better than Kwa-ling's usual fare. Even the approaching rail trestle, long repaired, presented no problem. So the journey should have been much more enjoyable for Matt. But it wasn't.

Over and over, he kept recalling the previous trip—when so many things had gone wrong and the real Sarah Macauley had been killed by the outlaws. Yet because of his recent encounter with Igor, he was now seeing the events in a new light. He must have been blind not to realize what was going on. How could he have taken Anya at face value, believing her to be the teacher, when, at every turn, she had given him such obvious clues as to her true identity?

But it had taken a lot of guts, he had to admit, to give up the small fortune in her purse, her social position, and the magnificent clothes in her valise. Despite himself, he laughed, remembering the oversized dress that had fallen off one shoulder, the monstrosity of a hat he'd made her throw away. It must have been even more difficult for her at school, assuming Sarah's responsibility to teach the children of Medora.

Matt could forgive all her deceptions—except one. But with Hettie Walsh's visit, Anya would see that he had already forgotten that night in the cabin and was now interested in someone else, equally beautiful.

Looking out the window, Matt noticed that the train was approaching the grave site where Sarah Macauley had been buried. On impulse, he left his private car, hoisted himself up to the catwalk, and crawled along the length of the train until he dropped into the cab.

"I want you to stop about a half mile up the track," he said to the surprised engineer. "You'll see a pile of rocks on the left."

"Is anything wrong?" the Pinkerton man riding in the engine asked.

"No. I need to check on a grave."

"Won't take long, will it, Mr. Bergen?" the engineer asked. "I'm just about an hour and a half ahead of another train."

"Fifteen minutes, at the most," Matt assured him. "That's all I need."

The engineer stuck his head out of the cab and watched for the rocks to come into view. With his hand on the brake line, he began to slow, the wheels groaning against the iron tracks.

"There it is," Matt said, pointing to the terrain about forty feet from the roadbed.

Within a few minutes, the entire train had come to a stop, causing the Pinkerton guards, immediately alert, to grab their weapons to defend the raw silk.

Matt jumped from the cab and began to stride toward the grave site. From a distance, the first thing he noticed was that the heavy rocks he'd piled on Sarah's grave were now strewn helter-skelter. Frowning, he continued walking until he stared down into the open pit. The bones had been dug up, not by an animal, but by human hands. Whoever had done it had not bothered to rebury them.

Sarah Macauley deserved better than this desecration. Making up his mind, Matt suddenly called out to a nearby guard, "I'll need a shovel and a box. Quick. We don't have much time."

Shortly before the fifteen minutes were up, Matt and the guard returned to the silk train, where the remains were stored in one of the boxcars. The cemetery on the hill overlooking the Double B Ranch would be safe from vandals.

As the silk train gathered steam and moved down the track again, Matt returned to his private car. He recalled how the Russian prince had been so insistent that Matt send him a map indicating the exact location of his wife's grave. After meeting Igor and his henchman, Torzhok, in Seattle, he suspected they had been the culprits, even though he had no way of proving it.

But with the wrong woman buried in the grave, they would not have found what they were looking for. Once convinced that Anya was dead, they would naturally suspect him, since he'd had access to her belongings. If Anya still had the papers, he hoped they were worth the risk. In his estimation, the prince had been more than willing to kill for them. For her own safety, Anya had better hope and pray her husband never found out she was still alive.

Toward the last of July, an impatient Stretch Hawkins decided he could wait no longer. He had grown lax, and Amelia was becoming suspicious, especially with the disappearance of the twin calves. He had not known that Diego had found them first and alerted Amelia.

"I can see how a mountain lion could have gotten one of them," Amelia had said. "But to have both disappear without a trace is highly suspicious." She had looked at him in an accusing manner, dismissing his lame explanation.

He would have to get her away from the house, somewhere on the range where Diego and the woman who called herself "Sarah" couldn't find her. But first, he had to set up an alibi for himself.

Three days later, as soon as they'd finished their early morning conference, Stretch said, "Amelia, there's a little piece of property being put up for auction on the courthouse steps in Bismarck tomorrow. I'd like a chance to bid on it, if you can spare me for the day."

Surprised, Amelia said, "That's fine, Stretch. You haven't had a day off in a long time."

"I'll more than likely have to spend the night."

"Then while you're in the city, you can do an errand for me."

A cautious Stretch said, "What's that?"

She lowered her voice to keep from being overheard. "Straight down from the capitol there's a monument maker and jeweler named Edwards. I'd like you to take a brooch to him and ask him to tighten the stones."

"I'll do that, Amelia."

"It's for Sarah's birthday," she added, "so I'd like it back within two weeks."

The next day, even before the sun came up, Stretch left the ranch and rode his horse toward Medora. In his pocket, he carried the brooch for the jeweler and also a note for Amelia, to be delivered a few hours later. He'd disguised his writing, pretending to be an unknown informant, requesting Amelia to come alone at noon that day to the arroyo where Mellie had drowned. There, he would give her information—proving that Matt had killed Mellie before she was actually found in the water.

If that would not bring her, nothing would.

One of Driscoll's men was waiting for Stretch several miles away near the fork. "Here's the letter," Stretch said. "Wait until you hear the train whistle, then ride in and leave it at the kitchen door—where Clara will be sure to find it. Then, ride out as fast as you can."

"What if somebody sees me?"

"Most of the hands are out on the range. Diego's the only one you'll have to worry about. Just keep your hat brim low, and pull your bandanna high around your neck. And don't linger."

Stretch hurried on, arriving in Medora with barely enough time to stable his horse and get to the station to buy a ticket.

"One round-trip ticket to Bismarck," he said, pushing his money through the slot.

"You staying long, Stretch?" the stationmaster asked.

"Just overnight. I'll be back tomorrow."

The train, crowded with passengers from Montana, pulled out from the station. Stretch finally found a seat in the last day coach. He spoke to no one. Soon he pulled out his bag of tobacco and a cigarette paper, rolled it, and struck a match. With the cigarette in his hand, he stood and sauntered toward the open door to the outside platform.

There, he looked out over the terrain, waiting for some of Driscoll's men, dressed as Indians, to appear on the tracks ahead. Their appearance would assure that no one would be watching him as he jumped from the platform and rolled down the knoll. The timing had to be perfect, the train slowing at that particular spot, for there would be no other opportunity on the wide, flat plains ahead.

The excited voices of some of the passengers told him that Driscoll had kept his bargain. "Look! Indians! Do you think they'll cause trouble?"

The train whistle gave a warning; the engine slowed. With all attention diverted to the track ahead, Stretch crouched and then fell from the train, his extra layer of clothing helping to keep him free of serious abrasions.

He lay still, waiting for the train to speed up as the Indians moved off the track. As soon as the last car had disappeared, Driscoll, hiding behind the knoll, came into view.

"Good mornin', Stretch. My, that was a mighty fine fall. If the train had been goin' any faster, you mighta broke your neck."

"What do you want, Driscoll? An extra bonus for doing your job?"

"Maybe."

"We'll talk about that later. You have a horse for me?"

"Yep." Driscoll brought forward one of the ugliest horses that Stretch had ever seen.

Immediately Stretch complained. "Couldn't you find a better horse than that for me to ride?"

"He's ugly, that's for sure. But don't let his markings fool you. He's the fastest thing I got."

Still grumbling, Stretch mounted the horse, and, with some further instructions for Driscoll, he began to gallop back across the prairie . . . in the direction of Sweet Grass Ranch and the dry arroyo.

* * *

For the fourth time, Amelia read the letter Clara had found. In the past hour, she'd also changed her mind four times, deciding first to meet the informant, then deciding to ignore the letter. Soon she would have to make up her mind one way or the other.

Could it be a trap? She didn't like the idea of riding into an ambush. If someone actually had information that would prove her daughter's death had not been an accident, why would that person wait five years before revealing it?

Amelia reread the letter for the fifth time. "Come alone, and do not tell anyone." She finally made up her mind. She would go, but she'd be a fool not to let someone know where she was going.

Hurriedly she sat down at her desk and penned a note to Anya. "If I'm not back by one o'clock, then get Diego to come looking for me." She put the sealed envelope near Anya's place at the dining table, where she would be sure to find it at lunch. Walking to the stables, she saddled her horse, slung her rifle across the pommel of her saddle, and set out in the direction of the arroyo.

Anya, busy painting a china plate as a surprise for Amelia, was unaware that the woman had left the house.

Chapter 37

"I'm glad you decided to come, Amelia," a familiar voice behind her intoned. "Don't bother trying to get to your rifle. Just step away from your horse and walk toward the bank. I'll tell you when to stop."

"You won't get away with this, Stretch," she said. "Somebody will find out."

He ignored her reply. "All right. Stop, and turn around."

Amelia obeyed him. She stared at the man who had been her foreman for fifteen years. At his side was the strange horse that she and Diego had seen the day her wheat field was set afire. Now she knew her suspicions had been correct. The man she'd trusted for so long was mixed up with the outlaws. "Why, Stretch?" she managed to say.

"Why?" he repeated. "Because time is running out. I've waited for fifteen years for this land, and that's long enough."

Amelia was reconciled to her own death. But she had to stall Stretch, to give Diego a chance to catch him. "Are you planning to kill me?" she asked, looking directly into his eyes.

Her words brought a momentary regret. "There's no

other way. But it's your own fault, Amelia. You should have married me when I asked you. I would have made a good husband."

"Marry the murderer of my own child?"

He did not deny her accusation. "You've blamed Matt all these years. You'd never have found out what actually happened."

"But I deserve to know the truth now, for old times' sake, Stretch," she argued. "Even a man waiting to be hanged gets one last request."

"Did you tell anybody where you were going?"

"No."

He looked at the sun high in the sky. "I reckon I have a few extra minutes before the next train comes along."

"I'm feeling a little weak. I'd like to sit down here on the bank while we talk."

"Suit yourself."

A few feet away, a cautious Stretch, with Amelia's rifle in his hands, also sat down. From his position, he was able to see anyone who might decide to ride in that direction from the ranch. His ego allowed him to be generous in answering Amelia's questions. After all, she wasn't going anywhere. And nobody would suspect him. He'd planned the perfect alibi.

Everyone knew how bitter Amelia had been since Mellie's death. When she was finally found in the arroyo, dead by her own rifle, people would assume that she had returned to the scene on the anniversary of the accident and done herself in.

* * *

At the ranch, Anya put away her paintbrushes and washed her hands in the basin, for the sound of Clara's bell told her that lunch was ready.

She hurried from her private quarters, down the long hallway, to the parlor. There, a steady breeze blew through the open windows, lifting the delicate lace curtains. Anya sat down and waited for Amelia. The bell rang again. After a number of minutes had passed and Amelia still had not appeared, she left the parlor to consult with Clara, who always took it personally when a meal was late in being served.

"If Amelia's goin' to be so contrary, that doesn't mean you have to eat your food cold, too, Miss Sarah. Go on into the dinin' room, and I'll serve you."

"I'm sure she'll be here soon," Anya assured her. Nevertheless, she followed Clara's instructions, for even Amelia acknowledged Clara's complete jurisdiction when it came to the kitchen.

As she sat down at her place, she saw the letter addressed to her in Amelia's handwriting. By the time Clara appeared, Anya had pushed her chair from the table. "Clara," she said, "Amelia's gone to the arroyo to meet someone. While I change and load my pistol, fly to the stables and get Diego to saddle up two horses."

"You think she's in danger?"

"Yes."

Clara set down the plate of food and ran for the door, her apron strings flapping behind her. "Diego!" she shouted.

* * *

Disobeying Amelia's request to wait for an hour, Anya and Diego raced toward the arroyo. The hooves of the horses pounded the dry earth, scattering the dust, putting scavenging birds to flight, and sending small animals into their holes. Clara's lament echoed in Anya's ears. "I knew that letter left on the doorstep this mornin' spelled trouble."

In the distance, Anya could finally see a stand of cottonwood trees. "How much farther? she shouted.

"Just beyond the trees," Diego shouted back.

At the arroyo, Stretch looked up. Coming across the prairie were two horsemen, riding at breakneck speed. "You lied to me, Amelia," he accused. "You told someone where you were going. But they won't get here in time to save you."

Amelia said nothing. Still proud, she would not give him the satisfaction of seeing her run. She merely watched Stretch lift the rifle and aim it.

A shot rang out, then a second one, causing Anya's heart to lurch. "Look, Diego. That horse. Someone is running away."

It did not take acute vision for Diego to see the horse with the strange markings. But his poor eyesight did fail to help him recognize its rider. Digging his spurs into his horse's flank, he wheeled in the direction of the fleeing rider, while Anya continued toward the banks of the arroyo.

"Amelia!" she shouted. "Can you hear me? Amelia, where are you?"

Anya finally saw her friend at the bottom of the gulch, in the dry creek bed that had lost all memory of spring rains. Tumbling down the bank, with her descent slowed only by an occasional scrub cedar, Anya reached the still figure.

"Amelia?" She began to cry at the sight of the white-haired woman with the mortal wound to her chest.

"Anya?" Amelia's eyes fluttered open. "You're in danger, Anya," she said in a weak voice. "You must go to Matt. He will help you."

"Who did this to you, Amelia?" she demanded.

The woman did not seem to hear her. Dazed, Amelia had her own priorities. "You remember, I told you once that we both had secrets to keep? Now I must share mine."

"Tell me who shot you, Amelia," she demanded again.

But Amelia paid no attention. "Before Mellie was born, I fell in love with Matt's father, even though I was married to Henri. We had a brief affair, and nine months later, Mellie arrived." Amelia coughed, then continued in a weaker voice. "Henri never said anything, although, at times, I thought he suspected. But he accepted Mellie as his own.

"When she fell in love with Matt, I knew they could never marry. So I used the feud as an excuse to keep them apart."

"Why are you telling me this, when I want to—"

"He loves you now, Anya. That's the important thing." Amelia's voice strained to be heard. "But my enemy is your enemy, too."

"Who is it, Amelia?" Anya leaned closer to hear the rasping, wheezing voice. "Who did this terrible deed?"

"It was . . ." Amelia's eyes fluttered and closed; a small, peaceful sigh escaped her throat. From the nearby cottonwood tree, a bird answered and then flew from the tree, soaring and sailing upon the sudden wind gust that swept down the arroyo.

A few minutes later, Anya's sobs told Diego that Amelia was dead. "The man got away," he said, looking down from the bank.

"Oh, how I wish Stretch hadn't left this morning!" Anya cried. "We need him so much."

Diego slid down the bank and gazed sorrowfully at Amelia.

"She spoke a few words, you know, before she died," Anya told him. "I don't think she recognized who shot her. But she told me to trust Matt."

"Then the feud is over. Do as she said—go tell Matt what's happened. I'll put Miss Amelia's body on her horse and take her back to the ranch."

Pushing Dreamer hard, Anya rode over familiar territory, past the boundary cabin and onto Bergen property. At times the tears obscured her vision, but she brushed them aside, praying for the ponderosa pine and stone ranch house to come into sight.

Fifteen minutes later, she saw the clearing and the steep-pitched roof of the Double B Ranch. She didn't take time to ride to the side. She slid from her horse and ran onto the front porch, where the two carved posts guarded the double doors.

"Kwa-ling!" she shouted, knocking at the door. "Kwa-ling!"

Belle Walsh, seated in the front parlor with Hettie, was startled by the insistent knock. "Heavens! Who could be makin' such a noise in the middle of the day?"

"I don't know. But whoever it is sounds as if she's in trouble," Hettie replied.

"Then I'd better go and see. Stay behind me, girl. We're not still in Denver, you know."

Belle warily ambled to the door and opened it. Standing before her was a disheveled hoyden, her wild, copper-colored hair blowing unchecked around her tear-stained face. "Yes?"

"I'm from the next ranch. Something terrible has happened and I must see Matt. Is he here?"

"It's not Indians, is it?" a suddenly fearful Hettie asked.

"No. There's been an accident," the woman answered.

"Matt isn't here," Belle informed her. "He and my husband Logan have gone on a shooting expedition to Montana and won't be back for several more days. But come in. You look exhausted. I expect you could do with a glass of lemonade."

"Thank you, Mrs. . . . ?"

"Walsh. And this is my daughter, Hettie. We're from Denver. Mr. Bergen invited us to see his ranch before . . ." She smiled as she allowed the sentence to remain unfinished. "He and Hettie are such good friends, you know."

"I'm Sarah Macauley, the schoolteacher in Medora."

"Then do come in and have a seat. Hettie, honey, go

and get that heathen in the kitchen to fix us all some lemonade."

"Yes, Mama."

Anya sat down in the chair offered her. She had not realized how weak she felt. Belle Walsh's droning voice seemed so far away.

"I'll be glad when Matt returns," Belle confided. "He's left the ugliest man I've ever seen in charge of the ranch."

"Travis?" Anya inquired.

"I believe that's his name. Matt took another cowboy by the name of Snake Man with him. He's supposed to be a good buffalo hunter, even though he has only one eye. I hope Matt's right, since my Logan needs somebody reliable to protect him."

Hettie returned to the parlor. "The lemonade will be ready in a few minutes," she announced, taking her seat beside her mother.

When Kwa-ling entered with the tray holding the pitcher and the three glasses, his eyes lit up as he recognized Anya. "Good afternoon, missee," he said.

"I'm glad to see you again, Kwa-ling."

"Something bad happen?" he inquired.

But before Anya could answer, Belle rebuked him sharply. "No conversation, Kwa-ling. Just set the tray down and go back to the kitchen."

Anya did not linger. As soon as she had finished the lemonade, she left. Mounting her horse, she trotted to the side porch, where she knew Kwa-ling would be waiting for her. Seeing him just inside the door, she said, "Amelia's dead. She was shot at the arroyo. Diego and I saw the man ride away. Since Stretch has gone to Bismarck, I didn't know who else to turn to."

"I send word to Lynx. He get up posse to chase culprit. But be careful yourself, missee."

"I will. Thank you, Kwa-ling." Then Anya asked, "Is Matt going to marry this Hettie Walsh?"

"I hope not, missee."

Late the next afternoon, as Stretch stepped from the train, a crowd of cowboys gathered about him. "Bad news, Stretch. Amelia Chaboillez was shot and killed yesterday. Lynx Mulligan got a posse together. They found the horse this mornin', but not the man."

Stretch was relieved, although his face didn't show it. He hadn't been absolutely sure that Amelia was completely dead when he'd ridden away. Pretending shock, he said, "How did it happen?"

"She got ambushed at the arroyo," the informant answered. "Guess you could kick yourself, Stretch, for bein' away when she needed you."

With the crowd following him to the livery stable, the foreman took long, angry strides. He struck his fist against his leather holster. With an anguished voice, he said, "I told Amelia it wasn't a good time for me to be off the ranch. But she insisted. She wanted to make sure the jeweler in Bismarck reworked one of her brooches in time for Sarah Macauley's birthday."

"Did Amelia have any relatives to leave the ranch to, Stretch?"

"No."

"Then I wonder who'll try to buy it?"

"Matt Bergen, maybe," Stretch answered. "He's always wanted it. Wouldn't be surprised if Matt did her in."

"Oh, he's still in Montana. So it couldn't have been him."

At the livery stable, the crowd watched Stretch saddle up and ride out of Medora in the direction of Sweet Grass Ranch.

"There goes a heartbroken man," the more vocal spokesman said. "He could never do enough for 'er." Agreeing, the others followed him to the saloon to continue the conversation.

"Won't seem the same around here, without 'er."

"That's for sure."

The cowboys raised their mugs and drank to the stubborn pioneer of the plains, Amelia Chaboillez.

Chapter 38

After Amelia was buried, with ranchers for miles around attending the funeral, the citizens of Medora discovered that the woman had left Sweet Grass Ranch to Sarah Macauley. The people who came into the post office were just as eager to discuss this latest development as the ones in the saloons.

"I can't believe it, either," Caulk agreed with Tom Meacham, the livery stable owner, not long after the news had spread. "I know Miss Amelia set great store by her, but it's not like she's blood kin."

"I hear she's already resigned as schoolteacher for the comin' year. Cyrus wasn't much for goin' to school, but even *he's* sorry she won't be returnin'. You know who they got to take her place?"

"Not yet."

At the Sweet Grass Ranch, Anya was aware of the talk in the town. She had tried to ignore the less flattering comment that she appeared to have wormed her way into Amelia's affections just so she'd be left the ranch. She knew it wasn't true, but there was nothing she could do to convince the few who chose to believe it.

Instead she worked hard, depending on Stretch to guide her as she learned about ranching. Things had not gone well, with many of the cattle disappearing. But since Amelia had chosen her as a steward for her land, she was determined to be more vigilant.

"Stretch, I want you to hire more men to patrol the boundaries at night. And we might as well buy a reaper. I intend to put more land into wheat, since that seems to be where the money is this year."

So with one hand, Stretch helped her, while his other hand stole from her. He was gratified that she'd had nothing to do with Matt Bergen, returning from the hunting in Montana after the funeral. But Stretch's attempt to fire Diego had not worked.

"No. Sweet Grass is the man's home. We're his family," Anya had argued. "Even though he can afford another place, I want to keep him on the ranch, just as Amelia would have."

Stretch did not argue. It wouldn't be long now before he made his final move. His negotiations with the Russian prince were going along quite well. Igor was not interested in taking over property in the middle of the West. He would allow Stretch to buy it, even though the land was entailed and couldn't be touched as long as Anya was alive. That meant only one thing. The woman would not be living long, once her husband got to her.

Poor Amelia. She thought she'd been so clever. But in the end, she'd signed another woman's death warrant as well. While he waited, Stretch realized he had to play his role convincingly, lulling Anya into thinking that he was her best friend.

Late one night, toward the end of summer, a tired Anya blew out her lamp in the turret bedroom and prepared for sleep. She knew the entire house was now hers, but somehow, she had kept putting off moving from the apartment. She felt safe there, not like an interloper, as she did in the other rooms, where Amelia's spirit was strong.

Stretch, watching for the light to go out, whispered to Driscoll from the darkness of the barn, "It won't be long now, before she's asleep. Give her about a half hour. Then you can start."

The torch to be used in the tunnel that connected the barn to the house had already been soaked in kerosene. With Clara and Jamie in the cabin at the edge of the yard, and Diego in the bunkhouse, Anya had to be taken without incident, kidnapped under their very noses, with no sound to alert them.

Prince Igor, and his man, Torzhok, were on their way and would be arriving in two more days. Stretch would meet them in Medora and take them to Driscoll's sod-roofed cabin, which was hidden in the hills. There they would complete their transaction. Then he would be a rich man, owning Sweet Grass Ranch, and the prince would have his wife back, to do with her whatever he wanted.

Finally the half hour was up; it was time to go. The full moon cast its glow over the corral, where a horse suddenly neighed. An owl, who'd made its nest under the eaves of the barn, hooted in answer. Other than that, no sounds disturbed the tranquil night.

Stretch pulled back a hay crib in one of the stalls. Lighting a match, he pointed to the little-used tunnel. "Be careful," he admonished, setting the torch aflame as Driscoll and two of his men moved into the tunnel. Then he settled down, waiting for them to reappear with the woman.

The men crept through the eerie tunnel. Driscoll, who'd always been uncomfortable in dark, enveloping places, swore as a rat crossed his boot. One of the men bumped against him, causing Driscoll to drop the torch. But he quickly picked it up and walked on. Behind him, sparks, encouraged by the draft, smoldered in the straw underfoot. A small flame slowly began to follow his path, fed by the continuous sparks dropping from the burning torch. But the three men did not notice, for the odor of kerosene was strong.

"There it is," one of the men whispered, coming to the door that led into the house. "Stretch said it would take only a push to get it open."

The hinges of the door creaked, despite the recent oiling Stretch had given them. The men quickly stepped inside the hall, leaving the hidden door slightly ajar.

The ornate silver candlesticks on the hallway table were too inviting for one of the men to pass up. He stuffed them under his coat before Driscoll could stop him. "We're here to get the woman. Not rob the house."

"Just a quick look-see," he begged. "Stretch won't know."

"All right. But be quiet. And remember, we all share and share alike." Driscoll did not want to be left out.

A sudden clatter of something falling to the floor in the dining room awoke Anya. She sat up and listened. Aside from the noise, she was also aware of a burning odor. Surely Clara hadn't left anything in the stove oven, but what else could it be?

Anya grabbed her wrapper and ran onto the porch. Flames were already shooting from the roof. "Stretch! Diego!" she shouted. "The house is on fire!"

Within minutes, the yard was filled with Clara and Jamie, Diego, Ward, and all the other hands who'd been asleep in the bunkhouse. They formed a bucket brigade, but the fire roared out of control, lighting up the sky for miles around.

By early morning, a heartsick Anya, her face blackened with soot, stood and surveyed the extensive damage. The magnificent house was gone, burned to the ground, as were the barn and the cabin at the edge of the yard where Clara had lived.

"What are you going to do now, Miss Sarah?" Jamie asked, holding on to her hand. "Where are you going to go?"

"I suppose I'll get a room at the hotel in town for a few days, until I decide what to do."

"You could always go to the boundary cabin."

"Perhaps later," she said, knowing that nothing would induce her to go back there.

"I wish we had room over my papa's store for you," he said.

Anya smiled through her tears. "I'll be all right, Jamie. It takes more than a fire to defeat us, doesn't it?"

"Yes, ma'am."

Anya called for Diego to harness the horses to the carriage. Barefoot, she drew a blanket around her body. While she waited, she turned to her foreman. "I'm relying on you to take care of things for the next few days without me."

"I'll do that, Sarah," he answered. "You can depend on me."

With Clara and Jamie as passengers, and the few belongings they'd been able to save placed in the back of the carriage, Anya left the devastated Sweet Grass Ranch.

Matt Bergen, on his last silk train run, wanted nothing more than to reach Medora and have a nice bath

and steak before going on to Fargo. He didn't know
what was the matter. All enthusiasm and excitement had
gone out of his life.

He'd sent Hettie Walsh back to Denver, for he
couldn't go through with marrying her just to get back
at Anya. She was dull and submissive, and he knew he
wouldn't be able to stand that in a wife. Even Kwa-ling
had been glad to see the family go. As for the filature—
he'd decided to sell it to Jean. The silk industry was in
the Frenchman's blood.

Perhaps he would travel, like Antoine and Medora.
Perhaps spend the coming winter in some warm
climate—Italy or Spain. Or he might even sail to Norway, to see the land of his ancestors and to look up
other blond-haired relatives by the name of Bergen.

By the time he arrived in Medora, the gossips had already gathered. "You'll never guess what happened
while you were gone, Matt. Amelia's place burned to
the ground."

"A pity," was all he answered.

As was her custom, Ruby had his bathwater ready.
Matt settled down for a good soak, ridding himself of
the soot and smoke of the trip. While he lit his cigar,
Ruby scrubbed his back. But something in his face kept
her from idle conversation.

As she turned to leave, she asked, "Do you want your
meal in your room, or downstairs?"

"Up here," he answered.

She nodded and closed the door.

* * *

He slept soundly, undisturbed, until an insistent knock awoke him. "Matt, let us in," Snake Man and Travis urged.

Irritated at being awakened long before the sun was up, a naked Matt stumbled to the door, shoved aside the chair, and motioned for the men to come inside. "You'd better have a mighty good reason for disturbing my sleep."

"We do."

Matt lighted the lamp by the bed and wrapped a sheet around his nakedness. "So?"

"We've just found out who Miss Sarah really is," Travis informed him.

"You're several months too late to surprise me." Matt started to climb back into bed.

"But she's in great danger. Stretch has sold her out to her husband. He'll be here in Medora any minute. We've got to find her and save her, Matt. He's plannin' on killin' her."

"How do you know, Snake Man?" Matt was immediately interested as he listened to his two cowboys.

"You remember you told us to keep particular watch on the north boundary while you was gone?"

Matt nodded.

"Well, it was Gus's turn last night. Only he got sorta drunk and let his campfire go out. In the dark, he overheard Stretch arguin' with a man that turned out to be Driscoll. They've been in cahoots, Matt. That's why so many cattle have been disappearin'."

An impatient Travis took over the story. "They didn't know anybody was around for miles. Gus said he didn't pay much attention to what they was sayin' until Stretch mentioned Miss Sarah's name. He said, 'Go back to robbin' trains and stealin' cattle, Driscoll. I'll take care of the woman myself.' Once they'd gone, Gus realized he'd better ride in and tell somebody."

"Driscoll tried to kidnap Miss Sarah earlier, but he burned down the house instead," Snake Man added. "So we've got to find her and hide her."

"She's here in the hotel," Matt informed them.

Travis groaned. "Then she's doomed. Ain't no sheriff in the world what wouldn't turn a runaway wife over to her husband."

Matt quickly made up his mind. "She won't be here when he arrives."

Relieved, Snake Man said, "I knew you'd think of somethin', Matt."

"While I get dressed, Travis, go down to the station and fire up the engines. The silk train is moving out."

"What about the guards?"

"We won't wait for them. Just wake up the engineer."

"What do you want me to do, Matt?" Snake Man asked.

"Stay here with me. I'm going to need your help."

In the second-story hotel room, with the wooden balcony overlooking the street, Anya slept soundly. She had stayed up far too late, for her brain had been in a whirl, tugging at the events that had happened, trying to fit the pieces of the puzzle together to make some sense.

Finally, in exhaustion, she had given up. Now, in the

early morning hours, she was still sleeping deeply. She had not progressed to that period of twilight sleep so common just before waking.

She did not hear the man hoisting himself to the balcony. She was unaware when he climbed through the window and stood over her bed. Anya's first indication that something was wrong came when a hand covered her mouth and she felt herself encased in her bedclothes, unable to move, unable to speak, or see the man who had invaded her room.

Chapter 39

"I believe you have someone there, Stretch, against her will. Let her go."

Startled to see Matt Bergen emerge from the shadows, with a gun pointed at him, the foreman tightened his hold on the struggling Anya. "Step aside, Matt. You wouldn't dare shoot. You might hit the woman instead." Stretch took several steps, but a second gun, suddenly poked into his back, caused him to falter.

"Put her down, Stretch," Snake Man ordered, pressing his own weapon harder against the man's spine. "She can't protect your back, too. Another step, and I'll shoot you myself."

Stretch knew he was beaten for the moment. He reluctantly gave Anya up to Matt.

"Now just keep walkin'," Snake Man ordered, while Matt, taking only enough time to remove the gag from Anya's mouth, carried her to the waiting horse.

As he began to gallop toward the train station, Anya struggled to free herself. "Be still," Matt ordered. "I'll get you out of these bedclothes once we reach the train."

"What's happening?" she whispered. "Why did Stretch do this to me?"

"He's sold you out to your husband."

"You mean Igor's coming for me?" a terrified Anya asked.

"He's probably less than an hour away."

"Oh, Matt. I wanted to tell you . . ."

"I should have kept the gag on. If you're not careful, you're going to wake the entire town before we get out."

Anya grew quiet.

The noise of building steam indicated that Travis and the engineer had been successful. As soon as Snake Man arrived, they could be on their way.

Tying Stretch to the fence at Antoine's slaughterhouse, where the butchers would find him when they came to work that morning, Snake Man headed out on foot for the station. Within a few minutes, he was running alongside the track. Travis, who'd been watching for him, held out his hand, pulling Snake Man into the rolling cab.

"Well, Stretch should stay put for a while," he said,

grinning at Matt and Anya. "How much time have we got?"

"There's an approaching train—probably Igor's—less than twenty minutes away," Matt said, causing Snake Man to lose his smile.

Jake, the engineer, added, "According to the telegraph, it's got three heavy engines pulling one private Pullman and one dining car."

"But it'll lose some time, stopping in Medora," Matt said. "If they decide to pursue us, they'll have to take on more coal and water. That should give us a slight advantage."

With Matt, Travis, and Snake Man all taking turns shoveling coal and firing up the boiler, the unguarded silk train sped through the open prairie. As the sun came up, bursting on the horizon to the east, Anya, with the bedspread covering her nightgown, kept watch, staring at the track behind them for any sign of Igor.

Driscoll's association with Stretch had not been a profitable one. The man was right. When it came to train robberies and cattle rustlin', he was the best. A pity he hadn't stuck to them, instead of teamin' up to kidnap that woman. But he'd make up for it now. And Matt Bergen, his old enemy, would be the loser this time.

Driscoll set about planting dynamite on the train track. No more hauling of rocks for him. It would be easier just to blow up the engine. Then he and his men could take away the raw silk in wagons and sell it later.

Once he'd finished, he straightened the wires that led

from the track to the detonator he'd hidden behind a large boulder some forty-five feet away. He'd planted enough dynamite on the track to blow up an entire train. Matt wasn't going to win this time.

Patiently Driscoll and his men settled down to watch. To shade himself from the hot, blazing sun, the outlaw had made a shelter from the limbs of scrub pines and an old tarpaulin the color of dirt. He had his canteen of whiskey beside him, too. He drank from it every few minutes, the strong brew relaxing him.

Hidden not far away were the wagons, ready to transport the stolen goods to one of his hideouts.

Lounging in the comfortable Pullman of his private train, a satisfied Igor had just finished his breakfast. He was in a good mood, for he felt he'd already won against the stubborn Anya. Soon now, she would be in his hands. His body trembled in excitement as he contemplated her punishment.

"Will there be anything else, my prince?" Torzhok asked, removing the empty breakfast tray.

"Go onto the platform and watch for the town," he said. "I understand there's a tall chimney that is visible for miles. As soon as you see it, come back inside and load my pistols."

A few minutes later, Torzhok returned. "Medora's in sight," he said, walking to the case that contained Igor's matched weapons. He proceeded to remove them from their velvet encasement, and once they were loaded, he handed them to Igor, who immediately strapped them around his slightly paunchy waist.

As soon as the train slowed and came to a stop, Torzhok rushed to place the step onto the ground for his master. He had entreated Igor to dress conservatively, for he knew, firsthand, how the townspeople treated foreigners dressed differently from them. Igor had only partially heeded him.

If Igor had trouble recognizing Stretch, who had been freed only a few minutes previously, the foreman had no such trouble with Igor. The Russian had worn his black polished boots and his hard-brimmed military cap, so different from the wide sombreros or soft-brimmed Texas hats that most cowboys wore.

Certain that it was the prince, Stretch strode forward to intercept him. He would not be pleased that Anya had escaped. But with the powerful engines at their disposal, they could catch up with the other train in no time, for its speed would be hampered by the boxcars of silk.

"Prince Igor?" Stretch inquired.

"Yes. I am he."

Torzhok, at his side, began to recite his pedigree, but one look from Igor stopped him.

"I'm afraid you'll have to continue the journey farther down the track," Stretch confessed.

"You mean you do not have the princess in custody, as you promised?"

"There's been a slight hitch. But we can catch up with her, once you take on more coal and water. I have it all arranged."

A disgruntled Igor turned on his heel and walked back to his private car.

* * *

The silk train puffed and chugged, demanding more steam to keep up its momentum. Despite their hard work, Matt realized that the other train, far more powerful, might come into view any minute.

A series of lights ahead signaled what he had feared. The engineer, reading the language of lights, said, "Matt, we're being asked to pull to the side track to allow a faster train to get by."

"But that must be the Russian's train," Travis said. "What should we do, Matt?"

"We'll obey the request," he responded. "But only long enough to get rid of the boxcars."

"You're going to abandon a fortune? I can't let you do that for me, Matt," Anya argued.

"You have no say-so in the matter. It's my decision. Jake, pull off just long enough for us to uncouple the cars."

"We're gaining on them," Stretch announced. "Soon now, she'll be in your hands."

"I have waited a long time for this," Igor replied, his good mood restored. He sat, with his head leaning out the window, watching for the other train. "What is that on the side track ahead?" he asked.

Stretch leaned out another window. "My God. Matt's abandoned his silk cargo. There's a fortune there in those boxcars, just waiting for anybody to come along and help himself to it."

Igor's eyes became calculating. He reached up and pulled the emergency brake, causing Torzhok to lose his balance and hit his chin on the floor as the train came to a crunching, groaning halt.

"What did you do that for?" Stretch asked.

"I think we might help ourselves to a few of the box-cars," he answered. "It is only fair that I exact some remuneration from the man for the trouble he's caused me. Besides, Anya cannot escape me now." Looking at Torzhok, he said, "Tell the engineers that I wish at least half the silk train to be attached behind my Pullman."

From Driscoll's lookout, a puff of smoke became visible in the distance. To make sure it was from the train, and not a mirage, he sent Bart to read the rails. Bending over, with his ear to the tracks, the outlaw heard a slight hum and felt the vibration that told of a train drawing near. He raced back to the hiding place. "It's the silk train," he announced. "Should be here in the next few minutes."

"All right, men, take your places," Driscoll ordered, moving to the detonator. He would trust no one but himself to set off the dynamite at the proper time.

Looking toward the west, he saw the train. But as it got nearer, he realized something was wrong. Two engines were linked together, but no boxcars trailed behind. It wasn't the silk train after all. Disappointed, he said, "Guess we'll let this one go by."

The engines passed, and Driscoll went back to waiting. But he sent Bart to the tracks once more. Within a few minutes, Bart came running back up the hill. "There's another train on the tracks," he said. "This time, I know it's the silk train."

Once again, Driscoll took his place at the detonator, his men ready to move out as soon as he ordered.

"There it is," someone whispered.

Driscoll flexed his fingers and then gripped the handle of the detonator box. As the engines reached the planted dynamite, he pushed downward with all his strength. The men around him put their hands over their ears, waiting for the massive explosion. For a few seconds, nothing happened. Had he made an error? The charges should have gone off by now.

Suddenly a massive explosion erupted, shaking the earth, splitting apart the three engines, the dining car, and the Pullman behind it. Iron boiler plates, giant wheels, flew through the air; a bell gave a last clang as it landed on the twisted track and rolled into a deep hole.

Driscoll grinned, despite the ringing in his ears. He'd used enough dynamite to blow up ten trains, causing the mules and horses to whinny in terror. As soon as his men had calmed the animals, they swept down to view the carnage. The occupants of the engines and the Pullman were unrecognizable.

A gloating Driscoll felt a momentary regret that Matt Bergen hadn't known what hit him. But he soon turned his energy to carting off the crates of raw silk.

Ten miles farther to the east, the rails reverberated and the engine threatened to jump the track. Anya and all the other occupants felt the effects of the catastrophe behind them. "What was that?" she asked.

"Sounded like an explosion, or a wreck," Matt answered.

The engineer, slowing down for the first time since uncoupling the boxcars, commented, "Whatever it was damaged the rails, I'll vow."

Travis and Snake Man, whose faces were black with soot, smiled at each other. "Then that means Miss Sarah is safe, don't it?"

When the engines rolled into the station at Bismarck and Matt walked inside, the stationmaster looked as if he'd seen a ghost. "You're supposed to be dead, Matt Bergen. The news just came over the wires. The silk train was blown up, with no survivors."

"It must have been somebody else," he answered. "As you can see, I'm a little dirty, but very much alive."

Chapter 40

Driscoll and his men wasted no time in transferring the valuable cargo of raw silk to the wagons. Although some of the crates had been damaged by the blast, most were intact enough so that they were not a problem. Only one other time had Driscoll been successful in stealing an entire cargo, but never one belonging to Matt Bergen, for his had been too well guarded. Evidently this time, though, the man had taken a chance, not believing that anyone would be daring enough to challenge him in broad daylight, in a more populous area. Too bad he would never know what actually happened—that Driscoll had finally paid him back for the vigilante raids on his men and the cattle he'd recovered. But with other trains due, he'd had to act swiftly, striking and then running.

As he kept pace beside the lead wagon, he looked at Bart, the driver, and grinned. "Feels kinda good, don't it, to be so successful?"

"Sure does. Whatcha gonna do to celebrate this fine cache?"

"Hide it first, where nobody can find it. Then break open that imported keg of rum," Driscoll answered. "But that ain't all. I aim to string up that Injun, Tall Tree. Reckon I could call it about even then."

Bart smiled. "I'd like to see the old man's face when you tell 'im Matt's dead."

"You will," Driscoll promised. "I been waitin' a long time for this. Too long."

"You know where to find 'im?"

"Pretty certain. I been scoutin' the lay of the land. Tonight, we'll take it easy. Then we'll head out before daylight tomorrow."

"A steak would be mighty good eatin' tonight," a wistful Bart offered.

"Maybe we'll find us a stray cow on the way back," Driscoll answered, feeling generous toward the men who had helped him. With pride, he looked at the procession of wagons, the crates hidden from view by a thin covering of hay.

* * *

That night in the hills, the lingering aroma of freshly cooked beef enveloped the low-lying land beyond one of Driscoll's hideouts. Around the campfire, the men who were already drunk began to dance and sing. As usual, Bart, dressed in his Indian blanket and feathered hat, was the most vocal, the most active, with the others attempting to keep up the pace he set. Finally Driscoll put a stop to the revelry.

"Calm down, boys, and go to sleep," he ordered. "Remember, we got another big day tomorrow."

Reluctantly the men who were still on their feet obeyed him. Within a few minutes, as the camp fire burned low, they spread their blankets on the ground, cushioned their heads on their saddles, and settled down for the remainder of the night.

Early the next morning, before the sun rose over the distant hills, Driscoll and half of his men rode in a southerly direction—toward the rocks and ravine adjacent to the Bergen property. Even though he'd never been able to find the Indian's shack, the outlaw had seen the old man searching for his herbs near the water plenty of times. If he waited long enough, he was bound to see Tall Tree again.

In the dim light, the riders seemed to have the land to themselves. But as the sun burst upon the horizon, they grew more cautious, looking from right to left, to make sure no one was tracking them. Finally, when they approached the sentinel of rocks at the side of the wilderness road, Driscoll gave the signal to hold up. Sending one of his men ahead to scout the area, he and the others waited. A few minutes later, assured that the way was clear, Driscoll and the rest of his horsemen set out in a gallop and didn't stop until they reached the rise near the river.

"Tall Tree likes to gather his plants before the dew is gone. He'll more than likely show up in the next few minutes, if he's comin' today."

"What if he don't?" Bart asked.

"I got all the time in the world," Driscoll answered. "If we don't see 'im today, we'll come back tomorrow."

But Driscoll did not have long to wait. The familiar figure, dressed in brown trousers and rawhide vest, appeared along the bank of the shallow river. As usual, the Indian seemed oblivious to everything but the gathering of his herbs.

In the air, a giant bird glided, its shadow skimming along the earth of sage and prairie grass, causing small animals to scamper to safety. A doe also sought cover, but a herd of buffalo on the opposite bank took little notice, preferring to graze peacefully on the dew-fresh grass.

"There he is, boys," Driscoll said. "Let's git 'im."

With the horses racing down the slope, the pastoral scene vanished in an instant. A shot rang out, followed by a bloodcurdling yell.

"Say your heathen prayers, Injun," Driscoll shouted. "Matt Bergen's dead, and you're gonna be next."

A slight turning of his head was the only acknowledgment Tall Tree gave of the outlaws and their intentions. He had lived a long time, full of grace and wisdom, aware of life and aware of death. But his own death would be one of his choosing. Slowly, with the basket of herbs in hand, he began to walk across the jutting rocks of the shallow stream.

"Look! He's crossin' the water and headin' straight for the buffalo herd."

"That idiot Injun! Don't he know he'll be trampled to death?"

Driscoll stopped at the bank and watched helplessly. He couldn't believe what he saw. On the other side of the stream, the old man raised his hand as if greeting the animals. Then his ancient voice took on a solemn chant that matched the rhythm of his moccasined feet.

A swirl of dust and a thundering sound accompanied his progress into the path of the stampeding herd, running parallel to the river. And when the animals had disappeared, no sign of Tall Tree remained, not even the basket that had contained his healing herbs.

A sober Driscoll stared at the devastation of the distant ground, void of any living thing. His victory was a hollow one, for although the Indian was dead, it had not been at his own hands. From the look on Driscoll's face, Bart knew not to say anything. It was better for the boss to speak first.

Driscoll sounded grim. "Boys, head on back. I got me one more little chore to do."

"Ya want somebody to go with you?" Bart asked.

"No. This is somethin' I aim to do by myself."

Trying to make Driscoll feel better, Bart said, "Well, at least before the old Indian died, he knew that you'd killed Matt."

Driscoll suddenly grinned. "Yeah, that's right, ain't it? He knew."

With his pride intact again, Driscoll urged his horse in the opposite direction of his men. He had not wanted anybody to come with him, for most of his men would think he was being overly obsessive, that he should stop while he was ahead. But he knew he would never be satisfied until he'd found the Indian's shack and burned it down. There was something so final about fire.

As Driscoll rode in concentric circles, ever wider, the sun directly overhead shone with a brilliant intensity, sapping moisture and energy from the landscape. Taking off his hat, Driscoll wiped the sweat from his brow with his dirty bandanna and then proceeded on. He was getting frustrated with the heat and the stinging flies and his inability to find the cabin that he knew was somewhere nearby. But he knew he would eventually find it. He'd just have to be a little more patient.

His persistence finally paid off. Suddenly, before him, the well-hidden log cabin came into partial view. The old man had been clever, that was for sure. A body had to be almost on top of it before seeing the structure. Driscoll dismounted and tied his horse to a scrub pine before continuing on foot toward the shack. His hand remained on his pistol handle as a precaution, even though the place looked deserted.

First he crept around the entire shack and peeked into one of the windows. He saw only the outline of herbs hanging from the rafters and a few pieces of broken-down furniture. No dog announced his surveillance; no other human being challenged him. So, with bravado, he stepped onto the front stoop, pushed the door open, and walked inside.

As his eyes became accustomed to the darkness, Driscoll looked around to see if the Indian had anything worth salvaging before he put the torch to the cabin. The decorated medicine pipe and the ceremonial knife on the mantel caught his eye, as well as the red trade blanket on the cot. Bart would enjoy having a medicine man's pipe and knife, he decided, and a decent warm blanket was always good to keep. He gathered them up, and then, seeing the cooking utensils, he decided to take them, too, wrapping them in the blanket.

Before leaving, he broke the flimsy furniture into pieces—the chair, the table, the wooden cot. Pulling down the dried herbs, he piled them high on top of the furniture before setting them afire. Making sure that the flames were going well, he picked up the blanket containing the stolen items and walked onto the porch.

"Driscoll," a voice called out from the small clearing.

Startled, the outlaw dropped the stolen goods and looked in the direction of the familiar voice. He not only saw one ghost, but a second one, as well. For standing before him was a stern Matt Bergen, with Tall Tree at his side.

"You're both dead," Driscoll shouted, his unsteady hand reaching for his pistol. "I killed you both!"

Matt laughed a harsh laugh. "No, Driscoll. You only *thought* you did. Just like you thought you'd gotten away with stealing my cargo of silk."

Driscoll's first shot went wild, richocheting against the large boulder beyond Matt and Tall Tree. Like a man possessed, he jumped from the porch and rushed them, firing bullets in rapid succession.

Taking cover, Matt aimed and fired in defense. He would have preferred handing Driscoll over to the authorities for hanging, rather than taking the matter into his own hands. But Driscoll had given him no choice. Matt's bullet found its mark. He saw the outlaw clutch at his chest and then fall in the dirt, his pistol sliding from his grasp.

With the glowing flames visible through the open door of the cabin, Matt and Tall Tree rushed past the fallen Driscoll, whose hand was still groping for his gun. Matt kicked the pistol out of reach and continued toward the cabin.

Later, after the fire had been subdued and the stolen goods recovered, Matt left his ancient friend. Driscoll lay where he'd last seen him, his greed and lawlessness his undoing. Knowing that Tall Tree would have to make a ceremony, purifying the ground where blood had spilled, Matt picked up the dead outlaw and tied his body to his horse. Then, slapping the animal on the rump, he sent Driscoll's horse on its way. That night, there would be no celebrating in the outlaw camp.

As Matt mounted his own horse and began the trek back to the Double B Ranch, where he'd taken Anya, he was grateful that the repair crew had been able to replace the damaged rails on the Northern Pacific so quickly. Otherwise he might not have discovered that Driscoll had murdered Prince Igor.

Surprisingly Matt felt no guilt for the unfortunate events of the past twenty-four hours. Some things, he had finally learned, were beyond a man's control. Yet through the outlaw's mistake, Anya was now free—free of the one who had caused her such pain, and free to look forward to a bright and certain future.

Chapter 41

Several months later, in the guest bedroom of the Double B Ranch, Anya dressed for her marriage to Matt. She was happy, and it seemed that her happiness had spread throughout the house. She could even hear Kwa-ling humming to himself in the kitchen as he finished icing the wedding cake.

On a chair lay her wedding bouquet, wildflowers and wheat tied with aubergine-and-gold ribbons to match her dress, symbols of the vastness of the prairie. Draped across the four-poster bed was the magnificent silk that Matt had given her for the housewarming. Until today, it had remained hidden in the clothespress at school.

She smiled as she remembered the misunderstandings surrounding the gift, for from the first, she had recognized its special significance—a present suitable for a wife from her loving husband. Although her trunk at the foot of the bed contained an entire new wardrobe, replacing the clothes she had lost in the fire, Anya had chosen to wear this particular dress on her wedding day as an offering of peace and love and acceptance.

Her clothes had not been the only victims of the fire. The papers detailing Igor's sins had also been destroyed. Without them, she had posed no threat to her husband. Yet she knew that had not mattered to him in the end. Because of his ego, her running away had demanded that he find her and punish her.

"Miss Sarah?"

She recognized the voice at the bedroom door. "Come in, Clara."

"Everything's ready," the woman announced, closing the door behind her. "The preacher's here. And you've never seen such dolled-up cowboys. I saw them in Matt's office as I passed by from the kitchen. Can you believe it? Travis has even shaved." Clara moved to help Anya with her dress.

"And Matt? Did you see Matt?"

She nodded. "Never have seen him so handsome. But my, is he nervous!"

Once Anya was ready, with the circlet of matching flowers framing her face, her bouquet in hand, Clara stood back to assess the picture of the bride. "Amelia would have been proud of you," she said, her eyes moistening.

"I wish she could have been here with us, Clara."

"Well, now," the older woman said, quickly brushing away a tear, "I'll go and tell them it's time to start. Just wait till Snake Man knocks at the door." As Clara left, she sniffed. "Too bad we don't have any music."

Snake Man, pleased to have been chosen to escort

Anya to the parlor, tugged at the borrowed collar that
was a mite too tight. He took a deep breath and said,
"Are you ready, ma'am?"

"Yes."

The walk was not far, merely the partial length of the
hall. But as she and Snake Man reached the entrance to
the parlor, Anya stopped for a moment. Matt stood before the decorated hearth, watching her. At his side was
Lynx. And seated in the chairs were the special friends,
a motley group, that they had invited to share in their
private ceremony.

Clara had already taken her place with Diego, Jamie,
and his father, Randall, Anya's new foreman. The parti-
tion in the boundary cabin had been removed, the place
enlarged for the Purdys to live in, until a suitable foreman's house had been built.

As she walked past other guests, she was aware of
Tall Tree in his ceremonial dress, and Kwa-ling in his
dark blue Chinese tunic. Gus, Travis, and the other
cowboys who had served as guards on the silk train
were all there, watching and waiting for the ceremony
to begin. They had closed rank to protect her from the
rumors that had flown after the wreck that had killed
Igor. And for that, she was grateful to each one. She
was part of them now, because Matt loved her.

With a sigh, Snake Man gave her up to Matt and took
his seat beside Travis. Then, the minister who had come
from Dickinson, the one to whom Prairie Dog had
given his tithe of gopher tails and magpie wings, smiled
and began. "Dearly beloved . . ." Outside the open window, a bird began to sing, causing Clara to smile.

But at that moment Anya was only aware of Matt, his tender look, as they pledged their love for each other.

Late in the night, after the guests had slipped away, and Matt and Anya were alone, they listened to the sound of the wind over the prairie. Only one secret separated them—the one that Amelia had confessed at the arroyo. But Anya promised herself she would not destroy Matt's first love.

But if Anya had come to terms with Mellie, Matt had not reconciled himself, yet, to her life with Igor. "I'm still jealous, you know, of your Russian prince," he said, holding Anya in his arms and kissing her.

"Actually you should direct your jealousy toward another man," she teased.

He suddenly stared into her eyes. "Who?" he demanded.

"The one I spent the night with in the boundary cabin. He was the first man I ever truly loved."

Her words began to heal his heart.

Toward morning, the lonely whistle of a Northern Pacific train, with its valuable cargo of raw silk, sounded as it traveled through Medora on its way east. Along the Little Missouri River, amid the badlands, herds of range cattle looked up, but continued grazing.

This was the golden era, when each man's dream was as wide as the prairie. For some, the dream was a mirage, destined to vanish. But for others, like Matt and Anya, the dream had only begun.